Her father is his sworn enemy, her capture his business, and her life his to guard. But when he suspects his client has more sinister plans, he changes the rules. He shows her the truth — about her father's crimes, the brutality of his own business, and the gulf between her life and his. Yet an even darker truth threatens to destroy his revenge, his business, and their lives.

Danya wants to travel, write, and find a man like The Werewolf, who's haunted her dreams. But no one measures up to the man who killed someone in front of her, swooped her up, and danced the tango with her. No one except her kidnapper. Now, captive and torn between fantasy and reality, Danya chooses reality: Caleb, the rough, lawless fixer.

Caleb seeks revenge on Danya's father for horrendous crimes he committed against Caleb's family. Having kidnapped Danya, Caleb plans to enjoy her for the thirty days he keeps her captive. But he has no room in his life for girlfriends. And Danya's gentle, trusting nature serves as a rebuke to Caleb's violent profession. Yet when they go on the road to escape their enemies, Caleb discovers how teamwork, trust, and tenderness give him new purpose. Will his belief in Danya enable her to save them?

Keeping You Captive
Copyright © 2024 Kathleen Haley
ISBN: 978-1-4874-4126-5
Cover art by Martine Jardin

Published by eXtasy Books Inc

Look for us online at:
www.eXtasybooks.com

KEEPING YOU CAPTIVE

BY

KATHLEEN HALEY

DEDICATION

To my sister Anna, who tirelessly reads all my novels, encouraging me in every way.

CHAPTER ONE: CALEB: SIX YEARS AGO

M urder. The job that paid enough to buy a semi-profes-
sional soccer team.

The only job that paid better? Kidnapping.

While I had zero experience in the latter, I had plenty in the former.

Handing my coat to the coat check attendant, I adjusted my werewolf's headgear. Tonight should go like clockwork — once I got used to this costume. I pocketed the coat check tag and moseyed into the atrium, where a waiter offered me a champagne.

A few minutes after entering the ballroom, I spotted my target. He flaunted his sleaziness like a '57 Chevrolet on a Sunday cruise. Even dressed as a colonial soldier, he was channeling Nixon. To judge from his shady record, it was a miracle no one had offed him before this. Taking bribes from opposing parties and then pitting them against each other when they questioned him was a pretty jackass move. Politicians thought they were untouchable. His bulbous nose and beady eyes reminded me of a proboscis monkey I'd seen on the nature channel. Pushing the comparison further would insult the monkey.

Sipping my drink, I moved in for the kill. My costume smothered me in fake fur and Lycra lining from head to waist. At least it was a frigid February in Philadelphia, and the headpiece left the face exposed. I'd grown out my beard a little and painted on heavy brows and a black nose, adding a couple of fangs to make me less recognizable.

1

I sauntered over, inserting myself into a small circle of ass-kissers and a lull in conversation. I thrust out a hand. "Congressman Hendricks? It's an honor, sir. Jack Donaldson."

I drew him into discussion about construction of the new sports complex, posing as one of the investors and praising the location he'd lobbied for. This naturally brought our talk around to his main political rival. Hendricks was clearly jonesing for a read on how much the financial community supported his opponent.

I edged closer to him, lowering my voice. "Before my team found out about that mistake he made ten years ago, we might've endorsed him. Now no one can stand him."

His bushy brows lifted a notch. "Mistake?"

I could smell his hunger.

I darted a nervous glance around the company present. "It's not general knowledge. I wouldn't want to broadcast anything here."

His eyes drilled into me before he bobbed his round chin towards a hallway. "Shall we go somewhere more private?"

I cocked my head, lifting an eyebrow. "As long as you're not wired."

He cracked a wry smile, leading us through the corridor to a door far down on the right. He'd obviously been here before. Having zillowed the hell out of this mansion, I applauded his choice of rooms. It was a cross between a library and music room, with bookshelves lining the walls and a piano in one corner. A nice quiet place for my operation.

He cricked the door closed behind us. "Now, Donaldson, do share what you know."

My foster sister had dabbled in theater in high school and taught me a few things about the stage. Now I decided to upstage Hendricks. Waltzing towards one of the floor-to-ceiling windows along the opposite wall, I garbled some nonsense with my back to him.

"What was that?" I caught his reflection in the dark windowpane as he closed the distance between us in a few strides, craning his neck to hear what I'd said.

Drawing an arm around his shoulder, I pulled him in as if to confide in him. Instead, I covered his mouth in a chloroform-soaked cloth. While waiting for him to lose consciousness, I gripped him tightly, murmuring a few parting messages to him from my client. After several minutes of weakening struggle, he crumpled to the floor. I was already wearing gloves for my costume. I tore off his shoe and sock, pulled out my hypodermic, and injected it between his big and second toes. Then I replaced his footwear, patting him on the cheek.

"Sweet dreams."

Whoever found him would think it was a heart attack.

Pocketing my equipment, I retrieved my glass of champagne and turned to leave. *The perfect murder.*

Only one problem.

In the doorway, wide-eyed and pale, stood a young 1920s flapper.

Danya

I froze like a rabbit before a snake. Deep down I may have hoped that by not moving I wouldn't attract the man's notice.

Did I just see what I think I saw?

The man sprawling on the carpet looked pretty dead.

My throat worked on a swallow, and I twisted the skirt of my dress in both hands.

All I'd wanted was a moment's peace in the library. For hours now Dad had continually lured Luis away and shoved rich, *eligible* bachelors in my direction. Since my shoes were pinching my feet after so much dancing, I thought I'd take them off for a few minutes, sink into a couch, and breathe a little.

But the sight in front of me punched all the breath from my lungs.

Then, as adrenaline pumped through my veins, I began to hyperventilate.

I whirled about, intending to flee. But a pair of strong furry arms banded me from behind, whisking me back into the room. My captor toed the door shut, clapping a large hand over my mouth. I wasn't all that small, but this man's powerful hold reduced me to a gift shop figurine.

A ridiculous notion entered my mind as he effortlessly carried me to the other end of the room — he smelled incredible. Anise, wine-stained wood, and musky masculine sweat invaded my nostrils.

I didn't bother to scream, with his hand muffling my mouth. Besides, my throat was too parched and my thoughts too jumbled for me to raise hell. Was he going to kill me too? Surely not in my own house with hundreds of guests present. Then again, he'd made it look pretty easy with his other victim. But my death would only make things messier for him. Or maybe keeping me alive would be the real mess . . . *Please, God, if I make it out of this alive I'll do everything I can to lead a purposeful life.*

He set me down facing the atlases in the geography section of the room. The musty smell of book cloth mingled with his yeasty, licorice-scented breath fanning the crown of my head. His free hand trapped my wrists behind my back, while his hard body pressed me into the bookcase.

A deep, gravelly voice rumbled at my temple, stirring molten magma in my core. Why was this man having this effect on me? "You're Walter Penwarren's daughter, aren't you?"

I froze again. Should I lie? Refuse to answer? I racked my brains trying to decide if I needed to protect Dad.

His hand slid to my nape, gripping it with a suggestion of snapping my neck. "Answer."

I managed a nod.

"I know a few things about your father that could get him locked up for a while. Do you want that?"

My breath hitched, and my heart skittered to a halt. His not-so-subtle threat made the fine hairs on the back of my neck stand on end, scattering goosebumps down my arms. Shaking my head, I croaked a "no" into his palm.

"The man over there died of a heart attack. Are we clear?"

"Mm-hmm."

"We were never in here. Understand?"

I nodded vehemently, murmuring my assent. He was going to let me go!

"Good." When he released me and stepped back, I felt his absence everywhere in my body. But not in the way I expected — not the way I should've. My skin tingled with chill after losing his scorching heat. My chest deflated like a balloon, and the lava roiling in my lower belly cooled to a simmer. Shockingly, my body craved his gritty voice vibrating through me and his massive chest encasing me.

That's why when he spun me around, pressed a hand into my lower back, and herded me out the door at this end of the room, my heart took a leap off the diving board and flipped in the air.

There's a reason he hasn't let you go, Danya, a warning voice chimed. *You're not out of the woods yet.*

"What are you doing?" I got out breathlessly as he ushered me down the hallway towards the ballroom at a brisk clip.

"*We* are dancing," he declared, as if the rest of the guests were busy murdering people.

"But . . . why?" I sputtered.

We'd reached a corner of the dance floor, where I halted, twisting from him. He molded me into an erect tango position, dragging me onto the parquet as my feet refused to move. One arm girded my back, the other clutching my hand as he plunged us dangerously into the fray of swirling bodies.

"What did you see in there, Danya?" His dark, throaty voice brushed against my ear, making me shiver. My name on his lips was equal parts ominous, tense, and thrilling.

"Nothing." So as not to draw undue attention to us, I placed my free hand on his shoulder blade, falling into step as he led me around the room.

He thrust us forward, then pulled me back, pivoting us. With our torsos flush, I was sure he could feel my clattering heartbeats. His gold-flecked hazel eyes darkened under my gaze.

"It's just us now. I want the truth." Rotating my body in ochos, he brought us around, closing with a corte. Then, holding my waist and stepping parallel to me, he spun me about and turned us till we faced each other again.

The surrounding music, talking, and laughter covered my words as I ventured to speak in shaky tones. "You were holding something to his mouth . . . "

He twisted us in opposite directions, then spun me into a low side dip, holding me there a moment before pulling me up. One hand held my waist from behind, and I tingled all over from his breath on my neck and his body at my back. Raising one of my arms, he slid his fingers along the underside, catching my hand at the end and whirling me back so our chests were inches apart. His eyes flared as they held my gaze. "Continue."

Who was this man who killed someone so calmly and then tangoed with such sultry passion?

"I—he sank, and then you . . ." I was too nervous and overcome by the memory to finish.

He pivoted me so we were both stepping forward, my back at his chest, his right arm on my belly. Then he twirled me twice and dipped me backwards low, his intense gaze boring into me. Giddy, my heart thudding, I anchored myself in the golden depths of his green-rimmed eyes. With a strength and assurance that sent shockwaves through my center, he pulled me up slowly, his hand sliding from my nape to my upper back.

He pressed his warm lips to my ear. "Remember what I said."

Tremors stole down my spine, replacing my knees with jello.

With that he turned and vanished into the crowd.

I only realized I'd been holding my breath when I exhaled again. I felt as if a supernova had occurred and a black hole had formed from the remnants of a dead star. The star was the Werewolf, and his departure the explosion. The resulting gravitational field pulled me towards him with a force I'd never experienced.

Remember what I said. How could I forget anything about the last thirty minutes?

Dad appeared at my elbow. "Who was that, Dani?"

Heat crawled up my neck to my ears. "I, um, didn't catch his name."

I'd be scared to know any more about him. And yet, a name would've made him more real, as if I hadn't just dreamed the last half-hour. Maybe it'd be better if I had.

"There are a few young men I'd like you to meet." Dad turned to introduce three twenty-somethings to me, all of them in finance.

This had been the refrain of the evening — of a number of evenings over the last few months.

One of the men asked me to dance. Though I was exhausted, hungry, and confused by my encounter with the Werewolf, I caught the steely glint in Dad's eye and his curt nod. I dutifully accepted, and we started to waltz.

Dad wanted me to marry soon and marry *well*—meaning, to a rich, successful man. I had insisted on going to college and pursuing a career. I didn't know just what yet, but I couldn't imagine leading the life of a socialite that Dad intended for me. Come the fall, I'd no longer live with him and my stepmom, Eve. After turning 18 a month ago, I'd bought an apartment in Rittenhouse Square with my inheritance from Mom. Dad didn't know about it yet. Something told me when he found out, all hell would break loose. And Luis, my stepbrother and closest friend in the world, was soon heading off to the Singapore branch of Dad's company. A lot would change in the next six months. Part of me was anxious, part of me excited by the imminent upheavals.

As I waltzed with my partner, half a dozen paparazzi snapped photos of me. Over the last two years, photographers had increasingly sought me out, not just at charity dos and balls like this, but while I went about my normal life in public. I knew it went with the territory of being Dad's daughter. Yet it still unsettled me because it fed into my image as a socialite.

Suddenly, a murmur arose at the back of the room. It spread to a buzz that energized the dance crowd. After a few minutes, my dance partner asked the couple next to us what was going on.

"Someone died," the woman gasped. "They think it was a heart attack."

Another wave of whispers followed, and her partner added, "It was that congressman—Hendricks."

Dad had already set aside his drink, his lips thinning into a line, as he stalked towards the source of the commotion.

The Werewolf's lips flashed before my mind's eye. They were full, shapely, and expressive. His nose had been painted black, so I hadn't caught its contours very well. But I could still feel the way he'd moved me across the floor—forcefully, smoothly, always in control. Power radiated from him like heat from the sun.

Who was he, and would he think of me at all again?

CHAPTER TWO: CALEB: PRESENT

The blonde currently lapping the slit of my dick was taking her sweet time about it. I'd give her another minute before I started fucking her mouth. I'd bought her a drink in the hotel bar solely because I'd wondered whether her wide smile indicated her ability to deep-throat. I didn't have time for more than a quickie tonight, since I was on call for the family.

She began to moan, sliding her tongue along the underside of my cock. While it felt great, it also felt like teasing, which I wasn't in the mood for.

Just as Sheila—Shirley?—set her mouth to work in earnest, my phone vibrated on the bed.

"Keep going," I directed, reaching for it and swiping up. "Yeah."

The kneeling blonde seemed to see my distraction as a challenge, taking me in deep while massaging my balls. Fine. I could multi-task. While talking, I knotted her hair in my fist and pulled hard. She whimpered, fighting to keep stroking me.

Benny sounded frantic. "Carlo and Sal are stalled at the point of interception. You need to go out there."

"How long?" Hitting the back of Blondie's throat, I stifled a groan. Not that Benny would've minded, but I didn't like to advertise my hobbies.

"Ten minutes. They were supposed to be in and out in two." I could picture Benny raking a hand through his salt-and-pepper pompadour.

"No word from Franco?"

"He's busy with the other job. You gotta handle this."

"Will do." I killed the call, just as Blondie suctioned my shaft to the point of no return. My balls tightened, and I slammed into the back of her throat, holding her head firmly in place. "Taste me for a few seconds, then swallow every drop."

She hummed, her eyes swimming with tears from her gagging. My hot cum spurted into her mouth, and I watched as her throat bobbed to swallow my spunk. It took a while.

I pulled out, tucking myself into my boxer briefs as she rose to her feet, her eyes full of hunger. "I'd love to take care of you, but I've got to go deal with something work-related. If you want to wait . . . "

Disappointment leached across her face. "It's okay. You have my number, right?"

"Mmm." I wouldn't be using it, however gifted Shelley's lips were. Grabbing my car keys, I nodded towards the mini-fridge. "Help yourself to anything you want. Or room service."

Since I didn't know what to expect at the scene, I called our doctor and two of the cops we had on payroll, giving them the GPS location of Carlo's and Sal's phones.

Half an hour later, I pulled over at the sight of lights from a patrol car. We were about ten miles from the interception point. The panel truck was parked behind the cops, two of its left-side tires blown out. Doc Amos's Mercedes was parked behind the truck. Amos himself was inside its cab.

I strolled over to where our officers were questioning a mustached man and a greasy-haired woman. "Listen, Edgardo, Shariq, can your powwow wait? We need to get the truck to South Philly by one."

"Problem is the truck, Cal," said Shariq. "It'll take time to fix the tire."

"I'll drive it to Merryen's. If one of you can drive my car

there." I figured if the truck could get ten miles to this point, it could go another twenty, however slowly I needed to drive.

Edgardo nodded. "I'll take it."

Shariq led the handcuffed man and woman towards the patrol car. "I got these guys."

Tossing Edgardo my keys, I ambled over to the truck, hopping up into the cab. "What's the verdict, Doc?"

Amos was busy dressing Sal's shoulder. It looked like a bullet had lodged in deep. White as a sheet, Carlo gripped his bloody right arm in the passenger's seat.

"They'll survive," Amos clipped.

"Can you keep working while I drive?"

Amos shrugged. "It doesn't matter to me whether we're moving or not. I have everything I need."

After disabling the truck's GPS tracking, I put it in gear.

Tens of millions of dollars' worth of opioids were in the back of this truck. No one was innocent in this scenario. Not the driver, not the holder he was delivering to, not the family, and certainly not me. But a job was a job. And this one paid extremely well.

On the way to the Passyunk depot, Carlo told me the whole story. They'd followed my intel and hijacked the truck, but a rival gang had apparently had their sights on the same delivery. After a shoot-out, in which Sal had been badly wounded, Carlo had let the driver handle the truck, but another member of the rival gang had showed up and blown out two of the tires. While Carlo dealt with him, the trucker's unseen girlfriend had materialized from behind the passenger seats and grabbed Sal's gun, shooting Carlo in the arm. Her boyfriend had driven the truck on wobbly wheels for ten miles, till the cops I'd called had pulled them over. Then Amos had arrived and begun to treat their wounds. No doubt a payoff and a warning from our officers would keep the trucker and his girlfriend quiet. I'd let the family deal with retribution from the distributors.

We crawled along at 30 miles per hour, our police escort shunting other cars away. Finally, just after 1 in the morning, we reached the depot, where Shariq, Edgardo, and their prisoners parted ways with us. For an hour I helped Benny and two others unload the truck, even though this was below my paygrade. After the earlier snafu, I wanted to make sure nothing within our power to go right went wrong.

Just as we were finishing, I got a call from the capo, Mario. "Everything good, Cal?"

"Yeah. We just finished unloading."

"Nice work tonight. I heard you saved the goods."

I swiped a few beads of sweat from my forehead. "Everybody had a part to play."

"Listen, I recommended you to somebody today. Said he has a job that requires a lot of finesse, if you know what I mean. I told him you're the best in the biz. He's gonna call you."

"Who is he?"

Mario chuckled. "The less said, the better."

That sounded promising. "Is he rolling in it?"

"Absolutely."

While I wasn't doing too badly as an *independent strategist*, I could always use more wealth. I was on retainer with the family and had about a dozen other regular clients, but I welcomed a chance to fill my coffers as insurance. Insurance against the evils my family had endured. Provision for my revenge against the man who'd caused those evils. Guarantee that Mom and Faye would be taken care of for life.

Money and revenge. The two goals that had driven me for the last twelve years. While steadily piling up the first, I had to bide my time for the second.

When I'd rung off with Mario, I nodded goodbye to the others, heading back to my house in Ardmore. Besides me, only Jeremy, my sometime driver, caretaker, and gardener, and his wife Marisa, my cook and housekeeper, lived here. Every time I entered it, I thought how wrong it was that Mom and Faye refused to move in. For seventeen years they'd stubbornly stuck to the same apartment in Germantown that Dad had last occupied. As if living there could bring him back. No amount of persuasion could get them to budge, even when I said they could still keep the apartment if they stayed here. The three-bedroom place had become a shrine to Dad and our family life before he died.

Settling into an armchair in my study, I pulled out a tin of the licorice mints I always carried and popped one in my mouth. Tomorrow I'd go see my mom and sister. Maybe I could come up with an argument that would finally convince them to leave Germantown.

Unlikely.

Danya

My gaze darted skittishly around the floor. My relentless, never-satisfied boss, Kari, didn't seem to be anywhere near. She was always prodding everyone to be *present on the job*. But for some inexplicable reason she especially picked on me. Gladys, the associate editor who worked in the cubicle next to mine, said it was because I came from extreme privilege. The chance to lord it over me, in my lowly position of editorial assistant, was too great a temptation for Kari to resist. But I thought she singled me out because she suspected the job was just a joke to me. Which made me try all the harder to prove how much it mattered.

I ventured to open up the personal email that had caught my attention. It announced that Anne Selznick, the famous travel vlogger and blogger, would be doing a book reading at a large downtown bookstore three and a half weeks from now. A thrill rolled through me, robbing me of breath. She was everything I wanted to be—had wanted to be for three years now. Having read, watched, and reacted to everything she'd produced, I was one of her biggest fans. I clicked on the link to buy a few tickets. Maybe my cubicle mates would go with me. I'd have a dozen questions ready for Anne, in case she'd entertain them.

A brittle cough sounded behind me, and I jumped in my chair. "Danya, I'd like to see you in my office please."

Shoot. Kari must be on the warpath if she wasn't chewing me out at my cubicle but in the privacy of her office.

Scooting my chair back, I followed her there, hunching my shoulders.

She indicated the chair in front of the desk and folded her small frame into the one opposite. "Danya, you've no doubt heard the expression *time is money.*"

"Er, yes." I opened and closed my clammy palms. I was in for it. She'd caught me spending work time to plan a social event using my personal email.

"I'll save us time *and* money by cutting to the chase." Kari leaned forward, folding her arms over her desk. "Perhaps you've heard that Ehsan is going on paternity leave starting next week."

That I didn't expect. "Yes, I had heard."

She regarded me over her glasses. "He was set to cover affordable Miami-area hotels and restaurants in two weeks' time."

"Ah, yes?" I prompted.

"Now he can't."

Where was she going with this? "Hmm."

She clasped her hands. "We have a tight schedule on our Southeast edition. So I'd like you to go down there."

Had I heard her right? "You mean write reviews?"

"Well, yes, that would be the main part of the assignment. Apart from the traveling."

I felt like leaping out of my seat and pirouetting around the room. As it was, I tried not to sound like a demented idiot. "Oh, that's—that's amazing. Thank you!"

She offered a curt nod. "Ehsan will brief you on all the notes he's made so far and give you the itinerary." She pursed her lips, her tone growing somber. "Danya, this is rather important. It's not just some fun excursion."

"No! No, I know." All eloquence had flown out the window. "It won't be fun. I mean, I'll give you really good pages."

She perused me a long moment. "Fine. That's all then."

I stumbled back to my desk in a daze. I'd just landed my first travel writing assignment! Just like that.

Blazing Trails operated differently from most presses, and its unique system was the main reason I'd jumped at the chance to work here a year ago. It staffed its own travel writers, grooming them through all phases of production, from research to copy editing. Before now, I'd never much cared about my slow progress. I was just happy to be working towards doing what I loved—traveling and writing about it.

Innes popped his head over the divider between our cubicles. "Good news?"

The grin splitting my face must've been louder than a bugle. "Yes! I'm taking Ehsan's assignment in Florida."

"Congrats. You deserve it." He high-fived me. "Drinks later?"

"Count me in," Gladys chimed.

Remembering that Kari could see everything from her office behind me, I completed my ticket purchase, closed out my personal email, and continued copy editing the piece from Kamau on Savannah.

At 5:30 PM, the four of us, including Kamau, headed around the corner to Mellow Yellow, our favorite bar. It was the sort of place Dad would've had conniptions over if he'd known I frequented it. Drink-stained wood everywhere, a popcorn maker in the corner, beer pong, pool, and bocce ball, with indie pop from all nations blaring over the sound system. The stuffy, reeking restrooms always had more toilet paper on the floor than on the rolls.

Our group loved it here.

Among other reasons, I loved it because it was the least likely place any paparazzi would find me. Ever since I was 16, Dad had pushed the paps on me at high-profile functions like charity galas, balls, and ceremonies. Whenever possible, he posed with me, calling me *Daddy's girl* and feeding people the line that I depended on him for everything. When in truth I'd used Mom's money to buy my own apartment and go to college, and now I supported myself on my salary. Dad jokingly told everyone my *school phase* and now my *work phase* were just ways to fill the time till I met the right man.

If this kind of press was the price of pleasing him, I was willing to go along with it to keep the peace. For he'd been livid when he'd found out I'd bought the apartment, pressuring me all through college to attend his high-society events at the expense of my studies.

But I didn't like stumbling upon articles that depicted me as an airheaded socialite with no purpose in life other than to look pretty and entertain people. I never recognized myself in those pieces. And I hated the gnawing loneliness I'd increasingly felt around Dad since high school, as if he had no clue who I was and didn't care to find out. Nor did I like my suspicion, whenever he set me up with men, that they were just trying to please him and marry into his money.

After carrying our beers to a table, the four of us toasted my windfall.

"To the next Elizabeth Gilbert!" Innes nudged my arm, a warm smile dimpling his cheeks.

"Where would you travel to next?" I twisted towards him.

"Australia. Hands down."

"I'd go to Venezuela." I sipped my beer. "I love the music, the food, and the beaches."

"We'll go together. The press is putting out a revised version of Latin America next year."

I sighed. "That sounds heavenly."

"*Hablas español?*"

My thumb met my index finger. "*Un poquito. Quiero aprender.* My stepbrother's half Mexican. I learned a little from him over the years."

His brows lifted. "*Te enseño.* Repeat after me. *¿Quieres salir conmigo este fin de semana?*"

I repeated the words.

He grinned. "Sure, Danya, I'll go out with you this weekend."

Blushing, I laughed. "How do you say *cheater*?"

"Ah, you'll never have cause to say that to me—in English or *en español*." He leaned in. "So how about it? Dinner, or a concert? Both?"

"Isn't there a no-fraternizing policy or something at work?"

He shook his head. "Nope. All good there."

I couldn't think of an excuse to say no. Innes was witty, charming, and good-looking, and he'd been flirting with me all year. "Just so long as things won't be funny between us afterwards."

His eyes twinkled. "So that's a yes?"

"*Sí.*"

Later, Kamau and Gladys headed off to their cars, while Innes walked me the mile or so back to my apartment. Spring buds studded the branches of the magnolias, dogwoods, and cherry trees lining the streets. Crocuses and hyacinths bloomed inside the iron grates on the boulevards. Though dark and moonless, the clear sky promised another biting, sunny day tomorrow.

Halfway home, I stopped and turned around slowly, scanning our surroundings. A prickly sensation coated the surface of my neck and arms. "Do you get the feeling we're being followed?"

His eyes widened. "No. Do you have any enemies?"

I knew he meant to lighten the mood a little, but I considered his question seriously. "Not that I know of. I guess my dad might."

As we continued silently walking, I strained my ears for unusual footfalls, sudden movements, or the brush of an unseen presence. I still sensed one lurking somewhere not far away, and I shivered.

Innes saw me into my foyer, where our doorman, Lev, stood reading a newspaper behind the desk. "Would you like me to come up with you?"

"No. Thank you for walking me back."

His lips kicked up at the corners. "So tomorrow night?"

I smiled. "Sure." I really hoped I wasn't about to lose a good friend by going on a date with him.

He wrapped me in a warm hug, kissing my cheek. "See you tomorrow."

I watched as his long legs carried him out the door. Maybe this time I'd feel some chemistry and sizzle. Since that night at the ball six years ago, I'd held every man up to a certain standard—and no one came near the mark. The Werewolf had ruined me for any other man.

Unbidden, my recurring fantasy played out in my mind— the Werewolf pulled up my skirts in the library as I faced the bookcase, fingered my soaking slit, and rammed into me from behind. Once he'd buried himself up to the hilt, he murmured in my ear, "Never forget."

It was like a promise and a curse. I never would.

CHAPTER THREE: CALEB

I swallowed the last licorice mint, tossing the tin in a garbage can as I approached the square. Faye had simultaneously laughed and wrinkled her nose at me for my obsession with all things anise-flavored. She said it could easily repel clients and women, since it was such an acquired taste. I shrugged and said they could take me as I was or leave me. Right after, we'd quarreled about Mom's continuing therapy appointments. Faye never wanted her to leave the apartment, regardless of the reason. But that was the thing about my sister — she could be so mature and wise one moment and stubborn and irritable the next.

I glanced at my watch. Time to act.

Passing the swanky pre-war building, I switched on all four channels of my jammer. After a minute, I turned around and passed again.

I saw the doorman going into his office, no doubt to investigate what had disabled the security cameras. Entering the lobby, I prowled behind his desk and chopped a hand into the base of his head. After he'd slumped to the floor, I fastened zip ties around his wrists and ankles, stuffing his mouth with a sock and covering his head with a dark sack. I hadn't put enough force into my blow that he'd be out any length of time. All I needed was twenty minutes. I left the jammer behind the front desk, covering it with a black cloth.

Finding the right apartment key on his office board, I took the stairs to the sixth floor. These days, I rarely accepted violent jobs like this. As a consultant, I knew enough rough types to refer clients to that I could usually remain in the wings, directing things. But this job came with the provision that I perform it all myself. It paid well enough that I didn't mind.

And far more than the money, it meant the beginning of my revenge.

I quietly let myself into the apartment, listening for movement. All was dark and still. I pulled the ski mask over my head. The subtle scent of jasmine lurked in pockets I passed through. There hadn't been time to prepare for this operation as much as I usually preferred. But I'd gambled that at 2 in the morning my victim would be asleep. Using a small LED flashlight, I found her bedroom and eased the door open, switching off the flashlight.

Now I knew where the jasmine came from. It must be her soap, or a body lotion.

Gentle breaths floated from the bed, where she lay on her back, her arms folded alongside her head like a saguaro cactus. I padded over, standing beside her to take her in. My heart might've skipped a beat or two. In the light of the streetlamps streaming through the large windows, thick, wavy locks of copper cascaded past her shoulders. She had a narrow, straight nose with an attractive knob at the bottom, naturally arched auburn brows, and apple cheekbones. Her jawline was a cross between a square and a diamond. Creamy skin and a long neck made me want to sink my teeth into her flesh. But most of all her lips made me stall. Like a full, pink crescent moon they curved upwards in a smile, as if she were dreaming of something pleasant.

So innocent, so naïve, and so vulnerable.

So fuckable.

The image whooshed before me—*I woke her up with a few caresses, stroked her glistening pussy, and made her scream for my cock. Then I straddled and impaled her till I shattered her sweet body into a million tiny pieces.*

Scenes from the night at her father's ball flashed through

my head. That was before I knew about Walter Penwarren or the extent of his crimes. The thought sobered me.

Ignoring my half-mast dick, I focused on business.

I slid my gloved hand under the covers, pulling her ankles together and tying them with a rope. Then I bound her wrists, securing them to a slat of the headboard. As she began to stir, I fastened a cloth around her head over her mouth. Her eyes flipped open, wide, ocean-blue, and full of fear. Her chest rose and fell like a stormy sea. A muffled scream tore at her throat, getting clogged behind the gag.

Danya

I'm being murdered in my own bed! Or raped, or tortured.

Lurid images stampeded through my brain, and my heart rocketed out of my chest. Panic squeezed my lungs in a death grip.

Wearing a black ski mask, he towered above me like the Dark Knight. I writhed and tried to escape across the bed. But my hands were fastened to the headboard. Trembling seized me, my teeth chattering into the gag.

This was how everything would end.

If he'd been able to get this far — past the cameras, past Lev, into my apartment — he could do anything he wanted with me.

What is he doing?

He was riffling through my dresser drawers, pulling out shirts, pants, underwear, and bras and stuffing them into a duffel bag. *Does he need my clothes to commit his crime — or did he tie me up to steal them?* Both seemed equally psychopathic. He ripped dresses and skirts from the hangers in my closet, adding them to the bag, which he slung across his chest.

Then he calmly advanced. *Oh, God. What now?*

Is a calm murderer better than an angry one?

I couldn't move. My muscles had seized up. But the hammering of my heart was deafening.

He cut the rope binding me to the bed and scooped me up, tossing me over one shoulder. Now was my chance to break free! His strong arm held my legs firm, but I flopped and wriggled my trunk. Until his free hand pressed my lower back into his shoulder blade, immobilizing me.

What's he doing now? Where are we going?

How long before he chops me up? Will he knock me out first?

"Shh," he hushed, as if my frantic thoughts were blaring from the rooftops. "Danya, you're going to be okay."

He knew my name. Was that scarier or not? The words could be reassuring or the signs of a very sick mind. But his tone didn't *sound* sick. It was gruff but warm. *Okay* was vague. But surely you wouldn't use it to describe a dead person?

Before long we were in the stairwell, his rapid footfalls echoing against the stone walls and steps. We passed through the foyer, where he collected something on the floor behind the desk, and then we were out the front door. He strode rapidly, as if he had a sack of potatoes draped over his shoulder. His back was constructed of granite, and his legs were like metal girders.

When we emerged onto the pavement, I raised my muted yell as much as I could, wearing out my vocal cords. But the streets were empty, and no one was near to hear my futile cries. All too soon we'd stopped beside a black BMW SUV. After dumping the duffel in the trunk, he opened the rear door and laid me along the seat, fastening my ankles to the drive-side door grip. As he bent over me, I caught whiffs of fennel and plum. Something pleasant—a memory?—stirred within me.

The fleeting sensation vanished. Despair coursed through my veins as he closed the door. The rear windows were tinted, so I couldn't see out, nor could anyone see in. Trussed up like a rotisserie chicken, I could only rotate from side to side. My situation was hopeless.

Crazy thoughts whirled and slammed into each other in my head. *He's taking me to a remote area to kill me. No — he said I'd be okay. He needs me alive and well in order to get his money. He lied. He's going to dress me up in my clothes, torture, and rape me. Then he'll bury me alive in the forest.* Anxiety pumped through my blood vessels.

Please let it be over quickly.

He removed his balaclava and gloves as he slid behind the wheel. Now I could see his profile. A trim dark brown sculpted beard framed his square jaw. A fade on the sides of his head led to a thick, long mass of hair at the top. His prominent ridged nose separated broadly spaced eyes under low brows. Permanent laugh lines bracketed his mouth, even when his lips didn't smile. But those lips . . . I thought I'd seen such lips before — shapely, plump, and bottom-heavy.

"I'm taking you somewhere nice, Diva." Examining the rearview mirror, he pulled out and drove slowly along the street. "You won't be uncomfortable." His lips twitched. "Unless you ask for it."

That's code for torture.

He turned on a country music station. The gesture and the choice of music humanized him — for better or for worse. I still couldn't tell what would reassure me most about a . . . rapist? Kidnapper? Murderer? But I wanted to hear more of his voice. There was something familiar about it.

I made incoherent sounds behind my gag.

"I realize this isn't what you planned on doing with your Thursday night." He sped up as if we were on a highway. "But I assure you, you'll sleep well where we're going."

Oh God, is "sleep well" a euphemism for something horrible?

He chuckled as if he'd read my thoughts. "No forced sex, no death, and no drugs, I assure you."

Not rape, not murder, not trafficking . . . or so he claimed.

Kidnapping, then.

"No, this is about money." He signaled a lane change. "And history."

His grim tone told me this was personal. Did that mean he wasn't just hired by someone to kidnap me? Or did his interests align with his client's?

With all the questions bombarding me, it was torture not to be able to voice them. He had to be some kind of desperado—or a total nutcase—to abduct the daughter of one of America's biggest biotech moguls, not to mention show his face to her. Short of murdering me, how did he see this playing out?

A spasm of fear racked my body. A large, warm hand steadied my waist, and the next thing I knew, my captor was laying a coat over me.

"Danya, I have a mother and sister." His rough voice contrasted with his tender words.

Or was I reading them too charitably? Maybe he was reassuring himself. Maybe this was the mantra he used every time he abducted a woman. He hadn't said he loved his mother and sister, or that he treated them well.

Though it was implied in his action.

I studied the fine contours of his face in the glancing lights of the highway. Who was this man? What did he want?

CHAPTER FOUR: CALEB

Now began the hard part of my assignment. The rough work was usually a piece of cake. It was the politics that always did me in.

The farmhouse near Dushore had a few lights on when I pulled the car up to the front door after our three-hour drive. Jeremy and Marisa had driven up yesterday and prepared everything. I left Danya in the car while I unloaded the duffel and my own bags, bringing them upstairs. When I returned, Marisa hovered anxiously by the front door in her robe, peering out through the glass, while Jeremy stood at attention behind her.

"It's pretty cold out," Jeremy husked. "Should I lay a fire?"

"I've put the kettle on." Marisa tipped her head towards the kitchen. "Bring her in there. The embers aren't yet dead from earlier. We can stir them up."

"You shouldn't have stayed up," I said in a gruff voice.

"Nonsense. Anyway, we only just woke when you pulled up." She opened the door for me, letting in a gust of 25-degree air.

In a few strides I was at the car, popping open the door and leaning over Danya to cut the rope binding her ankles to the opposite door. She didn't bother to fight this time — maybe because she knew she didn't stand a chance out here in the middle of nowhere in her t-shirt and short-shorts with her hands and feet bound.

"Now, Diva, I'm going to remove your gag. You can scream to your heart's content out here." *No one will hear except*

27

the screech owls, and they'll probably join you.

She gasped as I freed her mouth, noting the red chafing marks the cloth had made on her porcelain cheeks. She really was delicate. After gulping in a few lungfuls of air, she let out a loud scream that lasted a good thirty seconds. Taking a long breath, she yowled again, this time with a rattle to her voice. She had a set of pipes on her.

While she auditioned for the opera, I picked her up and carried her inside. Even wrapped in my coat, her curves made me itch to grope her. My hands would perfectly fit her hips, ass, tits, and narrow waist.

Though she stopped screaming once she saw Marisa and Jeremy, she tried to spring out of my arms. In an impressive display of core strength, she nearly succeeded. I threw her over my shoulder, pushed up the coat, and gave her a hard swat on her round springy ass. Damn, that felt good. After crying out, she kept silent till we reached the airy high-raftered kitchen, where I set her down on the vinyl couch in front of the fire.

She trembled violently, from fear, cold, or both.

I pulled a chair in front of her, caging her legs between my knees. Holding her chin in my hand, I pinned her with a firm gaze. "Let's get a few rules straight, Diva. First, as long as you're in my care, you obey me without question. If you fight me, expect consequences. I will punish you however I see fit. Understood?"

She tried to shake her head free of my grip, her cobalt eyes flaring. "In your *care?*"

My hand slid down the column of her slender throat, squeezing it. That, too, felt good. "The person who hired me could've hired someone far worse—far rougher—to handle this job. You wouldn't have fared so well with another man."

Her mouth slackened. "So I should be grateful to you? And what is *this job*? Enlighten me."

So she was feisty. Living up to the reputation of a redhead. I quirked an eyebrow. "You've been kidnapped."

My thumb brushed along the artery of her neck, registering her fluttering pulse. I imagined playing with her airways while making her come. What would those lips look like forming a perfect O?

"Then why are you talking about my being in your care? I'll be gone from here by tomorrow." She jutted her chin up.

I smiled, enjoying her fight. "I'm afraid not, Diva."

Her eyes flashed. "Yes. I will. You'll demand a ransom from my father, and he'll pay it."

Ah, she was so confident.

"We're on my client's timeline. Not yours. Not mine. Not your father's."

"What does that mean?" she choked.

"That for the next month you're mine." My dick twitched.

Enjoying Danya hadn't been part of anyone's plan, least of all mine. But plans changed. As of the moment I'd laid eyes on her tonight. And having her worked perfectly into the bigger scheme. I'd had a three-hour drive to decide on the matter. Never mind that my client had specified "no touching." Needs must.

In every sense of the phrase.

"No." She shook her head vehemently. "That's impossible. My father will pay you better than what your client is paying you, I'm sure!"

"It doesn't work like that."

Her brow crinkled. "But why?"

"I have reasons for going along with my client's plan. Reasons more important than money." *Revenge. On your father.*

"Whatever you need or want, my father will give it to you."

Poor little rich girl. She had no idea. "Oh, I'll be taking plenty from your father."

Including you.

Danya

"I want to call him." I extended my hands, as a reminder that he should unbind me.

A wicked spark lit his eyes, and his lips tugged up at the corners. "Two demands at once, Diva?" He tsked. "That's the second rule you'll follow while in my care. You don't make demands." He leaned in, pebbling my neck with goosebumps as he breathed in my ear. "You beg me."

My teeth and my thighs clenched. "I *never* beg."

As he moved his lips over my earlobe, I could hear the smirk in his voice. "You will."

A shiver of pure pleasure shot to my core from where his breath fanned my skin. Since it couldn't be from his words, which infuriated me, it must be from the vibrations of his voice.

I could've sworn I'd been in this situation before. What was so familiar about it? It must've been too long since I'd had sex. Definitely too long since I'd had pleasure.

The kindly dark-haired woman with snapping eyes who'd followed us into the kitchen brought over two steaming cups of tea and placed them on the table beside me.

"Marisa, this is Danya." His eyes never left mine.

She nodded. "Danya, you get yourself nice and warm. There's a thick duvet on your bed upstairs."

I reminded myself that she was on his side.

"Thank you, but I won't be sleeping," I clipped. *Or eating or drinking.*

To cave to any of my body's needs felt like capitulating. It would've been accepting that I was trapped here. If I could fast and go on a sleep strike, maybe I wouldn't be worth anything to anyone, and they'd have to release me.

Marisa smiled sweetly. "Well, in case you get the urge, everything's ready."

When she'd left, the man who'd upended my life reached for one of the mugs and held it to my lips. The fragrant aromas of jasmine white tea—my favorite—assailed my senses. Without thinking, I took a sip. Then another. *Oh,* that tasted so good.

Between sips, I challenged, "What's wrong, you don't trust me enough to free my wrists? Afraid I'll toss my tea in your face?"

"I don't take any chances, Diva." His gravelly voice was sinfully, decadently sexy.

Focus, Danya.

"Why do you call me *Diva*?"

His gaze dropped to my lips, lingering there. I felt heat seep into my face. "Because of who you are. Your ways."

"You mean because of my father. You don't know my ways yet."

He crooked a half-smile. "Your reputation precedes you."

He must be referring to the tabloids. Fine. If he wanted to think of me as a stuck-up, spoiled princess, he could go right ahead. I was all too glad to keep my true life and nature hidden from him. He already had too much power over me as it was. He didn't need to know who I really was. "What's your name?"

"Caleb." His ready answer startled me.

"Real name or assumed?"

"Assumed."

"What do you get out of this kidnapping?" I put bluntly.

His wicked grin turned feral. "Satisfaction."

My breath caught. "I thought you said *no forced sex.*"

Cupping my chin, he thumbed my lower lip. His intimate touch and searing gaze mesmerized me. Flames flickered in his now-amber eyes. "No force necessary."

I gulped, feeling a steady drumbeat thud between my thighs. All my blood rushed to my crotch. What was happening to me? I needed to quell my raging hormones and quick. This man had ripped me from my life. From work, my date with Innes, my first travel writing assignment, the chance to see my travel blogging idol. He was causing worry and grief among those who loved me—Dad, Eve, and Luis. And he'd tied me up like Houdini, minus a few locks. He also seemed to have some crazy idea that I'd submit to him without a fight. A month of captivity! I might not have a job to come back to.

No. There was no way I'd accept this situation. And not a chance I'd sleep with the enemy.

Tomorrow I'd plot how to get out of here. I already had some ideas. But now, as if my body taunted me, I suddenly felt the desperate need to crash. I stifled a yawn.

"We'll discuss rule number three tomorrow." My captor stood, gathering me in his arms.

I wanted to lash out again, make him work at getting me wherever we were going. But I was physically, emotionally, and mentally drained. As he carried me through the hall and up the stairs, to my embarrassment, I longed to nestle into his chest and fall asleep. He was so solid, warm, and masculine-smelling . . .

But my pride kept me awake. Just barely.

We entered a tidy room with a dark hardwood floor, a queen-sized bed, and two large double-paned windows. A dresser and desk lined the wall opposite the bed, and a door at the far end of that wall stood ajar, as though it led to a bathroom. A closed door beyond the bed suggested a closet.

"Need to use the bathroom?" Caleb bobbed his head towards the open door.

"Yes." I definitely wasn't passing up the opportunity to have my hands—and possibly my feet—freed.

"You haven't earned the right for that yet, Diva." As if he'd read my mind, he smirked, carrying me into a tile-floored bathroom with a clawfoot tub. "I'm going to loosen the ropes on your ankles so you can spread your legs." His salacious smile told me he'd chosen this turn of phrase. "But I'll wipe you. If you try anything, expect to be punished."

My thoughts raced. What could I do? The man was a Titan with endless shoulders, an iron-clad chest, and the glutes of an elite cyclist. The veins in his forearms had more tributaries than the Amazon River. If I used my wrists to strike a sensitive part of his head, I might knock him out briefly. But how would I untie myself before he came to? Maybe, once I had my ankle restraints loosened, I could shuffle out the door, down the stairs, and outside.

I decided to try it.

He set me on my feet in front of the toilet, pulling my shorts to my calves. Easing me down onto the seat, he untied the rope around my ankles. Then he nudged my legs apart. It was now or never. My heart sprinted, and my breath grew labored as I raised my hands to deliver a hard blow to the crown of his head.

Without looking up, he grabbed my right forearm, using it to twist my torso so I was pretzeled over the side of the toilet, and cracked his palm against one of my bare buttocks. I jerked and screamed, wriggling to break free of his hold. But he effortlessly pinned me face down so I sprawled sideways across the toilet. In another moment he was above and behind me, his scorching body cocooning me. Pressing a hand into my upper back to hold me in place, he rained a series of wallops over first one cheek then the other. Each one stung like a mother, and I hollered at the top of my lungs. Since his legs hemmed in my hips, there was no hope of escape.

With each spank, heat bloomed through my center. Every nerve, every cell of my body zeroed in on where his palm crashed down and the pain radiating from there. It was the most humiliating thing I'd ever been subjected to. I was utterly at his mercy, my ass exposed to him till such time as he deemed fit to cover it. And as the controller of my body and my pain, he controlled my mind. All I was aware of was his total power. He owned me right now.

The sensation of being completely subdued should've been unpleasant. But it wasn't. Instead, my core vibrated with need. My clit began to throb, and arousal welled from my pussy. The pain from the smacks was turning into want. I hungered for something only my punisher could give.

"*Please*," I whimpered.

I didn't know what I was asking for, apart from relief from this burning desire.

The flurry of slaps ceased.

He pulled me to a standing position, holding me up with one muscular arm. I would've flopped to the floor otherwise. His gritty voice rumbled into my temple. "What was that?"

"Please." Tears pricked at my eyes. Suddenly my emotions overwhelmed me, and I couldn't keep the tears in check. They spilled down my cheeks in rivulets, splatting on the tile floor. A sob racked me, and my chin dropped to my chest, my shoulders heaving.

He held me so close, we might as well have been one body. Now his soft tones were like the purr of a cougar. "What are you asking for, Diva?"

I was a mess of snot, hot tears, and saliva. "Release."

"There's only one kind of release I can give you." His lips fluttered against my cheek, making me tremble with yearning. "The others are off limits."

He meant he couldn't *release* me—from my bonds or from his custody.

"Yes, please. The first then." The gaping hollow that the Werewolf had left unsatisfied six years ago echoed my words. I'd only ever had pleasure thinking of him.

My captor spun me around, his eyes like twilit ponds. "That sounds a lot like begging, Danya."

I gulped, swallowing my pride, my eyes sliding sideways. "Yes."

He gripped my chin. "It takes courage to beg, you know. You're brave."

My brows crumpled together. "No, I'm not." *I'm a coward.*

He shook his head. "Asking for what you want when it's hard to do so. That's courage."

He pulled a sheet of toilet paper off the roll and used it to clean my face. Now shame covered me. Of course he didn't want me. I must be blotchy, tear-stained, and red-eyed. Totally undesirable. But still the pulsing in my groin craved attention. *His* attention. Never mind who he was or what he'd done to me. I was desperate for his touch.

"Diva, we're going to get some sleep." He kissed my forehead. "There'll be plenty of time for release."

CHAPTER FIVE: CALEB

She had to be strong, on top of beautiful, sexy, and smart. She'd taken my punishment like a soldier and turned it into something redeeming. With one word she'd bared her soul to me.

Fully aroused as I'd been, I couldn't take advantage of her in her emotional state. But seeing her ass cheeks tattooed with my handprints had nearly done me in. From her clit to her crack had been drenched. It was all I could do to keep from slurping up every last drop of her nectar. The air had been thick with the scent of her desire, and the tremor in her voice as she'd begged me to take her had shot straight to my cock and set it thrumming.

But this was a punishment for her trying to rebel. Rewarding her with sex would only encourage her to defy me again. And I had other reasons for keeping her hungry and on edge, notably her father.

After helping her use the toilet, I undid the rope around her wrists and replaced it with a thin scarf that didn't cut into her skin as much. Then I carried her to the bed, pulling down the covers and tucking her in.

Switching off the lamp, I climbed in beside her, brushing a lock of russet hair off her cheek. "Sweet dreams."

Danya

My eyes flew open, and I stifled a gasp in the darkness. Those words! That voice. *My God. No way.* Had I been that blind? Like rain that turns from sprinkles to a torrential downpour in seconds, dozens of details from the last few hours pelted through my brain, leaving no room for doubt. His honey-flecked hazel eyes. His arms around me from behind. His low, gritty voice that reverberated through my sex. His aromas of licorice and wine. His Olympian stature and mammoth presence. The way he handled me like a paper version of myself.

I'd been so dense.

But just as suddenly I saw why I hadn't figured out his identity before. I'd wanted to preserve my memory of the Werewolf as the man who'd inspired my first sexual fantasies—and all my sexual fantasies since. He'd always represented power, suavity, and daring. The way he'd electrified me then had kept me dreaming that he'd possess me for years after. I'd had a mental block tonight because I was dead set on not tarnishing that open-ended, hopeful dream with the harsh realities of the present.

Fury coursed through me. Caleb had ruined the Werewolf for me. In my dreams, the Werewolf protected me, cherished me, saw me for who I really was. Sure, I'd known he was a murderer, but the man he'd killed apparently had it coming to him. All the news sources stated that he'd had a number of enemies and his hand in many corrupt pots. In any event, in my fantasy, the Werewolf's cause had been just. I'd thought we were both on the same team. Our conspiracy had always tasted delicious. Now that he'd merged with my kidnapper, I'd become just another one of his jobs. A victim like that politician. Someone to coerce, threaten, and use. He saw me the way much of the public liked to see me—a rich, entitled brat. Didn't bother to dig beneath the surface. He was an insensitive brute who in one night had destroyed my whole narrative. I'd kept his secret that night and forever since—and *this* was how he rewarded me. By robbing me not only of my present and future, but my equally precious past.

I'd always hoped that just as the Werewolf was everything to me, I was special to him. Now it appeared I wasn't.

A tear trickled down my cheek as I lay on my side facing away from my captor. I stifled a sob, so he wouldn't wake and find me crying.

Even as it made more sense why I'd been lusting for him in the bathroom, I cringed from the shame of my undisguised, desperate need. Knowing that Caleb was the Werewolf, I recognized I was in more danger than ever. His nearness and aura acted like a lightning strike on my system, stimulating every nerve and neuron. Especially the bundles of nerves in my groin. And my entire spinal column. I melted in his presence. Nothing had changed in six years. If anything my susceptibility to him had intensified.

But he's disrupted your whole life, Danya! my conscience chided.

My lips set in a thin line as I stared across the dark room.

Don't worry, my stark resolve soothed my soul. *I have plans for escape . . . and payback.*

Blinding light lasered through my eyelid to my retina, jolting me awake. My eyes snapped open.

Holy mother of God in a birthday suit. My totally naked captor faced away from me while collecting his clothes from the dresser.

Shit. Two perfect, powerful globes stared straight at me like full moons. A broad, deeply sculpted V-back, tapering to a narrow waist, was Michelangelo's wet dream. Those bronzed thighs and calves were as edible as Kentucky barbecue. His tousled bedhead made my lady bits leak. I ogled freely, hoping he hadn't heard me waken.

"You can exhale now, Diva. Holding your breath isn't advisable, except when swimming." His gruff morning voice made my nipples pebble, even as his mocking tone jerked me out of my X-rated reverie.

How in hell did he know I was holding my breath?!

How had he known I was awake?

I swallowed a few much-needed gulps of oxygen, my mental cogs whirring. "If I can't breathe, it's because I'm in a living nightmare."

Pulling on a pair of navy boxer briefs, he swiveled slowly. *Oh. My. God.* The grid of his chest was like an oblong waffle iron with ten squares. A smattering of dark brown hair dusted the top of his sternum and funneled in a line down the center of his abs to a happy trail that disappeared beneath his waist. He was like one of those naked athletes on ancient Greek vases.

My first thought was *no fair*. He couldn't ruin my life *and* be this sexy. My second thought was *what's below the midriff?* My eyes scrolled down to his bulging package, and I found myself licking my lips.

A smirk nudged his lips sideways as he ambled over to me. He snapped his fingers. "My eyes are up here, Diva."

Blushing with the heat of a thousand fiery furnaces, I blinked, my gaze swinging to his taunting eyes.

The back of his knuckle grazed my jaw as he fisted my hair in his other hand and extended my neck. He leaned over me, mirth infusing his voice. "Maybe, if you earn it, I'll let you have some." He tugged hard, making my whole scalp tingle. "After some begging." His thumb pushed past the seam of my lips to my teeth, delving inside as he watched me intently, his eyes a blazing mahogany. "Suck, Danya."

Desire flooded my sheath, and the same desperate need for relief hammered at my core. I hollowed my cheeks and sucked his thumb while he pumped it in and out. My heart pounded as I imagined I was taking something else in my mouth. A moan escaped my throat, and I began to grind my hips. He popped his thumb out and pulled the covers down to expose my tightly peaked nipples through my shirt.

He pushed the t-shirt up above my breasts, his eyes darkening with lust.

His thumb lightly circled the areola of one breast, tracing lazy arcs this way and that. He kneaded and squeezed, all the while teasing me with his wicked smirk. If only he'd touch my nipple! He released my scalp and focused his other thumb on the other areola, playing with it and driving me insane. As his thumbs grazed my nipples at last, a zap of pleasure zinged to my sex. My whole body convulsed.

"Now, Diva," he gritted, "if you promise to follow my third rule, I'll let you come."

In my haze of arousal I struggled to decipher his words. "Third?"

A devious grin slunk up his face as he cupped my breasts, continuing to massage them. "The third is, I alone control your pleasure. Repeat that so I know you understand."

"But how would I—"

He pinched both nipples, pulling them hard. The pain was exquisite, and I bit back a scream. The gesture served to remind me that he did indeed control all my pain and pleasure. "We have a whole month ahead. I'm going to enjoy you in many ways. But you will never come without my permission. Repeat."

"You alone control my pleasure," I gasped, praying he'd pluck my nipples again. Anything to ease this torturous need building inside me.

He turned each nipple lightly like a radio dial. "In a few seconds, you're going to come. When I say you can."

My head lolled back from the hint of relief. "Please."

He bent down and bit one of my nipples while twisting the other, hard. I cried out, feeling waves of bliss roll over me. His head lifted, his fingers taking over where his teeth had left off.

"You may come."

My pussy contracted, and my entire frame shuddered as I gave in to the tidal wave that rocked me. It was euphoria, deliverance, and promise all rolled into one. And like last night, I was overcome by the power and skill of the man who could provide this. When he released my nipples, another spasm hit me, filling the room with my heedless groans. Panting, I slowly came down from my high, unable to believe I'd just come that way.

Amusement danced in his eyes. "We're going to have fun this next month, Diva."

I flushed, thinking of how I'd already begged twice in the last few hours alone. And I'd momentarily forgotten how angry I was at him. Things were not going as I'd planned. I needed to put my escape in motion.

Caleb

I turned away so my fully erect dick wouldn't be the elephant in the room, even if it literally was. Watching her come undone had been like shooting down the steep side of a roller coaster, where thrill and intoxication drown out all other feelings. Maybe I was drunk on my own power over her. My first kidnapping in a twelve-year career as a fixer, and I'd hit the jackpot. She was open, receptive, and sensual as fuck. Just now had been about exploring her, awakening her hunger, and getting her addicted to the pleasure only I could give.

The wide-eyed eighteen-year-old I'd danced with six years ago had grown into a highly sexual being.

I pulled on a pair of jeans and a white t-shirt. For Danya I selected hot pink lace panties and matching bra, black jeans, and a long-sleeved wine-red top. By the time I'd laid everything out on a chair, my raging hard-on was under control.

41

"Do you want a bath or shower, Diva?"

She seemed preoccupied. "No, that's all right."

"Come here, and I'll dress you."

"I think I'll just stay in bed." She wriggled to her opposite side, facing the window.

"That wasn't a request. It was a command."

She eyed me nervously, chewing her bottom lip. "All the same, I prefer to sleep. Seeing as how I'm not allowed to go to *my* job." Her emphasis lacked conviction, since there was a tremble in her voice.

My nostrils flared. "Your *job*, for the next month, is to obey and please me. In five seconds, you'll see what happens when I'm displeased."

She shivered, but stayed put as I counted down. At the end, she ventured an anxious glance at me, waiting.

I flashed the malicious grin I reserved for victims I was about to put through their paces. "You had your chance to be dressed in here, Diva. That chance has now expired."

Collecting her clothes on the chair, I stopped by the bed just long enough to scoop her up and throw her over my shoulder. She protested loudly as I passed through the door and descended the stairs, heading to the kitchen.

Marisa was kneading dough at the counter, and Jeremy was repairing a broken light fixture in the corner.

"Marisa, Jeremy, I'd like your help."

My long-faithful domestic workers dropped what they were doing and came to stand by the fire. Since they'd been happily married for forty-some years, I had no doubt they could handle what I was about to ask them to do.

"Our guest needs to be taught a lesson." My eyes telegraphed to them that I intended to discipline her. "She'll be dressed here, in front of you."

"No!" Danya bleated.

"No?" I set her down, holding her by the throat as I pulled

out my pocketknife and flicked it open. "So you prefer to be naked in front of Marisa and Jeremy? That can be arranged." Her eyes rounded with fear.

I sliced the scarf that bound her wrists, pocketed the knife, and pulled her arms above her head, wrenching her shirt off. Her arms flew to cover her breasts while I dragged her shorts down, cut the rope around her ankles, and rid first one leg then the other of the shorts. She tried to flee, but I flipped her around, trapped her wrists behind her back, and forced her to face Marisa and Jeremy completely naked. They stood calmly looking on, as if this were an everyday occurrence, training captives to obey.

"Marisa, don't you think she should stand up nice and tall? She has a body to be proud of."

"She does," Marisa agreed. "She'd look good in a gunny-sack."

Danya tensed and fought to break free. "I hate you!" Her voice cracked with rage and humiliation.

My cock jerked at her lower back as I held her snugly against me. Her naked body and feistiness were acting like amphetamines on my junk. "Jeremy, what color would suit her flaming hair, blue eyes, and milk-white skin?"

He tilted his head, scratching his stubbly chin. "I'd say red, or blue. Maybe black."

"I thought so too."

"Let. Me. Go." Danya seethed.

"What did I say about making demands, Danya?" I breathed hotly in her ear. A tremor passed from her head to her feet. "Marisa, Jeremy, I put the question to both of you — doesn't she look more attractive when she's furious?"

They chuffed a laugh, exchanging knowing glances.

"Brings color to her cheeks," said Jeremy.

"She's got gumption," Marisa pronounced. "Suits her well."

"Marisa, would you bring her bra over?" I nodded towards the pile I'd tossed on the couch.

Danya thrust out her chin, twisting her face away from her audience. "You can't do this to me. You'll rot in prison for the rest of your life."

I chuckled, enjoying her spirit. "You're the one committing indecent exposure, Diva." As Marisa held up the bra, I fed Danya's arms through the straps. "Jeremy, can you lend a hand with the clasps?"

"I'm not a child!" Danya spat.

I gathered her hair in my hand as Jeremy fastened the hooks. "Then stop acting like one," I advised in her ear.

"*Please*, let me dress myself." Her eyes jumped between mine, desperation swimming in their depths.

I smiled. "Too late for that. You'll submit to the rest of your punishment. Marisa, the panties."

Not surprisingly, Danya tried to kick me as I knelt down. Blocking her, I grabbed both her ankles and threw her back onto the couch, pulling her legs up so her ass was exposed to Marisa and Jeremy. "Ladies and gentlemen, the other end."

They chortled good-naturedly as I slid Danya's panties on.

Her eyes shot daggers at me. "You'll pay for this."

"Your father will be paying, Diva. Richly." I held my hand out for the jeans, which Marisa passed over. "Now, Danya. If you want a spanking in front of Marisa and Jeremy, the best way to get it is by struggling as I put on your jeans." She flinched, no doubt still smarting from her thrashing last night. "Hold out your leg."

She complied, and I pulled on her jeans.

"Stand up." She obeyed. "Arms over your head." Again, she did as directed, and I slid her shirt over her.

I turned her so she faced Marisa and Jeremy. "Is she acceptable for breakfast?"

Marisa laughed. "It's gone on lunchtime, Caleb."

Jeremy nodded. "She's gorgeous."

Cupping her chin, I turned her face to me. "You hear that, Diva? Do you want your restraints on over breakfast? Or are you going to behave?"

Her eyebrows leapt, as though the last thing she'd expected was to be granted momentary freedom. "I'll behave."

I'd broken her enough for now.

CHAPTER SIX: DANYA

So much for my plan to get Caleb to leave me alone in the bedroom for a while. I'd thought of finding something sharp to whittle away the scarf binding my wrists. From there I could undo my ropes and sneak out the front door.

Now, sitting at the kitchen table, I pinkened, reliving my utter humiliation of the last twenty minutes. I would never forget what he'd just done to me. Being naked in front of him in the bedroom would've been bad enough. But standing in the buff in front of his domestic help! In the *kitchen*. Being dressed by all three of them as if I were a toddler! Fury tore at my chest, and I gazed longingly at the knife Caleb was using to cut up an apple for me. How satisfying it'd be to hold it to his throat and make *him* beg.

His eyes crinkled at the corners. "What are you thinking, Diva? How to murder me?"

"Somebody ought to," I snipped.

A warm laugh tumbled from his throat. "Somebody probably will. But I assure you, it won't be you."

I narrowed my eyes. "What makes you so sure? After what you just did, I have plenty of motives."

Grinning, he slid the plate of apple slices across to me. "You're making things very complicated for yourself, Danya. You test me at every turn. You should know by now, not only do I mean what I say, but I get what I want. Always."

"Well, you can't make me eat." I arched an eyebrow, and his eyes glittered provokingly in response.

On to Plan Two — hunger strike.

Marisa set a plate of scrambled eggs, bacon, grits, and buttered toast before me. *Oh, God, this isn't fair.* Bacon was my favorite, bar none. My stomach grumbled. Loudly.

I poured cream into my coffee and took a sip, hoping it might make my cravings abate.

Smirking, he tossed a strip of bacon in his mouth. "I'll let your body do the forcing."

I pushed aside my plate and the plastic fork beside it. "How would your client like it if I died of starvation? On your watch?"

He hitched a shoulder. "More likely after one month you'd still be alive. Just." His filthy chuckle shot straight to my sex. "My question is, why put yourself through that?"

"As a statement of freedom. And rebellion." I tilted my chin up defiantly.

His expression blasé, he toasted me with his coffee mug. "Hear, hear, Che Guevara."

Though he ate and drank nonchalantly, his body seemed on the alert in case I'd throw something at him or try to wrest the knife away. His neck and forearm muscles looked ready to pounce, and his eyes skipped around, a forbidding gleam kindling them. I shuddered to think what he'd do if I attacked him now. My sore backside reminded me all too painfully of what he'd done for less.

Ignoring my insistent belly, I reveled in the free use of my limbs, folding my arms on the table. "Aren't you going to call my father?"

"He's the last call of the day."

I slanted my head. "You have more important calls to make?" I found this hard to believe.

"As a matter of fact, I do, Diva." He poured more coffee in his mug. "And while I'm making them, you're going to be tied up and under Jeremy's supervision in his studio."

My heart sank.

"Can't I stay with you?" I blurted. The question made no sense to me. Why would I want to stay with my tormentor? I should be singing hallelujahs at the thought of a break from him.

With a mischievous glint in his eye he snagged an apple slice, tossing it in his mouth. "Fond of me already?"

"Don't flatter yourself."

"Oh, but I do, Diva. After the look on your face earlier when I —"

"*Shh.*" My head snapped to where Marisa was humming to herself and putting bread loaves in the oven.

A sly smile crept over his lips. "If she didn't know before, she'll certainly know now."

I straightened my back. "After what you did to me earlier she'll know I hate you."

"Hate and lust make a potent mixture."

"Then I'm missing one important ingredient."

His tiger eyes bored into me as if they saw right through my lie. "Stand."

My breath hitched. "What?"

He tipped his head. "Now."

My chair scraped the floor as I stood, a quiver fluttering in my lower belly.

"Come here." Authority hummed and vibrated in his words.

I rounded the table, halting a step away from him. My heart raced, and my chest heaved. What was he going to do?

He slowly pushed to his feet, bolting me to his heated gaze. "Turn around. Slowly."

I traced a complete circle, warmth coiling outwards from my center and slickness pooling in my folds. I could feel the hectic pulse in my neck. Was his gaze, his dominance, or his whole presence doing this to me?

He leaned forward, his lips moving against the shell of my

ear. "Look down, Diva."

Pinpricks of awareness and arousal scattered along the surface of my skin. I glanced down to find my hardened nipples saluting him.

Instinctively, I threw an arm across my chest to hide my desire.

"And that's without touching." He curved an eyebrow.

I rallied. "Well, with my kind of hatred, any further lust is off the table."

He smirked, and I kicked myself when even his smug smile stirred glowing embers in my nether region. "I'll bear that in mind when you next beg me."

I opened my mouth to say — I wasn't sure what, but he was already glancing at his watch.

"Time to pick up another scarf and rope." Laying a hand on my tailbone, he led me back upstairs, where he tied me with the same chain gang-style looseness around the ankles and closeness at the wrists. Whether because his fingers had sent me into raptures earlier or I was succumbing to Stockholm Syndrome, I yearned for more of his touch on my wrists and ankles. His large, strong hands knotting the rope and testing the tightness of the scarf hypnotized me. That lustrous, molten-chocolate hair tempted me as he knelt, his head within reach of my fingers. I could weave them through his thick mane, burying my face in his clean, virile scent and not emerging for a long while.

As he stood, my hands grazed his crotch, sending a kick of lust to my heat. I took a step back to recover my breath. But he advanced, a wolfish glint gleaming in his pine-dark eyes. I shuffled back some more, and he moved towards me, till my back hit the wall. My chest rose and fell, my gaze drifting to his ruddy lips.

Placing his hands on either side of my head, he leaned in so an inch separated us. A flashback to our steamy tango surged up, and my throat suddenly felt parched. *Please kiss me. Please touch me.* I tipped my head up, my lips parting. *If he kisses me now, he'd be the Werewolf once more. I could forget where I am and why I'm here.*

"You may be worth fifteen million," he murmured, his lips millimeters from mine. "And maybe even worth the trouble."

My jaw dropped as I snapped out of my fantasy. He was talking ransom and pay? How stupid I was! He was determined to dance on the Werewolf's grave and leave me with nothing but bitterness for memories.

"Oh no, I'm not," I bit out. "I'll give you so much trouble that you'll wish you'd never set eyes on me."

The roguish quirk of his lips only incensed me further. "It's because you're so much trouble that you're worth so much."

Taking a few seconds to gather some spittle in my dry mouth, I took aim and spat in his face. More air than liquid hit his nose, but it was the gesture that counted.

His pupils dilating, he spat right back, with much more saliva than I'd mustered. His sputum landed in my eye, dribbling down my cheek.

"If you wanted to exchange bodily fluids, you only had to ask, Diva." A taunting fire lit his eye. "Though soon I'll mark your face with another kind." He pushed off the wall, his lips curving in a depraved smile.

"Never," I gritted.

He took a long narrow cloth from the dresser and stuffed it in his pocket. Was that a gag? My heart sped up.

"Never say never."

I had barely a few seconds to wipe the spittle off my cheek before he tossed me over his shoulder. The whole way downstairs I fumed. I didn't know what made me maddest. The way he reduced me to his captive, the way he put a price tag on me, or the way he canceled my Werewolf fantasy. I renewed my vow to get out of here and get even.

The study where he carried me was bright, warm, and cheery. Seated at a walnut desk, Jeremy worked on a laptop, wearing black-rimmed glasses with an absorbed expression on his angular face. Several brightly colored catalogs lay open beside him.

My nemesis set me down on a comfortable leather couch under built-in bookshelves. "Is planting late this spring, Jeremy?"

"Yup. Can't get things in till the ground can be worked, and everything's late this year," the older man grunted. "Just ordering more azaleas, asters, and such."

"If you want a book you can't reach, just ask Jeremy." My captor nodded to the shelf behind me, passing me a remote control. "The TV has no channels or programs. Only Netflix."

Internet! A way to communicate!

As if reading my mind, he added, "It's locked against the use or download of any other apps."

Damn.

I remained silent, glad he was about to leave. I wanted — badly needed — distance from him and the tumult of emotions and hormones he stirred up.

Caleb

Giving a nod to Jeremy, I locked the study door, sauntering towards my own office at the other end of the house. That spat with Danya — pun intended — came at just the right time. I'd known referring to her ransom would rile her. I needed her to look angry, hurt, and frantic later when I called her father. I couldn't afford to have her looking too comfortable. I had to stay on task.

Yes, her lips had been one of the more tempting prizes of my career. But claiming such a prize would cost me.

I settled into my office chair, opening my laptop. I'd connected to a VPN server in Lancaster, so my IP address was hidden. Jeremy's VPN server was in Harrisburg. Walter Penwarren would have an extremely hard time tracing our location. I had over ten burner phones to choose from for our video call to him. My client—for reasons known only to him—had specified that I was to call Walter every day starting today.

All in good time. Now for Gideon. I video called him on my laptop, waiting as the app's dial sounds rang.

"Mmrrmph." Gideon's messy blond hair and long, hawk-nosed mug popped up on my screen.

Was that . . . yep. That was drool encrusted on his cheek.

"You were sleeping." I smiled at my friend's nonexistent schedule. It was 2:30 PM on a Friday.

He yawned so I could see his tonsils. "It *is* almost the weekend."

"With *almost* being the operative word."

"What good is it being a professional hacker if you can't bend the rules? Circadian rhythms included." Fumbling around, he produced a brown-stained Star Trek mug, chugging its contents.

"Please tell me that's water."

His face contorted in a grimace. "You know me better than that. Water is the devil's brew. It's Diet Coke all the way, baby. From sunrise to sunset. Or, as the case may be"—he peered at his computer's clock as if he had no idea what part of the cycle we were on—"sunset to sunrise."

"Enabling your dentist to make the payments on his Florida condo?"

He grinned. "Colorado timeshare. It's all he talks about once he starts drilling."

I chuckled. "He's got you by the balls, so he rubs them in your face."

"Thanks for the visual."

"They're *your* balls."

He winced. "Not making things better."

"So. Speaking of balls. Did you get in?"

It took balls to do what Gideon did. He was known as the *Weissritter*, or White Knight, to cyber security experts across America, because his hacks tended to whistle blow on the corporations and companies he infiltrated. Those entities had plenty of enemies willing to pay Gideon for his services. So far, no one had the remotest clue to his identity, though a large bounty was out on his head. He'd been called the most gifted, elusive hacker of his generation, whatever the hell that meant. Now, as a favor to me based on our longstanding friendship—I'd known him since setting up as a fixer at age 18—he was hacking into Walter Penwarren's global biotech company, GenRev Technologies.

"Why do you think you found me asleep? I spent the whole night doing it." Gideon shoved a whole banana in his mouth, his cheeks puffing out like Dizzy Gillespie in his later career.

In Gideon-speak that was a yes.

"Find anything yet?" I couldn't keep the edge out of my voice, so much rode on this.

He held up a finger to signal he needed a second to mash up the fruit. When he'd swallowed, he washed it down with more Diet Coke. I wouldn't trade places with his gut if it were the last fallout shelter in a nuclear holocaust. "I've already found plenty of evidence of number one on your list."

I'd told Gideon to look for evidence of seven different crimes committed by Walter and his company. The first was shareholder fraud.

I felt as if my heart had cleared a hurdle in a track race. "Nice. How much?"

"Two cases, so far. I suspect that's the tip of the iceberg."

"I know you've got a few other jobs going, but you think

you can hack it?" Like me, Gideon loved a good pun.

His lips slid up in a half-grin. "You said we've got till the end of April first?"

"Yeah." The day to make a fool of Walter Penwarren.

"Leave it to me. Now, as for the other thing."

Gideon was referring to my request that he find a lucrative proprietary idea of Walter's company, steal it, and offer it to Walter's main rival, SciPulse.

My lanky friend leaned back in his swivel chair, his Adam's apple on full display as he lolled his head. "Any particular criteria, apart from *lucrative?*"

"Preferably multi-million-dollar, breakthrough, revolutionary . . . you get the idea."

He spun from side to side. "I'm no specialist in the field, but you think I'll know it when I see it?"

"Ping me when you see something promising, and I'll call you."

"All right. And, just so you know, I'm tracking all communications."

Read — *Walter's* communications.

"So if he's onto us at any point, we'll have advance warning."

"I take it you've done this before," I joked.

"Eh, just a few times."

"I'd say I'll name my firstborn after you, but I'll never procreate."

"Never say never."

As we ended the call, his words echoed in my head. That's right, I'd said them to Danya earlier. A grin tugged at the corners of my mouth. I was determined never to have offspring because of what had happened to me and my siblings. But pulling out and jetting my cum all over Danya's face would be a hot form of birth control. Literally.

My cock stirred in my pants.

I popped a licorice mint in my mouth and mentally prepared for the next item of business.

I glanced at my laptop. March fourth. Another year, another job with the Breadcrumb Client. When I'd completed the assignment a few days ago, he'd said he would give me the last piece of the puzzle today. For five years now he'd proven a stickler for tradition.

Chapter Seven: Caleb: Five Years Ago

M arch fourth. The only day of the year that's a command, as my foster father Clark liked to say. I needed to pay him a visit one of these days out in West Chester. Like me, he loved wordplay and double meanings. The sillier, the better. One of his favorites was, "If the devil ever goes bald, there's going to be hell toupee."

I'd just finished a major job the night before and was taking a blustery midday run through my neighborhood. March had blown in like a lion this year, and a lot of branches lay on the ground from a storm we'd had two nights before. When my phone rang with an unknown number, I stopped on the boulevard to answer it. If this was another job, it was coming at a perfect time. I had bills to pay for Faye's school, Mom's therapy, and the house I'd just bought.

"Yeah," I panted.

"Caleb Scott?"

"Speaking."

"I represent a client who wishes to remain anonymous. My name is Max Fischer."

I leaned against an elm trunk. "Go on."

"Can you meet at the Key Fountain in the Morris Arboretum at three?"

"I'll be there."

Two hours later, loitering beside the fountain, I found a

large-footed man in a three-piece suit and coat with wispy grey hair and one outward-turning eye. We shook hands and ambled down a walk lined with redwoods.

"Mr. Scott, my client has a job that needs delicate handling."

Words I'd heard a dozen times before. "He's come to the right place then."

"Let us call my client Mr. J. He has a large orchard outside Mifflinburg. You know, peaches, pears, apples, and so forth. He's owned the estate for fifteen years. The proceeds from the fruit and other products make for a good side business to his main one, which is in finance."

I nodded, plunging my hands in my coat pockets as a gust of wind sliced our faces.

"Mr. J. has had increasingly aggressive offers to buy his orchard over the last few years from a developer by the name of Salinger. He's turned them all down."

"Made in person?"

"Yes. Salinger waylaid Mr. J. at various locations in public and named a price. The last time Salinger approached Mr. J. about the property, a year ago, he warned him that things would be very difficult for him if he didn't accept Salinger's final offer."

I saw where this was going.

Fischer continued. "In January, the Pennsylvania Department of Revenue informed Mr. J. that he owed eight hundred grand in unpaid taxes relating to his secondary business, namely, the orchard, dating back fifteen years. Including interest, the total owed is one point four million dollars. When Mr. J. searched for the files that would prove he hadn't misrepresented his income, they'd been wiped from his computers and the cloud. The files mainly proved that all his claims for itemized deductions and employee business expenses were legitimate. They'd been selectively erased from his records."

I side-stepped a large puddle in the middle of the path, left from the storm. "And Salinger?"

"He *ran into* Mr. J. outside his work a week ago, offering him a price on the orchard that would nicely cover what he owes in taxes."

"Your client doesn't wish to fight this in the Tax Court?"

Fischer blew his nose into a handkerchief. "He has no evidence. Even if he took several months to try to dig up what he could from people he's dealt with over the years, he'd still fall far short."

I turned to him. "You want me to find something on Salinger."

Fischer met my eye. "As soon as you can. The revenue department has given Mr. J. another month to pay before they charge him with tax evasion."

"How much if I make the case go away?" A man like Salinger was sure to have shitloads of dirt that wouldn't take much digging to find.

"Mr. J. will pay you a hundred grand. He also has something priceless to offer."

"Namely?"

"Information."

"About?"

"Your father."

My brow furrowed. "Clark Williams?"

"No. Your biological father. Nathaniel Furness."

Caleb Scott was the name I'd assumed when I started out in the business, and it had remained my professional name ever since. Only Mom and Faye used my real name, Callum Furness.

A tingly sensation prickled at the back of my neck, sprinkling goosebumps along my arms. My father had been an enigma to us all. "He died." I avoided touching the excruciating nerve connected to how he'd died.

Fischer nodded. "Mr. J. knew him, and knows a great deal about the circumstances of his career. He knows why he committed suicide. Knows why your family suffered so much. Why you had to go into foster care."

The chill in the air suddenly felt raw, and I shivered. "How does he know all this?"

"He worked at the same company as your father for eighteen years. Though your father and he only overlapped for a few of them." Fischer's metallic voice began to grate on me.

"How can he be so sure *I* don't know all this?" I was equal parts insulted and fascinated.

"Because these are dangerous secrets known by very few and spoken of by even fewer."

"What's in it for him to let me in on these secrets?" Everyone had an angle, and I couldn't trust a person till I'd found out what it was.

"Two reasons—revenge and money. Mr. J. worked in the finance department of GenRev Technologies, owned by Walter Penwarren. Penwarren fired Mr. J. without cause in two thousand and five. Since Mr. J. witnessed many injustices during his time at the company—notably, the wrongs done your father and mother—he wants to see you redress a few of them." Fischer coughed into his hand. "As an anonymous shareholder in Penwarren's company, Mr. J. benefits from the shares' payouts through a trust. He believes Penwarren's dirty tactics are going to ruin the company."

"What exactly is Mr. J. prepared to tell me?"

"For this job, he's offering all the information he has on how Walter Penwarren first screwed your father over."

I side-eyed him. "For this job?"

Fischer bobbed his head. "He'll have more jobs for you. Each one will come with its own piece of the puzzle."

"Breadcrumbs," I mumbled.

"Hmm?"

"He'll give me breadcrumbs." The metaphor was apt because I was so desperately hungry for knowledge about my father, my stillborn baby brother Luke, and the onset of my mother's dementia at such a young age.

As for all the rest, I took full responsibility.

A week later, I sat in my kitchen gazing out at the pouring rain and waiting for a call from Mr. J., or, as I was now calling him, *the Breadcrumb Client*. It had been reasonably straightforward for me to dig up dirt on Salinger, and I'd had no trouble blackmailing him. I'd gotten him to replace all of Mr. J.'s tax files and convince the department of revenue to drop the case. Apparently Salinger had considerable pull with the department of revenue. But he hadn't been smart enough to avoid getting photographed over the years in compromising positions with numerous women. Unfortunately for him, his current custody battle with his wife required him to look squeaky clean. So much for his plans to replace Mr. J.'s orchard with a development.

I'd drunk three cups of black coffee but couldn't tell if my nervousness came from the caffeine or if it had driven me to drink more. I had no idea what to expect from this call. No idea who'd be on the other end of the line, how much they'd reveal, or if any of it would be trustworthy. I cracked my knuckles a few times, stood, and paced to the other end of the room. The hammering of the raindrops against the windowpane matched my heart rate.

The call came through at 4 on the dot.

I swiped up. "Hello?"

"Mr. Scott?"

"Yes."

"This is Mr. J., as I believe Max Fischer named me to you." His voice was a steady, strong baritone. "First off, I want to thank you for the way you handled that other matter."

"It was my pleasure."

"The information I'm about to share with you is confidential. Are we speaking on a secure line?"

"We are."

"Good." He cleared his throat. "I have the following on excellent authority, though I'm not at liberty to disclose my source. Your father, Nathaniel Furness, attended the University of Chicago at the same time as Walter Penwarren. Furness majored in biomedical engineering, while Penwarren studied economics. In their senior year, Furness invented a VR innovation for spine surgery, which he planned to develop with Penwarren's help. Penwarren beat him to the punch, obtaining a patent, creating a prototype, and marketing the device in record time. This idea and its wild success formed the basis for his company, GenRev Tech."

I didn't know how to process this news. Penwarren had stolen Dad's idea out from under him? I'd known my father invented things, but in the thirteen years our lives had overlapped, I'd only ever seen him make money from a desk job at GenRev. I'd always gotten the feeling he'd wanted much more from life—a chance to live off his creativity. From the few things Mom had told me about him, he was absentminded and impractical, but also laser-focused, ingenious, and dedicated.

"Why didn't my father take Penwarren to court?" I asked.

"He did." Mr. J. sighed. "That was a mistake. It's notoriously difficult to prove rights to an idea one hasn't patented. And Penwarren had so many more resources at his disposal, he was able to run circles around Furness in the legal arena. Furness spent seven years trying to prove he'd come up with the innovation."

Memories from early childhood filtered into my consciousness. Mom and Dad had repeatedly fought over tight finances, over *letting go* from Mom, versus *fighting for what's due to us* from Dad, and over the need to relocate to an apartment. That one especially reminded me how I'd puzzled over the word *refinance*.

Mr. J. went on. "I'm sorry to say the legal battle took a severe financial toll on your family, while Penwarren's pockets only grew fatter by the day."

I clenched my fists, remembering how we'd given up the house and downsized to a small apartment in the city. We'd gotten rid of the car, Mom had refused Faye the dog she'd wanted so badly, and Dad had begun to suffer what I later realized was major depression. The whole atmosphere at home had eroded like a sinkhole.

I believed what Mr. J. was telling me, because so many of his facts squared with what I knew to be true.

"I'm afraid, young man, that Walter committed four other crimes against your family."

I waited for him to continue. When he didn't, I prompted, "What else did he do?"

"The rest is for another time. I'll have more jobs for you. Each one will come with another piece of the puzzle."

I ground my teeth. "Why not just tell me now?"

"Because once you know them all, the revenge you take will be like an explosion that will reverberate across many lives."

"Better now than later," I huffed, growing impatient with this man's all-knowingness.

He chuckled. "My motives are selfish. But you'll understand them better in time."

And with that he hung up.

I threw my phone across the room, beginning to doubt the sanity of Mr. J. Sure, I'd gobbled up his breadcrumb like a goldfish. But who fed bits and pieces of the truth to a man as starved as I was? Only a sadist or a nutjob.

I planned to spend the next few days fact-checking everything he'd said. And I decided it was high time I found out who Mr. J. really was.

CHAPTER EIGHT: DANYA: PRESENT

Inactivity was definitely not for me. I might be kidnapped, but instead of sitting on the couch the way Caleb expected me to, I made it my mission to explore every nook and cranny of Jeremy's studio. After standing on tiptoe and craning my neck to read each title on the top shelf of the bookcase, I eased myself off the couch and shambled around the room investigating the trinkets and souvenirs Jeremy and his wife had collected over the years. Assuring me good-naturedly that none of this was private, he freely offered up information about their travels and their two sons. I asked him about the plants he was ordering for the garden at Caleb's house, and he sought my input on color schemes of flowers. After an hour of congenial talk, it was almost as if I hadn't stood naked in front of him earlier and he hadn't put on my bra. Though the memory still made heat crawl from my chest to my ears.

As the afternoon wore on, my hunger strike no longer seemed like such a brilliant idea. My brain converted every object into something edible. The metal stapler looked like a grilled rainbow trout. The antique dish resembled a bowl of pasta with clam sauce. The black-and-white checks on the antimacassar made me think of a sushi roll. *Mmm.* Spider roll. From the Japanese restaurant two blocks from my apartment.

Since my strike was by all accounts a resounding failure—I fully planned on devouring anything put before me at dinner—I turned to my next plan for escape—bring Jeremy and Marisa over to my side. They seemed like such decent folk, I couldn't imagine that part of them didn't flinch at what Caleb did for a living, not to mention this particular job.

"How did Caleb get into . . ." At a loss to describe what he did, I hoped Jeremy would fill in the blank.

"What, fixing?" He chuckled. "Since he makes no secret about it, I guess it can't hurt to share. He's been at it for twelve years — since he was eighteen. He's darn good at it, too." His voice brimmed with pride. "His foster father taught him everything he knew — about shooting, fighting, surviving, how the world works, you name it."

"How did his foster father know so much?" I wandered over to the window that overlooked a large meadow. Over the last few hours, the sun had retired, leaving the sky a dull slate-grey, as if rain or snow threatened.

"He was in the marines for eight years. Then he worked as a building inspector. He just retired this year."

"But doesn't fixing require contacts and experience?" I knew next to nothing about it, but it seemed like an odd profession for an 18-year-old to take up, just like that.

"His foster father's well-connected, and after a few jobs, Cal took to the work like a pro."

"It seems surprising that his foster father would condone . . . illegal behavior." I hoped this might lead to hearing Jeremy's own views on criminal enterprise.

A noncommittal grunt left his lips. "I'll let *him* tell you about all that."

"Isn't he ever worried one of his enemies will . . ." I searched for the phrase. "Take him out? I mean, since he works independently?"

"He's got the family's protection, for one." Jeremy sat back in his chair. "Then he keeps to himself, lives largely in a bubble. No one knows who he is or where he lives."

I knelt on the edge of a half-sofa. "It must be a pretty lonely existence."

He shrugged. "Guess he likes it that way."

"At least he has his mom and sister."

His eyebrows soared, and his mouth slackened. "He mentioned them, did he?"

I nodded. "As if he's close with them."

Smiling, he shook his head. "Wonders never cease."

Did he mean Caleb didn't usually talk about his family with victims — or didn't share this sort of thing with women? Either way, it was the first hint that he considered me something out of the ordinary, and I stowed this bit of intel away like a small treasure.

As if unwilling to talk any more about his employer, Jeremy resumed work at his computer. I felt flattered that he'd shared as much as he had with me.

Seeing him typing away made me think of all the work piling up at my own job. What was Kari thinking of me right now, when I hadn't called in sick? Innes probably thought I'd blown off work so I could bail on our date. Had they already assigned Florida to someone else? A lead weight plummeted to the base of my belly. All I'd worked for over the last three years had gone down the tubes in one day.

Did Luis already know I'd been kidnapped? I felt sure once he did, he'd fly back from Singapore and try to rescue me. I couldn't count on Dad the way I could on Luis. Luis and I exchanged dozens of texts daily and talked several times a week. We'd both been 9 when Eve and Dad had married, and he'd quickly become brother, best friend, and confidant. Nothing short of a war zone would stop him from trying to bring me back.

Maybe all wasn't lost. We were going to call Dad in a few minutes, Jeremy had grown friendly, Luis was on the way to save me, and across the house freshly baked bread had just been taken out of the oven.

I couldn't give up hope yet.

Just then a key sounded in the lock, and the door swung

open. Caleb stormed in breathing fire, his gaze swinging from the empty couch under the bookcase to Jeremy and then me on the opposite end of the room by the window. His face was murderous as he stalked towards me, his brows slamming down and smoke nearly blowing from his nostrils and ears. If I'd had the use of my hands, I would've clutched one of the cushions in front of me like a shield. But I had nowhere to retreat to.

A growl rose from deep in his chest as he fastened his malignant gaze on me. "Jeremy, you may leave."

Jeremy hopped up and exited faster than a lizard skittering into the shadows.

There goes my last hope.

"On your knees," Caleb commanded.

My eyes widened, and I blinked a few times. Surely he couldn't mean . . .

"You have three seconds." His voice was the ominous rumble of distant thunder.

Dumbstruck, I twisted my way from the couch to the floor, kneeling upright with my head bowed. My heart knocked at my chest wall with the urgency of a firefighter. What would I do if he ordered me to . . .

He took a step forward, fisting my hair and pulling so I had to look up at him. "Beg me to have mercy on you."

A swallow slogged its way down my throat. This was even worse than I'd thought. At that moment, I realized I would have willingly wrapped my lips around his length. But to beg, when I had no idea why, was an exercise in abject servitude.

The evil glint in his eye told me he'd read my thoughts. "That's right Diva. I can be merciful, or I can be vengeful. Right now I'm feeling *very* vengeful."

Seeking relief, I began to sink back onto my haunches, but his other hand cupped my throat and held me up. "I'll keep you kneeling like this all night. Until I get everything I want from you."

"What do you want?" I quavered.

"First beg."

My thighs quivered with the effort of keeping me upright. But still my pride clung to me. "Why am I begging for mercy?"

His lips curled in a sneer. "Your love and loyalties lie with a monster. And you hold part of him in you." His jaw clenched, his eyes wilding. "But I'll show no mercy to *him*."

"Please," I entreated, frightened by his words. "Please have mercy."

He squeezed my throat tightly, blocking my breath for a long moment. When he released me, I sputtered.

"Again."

"Please, Caleb. Have mercy." *On him and on me.*

"Not on him," he rasped, as if I'd spoken the thought aloud. He reached into his pocket and pulled out the long cloth from earlier, tying it tightly around my head over my mouth. "Stay in that position. Don't. Move."

What now? My abs and lower body ached from holding this pose for so long.

He tapped his phone and turned it around to face me.

My father appeared on the screen. "Danya?" His brows knotted. "Where are you?"

I choked out incoherent sounds from behind the gag.

Caleb

Seeing the fuckhole's face from above only enraged me more. Holding the phone in front of me, I remained out of range of the camera.

"Walter, as you can see, your daughter has her hands tied at the moment." I brought the phone even closer to Danya so he could see the fear in her eyes. "Spit out your questions and leave us to it."

I deliberately made it sound like we were having an orgy. I was beyond caring about the consequences. If I'd ever cared.

"What—what's going on?"

He got the C-movie lines.

"I believe the situation speaks for itself. Fifteen million, Walter. Wired to an account to be specified, on April first at eleven-fifty-nine PM."

"April . . . but that's a month away. I'll pay it now."

Hope flared in the diva's cobalt eyes.

I smirked, pulling the tin of licorice mints from my pocket and tossing one in my mouth. "Negative. April Fool's or never."

"But . . . why? What do you need a month for?"

"They're called rules, Walter. People occasionally follow them. You should try it yourself sometime." I nodded at Danya. "You may sit back. But keep your back straight."

Danya's chest heaved as she lowered her backside to her ankles with visible relief. She kept her tits high, just as I'd demanded.

It'd serve Walter right to watch her suck me off here and now. And the diva's eyes earlier had told me she'd rather be gagged with my cock than that cloth.

"I find that timing awfully suspicious," he muttered. "Our board meeting is on April first."

"Is it now?" My eyes swiped over Danya's edible curves. "Care to share the agenda, while you're sharing your calendar? Oh. Wait. I don't think I give a fuck."

"This is absurd," he blustered. "You don't know whom you're dealing with."

"A young woman who misses her loved ones?" I baited.

He snorted. "I'm speaking of myself. I'm one of the richest and most powerful men in the country. Do you have any idea how easily I could crush you?"

I chuckled. So he wanted to play chicken. "Ah, but who's holding your daughter now, Walter?"

He waved a dismissive hand. "That's beside the point. She'll survive. You're asking me to ruin my public image by not pursuing you. To look like a weakling and coward before my company, my shareholders, and my rivals. I won't do it."

"A virus set to infect your whole company's systems says otherwise. Of course, it only triggers once you bring in the authorities or the press, or otherwise take action to free her."

He scoffed. "Impossible! We have the best cyber security among the Fortune Five Hundred. Our team serve as international consultants."

The man was as wooden as a Russian doll. His daughter was tied up and gagged in the middle of nowhere, and he was bragging about having the cutting-edge version of IT security.

"Oops. Looks like someone was sleeping on the job."

He harumphed. "I don't know why you're wasting your time with my daughter. Clearly this is about my business. Call your crime what it is—ransomware."

"Go ahead and puzzle over semantics, Walter. Meanwhile I'll waste my own time with your daughter."

"I can't keep word about the virus from leaking." Walter loosened his collar. "Someone's bound to discover the threat."

"Let it leak, then. And by all means put your team to work trying to reverse it. I wish them luck." I advanced on Danya, plucking the erect nipples protruding through her shirt. Though Walter could see my forearm and hand, I didn't give a fuck. "Incidentally, your daughter got less coverage on this call than a pre-roll ad on YouTube. I'd love to see your main content."

I killed the call, pocketing my phone.

I now saw I'd been wrong to think of playing the long game with Walter. He was so wrapped up in his mega-corporate magnate fog that he forgot to care about his daughter. Not a word of encouragement, comfort, or support had left his self-serving lips. It was clear he was fine with letting her rot here, so long as his company's computer systems and his macho reputation remained intact. My client had specified that I was to call Walter every day, treat him politely, not touch Danya, and blah-blah. My call with the Breadcrumb Client had killed any possibility of politeness. And the last, well, Danya kneeling obediently, her lips at my crotch, was as tempting as it got.

No, it was time to move things along, Walter and my client be damned.

As I stroked Danya's mahogany waves, she let out a moan that activated all the nerve endings in my cock. Grabbing a tuft of her hair, I yanked, eliciting a long-drawn-out purr. "Not so delicate after all, are you, Diva?"

She gave a slight shake of the head. Her eyes, frantic with need, had darkened to glacial lakes. They pleaded with me, more vehemently than her begging earlier.

But I knew this time they weren't just pleading for release or mercy. They were pleading to forget. Because otherwise she'd have to think of what that call meant. She'd have to face the fact that her father was a shitty excuse for a human being, who considered her absence a mere inconvenience or liability—who likely even blamed her for his company's current predicament.

Well, she was about to need a lot of distracting, because she was in for plenty more rude awakenings about her father over the next four weeks.

Our interests were exactly aligned right now—we both wanted to forget Walter.

I undid the gag, tossing it behind Danya. I combed my fingers through her lush locks, pushing them off her face. Then I unknotted the scarf around her wrists. "Kneel up." When she'd done so, I reached over her, untying the rope that bound her ankles.

Standing above her, I gripped her nape. So exquisite, her features so rare, refined, and graceful. On the surface, Venetian glass. But the fire in her eyes told of the sexual creature lurking within. I suspected she had more diamond in her than I'd first credited her with. Still a diva, but just as much Athena as Aphrodite. Deliciously destructible, but capable of piecing herself together to fight again.

"Please me, Diva."

Her eyes flared with hunger. Without hesitating, she unbuttoned and unzipped my fly, dragging my jeans over my hips and freeing the erection that throbbed, thick and hard, against my stomach. She ran her tongue along her top and bottom lips, looking up for permission to uncover me. I nodded.

She peeled my boxer briefs down, tugging them and my jeans to my knees. Her mouth slackened and her chest heaved, like she'd just entered Ali Baba's cave. She breathed in deeply, closing her eyes as if my scent intoxicated her. When she opened them, I saw they'd dilated so the blue slivers of her irises rimmed gaping pupils. She swallowed, running her hands up the inside of my thighs. When her delicate fingers wrapped around my cock, I shuddered with relief. Her thumb swiped the seed spilling from my slit, sliding it along the veiny underside of my shaft. Pleasure tingled from my base to my balls, lighting a path of flames in its wake.

Cupping a ball in one hand, she fisted my girth with the other, twisting her fingers as her tongue lapped at my crown. She kneaded and teased my nut while laving my head on all sides. *Fuck*, that felt sublime. I groaned as she switched hands, massaging my other ball while rotating her fingers about my base. She tongued her way from my slit to my root along the same vein as before, licking the free ball and sucking it.

"Fuck yeah, Danya," I husked, half-hypnotized by the

sight of her mouth sheathing my ball. "More."

Holding my length in both hands, she wrapped her lips around my tip, taking half of me in a long, slow stroke. Her tongue rolled from side to side under my ridge as she descended, pausing where her lips met her fingers. A guttural sound rumbled from my chest, and my eyes shuttered. Her mouth was hot, slick, and velvety, and I wanted my cock buried in it to the hilt. I'd be patient, but not too patient.

She hollowed her cheeks, suctioning me as she climbed my dick, and *yeah*, I could take more of that. Lots more, further down, and faster. At the top she flicked her tongue against my head, sending a jolt of electricity straight to my bulb. *God-fucking-damn.* Puckering, she took me in again, descending a little further before hoovering me a little faster on the way up. I closed my eyes to focus on the sensations without getting distracted by her plump lips and curling eyelashes. A slight scrape of teeth here, a swipe of tongue there, now a tight channel of cheeks engulfing me, now lips closing around my shaft. My idea of heaven. I rocked my hips into her, my grip tightening on her neck and my fingers digging into her hair.

"So good, Diva," I praised hoarsely.

She hummed in response, taking me in deep and gagging slightly. *Ahh.* Now we were talking. My eyes flipped open to appreciate the tears and struggle as she tried to swallow me whole. Her eyes swam as she choked and sputtered. After a few more deep strokes, she recovered, visibly relaxing her jaw, and rose up, popping off to blow cool air along my cock.

I let her breathe a moment. Then I positioned her mouth at my tip, feeding my length in. Her eyes rounded, gazing up at me heatedly as I held her head still and began to fuck her mouth. With fast, punishing thrusts I drove in deep. Each time I hit the back of her throat I sighed with contentment, seeing and hearing her gag. She sucked, swirled her tongue, and serviced me like her life depended on it. Maybe tonight it did.

I sped up, swiveling my hips when I stabbed the back of her throat and holding her immobile when I pulled out. Pumping in and out, I took my pleasure, using her mouth brutally. I felt my balls drawing up, my girth full to bursting, and I paused mid-thrust.

I locked gazes with her. "Hold it till I say you can swallow."

She nodded.

Withdrawing a little, I slammed in. The barbs of my gathering orgasm turned into hot spikes, burning my spine and shredding my center. A growl tore at my throat. I came and came, my jizz ribboning across her palate as I made a series of rough partial thrusts. With each drop of release my limbs grew more spongy. Milked dry, I pulled out, watching her hold and taste my spend.

I held her chin between my thumb and forefingers. "Swallow all but a few drops."

Her throat bobbed as she drank my spunk.

"Open."

My cum coated her tongue. Dipping a finger into it, I drew a line from her eye down her cheek, where my spit had dribbled earlier.

"Never say never, Danya."

CHAPTER NINE: DANYA

His eyes glowed like white-hot coals, his lips curving in a vicious smile. He didn't forget a thing. Now he'd marked and humiliated me. Sorely as I resented him for taunting me with my earlier promise, my pussy wept too much for me to dwell on his words. My clit was a throbbing, swollen bundle of needy nerves, and all my focus centered on it.

He pulled his pants up, never taking his eyes off me.

I pushed to my feet, standing toe to toe with him. He probably pitied me after seeing how little interest Dad took in me. He was likely inwardly crowing that money couldn't rescue Daddy's little girl, even when apparently all Daddy was good for was money. That was how the public saw Dad and me, and I had no doubt my captor saw us that way too. He must be thinking, *If* that's *your support team, who needs opponents?*

While listening to Dad on the call, a myriad of emotions had swamped me. At first, hope that he'd save me. Then shock at his calm and lack of distress. Dismay that he valued his company and reputation more than me. Shame that he showed so little empathy, affection, or concern for me in front of my kidnapper. Anger at Dad, Caleb, and the whole situation.

If I was honest with myself, I couldn't say I was all that surprised at my father's apathy. It confirmed my growing conviction over the last few years that he didn't remotely understand me. After all, his heart had cooled towards me since Mom's death when I was 9. He'd always blamed it on me. But still, what kind of father saw his daughter bound, gagged, and likely being used for sex, and did nothing to stop the perpetrator?

After the call, I'd wanted to erase the pain of it, forget Dad, and forget where I was.

But I chose the wrong drug.

All I could think of while pleasuring my captor was my captor. The way he moved and acted as if he commanded the world. His power to destroy and give pleasure at once. His effortless control in everything he did. His colossal presence. Instead of transporting me away from here, getting him off had made me feel more in his thrall than ever. And tasting him had made me feel even more addicted to his essence — the aura, smell, and savor emanating from him.

I could reverse all of this right now. Stop him from pitying me. Extricate myself from his control. Show him I had supporters, even if Dad wasn't one of them.

I set my jaw in defiance, my eyes leveling with his. "My father was just in shock, you know. That's his way of receiving bad news. Anyways, he never displays his emotions strongly."

His eyes skipped between mine. "If that's what you need to tell yourself."

My chest squeezed. "No, I'm telling *you*."

To my relief, no hint of amusement flirted with his lips or eyes. If anything, darkness descended on his features. "You remember my words from earlier? Your love and loyalties lie with a monster."

My brows scrunched. "What do you mean?"

"Your father is guilty of horrendous crimes."

Unease trickled into my gut, and I swallowed to try to clear it. "What sort of crimes?"

"There are the professional crimes — the ones connected to his corporation — and the personal ones." He narrowed his eyes. "Those are by far the worst."

I reminded myself who I was speaking to. "You mean like kidnapping?"

He puffed out a dry laugh-breath. "Personal crimes that do real damage to people."

I knuckled my hands on my waist. "You've ruined my life. Is that not enough *damage*?"

"How?"

"I'll most likely lose my job, just when I got a great assignment. I'm supposed to be on a date right now—who knows what he'll think? Even if Dad doesn't look for me, my step-mom and stepbrother will—" I broke off, realizing I'd revealed too much. My heart tottered, and warmth seeped into my cheeks. What if the new terms of Caleb's threat would include Eve and Luis?

He cocked an eyebrow. "A date?"

Maybe he hadn't heard the last part. I tried to steady my breaths. "Yes, a date. It is Friday night."

His eyes dipped as he glided his knuckle down the column of my throat. "Who is he?"

"A co-worker."

"Name?"

I frowned. "I fail to see how—"

He cupped my throat snugly, causing a flutter to stir in my belly. "Name, Diva."

"Innes."

A slow, corrupt smile tugged at his lips. "I can't say I'm sorry that *Innes* doesn't get to take you out tonight. Do you care for him?"

I gave him an are-you-kidding-me look. "As if I'd tell you, thereby endangering him and giving you more leverage over me."

He thumbed my jawline, and I shivered. "Never mind him for now. Let's hear more about Eve and Luis."

The bottom dropped out of my stomach. He knew their

names. *Of course he does, Danya.* "I—there's really nothing to tell."

"Except that you seem to think they'll break my client's rules."

I tried to put him off the scent. "No, no. I'm sure my dad will convey to them that they mustn't contact any authorities or members of the press."

He flicked an eyebrow. "Or otherwise take action to free you."

My throat worked unsuccessfully on a swallow. "Er . . . that's right." *No!* my heart screamed. *They will!*

"Sounds as if we need to have a conference call with Eve, Luis, and Walter tomorrow. Just to make sure everyone understands the terms of this operation."

Eve may stand by Dad, but Luis will see me as far more important than GenRev. My heart soared when I thought of seeing Eve and Luis's faces tomorrow. "Fine."

Part of me hoped that my stepmom and stepbrother would show their worry and love enough that Caleb would see I had loyal supporters. But part of me feared that if they did, Caleb would tighten his vigilance in case they'd attempt a rescue. Or he might use my love for them against me.

"We'll make the call at eight in the morning so your stepbrother is awake and done with his day." Singapore was twelve hours ahead of Pennsylvania. Caleb's precision and knowhow sent chills down my spine.

A polite knock sounded at the door.

"Come." His eyes never strayed from me.

Marisa stepped in, bringing with her the smell of pork chops. "Dinner's ready."

"We'll be in shortly."

As she left, my empty belly rumbled loudly.

He cupped my chin, his hazel eyes like forests lit by wildfires. "Are you going to behave, or do I have to tie you up?"

"You don't have to."

He swiveled me, his hand grasping the back of my neck, and walked me over to the half-sofa where he'd dropped the rope and scarf. "Carry them in and lay them on the table by your plate. I'll use them, if necessary."

I flushed, picking them up and carrying them like a dog carrying its own leash.

I polished off the pork chop in record time, tucking into the mashed potatoes next. In case you've never tried it, eating a pork chop with a plastic knife and fork is no easy feat. But hunger makes even the most dauntless of tasks possible. A wealthy upbringing and a private school education had dinned into me that eating with my fingers was taboo.

"Back to the ways I've ruined your life," Caleb said amiably, as if we were discussing baseball. "You said you might lose your job. Don't you work for a travel agency?"

I put down my knife and fork. "Travel *press.* Blazing Trails."

"What do you do for them?"

"Reading, editing, a little bit of research and writing."

"And that's what you've always dreamed of doing."

I frowned. "Why do you say that?"

He smiled wryly. "You say I ruined your life . . . "

"I only work at this job because I can't do what I really want to do."

He arched an eyebrow, waiting for me to elaborate.

It wouldn't make any difference to tell him the truth. We were far from the realm of work now. And further than ever from the realization of my dream. "Since college I've wanted to be a travel blogger."

Since traveling with Mom when I was young, I'd loved going places. And in high school I'd discovered I loved to write. Mom and I preferred traveling simply, on the cheap, going to seedy hotels in colorful sections of towns across North America and Europe, eating street food and takeaway. Dad had deplored our style of travel and taken no part in it. But my happiest memories were of staying in inexpensive roadside motels on Mom's and my drives across the US. We swam in warm, aquamarine-lit pools at midnight where kids had pissed all day, eating pizza in our room while watching episodes of *Cheers* and old horror movies like *Halloween*. Thinking of those trips right now, a knot of nostalgia formed in my throat.

In college I'd gotten the idea of travel blogging. Not only did it combine my two passions, but it would've made Mom proud. And by blogging I'd be memorializing my best times with her.

"What's been stopping you?"

His direct question threw me for a loop. "I guess I'm just not good enough."

I hoped he'd leave it at that.

He leaned back in his chair, his eyes seeming to bore into my soul. "What do you like about the *idea* of being a travel blogger?"

I couldn't hold back my smile or the fizz in my tone. "The traveling, the writing. Connecting with other people passionate about travel."

"Do you do any of that in your current work?"

"Yeah. All of it."

"Then what makes you think you're not good enough to be a travel blogger?"

I lowered my voice, looking down at my plate. "I'm a perfectionist."

He tilted his head. "That sounds like a good thing."

"It's not." My gaze flitted to his. "It's paralyzing."

"Why aren't you paralyzed working for the press?"

"There's a set framework in place for everything at the

press—strict deadlines, well-defined tasks assigned by my boss, an established readership, and a marketing department."

"What does the press work not have that blogging would give you?"

I was sure he'd laugh at me. But I was too far into the thick of this conversation not to come clean. "Freedom."

He scrubbed a hand over his trim beard, his brow creasing. "So you want freedom. But when you get it, you're incapable of using it."

I nodded. "When I'm free, I put more pressure on myself to be perfect." I procrastinated at writing because putting words on the page meant making mistakes. I could only ever see the bad parts in my own work, none of the good. When aiming for goals, I set impossibly high expectations for myself that I could never meet. And goals were all or nothing—either I met them perfectly, or I didn't try. So most of the time, I was immobilized to act.

"What's the assignment?" Pushing his plate back, he leaned his forearms on the table.

"Hmm?"

"You mentioned a great assignment you'd just gotten."

"Oh. To write reviews of affordable Miami-area hotels and restaurants. It would've been my first travel writing assignment ever." I'd lost my appetite thinking of all the opportunities this job would've opened up for me. They'd proven to be mirages shimmering on the horizon that faded as I approached them. Then I remembered Anne Selznick. "And one of the greatest living travel bloggers will be in Philly in three and a half weeks. I'll miss her too."

I had no idea why I was spilling all this. To my kidnapper, of all people. Maybe I wanted him to feel some guilt for uprooting me from my life. *Guilt.* Apparently he wasn't capable of feeling it, since he must surely recognize me as the girl who'd kept his secret all these years. Yet he felt no guilt over returning the favor by kidnapping me.

Suddenly an idea shot up in my brain like a tightly sprung window shade. I had my way out! If I could use the secret as leverage over him, maybe I could induce him to let me go. Maybe the threat of being turned in would take priority over getting paid by his client, and he'd renege on his contract!

I sat back in my chair, gathering a few lungfuls of air by way of courage. "When I was eighteen, I witnessed a murder. I never reported it to the police. But now I think I might."

Only a menacing flash in Caleb's eye gave any indication that he recognized what I was referring to. He lifted his water glass to his lips with a steady hand, taking a sip before setting it down and turning it around. "What prompts you to report it now?"

"I was keeping it a secret as a favor to the murderer." My voice shook, and I closed and unclosed my hands in my lap. This might be either the brightest or the stupidest idea in the history of kidnapping negotiations.

"And now?" His gravelly voice hummed along the surface of my skin, riddling me with goosebumps.

I swallowed against the tightness in my throat. "Now the murderer has kidnapped me."

He propped his arms on the table, clasping his hands. "My advice? Forget about reporting it."

"Why?" A wobble fretted my voice.

"A jury has to believe an eyewitness's testimony completely in order to deliver a verdict of guilty beyond reasonable doubt. If there's even one problem with the testimony, the defense will bring it to light and convince the jury to find the defendant not guilty."

I soldiered on. "What makes you think there'd be a problem with my testimony?"

"Let me play defense while you play the witness." A

confident smile twisted his lips. "Now remember, you're under oath. Did you have perfect sight of the alleged murder?"

I wavered. "Well, not exactly. The defendant was partially blocking my view, and I couldn't see exactly what he was doing to the victim."

He perked one brow. "That's one strike against you. Is your memory one hundred percent accurate six years later? Can you confidently state, for example, what the victim was wearing?"

"I—no. I mean, I think he was in some kind of business suit."

He tsked. "Strike two, eyewitness."

Shoot. Hadn't he been wearing a suit?

My cross-questioner continued grilling me. "As the defense counsel, it's my job to impugn your character. You say you've kept this *secret* for six years and have only decided to come forward now. That's either an act of dishonesty or an axe you have to grind with the defendant, otherwise known as a bias. Can you deny either?"

With a trembling hand I reached for my water to relieve my arid throat. After sipping it, I stared straight ahead at the centerpiece of petunias. "No."

"Strike three." He reached out, turning my face towards him. His lips twitched, and a demonic gleam ignited his eye. "You're out."

My eyes slid sideways, as if by avoiding his gaze I could prevent the danger I now faced.

"Look at me."

My gaze snapped back to his.

"There's a heavy punishment for captives who threaten their captors and accuse them of murder."

My voice was so small, even I barely heard it. "Even when the captive is only trying to get back to living her life?"

"Especially then. Threats and murder charges are serious

offenses."

I rallied. "*I* think I deserve a reward. I kept your secret all these years."

He thumbed my lower lip. "Your reward was already factored into the contract when you were kidnapped."

It was? "How?"

He gave a brief shake of the head. "You'll find out when I return you." He rose from his chair. "Gather your rope and scarf and come with me."

CHAPTER TEN: CALEB

I led her out of the kitchen like a prisoner to the gallows, with my hand on the back of her neck. So she *had* recognized me. Over the last twenty hours I'd wondered if she would. For all that, I hadn't been prepared for her to threaten me. I had to hand it to her, she was brave. And resourceful. But now that I had a nice opportunity to punish her, I was going to enjoy it. So would she.

Since there'd been much speculation over the cause of the congressman's death and he'd been buried, not cremated, it was just as well I'd convinced her to keep quiet.

Over dinner I'd wanted to solve her perfectionism problem. After all, that was my profession — making people's problems go away. I now had the germ of an idea for how to help her, based on what she'd told me.

How wrong she'd been to think I would ever forget a favor done for me. No, I hadn't forgotten her. Not when my client had said the victim of the kidnapping would be the very woman who'd kept my secret.

The punishment I was going to give Danya would serve two purposes. It would remind her who was in control at all times here. And it would make her work hard for her pleasure.

Danya

He closed the bedroom door, wrapping an arm around my

midriff from behind and pulling me against his chest. "Give me a safe word, Diva."

My heart kicked into overdrive in my chest, and I tensed. "You mean, in case I'm in too much pain?"

He placed a hand over mine, guiding it to my crotch. Tingling instantly sprang up, as if my arousal had only been waiting to erupt again like a dormant volcano. "No pain. Only pleasure. But the safe word is in case you find the sensations too intense."

"I thought you said this was a punishment."

He glided our hands in slow circles over the surface of my groin. "It's delayed gratification after a lot of anticipation and strong feelings."

The now-familiar thud in my intimate flesh started up again. "What do I need to do?"

"A safety word, Danya."

"Oh." I thought for a second, before recalling the centerpiece at dinner. "Petunias."

I felt his chin bob over the crown of my head. "Step over to the bed and turn around."

His command ignited a spark deep in my belly, and I carried out his order without hesitation.

He leaned against the wall, twelve feet away, folding his arms across his broad chest. "Take off your jeans."

My fingers trembled from anticipation and excitement as I shimmied out of my jeans and stepped out of them.

"Your thighs . . ." His eyes flared, and I could see the bulge rising in his jeans. "They're grabbable, suckable, and biteable."

Heat spread from my neck to my hairline as I awaited further commands.

"Remove your shirt."

I peeled my shirt over my bra and off my arms, tugging it over my head and tossing it aside. Straightening and dropping his arms, he breathed in deeply through his nose.

His voice was gruff and guttural. "Unhook your bra, but don't take it off."

I did so, arousal welling from my slit.

His eyes hooding, he prowled towards me, stopping a few inches away. His gaze held mine as he raised his index fingers and touched my bra straps. Shivers ran from the touch points along my collar bone. Trailing his finger pads along the top of my shoulders, he slid the straps until they dangled over my upper arms. Then, hooking his middle finger in the center underwire holding my bra cups, he gave a tug. The straps slipped down my arms, and the cups fell with them, revealing my bare breasts.

As he dragged his hungry gaze over me, tendrils of heat curled about my center, and the ache in my pussy intensified.

"Touch yourself."

A blush leached into my cheeks. "I can't. Not in front of you . . . "

"Pretend it's me."

Maybe he could be the Werewolf again, after all. I'd made myself come enough times to images of him. Watching his twilit eyes, I slid my fingers inside my panties, coating them with my cream. He captured my wrist, holding my hand under his nose and inhaling. Then he inserted my slick fingers in his mouth and sucked, swirling his tongue around each, one by one. My sex thumped urgently.

He popped my fingers out, licking his lips. "You taste like honey."

His lips brushed the back of my hand, shooting bolts of electricity down my arm.

He placed my palms on my hips. "Take off your panties."

I swept them down to my feet, toeing them off.

My heart jackhammered in my chest as he stepped back, perusing me from head to toe.

A growl rolled from his chest, making me leak more desire. "Lie on your back on the bed."

I lay down, watching as he collected some scarves from a drawer.

He tied my wrists to the headboard so my arms formed a Y, his feral smile stirring glowing embers in my core. After fastening my ankles to the baseboard so my body formed an X, he stood beside the bed, taking me in. "I'll be back."

While he was gone, I closed my eyes and pictured what he might do to me in this position. He could straddle me and fill me with his cock. Maybe he'd finger and tongue me to orgasm. Maybe he'd cover my body in kisses, pressing his lips to mine at last. Frissons of expectation thrilled through me, and I sighed with longing.

When he returned, he switched off the lights, except for the lamps on either side of the bed. He placed a bucket on the floor at the base of the bed and a dark furry object on the bedside table. After draping some cloths over the edge of the bucket, he lit two candles in round tubs, setting them on the table.

His low, throaty voice rumbled in my ear. "Lights out." He fitted a snug sleep mask over my head, and all went black. My breaths came shallowly. Anything could happen now. What was he going to do? I braced myself for impact.

An incredibly soft fur brushed my belly. I couldn't imagine anything silkier. It slid along the contour of my waist, up my ribcage, and along my breast to my neck. But I could tell it was lined with hide, and amidst the fur were some thin strands of leather.

"*Mmmm*," I purred.

"This is a rabbit fur flogger."

"*Ohh.*" Something this furry could only caress. My anxiety began to ebb.

A few soft thumps fell on the underside of my breast—so

sensuous and velvety, like felt. A tickling caress of light leather accompanied each blow.

As he flogged my breast, I thought this was the best of both worlds — being punished in a gentle way. Eiderdown could hardly have been softer. But he was still controlling the sensations, still striking me. Rhythmic and precise, the strokes fell against each part of my breast. Sometimes he dragged the inside leather of the tails against my skin, which was delicious torture. He struck my peaked nipple over and over from what felt like different angles, making it ache for his touch.

Then the tails hit my other breast, like muffled leather. As if I were being massaged, blood heated the flogged areas.

When the blows of fur ceased, I immediately missed their impact. The flogger slid from the top to the bottom of my leg before I felt the thud of it against my inner thigh. *Ahh.* So near my sex! If it would only land there. It struck my rounded thigh repeatedly before he moved the tresses of pelt to my other leg, sliding them along the inside to my ankle. As they thumped my upper thigh, I began to long for *pain.* I wanted *actual* hurt. Like last night.

"Umm . . ." I interrupted the strokes.

The blows ceased.

"You don't have anything a little more . . . intense?"

I heard the smile in his voice. "I have more floggers. But tonight isn't about pain, it's about sensation."

But this bunny flogger is driving me insane! I kept imagining what it might feel like if it were just leather without the fur.

The satiny softness of the flogger thumped against the bottom of my foot, sending pulses to my groin. Then the flogger tails struck my other foot, slow and steady, teasing and promising.

Please, I inwardly wailed. *Give me more, harder.*

Warmth had spread from my breasts to my belly and from my feet to my middle.

The fur tails glided up my thigh, making me levitate with need as they approached my slit. They dragged along my opening, and I arched my hips into them, chasing friction and pressure. When their tips dangled against my folds, I writhed within the confines of my restraints, and a frustrated moan escaped my throat.

"Now that you're nicely warmed up, it's time to make you hot." His seductive voice sounded at my ear. "I'm going to drip hot massage wax onto your skin from a candle." I flinched. "It'll be about as hot as the water you shower with."

A melted massage candle meant a massage, which meant his hands on me. My heart sped up—not from fear but excitement.

Then I realized where the whiffs of cedar, lemongrass, and vanilla were drifting from. They grew more pronounced as he placed a palm on my thigh.

"Here's where I'll drip it. Relax."

I took a deep breath, letting my thighs unclench.

He removed his hand, and hot liquid dropped to the spot it had covered. His callused palm rubbed what felt like oil into my skin, eliciting a groan of intense arousal. His cool breath fanned the area he'd massaged.

"*Mmmm*." It wasn't so much the heat of the wax as the touch of his hand that inflamed me. "So good," I slurred, drunk on lust.

He dripped the candle over my inner thigh, moving his hand in slow, circular motions before blowing on the area. I thought I'd die from the sensuality of it. He did the same to my other thigh, his caress stimulating rather than soothing me. If he would only slide his palm up further and press my wet folds or my nub . . .

The bed dipped beside me, and I felt his heat above me. "Now your tits."

Oh, God, yes!

He lifted one breast and dribbled the hot liquid onto its underside. After a pause, he kneaded it into my flesh.

He flicked my pebbled nipple, drawing a whimper from me.

Dropping the wax over the top of my breast, he worked it in, stroking my areola. A spasm of desire overtook me. He was master of my body, controller of my senses. He savored me like a connoisseur, his movements expert and sure.

He shifted to the other breast, starting with the top and working his way around. I trembled with anticipation, recalling how he'd made me come this morning. Would he now?

And what would it be like if the wax were hotter?

Dribbling liquid wax up my sternum, he slid his palm between my breasts towards my neck, working the oil into the column of my throat. I loved having his hand on my throat, especially when he tightened it as if to choke me. Now, with all my senses heightened except my sight, I zeroed in on the heft of his hand and his warm breath on my skin. Masculine power radiated from him as he hovered over me.

His hand lifted from my neck.

My skin tingled from his attentions. Where would he drip the candle next?

His body shifted down the bed, and a moment later, hot wax landed on my lower belly. I sighed thinking of his hand there, near my pulsing center. He indolently massaged the oil into my flesh, the heel of his palm molding to the curve of my mound. *Ahhh.* A few more rubs and I'd explode!

He removed his hand, and a mewl of longing purled from my throat.

His deep voice resonated through my bones. "Now that you're hot, I'm going to cool you down."

Cool me down? But I wanted to be even *more* hot. Panting, sweaty, and steaming.

His fingers traced my pinched brows as if to smooth them out. "I'm going to use something cold to get you even hotter."

Ookaay. So far, everything he'd done had been pleasurable, if unbearably tantalizing.

"Prepare for a brief shock. Then excitement."

Hmm. That sounded intriguing. What could it be?

The bed dipped next to me, and ice-cold wetness hit my belly button. My torso sprang up, and I yipped. The solid, frosty object in my navel felt like ice. As he held it there and I grew used to its coldness, a slithery feeling of intense arousal slunk between my thighs. Flames licked my pussy, even as a flood doused them. He dragged the ice cube up my belly to my breasts, his hot tongue licking and sucking the path of melted water along the way. Fire and ice mingled on the surface of my skin—hot breath and tongue with freezing water, warring and merging into desire. I wriggled as he circled one breast with the fast-melting cube. He trailed it up to my nipple, holding it over my hardened peak till it had dissolved completely. Then he breathed hotly over my nipple and nipped it.

"*Caleb* . . ." I pleaded in a strained voice.

"Diva." His voice was pure, sexy gravel. A fresh ice cube landed under my other breast, causing me to flinch.

It was so much all at once.

The cube traced a slow path around my breast, swirling inward until it reached my tight bud. It circled my nipple before Caleb's warm breath blew over my peak. I'd never been so keyed up. His rough tongue lapped up the melt and swiped my nipple before he closed his teeth around it and tugged.

My back arched off the bed, and I cried out.

I felt him straddle me. The next thing I knew, his mouth was holding the ice cube against my throat. His warm lips and the frigid cube made a startling contrast of textures and temperatures as he dragged it along my clavicle to my chest. By the time he'd reached my bellybutton, the ice had melted. He drilled his cold tongue into my navel, then blew hot air into it. A reckless moan left my lips.

I heard the clink of ice cubes, wondering what next, when his warm lips kissed my mound.

"Oh, *God!*"

Frigid slickness chilled my skin as his mouth held the cube against my sensitive flesh. The cold went in and out, as if his tongue and lips controlled the ice. *So destructive, so in command!* His mouth dragged the ice cube to my clit, lingering there. My thighs quivered, my pelvis thrusting into him. Did I want more or less of this sensation? *More.* He held my belly down with his hand as he continued to trace a freezing path along my divide—slow, torturous, and burning. On the way back up, his tongue zigzagged along my opening, his beard scratching my lips and intensifying my need.

"*Please!*"

Numbing water dripped down to my crack. He swiped his tongue up from cleft to clit, sucking on my nub and holding one last small bit of ice against it till it melted. Lapping up the last of the liquid, he began to alternate sucking my clit with spearing his tongue into my channel.

"Oh, oh . . ." My orgasm started to build, like an accelerating freight train.

His fingers plunged into my depths, energizing all the pleasure-rich nerves. My inner walls began to flutter and close in.

His lips left my pussy as his fingers paused their pumping. "What do you say, Danya?"

"May I come?" I gasped.

Endless seconds ticked by, and I began to think that was it. I writhed and pushed up into his hand. A few teasing lashes of the tongue were all I got in response.

"*Please.*"

His answer, when it came, made my lower belly do a pole-vault. "You may."

He sucked forcefully and pistoned his hand in and out, sending me hurtling off the cliff, falling hard and fast into euphoria. I spiraled and spun, my bliss acting as resistance to keep me aloft. When I floated to earth at last, out of breath and spent, his tongue was lapping languidly at my entrance, and his fingers had slowed their strokes.

Removing my mask, he appeared above me with darkened eyes, his thickness spearing my belly. He produced a foil packet, tearing it with his teeth, and sheathed himself fully. "Are you on birth control?"

I nodded. "I just had my injection two weeks ago."

He untied the knots at my wrists and ankles, flipping me onto my belly. Spreading my buttocks wide, he smeared my juices along my crack. He kneaded and slapped my globes. "Such a fine ass."

As his teeth closed around a cheek, I shrieked and jumped, my hand flying back to stop him. Grabbing both my wrists, he extended my arms above my head. I heard the grin in his voice as it rumbled in my ear. "Aren't you used to submitting yet?"

My heart revved again, his total power exhilarating me.

After knotting a scarf around my wrists, he rolled his tongue down my spine to my cleft. Then he sucked hard on the area he'd bitten. When his mouth pulled away, I tensed in readiness, expecting him to bite the other cheek.

Instead, I felt the most exquisite feather-light touch of fingertips against my perineum. The touch tickled my folds, activating dozens of nerve endings. My butt wriggled, seeking more of this torment. At this point, he could do anything he wanted with me, and I'd submit. My body was no longer my own.

I began to grind desperately into the bed.

He yanked my legs in and straddled me, feeding his length into my sopping channel. When he filled me, I groaned with relief. Lowering himself onto my back, he caged me in. With one hand he fisted my hair, gripping my waist with the other. I was completely trapped, totally surrounded and immobilized. Just as my fantasy had envisioned, the Werewolf was taking me from behind. Only everything was infinitely sharper because it was happening and it was real.

He eased out, then slammed in, chasing the air from my lungs. He pulled my hair, extending my neck, and pressed his free hand into my lower back. "I'm going to wear this tight pussy out. Make you live, breathe, and dream nothing but my cock."

I moaned for more.

He tightened his grip on my hair, making my scalp tingle. Pulling out, he impaled me with a savage thrust. From then on, everything was a blur. Spearing me relentlessly, he grabbed and tugged my hair, waist, ass, and breasts as if they were extensions of his hands. He pounded me, rolled his hips, and rose up to repeat. But his breath was what did me in. His dirty words brushed my nape, filled my ears, and bathed every inch of my flesh like the spark to my fuse. My wick burned down, and I rocketed forth, humming through the air before exploding in an array of bright lights. The fireworks lasted awhile. Through the buzzing in my ears, I heard my groans and felt Caleb swelling inside me and dropping on top of me. His musky, yeasty scent filled my nostrils, and at the moment, I thought it was the best aroma I'd ever smelled.

CHAPTER ELEVEN: CALEB

Without pulling out, I rolled us so I spooned her from behind. "For coming without permission, you'll sleep tied up again."

She cracked open an eye, looking up at me. "I didn't know there was an option for me to sleep untied."

"There isn't, now."

She struggled to break free of me, but my arm banded her chest and my thigh penned in her legs.

"Let me go to the bathroom."

"Without me, Diva? I'd be remiss if I let you go unescorted." I pulled out, removing the condom and sliding us both off the bed in one motion.

"Because on the way there I might get abducted?"

"For instance." I didn't trust her not to lock herself in, unscrew a pipe from the sink, and bust the window open, using the glass to cut the scarf that tied her wrists and climbing out onto the roof. If she was that resourceful, she could find ways to get down to the ground and make her escape.

I decided to leave her wrists bound, gripping the back of her neck and walking her into the bathroom.

"Just how do you plan on getting away with this anyway?" She side-eyed me, her tone challenging.

I smiled. "Are you planning to carry out a kidnapping and need some tips?"

I had a pretty airtight method for erasing all evidence of the crime and my part in it, but sharing this with her would defeat my strategy.

Sitting on the toilet, she looked up at me hopefully. "Can you at least tell me why your client wants me gone a whole month? Or why I even matter in this? My father said it's just about the company."

"Even if I knew, I couldn't tell you." I wiped her, leading her to the sink, where I picked up the electric toothbrush. My client had refused to tell me these details when he'd hired me, though I would probe him again when I called him tomorrow. I squirted toothpaste onto the brush head.

"It's not as if *I* know anything about Dad's business. Nothing more than the public knows, at least." She opened her mouth to receive the brush, and I began to play dentist.

Now I could put that on my resumé too.

"He didn't want you to work at his company?"

"Unh-unh." She held up a finger, and I turned off the brush. "He groomed Luis for that. He wanted me to marry."

I resumed brushing. "Hmm. A traditionalist." *Aka. chauvinist.* No surprise, given his other offensive qualities.

I suspected it would take some time and delicacy to open Danya's eyes where her father was concerned. I hadn't yet figured out the nature of their relationship, but I had four more weeks to crack that nut. I'd kidnapped her for three reasons, and this was the third—to turn her against Walter. The first two being the sizable paycheck and the chance to distract Walter while Gideon hacked his company. When I'd accepted the job, I'd assumed Danya was the most precious thing to her father. Now, I was beginning to have doubts—though I'd bet she meant more to him than he let on. In any case, turning his daughter against him would be fitting revenge for what he did to our family.

When she'd rinsed out her mouth, she lit up. "Oh! You have multiple travel-sized everything!" She fingered the mini-toothpastes, dental flosses, shampoo, conditioner, and other stuff I kept for away jobs. "When Mom and I traveled, I always collected as many of these as I could and then used them at home to remind me of our trips."

"Couldn't you just buy them?"

Her laugh rose from her belly, warming my insides. "That would be no fun. It's like shelling. You can't just buy shells at shops. You have to find them on the beach."

She picked up a moisturizer, and I uncapped it, guessing she wanted to smell it.

She inhaled its fragrance, humming. "Would you put some on my face?"

I squeezed a dollop onto my fingers and worked it into her cheeks and forehead. Her skin was silky and even-toned.

Add beautician to my resumé.

"How do you keep your beard so neat?"

"I trim it every morning."

Her sapphire eyes had softened. "May I feel it?"

I nodded. She reached up her manacled hands and ran her fingertips along first one side of my jaw then the other. I hadn't expected the gesture to send an instant firebolt to my dick. But her nails scraping through my beard felt as erotic as a massage.

Her beatific smile was the same she'd worn when I'd stolen her from her bed. "I like its roughness."

"It's the opposite of you."

She thrust out her lower lip. "You think I'm a pea princess."

"Aren't you?"

Lowering her hands, she turned her head away. "Travel is my escape from being picky. It's an excuse to live simply. Regular life is full of complicated choices and endless options. The more traveling contrasts with everyday life, the more I love it." Her eyes landed back on mine. "I know some people want to recreate their normal life when they travel. Others want to upgrade to something fancy. I want to downgrade to something simple. Test my limits."

I cocked a smile. "When you say *simple*, are you talking a Michelin one-star restaurant instead of a three-star?"

She blinked slowly. "Of course you'd think that, given what everybody says about me." She swiveled, heading towards the door.

I reached over her, pushing the door shut. "Wait while I brush my teeth." I brushed and peed, then led her back into the bedroom. "So what *is simple* for you?"

"Anything that allows you to really *see* people from many different walks of life." Her face relaxed. "Long lines to events. Taxi rides. Street crowds heading to a celebration. Fish fries and fireworks. Open-air markets. Beach bars. Packed subway cars."

I arched an eyebrow. "What's wrong with the way the one-percenters travel?"

She shrugged. "Nothing at all, if you like that sort of thing. But everything at the top is streamlined. The hotels, the resorts, the experiences . . . they're all the same. I'm not interested in writing about something that anyone could predict before they even read a word. And I don't like to travel that way either."

Her reasoning made sense. If her everyday life involved complicated decisions over every small thing, traveling more simply must feel like a vacation. And if her goal was to meet different kinds of people and challenge herself, that style of travel fit the bill.

I unfastened her scarf and handed her panties and a t-shirt. While she dressed, I shrugged on a T and pulled on my boxer briefs, re-tying her wrists and guiding her back to the bed. I gestured for her to sit while I knotted a couple of scarves around her ankles, leaving them sixteen inches apart.

"Well, now you've got your out-of-the-everyday experience." I climbed in beside her, switching off the light. "And a nice test of your limits."

When I closed my eyes, thoughts of the Breadcrumb Client and my talk with him today returned. They'd been interrupted by the demands of this job.

Caleb — Four years ago

Shimmying down the suspension rope in the CrossFit gym, I hopped off and proceeded to pump out a set of wide-grip pullups on the high bars. From there I jumped on the rings and did one last set of dips. Dripping with sweat, I grabbed my towel and made my way towards the locker room. On the way there, my phone vibrated. *Gideon.*

"What's up?" I strode over to an empty corner of the gym where no one could hear me.

"I know you've got your call with the breadcrumb dude in an hour." Gideon was doing that annoying thing where he clicked and unclicked his pen at bullet speed. "I just wanted to say, no luck so far in finding anything more on Ian MacLamare."

Last year I'd spent some time after my conversation with Mr. J. researching employees who'd worked in the finance department at GenRev's headquarters for any considerable length of time. Fischer had said Mr. J. had worked there for eighteen years. I'd come up with a 57-year-old named Ian MacLamare who'd left the company in 2005. When I'd found no useful online records for him, I'd done the kind of in-depth search a PI does. The upshot of my investigation was that MacLamare had disappeared without a trace in 2005 — the year my father had died and I'd gone to live with Clark. Whether MacLamare had changed his identity, gone off the grid, or moved abroad, his whereabouts and status were unknown.

"You weren't able to trace his phone?" I'd had Gideon try to track Mr. J.'s location from the number he'd called me on last week to assign me the job.

"Wherever he is, he doesn't seem to have any info on public databases. Can't get him through *intext*, White Pages, or any of the searches I use for other countries. I'll keep trying, though."

"Thanks, man. In an hour I may have a new number for you to trace."

We rang off, and I went to take a shower. My job for the Breadcrumb Client this last week had been relatively easy. He'd only wanted me to extricate a friend of his from the teeth of a loan shark. By giving the shark a taste of his own medicine — a few threats reinforced with some of the violence he used on borrowers — I'd cleared Mr. J.'s friend for the time being. This apparently satisfied his friend, who anticipated being able to pay back the money to the shark in a month.

When I got out of the gym, I walked over to a nearby park and took a seat on a bench, eating a sandwich I'd bought at a deli down the street.

Mr. J. called at 4 on the dot, as if to match the date of March fourth. After thanking me for cooling off the loan shark, he launched right into his continuation of my father's story.

"Last year, I told you how Penwarren stole your father's invention and hounded him in a bitter lawsuit that lasted seven years and considerably reduced your family's means." Mr. J. had the kind of speaking voice that compelled you to listen. He sounded as if he was summing up an argument in court. "Had Penwarren left Furness alone, no doubt Furness would've found a high-paying job at some other biotech firm. But Penwarren managed to get your father blacklisted at all the companies within a two-hour radius of Philadelphia. Short of moving, your father was stuck. Unless he was willing to work in a field other than what he was trained in, he had to accept the only available position in biotech — working for Penwarren."

My lips curled in a snarl. "Why did he force him to work at his company?"

"Partly to have your father under his thumb, partly to keep him close so he could spy on whatever new ideas Furness might develop."

Of course. The asshole probably counted on stealing another of my father's inventions. Bile rose in my gut at the injustices done to him.

"My mother also worked for GenRev." I threw this out to see how much Mr. J. knew.

"Yes. Lucy Furness was hired in the design department at the same time your father was hired in the engineering division." He paused. "But that's a story for the next job."

"Wait." I knew he could hang up any second. "What's your real name?"

"You'll find out when you enact your revenge on Penwarren. For now, know that I'm acting on behalf of someone else."

He ended the call.

Someone *else*? *Acting* as in giving me these breadcrumbs of information? My head spun at the thought of all the areas my research would have to cover if I tried to figure out whose interests he was representing.

But I was determined to tackle the task.

Caleb — Present

Waking at dawn the next morning, I fastened Danya's ankles to the baseboard and left her sleeping while I showered, trimmed my beard, and dressed. Since she was still asleep when I emerged from the bathroom, I stepped out of the bedroom, locking the door, and sat in a chair down the hallway where I couldn't be heard if I lowered my voice.

Arnold Black, my client, was always up early.

Talk about another Howard Hughes type. He lived on a small island off the coast of Massachusetts with twelve other inhabitants — his wife and staff — and had supplies brought in by boat twice a week. He'd made millions in investment banking and retired two years ago at 53. Looking into his connection with Walter Penwarren, I'd found out that not only had they been in the same class at Yale, but they'd belonged to the same club in Philly. I couldn't find evidence of rivalry, animosity, a business relationship, or even a former friendship, and Black had withheld details as to why he'd commissioned this assignment.

"Scott." Black's voice was on the higher side. "How's the job coming?"

"Fine. She's asleep now. We're having a four-way with her stepmother and stepbrother at eight."

"Why?" he clipped.

"Because she's pretty sure Penwarren will tell them, and they can't be trusted not to pull something."

"I don't think this is advisable . . . "

"I need to warn them to keep quiet." My firm tone said I wasn't budging on this. "If the job is to be done, it has to be done right."

Silence followed. "If you're sure . . . "

"I am."

"All right. Have you been following my terms? You call Walter every day, you're polite to him, you haven't touched Danya, etcetera?"

"Yes." I suggested I was answering all questions, while truthfully answering his first. Then I moved on quickly, the way politicians often did. "She's asking why she's been kidnapped when this is a case of ransomware. She also wonders why it's for a month."

"She can keep wondering." *Read – so can you.*

"That's about it then." This didn't mean I'd let it go. I'd have Gideon look into the security threat at GenRev.

"Good. Keep me in the loop."

We ended the call, and I went to wake up the diva.

Chapter Twelve: Danya

Waking to find no sign of Caleb, I sat up and went to work trying to loosen the knots fastening my ankles to the baseboard. The knots were far more complex than anything I'd ever seen. I'd only gotten one undone when the key turned in the lock and the door swung open.

"Morning, Diva. I see you're up and trying to escape," he greeted genially, sauntering over with an outlaw's smile. "Did you dream of me?"

"Yes. I was stabbing you with a pitchfork I found in Jeremy's shed."

My breath caught at his easy morning sexiness. Mint, fresh soap, and manliness emanated from him. Clad in a black button-down shirt, grey chinos, and trail-running shoes, he looked ready to slay. Not just me, but the world. His clothes hugged his body just so, everywhere hinting at the muscles beneath. He'd rolled up his sleeves, so that the popping veins of his forearms felt like a third person in the room.

He chuckled, undoing the second knot with a flick of his wrist. "You can work off some of your hatred on me later."

That sounded too good to be true. "Oh, yeah?"

"No weapons allowed, though. Just your body." His hand rounded my breast through my t-shirt, his thumb brushing my puckered nipple.

Heat zinged to my center, but I tried to focus. "I won't be tied up?"

"Nope." He made quick work of the knotted scarves, freeing my feet and hands. "But a shower, breakfast, and a talk with your family are the first orders of business."

"What's after that?"

"I'll be gone until dinner."

My stomach arced and swooped. Maybe this was my chance to escape! "Where?"

He cupped my ass, propelling me towards the bathroom. "A personal matter."

I'd have to think how I could use his absence to the greatest advantage.

The hot water cascading over my body felt heavenly. Almost as amazing as the free use of my limbs to soap and shampoo myself. Of course, the whole time my jailer stood just outside the shower, leaning against the wall and watching me. But even his surveillance couldn't upset my momentary sense of calm. Getting clean seemed to be a primal pleasure of all creatures, from hippos to ants.

After toweling myself dry and brushing my teeth, I chose a pair of white jeans and a close-fitting midnight-blue knit top that would keep me warm even in the cooler areas of the large house.

"Good choice," my captor appraised, once I'd dressed.

I flushed under his sizzling gaze. "Why are you letting me do everything myself today?"

"Because you're following directions."

"So I've graduated from toddler to adult in one day?"

He flicked an eyebrow up. "Just to teenager." He glanced at his watch. "Time for breakfast." Grabbing a rope and a few scarves, he led me out the door, his hand on the small of my back.

Marisa's fresh bread tasted unbelievable with butter and jam from a nearby farm. Today, I wolfed down the crisp strips of bacon.

I wondered if Caleb's current edginess related to me or to the *personal matter* he was taking care of. His jaw ticked, the arteries in his neck pulsed, and his body looked ready to spring, like a panther eyeing its prey.

"Going to see a girlfriend?" I asked in a casual tone.

"Nope." He sipped his coffee.

"You seem keyed up."

"However tense I seem, I assure you I'd be much more tense if I had a girlfriend."

"Why?"

While I myself hadn't had a relationship in over a year, I remembered it as a calming experience. *Maybe too calm*, a devilish inner voice suggested.

"For one thing, a girlfriend is a liability in a profession like mine. For another, girlfriends are too high-maintenance. Women, in my experience, are for sex only. When they expect more—like dates, communication, or an investment of feelings—they get entitled, clingy, and nagging."

"That view seems awfully reductive. It reflects on you more than on women. You're missing out on the best parts of a relationship." Though I didn't speak from vast experience, I felt the need to defend meaningful connections.

"And what might those be?" He poured more coffee into his mug, sipping it black.

I thought of the highlights of my two college relationships and the one I'd had for the year after graduating. "Being appreciated and understood by someone. Being supported. Learning and growing by their side. Feeling needed."

Feeling loved. I especially missed that.

"You're talking about an ideal that rarely plays out in reality. Even when it does, it's more work, stress, and grief than it's worth."

"Grief?"

"Love means loss. When you love, you weaken yourself. You open yourself up to heartache. You become dependent on someone." He shook his head. "Not for me."

"You sound as if you speak from experience." For some reason, my heart sank after hearing his views on women and love.

His lips drew into a line, but he didn't say anything. Pushing back his chair and standing, he tossed one of those licorice lozenges into his mouth that he always kept in his pocket. I'd noticed he tended to suck on them when he was on edge, as if they soothed him.

"Bring your rope and scarves."

We traipsed to Jeremy's study, where Caleb told me to stand and wait in front of the half-sofa by the window. He stepped over and murmured something in Jeremy's ear. Jeremy asked him a question, and they conferred for a few minutes. I strained to hear what they were saying, but I got no sense of even the subject matter.

After Jeremy had left the room, Caleb locked the door, pocketing the key. He drew the curtain over the window behind me, leaving the room much darker. Tension radiated from him, making blood rush to my head and drum a frenzied pulse in my ears. What was he planning to do?

"Hands out."

I extended my wrists, which he bound with one of the scarves.

"Feet together."

I closed my legs, and he tied the rope around my ankles.

Flames flickered in his gold-green eyes. Cupping my chin, he pressed his thumb pad into my lower lip. "Such an obedient girl." Warmth rushed to my core, as if his words were Mickey Mouse's powerful arms in *Fantasia*.

I had no time to puzzle over my reaction to his praise. He gagged me with a scarf, lifted me, and arranged me in a side-sit position at the end of the half-couch.

"Let the games begin." Pulling up a chair, he tapped his phone.

Dad's voice boomed out. "Hello?"

Caleb touched the phone again, and Eve's smooth voice poured from the speaker. "Hello?"

He tapped it once more. After a moment, Luis's soft voice greeted me. "Hello?"

Caleb turned the phone towards me, holding it between his legs. He touched one more button, and each person's picture appeared, occupying a third of the screen.

My muffled sounds from ten feet away were me trying to say hello.

Everyone talked at once, Eve and Luis calling out "Dani!" and Dad scolding, "Eve, I told you not to get your son involved in this."

Eve said, "He was going to find out anyway! It's your company. And it's a whole month."

Luis narrowed his eyes. "Are you being mistreated, Dani?"

I shook my head.

His jaw clenched. "I'm flying out late tonight. I'll come find you."

I could feel the love vibrating through his voice, and my chest expanded.

Dad broke in. "Absolutely not. She's doing fine. That derelict laid out the terms yesterday. Let him tell you."

Caleb began whistling *Take Me Out to the Ballgame*. What was he up to?

Dad huffed, "You see what we're dealing with. He won't even speak today. *Speak!*"

Caleb's dry raspy chuckle was the only sound in the room.

Eve murmured, "How frightening! Maybe it's best you keep clear of this, Lu."

Luis's eyebrows nosedived. "No way. He doesn't scare me. Don't worry, Dani. I'll come get you."

Dad's face had purpled. "See here, Luis. We worked it all out yesterday. This is none of your concern. The entire company's security systems are under threat of a virus that'll publish all our sensitive information. Billions would be lost in a minute, and the company would be ruined. Hundreds of families would suffer."

Caleb snorted.

"What do they want with Dani?" Luis shot back.

"Who knows? Those are their terms." Dad waved his hand. "It's that weasel at SciPulse, Ben Yosevich, who's behind all this, I know. He'd like nothing better than to make our company look like it's going to tank and have all our shareholders sell. He's trying to make me look bad. And he wants to stop our takeover of his company. He knows Dani's my weakness, and he's hitting me there to make me suffer."

Caleb chuffed a laugh. I didn't know whether I was more insulted by Dad or Caleb's mocking reactions to him.

"If that's the case, why isn't Yosevich just ruining you, instead of threatening to do so?" Luis put.

"As I said," Dad repeated with exasperation, "he wants to make me suffer slowly—first in the public eye, then in my heart. And fifteen million is nothing to sniff at."

Caleb placed a hand over his heart, lifting his eyes to the ceiling. I glowered at him.

"Anyway," Dad went on, "Yosevich probably figures we'd find him out and come after him. This way, he gets to have his cake and eat it too."

"What do *you* propose to do about it?" Luis challenged Dad.

"Nothing. Or, rather, get Drake Arthur to reverse hack these criminals." Dad looked at me for the first time, his voice stern. "But, Dani, this is important. If I ask Drake to do that, then you have to agree to see him. He's been wanting to take you out for a year now, and you always have some excuse. He's a fine young man. Rich, successful, the best there is at cyber security. You couldn't do better for a husband."

I groaned. Here we went again with Drake Arthur, who was on retainer at GenRev. Dad had been pushing him on me since I'd started working at Blazing Trails. Dad had been so offended that I'd taken a job instead of marrying that he'd upped the ante in pressuring me to date Drake. There was nothing *wrong* with him—he was good-looking, smart, and nice enough. But he was irremediably tainted by the fact that Dad had chosen him. He was the last in a long line of young men hand-picked by Dad for the sole purpose of marrying me off to wealth.

Drake would be Dad's dream come true, since he had a reputation for the best cyber security available.

Dad continued his lecture. "Dani, you'd be lucky to be chosen by a man like Drake. But you've got to give up your bohemian habits. He won't allow you to stay in rundown hotels. Might not even approve of you doing that silly job you insist on going to. After what's happened now, I'm sure you agree you've got to move out of that shabby apartment. Had you been living with us, you never would've been kidnapped."

Was *this* what Dad thought of my life? A silly job, a shabby apartment, bohemian habits, choices that landed me where I only deserved to be—kidnapped and held for ransom? I felt as if my chest had been ripped open and an internal wound exposed to the air. My eyes burned, and tears threatened. A tightness constricted my throat.

"That's enough, Walter," Eve said sharply. "You can't blame her for this."

"Enough talking," Luis broke in. "We're getting nowhere. We need action."

"No!" Dad slammed his fist on the desk in front of him, making a few paperweights rattle. "That's just what we *don't* need. No one is doing anything. We're going to sit tight and wait for Drake to crack this. Dani, do I have your word that you'll date Drake?"

Unable to shake or nod my head, I focused on not crying in front of my family. In front of Caleb, who must be laughing at our bickering.

"Dani, sweetheart, you're strong," Eve soothed. "You'll get through this."

"I'll get you out of there, Dani. Hang tight," Luis reassured.

"So help me, if he does anything foolish . . ." Dad seethed.

"Time to say goodbye, Walter." Eve kissed her hand and held it up to the camera. "We love you, Dani."

"Dani, think about what I said," Dad said gruffly.

Caleb ended the call.

"Errrgghh!" I growled in frustration, wanting to tear the roof down with a yell. I was furious at Dad, and even madder at myself, as I seemed incapable of keeping the tears from falling. I twisted away from Caleb so he couldn't see them skidding down my cheeks.

Why was I crying? It must be because Luis was so loyal, brave, and loving. Or maybe because Dad was so horrible. Maybe because part of me believed that some of the things Dad had said were true. He'd always said I was partly to blame for Mom's death. Maybe this was just another case of my recklessness having grave consequences. My apartment building *was* old and probably didn't have the most up-to-date security cameras. Maybe my job *was* just a joke. Maybe my style of living and traveling was frivolous and irresponsible.

I had a flashback to fifteen years ago. Mom and I had traveled to Sofia, Bulgaria, and met a fascinating couple at a park. They'd offered to take us around the city and show us lesser-known sights. While we were in a particularly busy section of Sofia, the car the man was driving got smashed into by another vehicle on the rear passenger side, where Mom was sitting. She'd been rushed to the hospital, but she'd died a few hours later. Dad had raged that I was unable to keep Mom safe, make good judgment calls, or read people. Part of me always suspected he was right.

Dad could never love me nearly as much as Mom had loved me. And I was to blame for that. The hollow I carried around inside always reminded me of this fact.

The gag was removed, and a callused hand brushed the hair off my face. I buried my face in the cushion, sobbing and heaving. "I just want to be alone."

"Sorry, Diva. I can't leave you alone. But I'll leave you with Jeremy. I'll be back by six at the latest."

I was beyond caring about his pity. But the shame of it all, the embarrassment of my breakdown, prevented me from showing my face. Caleb had rightly mocked me and Dad throughout the call. And I'd had to sit propped up like a doll to hear Dad's comments and Caleb's laughter.

The door creaked open, and I heard footsteps as Jeremy entered, murmuring something to Caleb. A moment later, a blanket was draped over me. I didn't know who put it there, but I was grateful for the chance to hide.

Then all was quiet. For a few minutes I wallowed in the stillness. Risking a peep behind me, I saw that Jeremy was working at his laptop and Caleb was gone. Relief washed over me. Now at last I had a chance to collect my thoughts.

CHAPTER THIRTEEN: CALEB

Shrugging on my coat, I stepped out into the raw cold and pressed the key fob for the car. My shoes crunched on the gravel as I rounded the beamer and popped open the door, sliding behind the wheel.

That had been the ultimate exercise in self-control. Keeping my mouth shut in case someone was recording the conversation, while the whole time all I wanted was to mess up Walter's grey-mustached face. Everything about Walter was grey—his complexion, his combover, even his eyes. I liked to think his features reflected his crimes. He'd be a lot greyer once I'd finished with him.

I had let Walter warn Eve and Luis, as I'd known he would. He'd barked so much at his wife and stepson that he'd done the job better than I could've. My silence, in many ways, was the most threatening communication of all. It sent the message that the man behind the crime was no fool who'd stumble into a trap or who felt he had to browbeat people to get his way. Less was more in this case, and Danya's carefully staged position on the couch told them everything they needed to know: she was being looked after by someone who meant business.

Turning on one of the blues satellite stations, I headed towards the main road out of town. If I had more time or headspace, I'd replay some of those awkward moments in the conversation, where it was clear Danya's parents were just trying to look suitably upset, and where Walter was obviously furthering his ambitions. Setting his daughter up on a date while she was bound and gagged took the cake for opportunism. As for her stepbrother, I couldn't tell if he was the sort to take action or not. Even if he reported this to the police, they'd have nothing to go on. If he sniffed around on his own, he was more likely to get himself into trouble than cause trouble for me.

"Call Gideon," I said to my phone.

A moment later, the call connected.

"Yoooo," my friend half-yawned, half-greeted.

"Is this a bad time?" I merged onto the main highway.

"A little early, but otherwise, no."

"You going to Finney's later?"

Gideon had a group of computer nuts he hung out with at a dive bar in Passyunk Square every Saturday night. In the past, I'd joined them there for pool and poker.

"Yeah. Tonight's ghost and ghoul trivia."

I chuckled. "You'll kill it. I feel sorry for the other teams."

As we discussed another job he had hacking for a hotel workers union, he told me about some of the dirtier union busting tactics used by corporations.

"How was your talk with the breadcrumb dude?"

"Not great." I shoved a hand through my hair. "Pretty fucking awful."

"You wanna talk about it?"

"That's all I'll be doing for the afternoon."

"You going to see Lucy and Faye?" Gideon knew I saw my mom and sister without fail every Saturday. They both loved him.

"Yeah. I don't want to make Mom relive anything too painful. But I have to know the truth."

I'd confided in Gideon about everything I'd heard from Mr. J. except for yesterday's bombshell.

A hiss blew through his teeth. "The truth can be brutal."

"You oughta know."

"Speaking of, I found some more damning evidence on Walter's company."

My pulse spiked. "Yeah?"

"For over twenty years GenRev has been giving kickbacks to surgeons and doctors who order GenRev's medical devices and drugs."

"I thought all the big companies did that."

"Nuh-uh. It's a pretty serious offense these days."

I smiled. "Day two, and he's already racking up the crimes." Then I remembered the other thing. "Can you look into a virus set to attack GenRev? My client has taken their systems ransom."

I could hear the grin in his voice. "I'd love to know who the architect is behind that. This just isn't Walter's month, is it?"

"Or his decade."

"How's his daughter doing?"

"It's not her month either. She's about to have her bubble burst where her father's concerned."

A long tinkling told me he was in the can. "Judging from all the pictures of her online, I'd say she's hot and rich enough to cope just fine."

Her nipples saluting me through her shirt this morning flashed through my brain. Then the feel of her tight mouth around my cock. "Mmm."

A roar of laughter surged from him. "You're banging her."

I lane-surfed through some slow-moving cars. "There's nothing else to do when you're watching someone twenty-four-seven. You try it sometime. Even an ape starts looking good."

"This chick is no ape. And you're not desperate. Not by a long shot. Me, on the other hand, I've had to switch *to* the other hand, because my right was getting carpal tunnel."

"Now who's giving unwelcome visuals?"

"Point is, I'm not buying your whole my-job-sucks shtick,

because no doubt you're getting sucked. By a hot piece of ass."

"It's just one more way of flipping the bird to her old man."

"How sweet it is! Revenge, I mean." He cackled.

For some reason, it didn't sit right going on about using Danya. Not when an image of tears streaming down her reddened cheeks hovered in my head.

"Don't you have some hack job you should be at? I won't keep you," I told him.

"Hey, you called me. You woke me from a dream where I'd hacked into a deep neural network that exactly replicated Putin's brain. Suddenly I had the most valuable secrets on the market."

"What did you do with them?"

"I don't know. That's when you buzzed."

"Sell them to Bill Maher."

"I'll think about it. Later, man."

After we'd ended the call, I turned up the music. Danya had been perceptive when she'd noticed I was on edge. Asking Mom about what the Breadcrumb Client had told me yesterday was going to be painful for everyone.

But there was no going back now.

Danya

My gaze swerved to the clock on Jeremy's desk. *9:05.* I had nine long hours to kill. I spent the first fifteen minutes opening the curtain on the window behind the half-sofa, so the sun bathed the room again. I used my teeth, hips, and shoulders, but I got the job done. Then I hopped over to the couch beneath the bookshelf, kneeling up to find something to read.

Not for the first time, I found myself puzzling over the titles on the shelves—physics and engineering manuals, survival narratives, US history books, and memoirs and fiction by American greats like Mark Twain, Jack London, and John Steinbeck.

"Are these all your books, Jeremy?"

"Just the ones on the top shelf. The rest are Caleb's."

I thumbed the well-worn spines, finding many of the volumes dog-eared. *Tortilla Flat, The Valley of the Moon, Roughing It*—Caleb must really enjoy American writers of a century ago. Sliding out a collection of short survival tales of the American West, I noticed something behind the books. I dropped the story collection to peek through the empty slat. One of those black-and-white composition books middle and high school students use stood on its side against the back of the bookcase. Glancing over at Jeremy, I saw he was immersed in whatever he was working on. I had to remove several more books to make room to reach my tied hands in, but eventually I nudged the composition book out.

I turned my back to Jeremy so I could hide the notebook, slumping onto the couch. Had I just discovered Caleb's private journal? Some secret record of his thoughts that would shed light on who he was? Maybe the key to the mystery of how the boy became the Werewolf and the Werewolf became the kidnapper lay in these pages. My heart beat wildly, and heat swirled up my spine.

With my wrists bound it took many awkward attempts, but I managed to flip through the notebook. Not a single pen mark interrupted the continuous blankness of the lined pages. No name or date appeared inside the cover, and nothing signaled that the book had ever been used.

Now a different kind of excitement thrilled through me — the kind I used to feel in high school when I cracked open a new notebook and envisioned filling it with writing. So many thoughts pressed at the gate of my mind waiting to be poured out in words that I panted for a pen or pencil. I cast my eyes around the room, spying a cylinder among the picture frames and plants on the table next to the door. With some trouble I covered the composition book with the short story collection and slid off the couch, scooting over to the table.

Several pens and a pencil stood in the cylinder!

I picked up a pen like a cigarette between my forefingers and jumped my way back to the sofa. Now to figure out how to write.

I soon discovered that if I knelt on the floor with the notebook open on the couch and leaned over to the left, I could grasp the pen in my right hand and scrawl words slowly. I propped up several books as a barrier to hide what I was doing from Jeremy. Every fifteen words or so I shook out my hands to keep them from cramping up. It was a painstaking process, but determination made me patient.

Knowing no audience would ever read what I wrote or judge me for it, and knowing I wouldn't be able to take any of my writing away with me, I composed more freely than I had in years—despite the fact that I was bound. I planned to hide the notebook where I'd found it so I could add to my reflections whenever I had a chance.

Here were some of the jumbled thoughts I recorded—

College papers killed inspiration. They ruined writing. Grades, arguments, footnotes, pre-assigned topics—they allowed little creativity. I wrote everything the night before, or four days too late. None of it any good. The day I'd produce a good, well thought-out paper was always just around the corner and always out of reach.

If I marry, I want my husband to be someone I choose, someone who sees me and accepts me for who I am. Dad's choices of husband would try to change me beyond all recognition. Or, worse, they wouldn't even factor me into the equation but would consider only the money I'd bring them.

Maybe love and a fulfilling career are like that huge stuffed animal prize at the fair. Only a few lucky people land the ring around the duck's neck, but everyone tries for it because they've seen people walking around with the prize and think they can win it too.

If this were my blog, I'd start by revisiting the motels Mom and I stayed at, the small-town diners and roadside restaurants, and the local establishments where people pin flyers announcing community events. Sandusky, Ohio; Eau Claire, Wisconsin; Dickinson, North Dakota; Billings, Montana; Twin Falls, Idaho; Winnemucca, Nevada; Nevada City, California. Then, returning east via the southern route, Tombstone, Arizona; Sheffield, Texas; Ponchatoula, Louisiana; Laurel, Mississippi; Fort Payne, Alabama; Blountville, Tennessee; Lexington, Virginia.

If time permits, I could avoid the interstates altogether and take country routes through even smaller towns, staying a full day at some of them. Maybe that's what travel really boils down to — chasing the chance to imagine living in a place permanently.

Would the Werewolf have accepted me as I am? Or was he like a place you stop at on the road and romanticize as you imagine living there long-term?

I filled four pages with messy print and disjointed thoughts. When I looked over at the clock, it was already noon. I covered the notebook in books and pushed to my feet.

Just in time, since a knock sounded, and Jeremy went to the door to unlock it. Marisa entered with a tray filled with glasses of what looked like lemonade and sandwiches. She locked the door behind her, placing the key in her back pocket.

"Let me untie your hands for lunch," Jeremy offered kindly.

"Thank you." My jaw slackened. He trusted me enough to free me!

I shook out my liberated hands and stretched my arms. I could've unknotted my ankles and tackled Marisa for the key. But somehow their trust and kindness made it hard to think of offering violence, even for my own escape. Maybe that famous poet—I couldn't remember her name—had been right when she said that every prison is of our own making. This room hadn't been a prison at all for the three hours that I'd been filling the pages of the composition book. Not for one moment had I chafed to be set free.

The three of us sat at a table Marisa pulled out, eating her roast beef sandwiches and talking about our favorite things to do in Philly. Marisa loved visiting the Barnes museum, while Jeremy loved birdwatching at the John Heinz National Wildlife Refuge. I liked buying a cheesesteak in South Philly and wandering around Little Italy.

After lunch, Jeremy either forgot to re-secure my wrists or didn't bother to. My bound ankles seemed to signal that we were going on the honors system for the rest of the afternoon. Whether Caleb had sanctioned Jeremy's lenience or not, I took full advantage of it. I hopped over to the window to watch the finches and sparrows using the feeder in the back garden. Then I made my jerky way back to the couch, where I sat down and placed the notebook on my lap to continue writing—still behind the wall of books I'd erected.

I wrote out lists of blog topics I could tackle and bullet points to cover with each theme. After matching travel spots to themes, I brainstormed names for my blog. The exercise was purely fanciful, as I'd likely never put these plans in motion, nor would I have access to them later. But ironically, knowing they were impossible freed me up to imagine and write without censoring myself.

Then I wrote about Caleb. I speculated where he'd gone, preferring to think he was doing a not-too-dangerous job, rather than meeting up with a woman. I tried to guess at why he hated Dad so much. I came up empty. I explained his silence on the call as him protecting himself from being recorded. And I pictured him on the road collecting and using all those travel-size containers. What sorts of jobs required a fixer to travel? Apart from kidnapping.

I wrote about how frustrating it had been to want to please

two opposing teams at once — Caleb and Dad — and leaving both indifferent and unimpressed. I even confessed, with plenty of guilt, that I missed Caleb more than I missed Dad.

Thoughts of Dad and Caleb were inextricably intertwined.

I checked the clock, finding it was 5:30. Time to hide all evidence of my day's activities. Replacing the notebook with the pen inside at the back of the shelf, I set the books in front of it, just as they'd been before.

Jeremy stepped over. "I should fasten the scarf again . . . "

So maybe my temporary freedom was our secret. That was fine with me. I wouldn't tell on him or abuse his trust. I held out my wrists so he could tie me up.

No sooner had he bound me than the key turned in the lock and the door opened to reveal Caleb, pulsating with power and intensity as he stood on the threshold. I recalled how the Werewolf had created a black hole of energy when he'd left me six years ago. But this gravitational pull was ten times stronger. My captor's eyes were fiery orbs of bronze and malachite.

He crooked his finger. "Come here."

I didn't hesitate to hop in a most undignified way towards him. My pride had apparently gone the way of Woodstock in 1999. Whether because I was insanely attracted to him, because he'd punished me roundly on four occasions, or because I actually *liked* following his orders — maybe all three? — I obeyed him without question.

He bobbed his chin towards Jeremy. "We'll be in shortly."

Jeremy swept past us, closing the door behind him.

My thoughts of the afternoon swirled to the surface like a whirlpool. It was all I could do to muster the courage to voice them. "Why do you hate my father?"

Caleb hooked a finger under my wrist scarf, tugging me forward so I leaned against his thigh. "The truth, Diva, is precious and painful. Before I give it to you, I need to know three things. Are you strong enough to hear it? Do you want it enough? And will you recognize it for what it is?"

I gaped at his assurance. "I was asking for *your* truth. A relative truth. You speak as if it's *the* truth. Positive and absolute."

He stepped backward, releasing his fingers from my scarf. Losing my balance, I toppled forward. The room tipped and spun. In that instant I knew I'd fall head-first to the floor. I nearly did, but at the last second, a strong arm blocked me.

Doubled up over his arm, I panted, adrenaline coursing through my veins.

His cool tone bordered on mocking. "I think there are some truths we can agree on, Danya. That you would've fallen and hit your head just now is one." He stood me upright. "That you were afraid is another."

Heat seeped into my face.

"Are those positive and absolute enough for you?" He turned on his heel, breezing out the door and leaving me more unsettled than ever. Now I got to add supreme embarrassment to my confusion and ignorance.

Hobbling to the kitchen took ten minutes.

Chapter Fourteen: Caleb

Jeremy reported that Danya had spent the whole day writing in the composition book I'd had him buy at the town's grocery store that morning and place behind the books in the shelf. I'd also instructed him to put pens in the pen holder so she could sneak one for writing. And I'd told him to untie her wrists in the afternoon if she'd cooperated during the morning. In my experience, the best way to get someone to do something was to forbid it—or to make it so hard to do that the challenge made that person more determined than ever to accomplish it. I'd directed Jeremy to pretend not to notice that Danya was writing in the notebook. Since, according to him, she'd immersed herself in her writing, she must be getting over her block.

It was in my own best interests to keep her occupied during the daytime. I didn't know how often I'd have to leave or for how long, but knowing she wasn't giving Jeremy trouble or trying to escape would make everything easier. Plus, a month was a long time to hold someone who was completely unwilling. Letting her have her writing—especially if writing came hard to her in everyday life—would make her a good deal more manageable.

We passed the first part of dinner in silence. Since the diva had shown that she neither wanted the truth enough nor was ready to recognize it as truth, I wasn't about to waste my breath telling her about her father.

She ate heartily, cleaning a plate of Cornish game hen and colcannon. When Marisa served the spinach salad, Danya grew talkative.

"Marisa, I know you're from North Philly, and Jeremy said he's from Quakertown. What about you, Caleb?"

"West of Philly," I said vaguely. Five years ago I'd bought the house that most closely approximated what Mom and Nathaniel had owned in Ardmore before relocating us to an apartment in the city when I was eight.

"My stepmom's cousins live out in Rosemont," Danya offered. "They're not too fond of Dad, and the feeling's mutual, so I've always had to sneak visits with them."

"Are you close with your stepmom?" Since Eve had worked as an administrative assistant in the marketing department of GenRev at the same time Nathaniel had been in the R&D department, it was possible she knew something about my father.

A quiet smile unfurled across her face. "Yeah. Eve's amazing. She never tried to be a replacement for Mom. Just a good friend and mother figure. And she showed me the same love she showed Luis. Even though she quit working at the company when she married Dad, she's always been active for charity. For nine years now she's worked hard for an organization that funds Alzheimer's research. She's really inspiring."

"Does she have a personal history with Alzheimer's?"

Danya's lips thinned into a line. "Her great-aunt died from it."

I thought of my own mother's battle with early-onset dementia and the alcoholism that had likely caused it. Over the last twelve years, through cognitive stimulation therapy and cognitive behavioral therapy, she'd made enormous progress towards recovery from both. "I'm sorry to hear that."

She sipped her water. "I never met her. But I did meet her son once. He was one of the most serious people I've ever talked to. And that's saying a lot, since most of Dad's finance friends are *very* serious."

"Money will do that to a person."

"Either that or they remain completely unfazed by it." Her soft laugh rippled through the space between us. "A friend of mine, Alex Choo, is independently wealthy. But he still walks dogs for a living. When another friend asked him why, he said he used to be much heavier, and dog walking got his weight under control. So to keep his weight low he continues to walk dogs."

"Which sort of person are you?"

"Whenever I've had money in the past, I spent it too fast to find out." She smiled ruefully.

"On what?"

"An apartment, college, a charity I started."

"What's the charity?"

Her eyes flicked to mine. "Kids Crossing Countries. It provides opportunities for kids to study foreign languages starting in elementary school. And for teens to travel internationally."

"Is it big?"

"Not yet. But I'm hoping to grow it."

"With all your connections, I'm sure you'll have no problem."

She twisted her lips. "They're all Dad's connections. I don't like using them."

"Why not?"

"Dad's help comes at a price. One I'm not willing to pay." She tilted her head as a sly smile slid up her face. "We always return to talking about me. You're good at deflecting questions away from yourself."

I fished out a tin of licorice mints. "In my line I have to fly under the radar as much as possible."

"Can I try one of those?"

I held the tin out, and she took a mint, sniffing it before

placing it on her tongue. I watched as she closed her lips around it, hollowing her cheeks to suck. My dick throbbed, reminding me it hadn't seen action since last night.

"Two things." She held up her fingers. "One, if you want to fly under the radar, it's probably a good idea not to have licorice as your signature flavor. And two, it's impossible for someone like you to fly under the radar."

I perked an eyebrow. "Someone like me?"

"Who dances the tango, looks like you" — her gaze meandered over me — "and ties the most complicated knots like you're tying your shoe."

My eye met Marisa's, and I nodded to her. Drying her hands on a towel, she left the kitchen. I tapped a playlist on my phone, accordion notes sounding the start of a tango song.

"Which is it, Diva? You want to dance or stab me with a pitchfork?"

Crimson spread across her cheeks. "Dance."

I rose, taking her by the hand and leading her out to the floor in front of the fire. Pulling her into a close embrace, I whirled us around while sweeping her to the opposite wall and back.

I spoke in her ear, my palm gliding up her back to her nape. She shivered. "What did you do all day?"

Her low voice quavered. "Thought about stuff, read, talked to Jeremy and Marisa."

I twisted her so she faced forward in front of me, my fingers skating her arm as she extended it behind her while my other hand pressed into her chest below her breasts. I brushed my lips against her temple. "What did you think about?"

"Traveling, writing, Mom, Dad . . . you."

I spun her twice and dipped her low. When I'd pulled her back to my chest, I murmured into her hair, "Let me guess. You thought about how much simpler everything is when you're tied up. How it saves you having to make all the complicated decisions you usually have to make."

Her wide eyes and slack jaw told me I'd hit the nail on the head. As the tempo picked up, I led her in a rapid series of boleos, followed by a turn. Then we did a run with mirror steps, and I pulled her up, seating her on my bent leg. I spun us, rounding to a close in an open-leg stance so her thigh wrapped around mine as she leaned into me.

Those brilliant aquamarine eyes gazed back at me, her lush lips hovering inches from mine. She was begging to be kissed. And I came closer to giving in to temptation than I had in a long time. She was heart-stoppingly beautiful, soft waves of flaming hair framing her face. Her shapely thighs molding to my legs made my cock stand forth and report for duty. But in my experience, kissing lips led to tenderness, which led to a woman making emotional demands. That wasn't what this was about.

Danya

I hungered for his lips with a need that sang from every pore of my body. When he stepped back, releasing me from his arms, the heat of rejection crawled up my neck to my ears. Bereft of his touch, I ached for some affection—any attention—that would fill this hollow inside me. But only from him. He was all I craved.

When his commanding tone sliced through the low-playing tango music, my heart leapt. "Strip and bend over the couch, spreading your legs wide."

Much as I longed to comply, I held back. "But Marisa and Jeremy—"

"Know to stay out of here until we leave." He swatted my ass. "Move."

Blood rushed to my sex and set it pulsing as I scurried to

obey.

He stepped aside, watching while I disrobed, starting with my shirt and jeans and finishing with my bra and panties. I propped myself on my hands, but he leaned over and folded my arms so I rested on my elbows. Fondling my breasts, he flicked my peaked nipples. He kneed my legs wide apart, pulling my hips towards him while dragging his fingers over my drenched slit.

"Such a good girl," he breathed in his gravelly voice. "So ready to receive my dick whenever I choose to give it."

His praise stoked the flames licking at my center. Did he know the effect his words and tone had on me? He must. Hearing the swish of his jeans and boxer briefs as he swept them down, I twisted to see him stroking his behemoth cock from root to tip. He tore open a foil packet with his teeth and sheathed himself in one motion.

Bending over me, he caged me in with his blisteringly hot trunk. His tip pricked and teased my opening as his gruff words shot tremors down my spinal column. "Fight me now, Diva. This is the hate-fuck session I promised you this morning."

Fighting him was the last thing on earth I wanted — short of having my clit pierced.

"Can I take a raincheck on that?" I mumbled.

An arousing laugh tumbled from his chest. "If you don't fight, then you beg."

"There's nothing in between?" I tried.

His teeth closed on my earlobe, and his hot tongue swirled in my ear. What was left of my spine disintegrated with his searing breath. "Nothing."

A desperate moan climbed from my throat. "*Please.*"

His girth prodded and traced my entrance. "Please what?"

By now I suspected he preferred directness and honesty.

I swallowed. "Please give me . . . your cock."

Fisting my hair, he extended my neck, his rough voice resonating in my ear. "And why should I do that?"

"Because I need you!" I cried.

He pinned my arms flat on the sofa, over my head. "I happen to be keen on fucking *you*, Diva."

Thank God! I rejoiced.

He fed his length into my pulsating pussy, and as fast as he filled me I consumed him. He pounded me harder than a battering ram, hitting my sensitive spots over and over with punishing force. His hips rocked, swiveled, and thrust, holding me in place as he worked us both up to a pitch of delirium.

Pleasure swelled and twisted within me like a funnel cloud preceding a tornado. I had no choice over where or when it touched down. His forceful attack acted like the destructive, high-speed winds that demolish everything in their path.

He yanked my hair hard, making my scalp tingle, before pulling out completely. "What do you say, Danya?"

"Please . . . please may I come?" My voice was hoarse and scratchy. His virility surrounded and filled me, turning me into pure animal.

"You may." He slammed into me, connecting the funnel to the ground and shooting me upwards in a whirlwind of rapture. I corkscrewed around, ripping apart and flying out from my center. My groans peppered the air as pleasure tore through me. His body seized up and he growled, finding his own release. Something about his primal noises, the feel of his engorged cock inside me, or his continuing strokes unloosed another cyclone of ecstasy, and I came again with a vagabond moan.

Though Caleb had done all the work, we were both out of breath and sweaty. Panting, we slowly recovered from our efforts. Since the music had stopped, the only sounds besides our breaths were the crackle of the fire and the hum of the refrigerator. Peeling himself off me, he pulled out, removing and disposing of the condom.

I stood woozily, wishing we could cuddle in front of the fire. I had so many questions to ask him, but he always turned the conversation back to me. There was no point in asking.

After I'd dressed, Caleb nodded his head towards the door. "Since you've been good, I'll let you sleep with just your ankles tied."

A little later, as I drifted off to sleep, I wondered why he'd trusted me so much tonight. He had no way of knowing my mind was more on writing than escape. No way of knowing I'd rather please than anger him. Or knowing how much I was starting to like Jeremy, Marisa, and the simplicity of life here.

He'd no idea how many glimpses of the Werewolf I'd begun to see in him.

Caleb — Three years ago

I chuckled as I read the note accompanying the last of the three cases of hard apple cider the delivery guy had set down in my front hall. The Breadcrumb Client had a sense of humor after all. He'd always struck me as incapable of cracking a joke. Maybe this was his way of telling me I'd need a little alcohol to hear what he was going to share with me in fifteen minutes.

Two weeks ago, Mr. J. had called to say municipal authorities in Mifflinburg were giving him grief because of the hard cider he sold at his orchard without a license. Apparently every year he'd applied for a license and been denied each time. So he kept his sales on the down-low, producing a limited amount of cider each fall and not advertising tastings. By spring he'd always sold out, and this year looked to be no different. But a month ago the county had threatened to report him to Harrisburg unless he paid them a *fine* of 250 grand.

A trip up to Union County, a few discreet talks with borough officials, and a couple of greased palms had cleared things up. I'd managed to convince the local officials that Mr. J.'s hard cider boosted tourist revenue, persuading them to overlook all unlicensed sales to date. Meanwhile, I'd paid someone in Harrisburg to ensure that Mr. J. would receive his limited winery license by the end of April.

Mr. J.'s note read, *For closing the cider case, you're invited to open one.*

I cracked open one of the unlabeled brown bottles, taking a sip. I was no hard cider buff, but I'd describe the taste as bright citrus notes followed by astringent floral flavors. It was dry but complex. Clark would appreciate this, since he liked tart apples. I'd bring him a case this week.

At 4, Mr. J. called, and I swiped up.

After thanking me for handling the borough authorities, he asked what I thought of his cider.

"It's good. Does every batch turn out different?"

"I'm getting better each year at zeroing in on the exact taste I want. This year's recipe was spot-on."

I swigged some more, waiting for Mr. J. to give me the latest breadcrumb.

He cleared his throat. "Last year I told you how Walter Penwarren virtually forced Nathaniel Furness to work for him so he could keep tabs on him. Penwarren closely monitored everything Furness did. Furness spent considerable time on his own developing a new kind of augmented reality treatment for Alzheimer's patients. It improved on the current calming experiences, memory aids, and cognitive stimulation therapy. Had Furness developed this idea, he would have made millions. What he didn't realize was that Penwarren had hired someone to hack into Furness's private computer and monitor it too."

I spluttered the cider I was swallowing, plonking the bottle on the counter. "You mean Penwarren stole his invention out from under him? *Again?*"

"I'm afraid so. Penwarren went about developing and marketing it, and by the time your father realized what was going on, his employer had the upper hand. Furness filed another lawsuit claiming that he'd invented the idea. But Penwarren countered that Furness had developed it on company time with company resources. And he produced plenty of proof in the form of time stamps, file directories, emails, and so forth — all trumped up by his hacker. Furness didn't stand a chance."

My limbs tensed, and the blood vessels in my neck threatened to burst. I wanted to torture Penwarren slowly and painfully, till he begged for mercy. Suddenly drinking that cider seemed like a bad idea, as my head felt ready to explode. "What happened?" I forced out through clenched teeth.

"That's for next time. Meanwhile, enjoy the cider." Before I could get a word in edgewise, he ended the call.

"Fuck!" I slammed my phone down.

Stomping out of the kitchen, I took the stairs two at a time to go change into my running clothes. I needed to pound the pavement till my legs gave out. Anything to escape this feeling of powerless futility. I was sick and tired of Mr. J.'s games. Next time he could find some other fixer to dangle on his hook.

The problem was, the hook was so deeply embedded I could no longer break free.

CHAPTER FIFTEEN: DANYA

As the days went by, we fell into a routine of sorts. Caleb always rose before me, working on his laptop for a while before waking me for morning sex. His tongue, fingers, and cock roused me to consciousness before making me nearly pass out again. Afterwards, when we took a shower together, he maneuvered me into various positions under the steaming jet of water — standing with my back against the wall, bent over bracing my hands on the ledge, facing the wall with my legs forming a chair, sitting with my thighs wrapped around his neck — and brought us both to climax again.

After breakfast, Caleb would leave me for several hours with either Marisa or Jeremy in Jeremy's study. I suspected he was working somewhere in the house, because soon after Jeremy led me into the kitchen for lunch, Caleb joined us. Then followed another few hours in the study, during which time I continued my writing. My wrists were always left unbound now, while a rope with complex knots loosely bound my ankles. I planned out my blog as minutely as if I were actually starting it, brainstorming angles for various pieces and trips, sketching out designs, and listing content I'd embed in my site. Around 6, I always hid the notebook in the same location, replacing all the books I'd used as a wall to block Jeremy's view of my writing activity.

Directly before dinner, Caleb would come into the study, bind my ankles more tightly, tie my wrists, and fasten a gag around my head. Then he'd video call Dad, remaining silent while Dad rambled on about how hard Drake Arthur was working to identify the virus and reverse hack the culprits. Dad spent a good ten minutes singing Drake's praises and laying into me about getting married. Then he went on a rant about his rival company, SciPulse, and its owner, Ben Yo-sevich, threatening to bring them down once he could prove they'd masterminded both the virus and my kidnapping.

I'd stopped expecting relief or sympathy from Dad's ti-rades — which was a good thing, since they were as far from soothing or sensitive as Perth, Australia is from the Bermuda Triangle. I wished he'd tell me how Luis and Eve were, or tell me he'd stopped by my apartment to pick up my mail and water my plants, or any other mundane, affectionate gesture. But Dad operated on a much higher plane. Daily life and fam-ily ties were liabilities, for which my kidnapping was a case in point.

Emotionally drained by the time Caleb killed the call each evening, I was grateful for his, Marisa's, and Jeremy's slight-est kindnesses. Over dinner, I told stories of best and worst moments from my past travels and tried unsuccessfully to find out more about my captor. He remained more tight-lipped than ever. After dinner, Caleb and I played gin rummy and competed in building card houses on the living room car-pet out of the many card decks Marisa had collected over the years. We also danced the tango, swing, and salsa. Dancing invariably led to sex — on the floor, sofa, chairs, and, one night, on top of the piano.

Caleb

We sat at breakfast on Wednesday, day six of the kidnapping. Marisa had made banana pancakes and sausages. My phone buzzed midway through the meal, and I paced from the room to take the call.

It was Faye, saying that Mom was sick. "I think it's the flu. The Kalinskys all had something similar last week."

Her voice was laced with that edge of panic she got whenever something out of the ordinary happened. A new neighbor moving in across the hall. A dog that hadn't stopped barking during the night. A construction project that had started on the building opposite in back. Faye liked things to remain the same, deeply mistrusting anything new. Change was unstable, and stability kept Faye sane.

My sister didn't drive. Her part-time job of delivering groceries locally for the store down the street allowed her to walk or use an electric scooter. She never left home for more than a few hours at a time, for fear that she'd come back to find Mom gone. And, for the same reason, she grew antsy whenever Mom was out for more than several hours. Schedules were my sister's lifeline, while anything that upset routine was anathema to her.

According to Mom, Faye had been like this since soon after I'd been placed with Clark and his family, when I was 13 and Faye was 10. By the time I'd come back, five years later, Faye remained emotionally arrested at age 10, as if an evil fairy godmother had cast a spell on her. I'd managed to send her to a Catholic all-girls' school to graduate high school. Under the extra care and kindness of the sisters, she'd thrived.

But the last nine years had seen her dependency on Mom take an increasing toll on our mother's mental health. Besides trying to get Mom and Faye to live with me in Ardmore, I'd been trying to involve Faye in activities with people her own age. She refused to see a therapist, but people I'd talked to about her arrested development had suggested that active forms of therapy could do her a world of good. At least she knew a lot of people in the community. The trick was getting her to participate in organized activities with them.

I was grateful Faye had used her phone to call me. It had

taken several years to convince her that using a cell phone didn't require the skills of a rocket scientist. Now, occasionally, she even tapped out a short text to me.

I glanced at the time. "I'll be there no later than twelve-thirty." I knew that Faye would be too worked up to take Mom's temperature. "Can you find the Tylenol bottle in the medicine cabinet and give her a couple? And wet a washcloth with cold water — place it on her forehead?"

"Okay."

I wasn't sanguine about her following my directions.

After we'd ended the call, I returned to the kitchen, where Jeremy met me with a look of alarm in his dark-brown eyes. I glanced over to the table to make sure the diva was behaving. She was chatting with Marisa, demonstrating something with her delicate hands.

"Maybe we'd better go into the other room," he suggested.

We stepped into the dining room, and Jeremy closed the door. He rubbed the back of his neck, avoiding my eyes. "I'm sorry, Caleb. I messed up."

My brows bunched. "What's wrong?"

"You remember that independent film *Black Horizon* that I told you about?"

My jumbled thoughts grew more confused. "What?" Why was he talking about indie films?

"We agreed to let them film here on the farm." Jeremy scraped a hand through his thin hair, making it stick out at all angles. "It was a whole year ago, so I kinda forgot."

I waited as patiently as I could for him to get on with it.

"Turns out, the date they set to film is today."

"Here? Today?" My index finger pointed at the floor. I tried to keep my voice down, but I couldn't hide my agitation.

He gritted his teeth. "Yeah. They just called to say they'll arrive at nine-thirty. I can't really put them off, because they paid in advance and it's all in the contract."

"*Fuck.*" It was my turn to rake my fingers through my hair. "I have to leave for Philly in the next half-hour. Mom's sick."

"I'm sorry, truly, but Marisa and I'll need to make sure the film crew have everything they need." Jeremy shifted from one foot to the other uncomfortably. "It'll be a little difficult to hide *her.*"

Gagging and tying up Danya for a whole day would only have been possible for the first day or so of her captivity. In the last five days we'd moved beyond that to another kind of arrangement. Plus, I didn't even know if I'd be back tonight — it all depended on Mom's health. And I couldn't very well ask Marisa and Jeremy to watch Danya overnight. I was doubly stuck.

"I'll handle it." I strode back out to the kitchen, catching my captive's eye. "Diva, come with me to the sun porch."

The 1950s south-facing addition to the farmhouse had plenty of sunlight during the day. I had a feeling the view of the fields and groves to the South would impress Danya.

I wasn't wrong.

When we reached the porch, she clasped her hands. "Wow. This is breathtaking. In a few weeks' time, all those dogwoods and cherries will be blooming. It'll be a magical field of white and pink."

"Take a seat." I indicated a bench swing that hung from the rafters.

She folded herself into the swing, toeing it into gentle motion, her gaze clinging to mine.

Wearing a powder-blue wool dress that hugged all her curves, she had her hair swept back from her face in a clip Marisa had given her. Her stunning cheekbones and shapely calves showed to mesmerizing effect.

I stood directly in front of her, cupping her chin. "When I brought you here, I promised you I wouldn't drug you. I want to keep that promise."

Her rounded eyes blinked. "Why would you need to drug me?"

"We're going back into the city. I need you to come quietly with me while I make a visit to someone." I couldn't leave her in the car. Someone might see or hear her, and she might catch cold. Especially if I stayed for any length of time.

"Who are you visiting?"

I debated whether to confide in her and potentially gain her sympathy or keep her in the dark. In the end, the immediate advantages of telling her outweighed the long-term risks. "My mother and sister. Mom's sick."

"Oh." Her gaze dropped from mine, and I could see the cogs whirring in her brain.

"I understand you will try to escape if you can, Diva. But then I'd have to drug you to make sure you don't." I put the problem in terms of our respective roles of captor and captive. "I don't want to have to do that."

A swallow tracked its way down her lily-white throat as her earnest gaze cut back to me. "I won't try to escape."

"You won't make a scene or cry out?"

She shook her head. "I promise."

My gaze jumped between her eyes. "At the first sign you're going back on your word, I won't hesitate to give you an injection. As long as you keep your word, I'll keep mine."

Her eyes blazed, and her voice sharpened. "You have my word. That's good enough."

I nodded. "Gather some things to stay overnight. We need to be out of here in the next ten minutes."

There was a chance I was making a huge mistake. But if I was any judge of character, the diva meant what she said and would be true to her word.

Using the same loose ankle binding I'd secured Danya with for the last few days and fastening her wrists in a scarf, I left her mouth ungagged but blindfolded her. In return for putting her through all this, I let her ride in the front passenger seat. Though I tinted her window so as not to draw attention to her blindfold from passing vehicles.

"Can we listen to classic rock?" she requested.

"Sure." I tuned in to one of the satellite stations, and the snarling guitars of Jimi Hendrix's *Lover Man* blared forth.

"Is it just me you're quiet with, or are you usually this reserved with women?"

I merged onto the highway, speeding up. "I wasn't aware I was quiet."

"You never answer questions. You're always asking *me* questions. It makes me feel very uninteresting."

I shot her a wry smile and a squint that she couldn't see. "I'd think it would have the reverse effect."

"I thought so too." She shook her head. "But I'm starting to realize that the more interesting a person is the more they're *interested* in other people." She turned towards me. "You're not letting me be interesting."

"Sorry to hamper your expression. Kidnapping tends to do that."

"Just so you know how interested I am, here are the questions I'd ask you if I thought you'd ever answer them." As she settled into her seat, I looked forward to hearing more of her mellow voice. I was coming to appreciate its calming effect. "How did you get into fixing? Have you ever been in love? What do you do for fun? How did you learn to dance? What's your ultimate dream or goal in life? What's the funniest movie ever made, in your opinion?"

"It's a toss-up between *Inglourious Basterds* and *Snatch*." I opened a new tin of licorice mints, lobbing one in my mouth. "With *Fight Club* as a close runner-up."

She laughed. "You like violence and Brad Pitt."

I shrugged. "They're both hilarious."

"While you're opening up, any other questions you'd like to answer?"

I checked the rearview before switching lanes. "I'm good."

"Hmm. What you avoid answering tells a lot about you too."

"Or it tells you who I don't trust."

Swallowing, she faced the window. "I'll try not to take that personally."

As a Black Sabbath song filled the car, she was silent, visibly soaking up the music.

When the song ended, she twisted back towards me. "I'll bet you think I write about rarefied stuff that has no bearing on the real world. You think I'm a spoiled brat with no experience of real life — that I only hang out with privileged people. That I have no useful skillset and lack direction."

What was she going on about? Was all this because I said I didn't trust her?

My brows soared. "Is that what you think of yourself?"

Her voice wobbled. "Is it true?"

"What does it matter what I think, Danya?"

"I was right. You despise me." She sounded distraught.

"I don't despise you." This was why I didn't do girlfriends. Well, apart from doing them.

"Because I look up to you." She reached her tied hands up and wiped her nose with the back of one. "And it's not fair, you know. Our situation."

"Not fair to you?"

She opened her mouth and closed it, as if she thought better of saying something. That was when I knew she was going to say "not fair to us." Time to nip that thought in the bud.

I scrubbed a hand over my beard. "Look, Danya. Our situation isn't remotely about *us*. There's no trust allowed between a kidnapper and kidnappee. It's in my best interests to keep a major power imbalance between us. I'm using you.

Our interests clash completely. None of that makes an *us* possible."

She bowed her head. "Well, if we weren't in this situation, would there be an us?"

Absofuckinlutely not.

"I told you," I practically growled, my fingers drumming the steering wheel, "there's no place in my life for a girlfriend."

Simplicity was best here. No need to add that when it came to personal relationships I was the world's worst communicator. Look what I'd caused to happen to Faye and how things had ended with my first and only girlfriend, Gillian.

And no need to mention that if I *did* do girlfriends, the diva was among the very last women I'd date.

That was *if* I did girlfriends.

The Who's *Behind Blue Eyes* began to play on the radio.

"I hear you, Pete," Danya murmured.

Chapter Sixteen: Danya

Caleb parked the car, untied my wrists and ankles, and led me, blindfolded, up some steps and through a door.

He kept one arm wrapped around my back, speaking in my ear. "You're doing very well, Diva."

"Somehow I've managed to remember how to walk, though I've been out of practice recently," I chaffed. "It must be like riding a bike."

His earthy chuckle stole through my veins like red wine. "We're stepping into the elevator now."

After a short ride, he guided me down a cool, stone-floored hallway. As we paused and turned, he murmured, "Go along with my story."

I nodded. It was the Werewolf all over again. I savored our collusion, without fully considering what it might mean to do so.

He rapped on the door and removed my blindfold at the same time.

A petite, dark-haired woman with large, solemn brown eyes and a wide mouth pulled open the door. Caleb's nose and bone structure found their replicas in her face.

She threw her arms around him, hugging him tightly. "Cal. Mom'll be so happy to see you." She stepped back, surveying me with a shy smile.

"Faye, this is Diva. Diva, my sister." Caleb led me in, shutting the door. "Diva's driving to upstate New York with me."

Hmm. New Paltz? Poughkeepsie? These would be about the distance we'd driven, by my estimation. Then again, he was already telling his sister a few fibs.

I shook her hand. "Pleased to meet you."

A frown creased her brow. "But Mom—"

"Don't worry," he soothed, coiling an arm around her back as he kept an arm on my shoulder. "We'll stay as long as she needs. Diva doesn't have to get there in a hurry. Nor do I."

"Don't either of you worry." I looked up, telegraphing with my eyes that he didn't have to shepherd me everywhere. "I'm not going anywhere."

Knocking lightly, he pushed open a door that was slightly ajar. "Mom?"

A wiry middle-aged woman with Caleb's hair, lips, and eyes lay in a large bed covered in a duvet. Her attractive features looked haggard.

I hung back a little, out of deference to his mother, as Caleb advanced to her bedside.

"Cal, you didn't have to come," she husked. "It's probably just the flu. Who do we have here?" She trained her green eyes, dulled by sickness, on me.

"Mom, this is Diva. She needed a ride to upstate New York, and since I was headed there, I offered to take her."

I nodded. "I'm sorry you're under the weather, Mrs . . . ." I trailed off, realizing I had no idea what Caleb's last name was.

She coughed lightly into her hand. "I'm Lucy. Don't you two worry about me. I just need to sleep off this fever. I'll be right as rain tomorrow."

Caleb had disappeared into the adjoining bathroom.

"Can I get you some cold water or tea?" I offered.

"Cold water would be nice. And if you could . . ." She turned towards the bedside table, where a damp washcloth lay.

"Of course." Taking up the cloth, I headed towards the bathroom.

Caleb emerged carrying a Tylenol bottle and a

thermometer, and we brushed arms in passing. Surprise and gratitude flitted through his eyes.

After running the cloth under cold water and wringing it out, I folded it and returned to the bedroom, placing it on Lucy's forehead.

She had the thermometer in her mouth. When it beeped and Caleb removed it, she sighed. "That coolness feels good."

I turned to find Faye behind me. "Faye, would you show me where the glasses are?"

Nodding, she pivoted, leading me out through a living room to a comfortable kitchen with sunlight pouring in over a breakfast nook. She pointed towards a cabinet. "The glasses are in there."

"Thanks." I opened the cupboard, took down a glass, and filled it with water. For good measure I found some ice cubes in the freezer, adding them to the glass.

Faye chewed her lower lip, her gaze darting to mine. "Is Mom going to be okay?"

"She looks strong and basically healthy, so I would think so." I hoped I wasn't overstepping, but Caleb's sister clearly needed reassurance.

"Mrs. Kalinsky was sick for a whole week."

"Well, the same sickness takes a different form with each person. Your mother may be better in a couple of days." As I trekked back to the bedroom, she trailed behind. "Sleep often does wonders for a person."

Caleb placed a few pills in Lucy's palm, while I handed her the glass of water. When she'd swallowed them, Caleb pulled the covers up to her chin.

"Get some sleep, Mom."

"As for dinner—" Lucy began.

Caleb interrupted her. "Don't worry. We'll figure it out."

"But the lamb needs to be cooked tonight," Lucy insisted, anxiety infusing her voice with urgency.

"I can do it," I piped up. Remembering what my roommate Keiko taught me in college, I added, "I'll be sure not to *over-cook* it, either." That seemed to be the usual worry of cooks when it came to lamb.

Lucy relaxed back onto the pillow. "All right. You'll find asparagus in the crisper. And Faye knows where the roasting pan is."

In a matter of minutes her short breaths were the only sound in the room.

Faye stood beside me, clasping her hands in front of her. "Good thing I finished all my deliveries early today. Mrs. Jatnieks said I should get back to Mom."

Caleb stood. "If her fever doesn't improve by this evening, I'll call Dr. Sedona."

"Oh, no." Faye shook her head vehemently. "She won't need him."

"Doctors are just like everyone else," I told her, "only they have a little more knowledge. He may have a few suggestions for how to make your mom feel better faster." Though Faye looked a little older than me, she seemed emotionally much younger.

Faye tilted her head, searching my eyes. "He won't take her to the hospital?"

"That's what a home visit is for," I reassured. "To make sure she doesn't have to go."

"Okay." Faye seemed satisfied. She followed us as we tromped into the living room. "When Mom makes roast lamb she always puts carrots with the potatoes."

"If you'll direct me how, we can make it just as your mom likes it."

A beam lit her entire face. "When she wakes up, maybe she'll feel like eating."

I smiled. "There's nothing like the smell of roast lamb to sharpen the appetite."

"Then we'll need Frank Sinatra too. That's what Mom listens to when she cooks."

"Sinatra it is." I caught Caleb dividing a thoughtful look between us.

While Faye put on a CD, I found the beef broth, rosemary, onion, garlic, and olive oil, then unwrapped the leg of lamb. Keiko had shown me how to slow-roast lamb for five hours on a low heat so it was fall-off-the-bone tender.

I preheated the oven and prepared everything, as Faye told me the likely at-large teams to be selected for March Madness. She and Caleb disagreed over a few of the candidates, but Faye had so many statistics to back up her arguments that my money was on her projections.

"Faye, how do you know so much about basketball?" I stuck the roast in the oven. "Do you play?"

"She knows the stats of every major American athlete on college and pro teams," Caleb boasted. "Cycling, swimming, football, baseball, soccer, you name it."

Faye blushed. "I like watching sports. I don't play anything now, though I did play shortstop in softball at St. Catherine's."

Caleb leaned against the bar counter that separated the kitchen from the living room. "I told Faye she should join that adult league softball group in West Philly."

"Oh, I've heard about them." I poured a couple of glasses of water and slid them across the counter to Faye and Caleb before sipping some myself. "A friend in college joined them when she graduated. They're really friendly, and they're all about the community."

"I don't know." Faye turned her glass around. "I'm out of practice. They probably want people who've kept in better shape."

"You're in great shape," Caleb countered. "You deliver groceries six days a week on foot and on your scooter, and you never use elevators." He held up her arm with a grin. "Look at these guns, Diva."

Faye giggled, her adoration for Caleb palpable in her glowing eyes, warm tone, and relaxed posture.

Their conversation turned to people in the neighborhood who, Faye claimed, had asked after *Cal* and said to tell him hello. Faye seemed to know everyone, from the regulars who frequented the grocery store where she worked to the local postal workers and residents of her building. Caleb listened to her gossip, drawing her out with questions that she answered animatedly.

"If you like the puppet theater, you might consider volunteering there," he suggested, pouring roasted almonds into a dish and popping one in his mouth.

Faye's eyes lit up. "Maybe! Mr. Weisenheimer says he can't book enough performances for all the kids."

Caleb tipped his head. "He may just need more help."

"And the theater is only three blocks away, so I wouldn't have to leave Mom for long."

It became clear that he was encouraging his sister to engage in more activities around the community—possibly to get her out of the house more, or to give her more interactions with people. Maybe to help her mature emotionally.

His patient attention, good humor, and keen focus hinted at his own deep love for her.

She stood from her barstool. "Diva, do you want to see some pictures of our family?"

I looked to Caleb, who nodded his permission. "I'd love to."

As Faye showed me photos of her and Caleb when they were younger and of their parents, I got the sense that Faye's mind, like the apartment, memorialized a time past when their family had been a unit. Since she spoke of their father in the past tense, I gathered he'd died. She proudly showed me his biomedical engineering books, his large collection of beetles—thankfully dead—and his albums of photos taken on trips across North and Central America.

"We went to Monterrey, Mexico when I was four." She pointed to a picture of the four of them on a mountain. "I don't remember it, but that's me."

"I've always wanted to go there. My mom and I used to travel a lot around the States. But we never visited Mexico." I laughed at a picture of what looked to be a seven-year-old Caleb seated on a burro, wearing a straw hat and looking very serious. "I can't tell whether he looks more upset at not moving or the donkey more upset at having to carry him."

"Both," Caleb's gritty voice sent tingles from my neck to my tailbone. His large hand cupped my waist as his scorching body curtained mine from behind. "It was ninety-six degrees that day. The burro didn't want to budge, and I just wanted to go. Anywhere to escape the heat."

I instinctively leaned into his touch. "Whenever I remember the feel of things, my memories always conflict with the photos. In the end, I prefer what I remember to what the picture tells me must be true." I laughed to think how inexact my memory was. "My mom's father had a high-raftered attic where I used to sleep whenever I visited him. I stayed up half the night imagining I was on a ship and the timbers were masts. I traveled all sorts of places once everyone else had gone to sleep. But there was just one problem. When I looked at photos of that house years later, it turns out it only had two stories, and neither was high enough for what I remembered. And there were no timbers!"

Faye's eyes widened. "They probably removed the attic when they found out you knew where it could take you."

She was a wise soul. I took hold of her hand and squeezed it. "I think you're right, Faye."

"Do you remember the Hexagon Museum, Faye?" Caleb

reached over my shoulder and flipped the album a few pages forward. It looked as if everyone was a few years older, and they were inside a well-lit space.

Faye shook her head, peering at the photos.

"A museum in Arlington, Virginia where all the things hexagonal in nature and the arts make an appearance." Caleb pointed at a picture of a honeycomb with bees crawling over it. A young Caleb and Faye stood with their hands pressed to the glass, examining the display. "Another example of the photo not capturing the memory." He was so close that his warm, anise-laced breath fanned my forehead. "I remember Dad explaining carbon nanotubes to us. Tubes wrapped with hexagons. The material with the strongest tensile strength known to humans and, equally important and mysterious, electrically conductive."

Suddenly the engineering books in Jeremy's study made sense. They were a part of Caleb's father. Caleb's mystique had never been so potent as now, when he summarized in a few short sentences what his father had said some twenty years ago about the structure and makeup of carbon nano-tubes. His complexity ratcheted up my pulse and sharpened my awareness of everything from my toes to my breath.

I swallowed. "I'd say your memory was far better than any photo could ever be."

After putting away the last album, we all went into the bed-room to check on Lucy. Since she was chilled, Caleb found a wool blanket and draped it over her. I made some herbal tea and brought it in.

"Do you have a hot water bottle?" I asked Caleb.

He nodded, following me into the bathroom and showing me the cabinet beneath the sink. I heated the water to scalding temperature and filled the bottle two-thirds of the way, cap-ping it.

"Here, Lucy, this may help." I held the water bottle out,

and she lifted the covers so I could place it on her belly.

She groaned. "My God, that's incredible."

Caleb drew up two chairs for me and Faye to sit beside the bed. He sat down next to his mother.

Lucy sat up to sip her tea. "Today is Wednesday." She pursed her lips. "I need to have that write-up in by the end of tomorrow."

"What write-up?" Caleb leaned forward, resting his forearms on his knees.

"The center asked me and two others who've been through the whole course of CST — cognitive stimulation therapy — to write two pages on our experiences. I want to show the path I've covered from early days to now, so I can inspire others to make the same progress." She looked over at me. "You see, Diva, I've been recovering from dementia and alcoholism." She set her tea on the bedside table, lying back down. "*Ahh,* that hot water bottle! The write-up is due by two o'clock tomorrow, to accommodate their deadline of next week."

"Tell them you'll get it to them by Monday." Caleb sounded unimpressed.

Lucy shook her head. "No. I'm not risking them not including my story. This is important."

"What do you have so far?"

"Nothing."

"Then how do you expect to have it done by tomorrow at two?"

She set her chin. "I'll be better by then."

As she hacked a cough, Caleb held the glass of water to her lips. "Mom, you're in no condition to worry about deadlines."

Silence followed, in which only the obstinacy of mother and son reverberated through the space.

Taking a deep breath, I cleared my throat. "Lucy, if you tell me your thoughts and experiences, I can jot them down and write them up in two pages."

Her brows crumpled. "Why? I thought you were a yoga instructor."

I tamped down a laugh. "What made you think that?"

"Your name, your physique, the fact that you're headed to upstate New York."

"I *wish* I were a yoga instructor. I'm just a travel writer." I decided that was what I'd call myself in this limbo.

She held up a finger. "Never say *just* when describing your profession."

Shooting me a warning look, Caleb cut in. "Diva will be too busy with her own work tomorrow, Mom. You can't ask her to take on an extra task."

Curiosity, the urge to help, and a longing to use my skills acted like a drug on my system. I ignored his look.

"As it happens, I have no other work tomorrow," I amended. "I'd be only too happy to help you complete this write-up."

Caleb's eyes narrowed, bringing his brows down with them. Tension radiated from him, and I knew I'd pay for my defiance.

Lucy smiled weakly. "In that case, I'll take you up on your generous offer. Let me just get some more sleep, and I'll tell you everything."

Settling back into the pillow, she drifted off within a minute.

Sleep. The best defense against illness.

As we all stood, Caleb kept close at my back while we filed out. I feared I had a battle of another kind on my hands, one sleep wouldn't help me fight.

CHAPTER SEVENTEEN: CALEB

Until now everything had been going smoothly. Faye and Danya got on like a house on fire, Mom's fever had kept within the 101.5 to 102 range, and I'd managed to keep the two sides of my life from leaking into one another. Danya hadn't blown my cover—she'd even refrained from calling me *Caleb* in front of my mom or sister—and she'd been sympathetic, attentive, and helpful.

But just now, she'd been *too* helpful. If Mom told Danya of her struggles with alcoholism and dementia, she might let slip any number of sensitive pieces of information. About Dad, Luke, me, Faye, and Walter. Even if I sat in on Mom's confessional session—and I fully intended to—I could only do so much damage control if she blurted out details about our family's past. Mom, when healthy, was rarely tactful. When she had a fever, I'd no doubt her lips would loosen like a worn-out spring.

Persuading Mom not to do this write-up was out of the question. She was more stubborn than the burro I'd ridden in Monterrey. So I had two other options. One was to convince Danya to bow out. Failing that, the other was to talk to Mom and warn her to stay on topic. I decided to knock out the first task while Mom slept.

Danya seemed to sense I was on the prowl. As we entered the living room, she said brightly, "Faye, shall we prep the potatoes and carrots and start them roasting?" Her body sprang from mine.

I clamped an arm around her waist from behind, pulling

her into me. "Faye, would you check the fridge to see if we have mint jelly?" I suspected we didn't. "If not, maybe you could go to the store to get some."

"Hmm." Faye scanned the contents of the fridge door. "No. Mom forgot to buy it. I'll go. You can't have lamb without mint jelly!" She grabbed her satchel and headed out the door. "I'll be back in half an hour." She smiled at Danya, trapped in my arm. "Don't cook without me, Diva."

"I won't," the diva replied tightly.

Faye would stop and gab with everyone she knew on the way, in the store, and coming back.

When she'd closed the door, Danya struggled to break free of me. "What will your sister think?"

"Her mind is innocent." My free hand cupped her throat. "Her idea of sex is what happens in a nineteen-fifties musical."

The diva's pulse jumped beneath my fingers, and my dick stirred. Not even a week into this kidnapping, and my body reacted to her like a flame doused with jet fuel. Usually I grew bored with a woman quickly. Danya had the opposite effect on me. I couldn't get enough of her.

"I need to check on the lamb and baste it," she warbled.

"The lamb can wait." From her waist, my palm roved to her heat. Cupping her crotch, I moved my lips against her cheek. Her eyes shuttered, and her chest heaved. "I don't want you to write that piece for my mother."

"Why not?" she croaked.

"Personal reasons." I tongued her jawline, swirling the tip of my tongue in her ear. Her whole body shuddered as she groaned. I hiked up her dress, my hand coasting along the inside of her thigh. "Give her an excuse for not doing it."

She mewled and grasped my forearms while my fingers dipped into her panties, sliding back and forth over her creamy pussy.

"*Ohhh,*" she moaned.

My full-on boner stabbed her lower back. "So I have your word you'll tell her no?" As soon as I had her promise, I could bend her over the couch and fuck her. I planned to demolish her panties and carry them in my pocket to smell later.

"No," she murmured, rocking her hips into my hand.

I stopped slicking my fingers over her swollen clit. "No, as in that's what you'll tell Mom?"

Her eyes fluttered open. "I mean no, I won't bow out of doing the write-up for her. I have personal reasons for wanting to do this favor for her."

"Which are?" I circled my forefingers lazily around her nub. If she was going to put up a fight, then Plan B would go into effect.

She gyrated to catch the pressure of my finger. "If you tell me your personal reasons, I'll tell you mine."

"Not a chance." I sank three fingers in her channel, finding her G-spot and pressing it.

A guttural moan escaped her as she leaned back into my chest. "Then I can only say" — she panted and ground her hips into my hand — "this means a lot to me — *ahhh*" — her pelvis thrust into me — "and I always do what I say I'll do. Like you." She swiveled her hips, chasing the friction I gave her. "I told your mom I'd do this for her, and I intend to stick to my word."

My hand tightened on her throat as her pussy continued to pump my fingers. "I told you my three rules that first day, Diva. As long as you're in my care, you obey me without question. If you don't, you can expect punishment."

Her eyes glittered with resolve. "Then I'll take your punishment."

As I held my fingers steady, she rode them like a wild woman, huffing and grunting. I squeezed her throat, stopping her breath. Her movements became erratic and jerky, and her

155

inner walls began to close in on my fingers.

I pulled them out, releasing her throat. Gasping, she stumbled forward, confusion smeared across her face. She tried to reach into her panties to finish the job, but I pinned her wrists behind her back, yanking her into my chest.

"Unh-uh, Diva. If you break rule number three as well, I'll use my thin flogger on you." She shivered. "That's right. It's very different from the rabbit fur flogger."

Her cheeks were redder than lobsters, and the sight of them shot more blood to my cock.

"There is no place on earth you can hide that I won't hunt you down and have my revenge," she choked.

"Hide, Danya?" I tilted her chin up, bolting her gaze to mine. "I don't hide. Ever. You must be mistaking me for your father." I chuckled darkly. "Anyways, I look forward to seeing you try to have your revenge on me."

Her nostrils flared. "You think I'm a joke. Something to be toyed with."

My eyes flicked between hers. "You're far too dangerous to toy with."

I stepped away, watching her angrily adjust her dress. Her bunched brows and huffs of breath told of her frustration. The high color in her cheeks suggested embarrassment. Her coppery waves flew off crazily in all directions like Medusa's— as if she'd been thoroughly fucked.

Only she hadn't.

All in all, an effective punishment.

A few minutes later, Faye returned full of news from Sal's.

Danya

I hated him. Fiercely, passionately, and incurably. Regardless of what he claimed, he was clearly laughing at me and all he thought I stood for. Although *he* filled all my waking thoughts and controlled my body utterly, I had no claim on his mind. Maybe a little on his body — I'd felt his erection poking me — but he mastered the urge far better than I could. He didn't want to allow me this small expression of my character, this chance to write for his mom. And in return for my keeping my word, he'd punished me with the most humiliating, frustrating non-climax in the history of almost-orgasms.

The worst of it was, I had no chance to seek revenge now. I wanted to make sure his mother got well and had her write-up done to her satisfaction. I found Faye lovable and captivating and would not say no to anything she asked for. As for Caleb, he could do anything he wanted with my body, and I'd roll over and beg him for more.

I chopped carrots ferociously, adding them to the diced potatoes in the pan. Faye was chatting about someone who'd lodged a complaint against the construction project on the building opposite in back.

My thoughts ranged to the *personal reasons* I'd mentioned to Caleb for helping Lucy. I'd spent the last five days recording random thoughts and dreams in the notebook, but my scribbling had only made me impatient for a keyboard and the internet. I missed writing with a clear goal and deadline. This write-up for Lucy was a way I could use my skills to be of service to someone.

And if the piece would make a difference to the lives of people seeking treatment for dementia, it might have a powerful impact. One that resonated with me personally.

This was also a way of reclaiming my lost character. Being kidnapped, tied up, and held for ransom had hobbled my ability to act and express myself. As I'd said to Caleb in the car, I felt very *uninteresting* right now.

This was my chance to become interesting again.

After Faye had put a Nat King Cole CD on, I served up the

157

lamb, potatoes, carrots, and asparagus with the gravy I'd made. Since Lucy was still sleeping, we didn't disturb her. The lamb had turned out pretty delicious, if I did say so myself.

"Diva, if writing doesn't pan out for you, you might try your hand at the restaurant business." Caleb helped himself to more meat and potatoes.

Faye popped an asparagus in her mouth. "You cook as good as Mom."

I smiled. "That's high praise, I'm sure."

"It is." Caleb speared a potato. "But it's true."

After dinner, Faye and Caleb danced the cha-cha-cha to a Nat Cole song. If I'd had my cell phone, I would've taken pictures of them, they were so sweet together. Caleb was a different person with his mom and sister, that was for sure.

Lucy awoke briefly to use the bathroom, during which time I laid a fresh cold washcloth on her forehead, fetched her another glass of ice water, and replenished her hot water bottle. When she'd fallen back asleep, Faye retired to her room, and Caleb led me to our own bedroom.

"My foster father had me learn," he said, once we lay side by side in the darkness. "At the local Elks club."

I twisted towards him. "Learn what?"

"You asked earlier how I learned to dance."

"Oh." I felt as if a forbidden door were opening a crack and I needed to get my foot in. "It seems he taught you a lot."

A wistful smile crept up the side of his face. "You could say that."

"Are you close with him?"

"Yeah."

As he rolled to the side, giving me his back, I knew the conversation was over.

But the fact that he'd shared this glimpse of his early life with me made me inwardly glow. It was impossible to hate him in that moment.

Caleb — Two years ago

Gideon pushed open the door to Finney's, and I followed him in. Since it was only 3 on a Wednesday afternoon, hardly anyone but a couple of deadbeats occupied the bar. A few bums were playing pool in back, Ginnie was stocking the bar, and Val was blasting heavy metal to his heart's content.

Ginnie sidled over, her ample tits nearly exploding out of her low-cut white bartending blouse. "Gideon, *mio amore,* you still drag your feet in setting a wedding date." Her voice was dusky and seductive, and her thick blonde waves tumbled down her back from a hair tie.

Gideon grinned, leaning in to kiss her cheeks. "It's my job, *cara mia.* If I had my choice, I'd marry you *domani.*"

Her plump lips pouted. "You refuse to tell me what you do. MI5? FBI? KGB?" She reached up and threaded her fingers through Gideon's messy locks.

Not something I would've attempted, given the last time he'd showered was probably the night Penn beat Brown at basketball. I'd said I wouldn't watch it with him if he didn't clean up first. I hoped Ginnie planned to wash her hands before serving drinks.

Gideon hummed. "If I told you, *principessa,* I'd have to kill you."

"And you've come with your fellow spy, Caleb." She nodded at me. "Please, Caleb, tell this man to take a break and make an honest woman of me."

"You could sooner make an honest man of him." I leaned against the bar, crossing my legs. I always enjoyed Ginnie and Gideon's routine, but today was even better than usual.

Her hand cupped his face, her voice rising with urgency.

"Then let's live the dangerous life together, *cuore mio*. We'll move to the mountains and raise goats."

He kissed her palm. "I have one more mission, *tesoro mio*. Then I'll come for you, and nothing your father says or does will stop me from taking you away."

She sighed. "Gideon!"

Val barked, "All right, all right, show's over, Romeo and Juliet. Customers at five o'clock." He turned up the music.

Winking at Gideon, Ginnie slid some IPAs across the bar, and we downed a third of our beers in one pull.

When she'd sashayed down to the other end of the bar to help the new customers, I said, "Remind me again why you haven't gone on a date with her?"

Gideon shrugged. "Our schedules never seem to overlap."

I glared at him through my lashes. "Seriously? *Make* them overlap."

He cocked his head. "You think she's interested?"

I pretend-pounded my forehead with my fist. "If she hinted anymore, she'd be fastened to your dick."

Gideon groaned. "But it's like, I play everything out in my head in advance, and I *see* the end of it all in the beginning. I can see her getting sick of my non-stop programming, my weird hours, my . . . habits. You know."

"Yes, you're weird as shit. Yes, your habits take getting used to. Yes, you're wedded to your job. But she sees something in you she likes. Let her decide if she can take the full you or not." I tipped back my glass. "The hard part's over with. You know you have the same sense of humor. You know she likes you. Just ask her out already."

Gideon rolled his shoulders back, clearing his throat. "I need to get a few more drinks in me first." He sipped his beer. "Tell me what the breadcrumb dude had you do this time."

I threw another glance behind me to make sure no one could hear. "About two years ago, one of Mr. J.'s accountants discovered an offshore account Mr. J. holds that shields funds from the IRS. He tapped into it, siphoning off small amounts monthly. The amounts he's taken have added up to about one hundred and forty grand. Mr. J. asked me to look into the missing money, and I traced it back to this accountant."

"What did you do?"

"Posing as an IRS criminal investigator, I arranged to meet the accountant—let's call him Mel—at the office of an acquaintance of mine who's an attorney. I showed Mel evidence that he'd laundered money from Mr. J.'s illegal offshore account in the amount of sixty-five grand. I cited the criminal penalty for such an offense, namely, twice the amount of the money laundered, or one hundred and thirty grand. In addition, he was liable for a civil penalty of ten grand. I provided him with five different ways to pay—including money order."

Gideon's brow crinkled. "But what if he looked into it?"

"The terms of the fines were accurate. So was the evidence. I suggested he'd only laundered sixty-five grand so that he'd be afraid to call attention to himself and trigger further investigation that showed he'd actually stolen a hundred and forty grand. And have you ever tried to follow up with a specific person at the IRS? It's easier to hit a fastball." I chuckled. "He came up with the money within two weeks and paid the so-called fines in full." I drained my beer. "Of course, Mr. J. fired him. So far as Mel knows, Mr. J. is paying his own fine for tax evasion as we speak."

"Sounds like his own guilt trapped him better than you could've done."

I nodded, standing from my barstool. "I'd better go take the call. I'll be back in a few."

No sooner had I reached the quiet back garden of the bar than my phone buzzed. *Mr. J.*

He congratulated me on my resourcefulness in handling

his former accountant. Then he launched right into giving me my fourth crumb.

"After Walter Penwarren stole your father's second invention from him, Nathaniel Furness tried unsuccessfully to sue him. This time the stakes were much higher for Furness. He wanted to send you and Faye to independent middle and high schools. He had an idea for another innovation that required extensive research in Chile. And he'd begun to chafe at working for a relative pittance for Penwarren, doing a desk job, when he longed to do more hands-on development." Mr. J. opened a creaky door. "Needless to say, the lawsuit drained more of Furness's resources. Then, at a point when he was more heavily in debt than ever and financially at his wits' end, Penwarren laid him off."

I ground my molars. "Did he tell Penwarren where to stick it?"

"He couldn't afford to. Lucy Furness, your mother, was still working for Penwarren, and she was now the sole breadwinner. Your father didn't do well as an unemployed stay-at-home father. He spiraled into a worse depression than he'd suffered during the first lawsuit." Mr. J. lowered his voice. "Meanwhile, Penwarren's company, GenRev, gouged patients for the AR treatment Furness had developed, because they had a monopoly on it."

This hit even closer to home, because we'd had to pay so much for Mom's therapy over the years. The irony that Dad had been the one to invent it made me even more bitter.

Mr. J. hemmed. "So that's where everything stood when the last series of tragic events occurred. But I'll save those for the next job."

"Wait. How does the person you're acting on behalf of know all this?"

"Through a combination of firsthand and secondhand information."

"And how did he or she know my identity?"

"I'm afraid I can't tell you that. I wish you a good evening."
With that he rang off.

I raked a hand through my hair, stuffing my phone in a
pocket.

These events in themselves would've been more than
enough to drive my mom to drink and my dad to commit suicide. But Mr. J. claimed there was yet more to come.

I dreaded hearing what he had to say next time.

CHAPTER EIGHTEEN: DANYA: PRESENT

Reading the thermometer, Caleb gave a satisfied nod. "One hundred point six."

I set the hibiscus tea on the bedside table. "Let me help you sit up."

"Faye, can you get a few cushions from the living room?" Lucy had claimed she was ready to work on the write-up, and informed me, "We have four hours before the deadline."

As Faye brought in the cushions, I created a bolster under Lucy's pillow, propping her up against the headboard. Caleb took a seat in an armchair to the side, while Faye tucked herself into another chair. I sat in a chair at the foot of the bed with a blank notebook and pen in my lap.

Lucy seemed as unfazed by her audience as she was unshy of telling a near-stranger her story. "When my son finally convinced me to see a doctor about my dementia, I was forty-three, and had been an alcoholic for six years. I hadn't held any job for longer than a few months because I lacked the necessary mental abilities. Reading and writing, making decisions, solving problems, focusing — all of it had become difficult. One day at my job — I was a clerical assistant — I broke down sobbing and couldn't stop. That was when I knew I needed help. Dr. Jackson recommended I treat my alcoholism and young-onset dementia together." Sipping her tea, Lucy went on to describe how at first she'd dragged her feet at doing the individual and group therapies the doctor prescribed. Then, as she began to see improvements in her cognitive skills and her mood, she applied herself intensively to recovery. She talked about setbacks she overcame along the way, periods when she was impatient with how slowly she was progressing, and ways that the struggles of fellow members in her CBT group inspired her. And she gave examples of the CST methods that had worked best for her particular needs. "Now I'm teaching myself the new design software used by biotech firms in case I get up the courage to apply for another position like what I had—"

"Before," Caleb broke in. "When you were working in biotech."

Her eyebrows jumped as she shot him a startled look. "Yes, before. It's hard because I'm fifty-four now, and it's been years since I worked in the field. But I never would've had the ability or confidence to try again without the therapy, the center, or the support of my groups."

I looked over my notes. "Would you like me to include the bits about CBT, even though the write-up focuses on CST?"

Lucy nodded. "It's important to show how the two worked together. I don't think the stimulation therapy would've been so effective without the behavioral. And since my young-onset dementia was likely caused by alcohol, I want to tell the full story."

Caleb pushed to his feet. "I'll set you up on my laptop, Diva."

Lucy's warm smile matched her softened eyes. "Thank you for doing this."

I smiled. "I'm happy to help."

Fatigue seeped over her features. "I may take a nap now. But please wake me when you've finished, so I can read it."

Caleb turned off his internet and closed out everything other than the office program on his computer. He sat down beside me at the dining table, working on his phone while I transformed my notes into an informal two-page essay. Faye had left to make her grocery deliveries for the day.

After finishing and reading through my draft, I read it aloud to Caleb.

When I'd reached the end, he was silent for a moment. I looked over to find him gazing intently at me.

"Yeah. You are a writer." His lips saying those words—or maybe it was his gravelly voice—had the same effect of him drilling his tongue in my ear. A shiver skated down my spine, and my heart rate ramped up. How did he manage to make five simple words sound so sexy?

The amber depths of his eyes pulled me in like a magnet. "I hope your mom likes it."

"I don't see how she wouldn't." He reached over, tucking a curl of hair behind my ear.

As his rough fingers lingered at my cheek, I leaned into his palm. His gaze dipped to my lips. What would those sensual lips feel like pressed to mine? I'd spent so much time with Caleb this last week that the reality of him had begun to supersede my fantasy of the Werewolf. Now I had to work to recall what I'd imagined over the years. His charisma commanded my full attention when we were together, and when we were apart, new impressions of him overpowered old memories.

"Maybe you were right to help." He thumbed my lower lip, cupping my chin. "Mom would never have slept easy knowing this was left undone."

Once more he seemed to be opening a door for me. I seized on the chance to enter his world. "Why were you against it?"

"You're part of my professional life, Diva. This is my private life."

"I understand. You want to keep the two apart."

"For everyone's safety." As he rose, I missed his touch already. "I'll see if she's awake."

Lucy awoke half an hour later and read through my essay.

"Yes. This is just what I wanted." Gratitude brimmed in her eyes. "My write-up will be the most polished, because a professional writer did it." She flashed an eager smile. "Well, let's send it off. It's nearly two."

After Caleb sent it, Lucy was in a sociable mood.

"Diva, what takes you to upstate New York?" Her eyes flitted to Caleb and back to me.

"She's ghostwriting the memoir of a woman who's led a very interesting life," Caleb explained. "The woman lives in the Catskills."

I hoped Lucy didn't probe any deeper about the woman, because I'd probably make a mess of things if I had to elaborate.

"How did you two meet?" Lucy's eyes had the same sharp, knowing glint that I'd often seen in Caleb's. "And, Cal, I'd like to hear from *her*."

Since Lucy no doubt knew we were sharing a bedroom, I didn't try to pretend I'd found Caleb on a ridesharing app or through a business transaction. Plus, I had no idea what business she thought her son was in. I stuck as close to the truth as possible. "We danced the tango together at a party."

Her tickled smile resembled Caleb's so much that it took my breath away. "He is a gifted dancer. I'm glad he's putting his talents to good use. Cal, I hope you're planning to stay upstate."

His lips twitched. "Diva will find it hard to get rid of me. My work takes me where she is."

Lucy nodded. "Good. I'll be honest with you, Diva. You're the first woman I've seen Cal with in a long time. Not to scare you away. He works very hard and doesn't have much room for romance. But I can see you're something special."

I could feel the heat spreading through my cheeks. Suddenly it felt like a very bad idea to be lying to his mother. She didn't even know my real name. "He does seem to work hard."

"Has he shown you his house yet?" Lucy gushed. "It's—"

"Mom, Diva has a video call to make," Caleb cut in.

Caleb

That was close. I'd interrupted just in time as Mom was about to tell Danya where I lived. "I need to set her up in the other room."

"Oh! Don't let me keep you." Mom waved her hand. "We can talk later."

It was a good time to call Walter. Faye would get home in an hour, and if Mom continued to improve, Danya and I could be on the road by 7. I hadn't called her father yesterday—the first day I'd missed—so I wanted to make it a priority today.

Leading Danya into our bedroom, I locked the door. "Hands out, Diva."

Her eyes danced mischievously. "Did you practice saying that in a suave, seductive way before becoming a kidnapper?"

Tying the scarf around her wrists, I smiled. "If it's suave and seductive, that's a bonus."

"It certainly is a bonus," she replied, stepping wider, as if daring me to say *legs together.*

This new, kittenish side to her shot all the blood to my cock at lightning speed. I leaned in, smoothing her hair back and brushing my lips against the shell of her ear. "Be careful, Diva. You're playing with fire."

The fine hairs of her neck stood on end. "I like fire."

Through her thin shirt my thumb and finger closed on one of her pert nipples, pinching it. Her breath drew in sharply. "Just make sure it likes you."

My hands sloped along the curve of her waist, rounding

her ass cheeks and squeezing. My daily dose of Vitamin Diva.

I jerked her hips together, squatting to knot the rope around her ankles.

She messed my hair up while I fastened the knot. "How long do you let your hair grow before you cut it?"

Standing, I spun her so her back was to my chest. "The best way to be ignored by me is to ask pointless questions. Do you want me to ignore you?"

"I was just having a little fun." She wriggled in my grasp. "Anyways, you can't ignore me. You've kidnapped me."

I tied the gag around her head. "Ignoring you would be a cinch. If that's a challenge . . . "

She gave a forceful shake of her head, her eyes flaring. "Unh-unh!"

A week of submitting to me had taken the edge off her pride. I smiled at her transparency. "Hmm. We'll see." I swiveled her. "Down on your knees, Diva."

When she'd knelt on the floor, I tilted her chin up. "Keep your back arched and your chest high."

She could flirt all she wanted, so long as she remembered who was in charge.

I put the call through to Walter, turning the camera so Danya was in full view.

"Hello, Dani," he said hoarsely. "Finally you've called. I have some news, and it's best that your kidnapper hear it too. Two of my C-suite officers were closing a deal downtown yesterday evening, and they overheard a conversation between a couple of lowlifes in a bar. When my men heard your name mentioned, one of them pushed record on his phone."

There was a pause while Walter pulled up the file on his phone and pressed play.

One of the voices was deep and round, the other nasal and midrange. I vaguely recognized both of them but couldn't put my finger on how.

Nasal Voice said, "He's hired a guy to kidnap her and hold her till April first. But when Roddy and Vic offered to rent her, he decided to cut them a deal. He'll extend the kidnapping by a week and let them have her for a month for three mill."

Deep Voice grunted a laugh. "At the rates Roddy and Vic charge, if four or five guys a day score her, they'll more than get their money back."

"Plus she's good for business. You've seen this bitch all over the magazines. Half the dicks in the country wanna bone her."

Deep Voice snickered. "Rich-girl pussy tastes different. It's sweeter."

Nasal Voice twanged, "The deal is, we head up there and pick her up. Drop her at their place on Friday."

"Does the guy who kidnapped her know we're coming?"

"No. The boss said he can't know, or he'll run. He likes to keep a low profile, and apparently his conscience bugs him when it comes to selling tail."

Deep Voice grunted. "His neck isn't on the line. What gets me is, the boss is loaded already. He's got a friggin' island. What does he need with another three mill?"

Nasal Voice scoffed. "That's why he's rolling in it and you're not. Rich people know every bit counts."

"Are we taking her back in a month?"

"That's what the boss said. He also said no freebies on the way."

Deep Voice snorted. "That's what he thinks. If I feel like a nice piece of ass, I'll take it."

"More like a multi-million-dollar ass. You can't afford it."

The conversation devolved into talk of horse racing, and Walter hit pause.

Walter's voice sounded more urgent than we'd heard it all week. "My men didn't confront or follow these thugs, because it wasn't their place to do so. But you see what's at stake. So whoever you are who's holding Danya, please consider my daughter as if she were a woman you cared about. Consider what you'd do to make sure this didn't happen to her. She's about to be used and abused by many men. I've got to report it to the authorities."

Since I agreed, I didn't bother to say anything. If my client had changed the terms of our contract without telling me, then all bets were off. Walter couldn't be expected to sit by while his daughter was sold for sex. Though I couldn't wrap my head around the idea that Black had ordered this. I'd be calling him as soon as we got off this call with Walter. True, it'd been three days since I'd talked to Black—he could've made any number of plans in that time. And I didn't know him well at all. If he had connections in the sex trade, he might be tempted to make more money off this operation.

But one thing was clear—no one was taking Danya.

All signs pointed to Black being *the boss* in that conversation. Not just the references to his being a millionaire and having an island, but the dates mentioned and the comment about me keeping a low profile and not getting involved in sex trafficking.

"Wherever you are, please make sure these criminals don't get hold of Danya. I'll add on a five million dollar reward if you keep her safe."

Anger surged in my chest, and my neck muscles tightened. I wouldn't be Walter's pawn or his paid lackey. I would protect Danya because she deserved it, not because I hoped for a bonus. But of course money was the only currency Walter dealt in. I knew that after five years of breadcrumbs and seventeen years of watching my family suffer.

Maybe this was his way of showing he cared after all. For the first time he seemed genuinely worried about his daughter.

This isn't just about revenge now. It's about Danya's safety.

Tamping down my urge to lay into him, I ended the call.

The diva looked more frightened than I'd ever seen her—even on the night I'd kidnapped her. Her eyes had rounded, her face was ghostly, and her whole body trembled. Goosebumps speckled her arms and neck.

Raising her up, I removed her gag and untied her ankles and wrists.

"Caleb . . ." Her voice caught in her throat as she launched herself into my chest, flinging her arms around me.

I cupped the back of her head, hooking an arm around her and pulling her closer. "You have nothing to worry about, Diva."

Beneath the lavender soap we both used, I caught whiffs of her own unique scent of sweet marjoram and sun-baked granite. I didn't realize till now how clean and home-like her natural aromas were. I wanted to nestle in her skin and hair till I'd gotten my fill of her taste.

"But you heard Dad. They'll find me and sell me to those men." Her body tensed before a spasm racked her.

"They'll be dead before they touch a hair on your head." I stroked her hair, my thoughts whirring on possible solutions. "I need to make a few phone calls. I'm going to leave you with Faye." I tilted her face up, finding her usually-luminous eyes clouded over with anxiety. "Don't go in to see my mom till I come with you."

I hoped I wouldn't regret leaving Danya alone with Faye. But I had no choice at this point.

"Okay."

I ironed out the kinks in her brow with my thumb pad. "You have my word I'll keep you safe."

Her eyes searched mine, but she said nothing. I didn't have any more time to reassure her. I had to get a move on.

Faye and Danya started a game of Chinese checkers at the

kitchen bar counter while I stepped out onto the covered balcony, pulling out my phone.

Just as I was about to call Black, a call came in from Jeremy.

"Everything okay?" I half expected him to say Black's hired goons had showed up already.

"A tall guy named Luis darn near beat the door down about twenty minutes ago," Jeremy huffed. "I told him he couldn't come in. He said he wanted to see Danya. Said he was her stepbrother, and he knew she was here. I said there was no one here but my wife and me. He said he'd be back, with or without law enforcement."

"Thanks for handling that." I shoved a hand through my hair. Things were heating up in Dushore. Clearly it was no longer a viable hideout. "The sooner you and Marisa can pack everything up and head back to Ardmore, the better. I don't want you there when people start crawling all over the farmhouse."

There was no need to worry him by mentioning what Walter had shared.

"All right. Let me know if you need us to do anything else."

No sooner had we rung off than Gideon called.

I swiped up. "What's up, Gideon?"

"Thought you might like to know. I've been monitoring all Walter's communications, and three hours ago a detective Moeser called from the ninth district. He told Walter his daughter's apartment had been broken into and thoroughly ransacked. We're talking plants and pictures slashed with a knife, smashed appliances, the works. Apparently a neighbor reported it this morning. Moeser found a note on the table addressed to *Walter Penwarren*, which is why he contacted him."

This news jarred me far more than Jeremy's. After all, Luis was just trying to protect his stepsister.

My stomach dipped and tilted. "What did the note say?"

"I don't know. He called Penwarren into the station to look

at it."

I took a few deep steadying breaths through my nose. "Did they take anything?"

"Moeser said obvious valuables like her phone, laptop, and jewelry were strewn around the apartment. Like they didn't care about stealing stuff."

Fuck. Danya could've been hurt or killed.

"We just got through talking to Walter, and he didn't mention it. What was his reaction to the detective's report?" I wanted to get a thorough read on him.

"He said, and I quote, *Doesn't surprise me one bit. Rundown, shabby, poor security. That place is practically inviting burglars in.*"

That sounded consistent with Walter's stance on Danya's apartment during our phone calls.

Interesting that he hadn't mentioned the kidnapping to Moeser — at least not over the phone. He'd known about Danya's risk of getting used for sex since yesterday evening. Maybe when we called he'd only just decided to report her abduction to the police. Or maybe he'd already filed the report when he'd gone to see Moeser and had just made it sound to me and Danya as if he intended to do so.

Had he deliberately refrained from worrying Danya by telling her that her apartment had been broken into? Had it slipped his mind in the midst of his greater anxiety over the sex traffickers?

I filled Gideon in on the call with Walter and Jeremy's news from the farmhouse. "You think this is all just coincidence?"

Gideon grunted. "I don't know, man. Shit has a way of happening all at once. Hard to say at this point if there's a correlation. Have you called Black yet?"

I leaned against the balcony railing, looking out over the courtyard between the buildings in back. "He's up next. If he doesn't call me first. Everyone seems to be beating me to the punch today."

Sure enough, while I was finishing my talk with Gideon, a call came in from my client.

CHAPTER NINETEEN: CALEB

"That's him on the other line. Gotta go."

"Good luck." Gideon hung up, and I accepted Black's call.

"Scott, there's been a leak," Black opened. "Danya's stepbrother, Luis Fuentes, was snooping around the city this week, sniffing into her whereabouts."

"Go on."

"He paid someone for the address of the farmhouse. If he's not already there, he's headed up there."

"How do you know?"

"Mario told me he talked to Sal, who saw one of the guys who helped you handle a job last year up in Dushore — Stefano, I think was the name — talking to Fuentes."

It was true that one of Mario's soldiers knew of the farmhouse. I could imagine the conversation between Luis and Stefano going something like this. Luis asks him, if he wanted to do a kidnapping, who would he hire and where would the guy take the victim. Stefano thinks for a second and comes up with my place in Dushore, possibly even mentioning my name.

"When was this?" I questioned.

"Yesterday morning."

"Why are you only telling me now?"

His breath exploded on the other end of the line. "I've tried to call you five times since then. You haven't picked up."

It was true I'd been preoccupied with the film, Mom, and Danya. I'd dropped the ball.

"I'll deal with Fuentes," I clipped. "Did you have anything else to tell me?" I crossed my legs, twisting to look down over a narrow street where three cars had gotten tangled up together.

"No," Black grated. "What do *you* have to tell *me*?"

Time to lay it all on the line. "We talked to Walter today, and he played back a conversation of two scumbags who say they've been hired by you to sell Danya for sex for the next month for three million."

Black harrumphed. "Not likely. You know the terms of our contract. Sex trafficking isn't part of them."

After twelve years of mixing with people from all walks of life, I'd learned to focus on what they weren't saying—their other tells. Black struck me as a man who kept his cards close to his chest and went on the offensive when he thought people were attacking him. These qualities, plus the fact that we were talking on the phone, made it hard to read him now.

"Then how did they know so many details of our operation? They knew dates, they knew about you and your island, and they knew bits about me. They named Danya specifically as the kidnapped victim. And they sounded as if they knew our location."

Black's tone was dismissive. "Fuentes' inquiries must've tipped them off. Some trafficker figures he can horn in on my kidnapping and make a few million. You of all people must know that once you dirty your hands, all kinds of sleazy types show up to help you get them dirtier."

My client's lack of curiosity, concern, and surprise put me on the alert. He was ready to write this off as some wannabe sex trafficker who didn't pose a real threat to our operation. Nor did he seem upset that these deadbeats knew so much about him. Something didn't add up.

"How do you want me to deal with this?" I said blandly.

"Just focus on staying out of Fuentes' way. He's caused

enough trouble. Everything else okay with her?"

Of course I omitted that we were at my mom and sister's apartment. "Fine."

"Where are you now?"

The question was so casual, it raised all kinds of red flags. It came too late—he should've been worried about our location earlier, when he mentioned Luis. And he asked it as if he didn't want to alarm me. Either he suspected we weren't in Dushore and wanted to track us more precisely, or he already knew where we were and wanted to see if I'd lie. I looked around in case I could detect a sign of him nearby now.

"Dushore," I lied. "But we'll clear out within the next hour."

"Good. Keep me posted on where you go."

Yeah, we'll see about that. "I have one other question for you," I added.

He waited.

"What do you know about the break-in at Danya's apartment?"

"What makes you think I know anything?" he replied testily. "This is the first I'm hearing about it."

I let silence pulse between us over the line.

"I'll be in touch."

We ended the call.

This wasn't the first time I'd mistrusted a client. Luckily, trust wasn't usually necessary to get a job done. In the past, I'd had men I didn't trust from the outset and men I'd come to suspect over the course of a job. But more rode on this assignment than on those other jobs. For one thing, Danya didn't deserve to suffer, and for another, I was more determined than ever to screw Walter over.

I planned on fucking with Arnold Black. Since it was very likely that he was fucking with me.

Danya

Faye and I had just made sandwiches out of leftover lamb, red onion, feta cheese, tomato, and arugula, when Caleb pushed open the balcony door and stepped into the living room. For the last hour and a half, playing Chinese checkers, talking to Faye, and preparing dinner had been the only ways I could distract myself from the scariness of my situation. It wasn't that I didn't trust Caleb to follow through on his promise to try to keep me safe. But what if circumstances beyond his control overruled his will? What if the other men his client had hired outmaneuvered him?

"Diva, come with me." Caleb nodded towards our bedroom, where I followed him.

Closing the door, he gestured towards a chair, and I took a seat. My heart beat erratically as I wondered what he'd found out during his phone calls. I'd seen the tension emanating from him out on the balcony, his taut features and grim expression. He could only have worse news to pile on top of what Dad had shared.

"The rules of this kidnapping have changed." He ran a hand over his beard, pacing to the bed and back. "I no longer trust my client. He may in fact be up to no good. So I'm taking matters into my own hands."

My heart flew up into my throat and lodged there. I tried to swallow, but it was too tight. "What do you mean?" I rattled.

"Under the old terms of this job, my client considered your safety. Now, he may not give a fuck." He dragged a chair over and sat down opposite me, his legs bracketing mine. His eyes were storm-tossed oceans lit by lightning streaks. "It's up to me to keep you safe, and I intend to do it, while fulfilling all of my own goals."

179

"You mean keep me safe from . . . what those men talked about?" Speaking the words would make their plans more real.

His brows dove down. "And other dangers. Your apartment was broken into and ransacked. The perps didn't take anything valuable, but they left a note addressed to *Walter Penwarren*. It sounds like a warning that they're watching you."

I shivered. "Who would've done that?"

"Not your average burglars."

"I suppose the police won't be able to help catch the men we heard in the bar?"

He shook his head. "Not on the basis of that phone conversation. They need probable cause. If those dirtbags plan on doing what they claim, they'll be well underway before the law can catch up with them. I need to keep a few steps ahead of them so they never get the chance to lay their hands on you."

I slumped back in my chair, clutching my brow. "I miss the calm of the farmhouse. When life was simpler and I was just kidnapped."

"Those days are gone, I'm afraid." He glanced at his watch and stood. "We need to be out of here in fifteen minutes."

We packed our things, wrapped up some sandwiches, and said goodbye to Faye and Lucy. When Faye had closed the door to the apartment, Caleb blindfolded me once more, leading me down and out to the car.

After driving for about an hour, he pulled over and killed the engine.

He undid my blindfold, and we sat in the darkness of a rural road, listening to early country music from a playlist on his phone while eating our sandwiches.

As we finished, for the fifteenth time he glanced in the rearview mirror.

"You think we're being followed?" I ventured.

"I'm not taking any chances." He reached across me, opening the glove compartment, and slid out a pistol. While he loaded it and checked to make sure a round was in the chamber, I stopped breathing.

He tucked the gun in a holster I hadn't noticed inside his waistband with the same ease that he might pocket his wallet.

I could feel the blood hammering in my head. "Do you often use that?"

"When I need to." As his eyes slanted to mine, I could see the roguish gleam in them.

My thighs clenched, and all the blood rushed away from my brain and down to my sex. I was getting turned on by him carrying. He seemed fully in his element when in danger, his fearlessness making him even more powerful.

Since I couldn't walk off this extreme horniness, I put my feet up on the dash and changed the subject. "Does anyone know both your identities?"

He started the engine, pulling onto the road. "Just one person, so far as I know."

"Who?"

"A mystery client whose name I don't even know."

"How did he or she find out?"

His assessing eyes cut to me. "My best guess is that he followed the history of my family, putting two and two together when it came to my double life."

I gazed at his strong, sinfully handsome profile. "I'll never tell anyone about Faye and Lucy."

"I know you won't."

Around 10:30 we pulled into a motel near Greensburg, Pennsylvania that had a lit *vacancy* sign.

When he'd parked in the lot, he let the engine tick. "Do you have plans to try to escape?"

I considered what awaited me if I hitched a ride back — sex traffickers, intruders who were monitoring my movements, a ruined apartment, and joblessness. By contrast, going wherever Caleb went meant convincing him to tell me why he hated my father. It meant showing him more sides to me and breaking down a few of his barriers. And it meant traveling.

"No."

A corner of his mouth crooked up in a dirty smile. "Good. Because you won't succeed."

Ten minutes later, Caleb keyed us into our room, where I quickly located all the notepads, pens, mini-shampoos, soaps, and other goodies I was obsessed with.

I held up a pad. "Can I write a little before going to bed?"

"Sure. I've got emails to check."

I gathered the courage to ask him what I'd turned over in my head for our whole drive here. "Could you check my personal email and scan it for important-looking messages?"

"Like what?"

"From my boss, Kari, for example. Or Gladys, Innes, or Kamau, my co-workers."

He sat on the bed and opened his laptop, turning the screen away from me. I seated myself in the chair opposite, waiting.

After a few minutes, he asked for my email service, username, and password. I gave them to him, and he perused my inbox.

Finally, he read aloud a message. "This is from Kari Showalter. It came in last Friday morning at nine-thirty-five. She writes, *Danya, I was shocked and disappointed to get the message you left on my phone this morning. Are you sure you want to put in your resignation? You're making excellent strides in editing, research, and writing. And I'd looked forward to seeing what you came up with for the Florida assignment. You say you're thinking of changing fields altogether. But you never spoke with me about this, and it seems very sudden. I welcome some dialogue and engagement. Please call me at your earliest convenience so we can talk about this."*

My jaw had dropped to my shoes, and a stony coldness seeped through my toes and fingers, making me unable to move. When I finally regained the use of my tongue, I stuttered, "Did you do this?"

Caleb's brow furrowed. "Do what?"

"Call in and quit for me last Friday morning?"

"How could I have done that when she says you called?"

"But I can't have called, because I was tied up and asleep at your farmhouse!"

His eyes narrowed, and his nostrils dilated. "No. You can't have. Someone else called in pretending to be you."

Icy chills shot through my upper arms, chest, and thighs. *Someone else called in pretending to be me.* Someone else quit my own job and told Kari I was thinking of changing fields. And they'd done this the very morning after I'd been kidnapped.

"Who?" I wrapped my arms around my chest, gathering in what warmth I could.

"Someone who knew you'd be gone anyway," Caleb said slowly, as if he were catching thoughts racing through his head while he spoke. "That doesn't leave many options."

"But how did they recreate my voice?"

His tongue moistened his lower lip. "There are ways. Deepfakes. I have a friend who deals in them all the time."

A tremor stole through my body. "Doesn't that mean this person also had access to samples of my voice?"

"Probably."

"But why would they do this?"

"Identity theft. Very lucrative for extortion." He clearly spoke from experience, a fact that made me shiver more.

"You mean someone's about to extort something from me?" I bleated.

"Given what happened to your apartment, it's likely."

What could anyone possibly extort from me? My

183

apartment was my only real asset. Suddenly I remembered the question I'd been meaning to ask earlier. "How did you know my apartment had been broken into? Dad didn't mention it in his call."

"It's my job to keep tabs on that kind of thing."

"But *how*?"

"I can't tell you, Diva."

I felt like a rider in the Gravitron at the point where the G forces plaster you to the bed and you try to move. Dizziness met me as I attempted to stand.

Caleb's strong forearm shot out to steady me. "Time for bed, Danya."

He helped me into my t-shirt, tucking me in and turning off the light. Fatigue rushed up and clamped its large claws around my limbs, leaving me with no time to review the devastating news of the day.

My last thought was that there was a loaded gun within a few feet, and Caleb might have to use it at some point on this trip.

Chapter Twenty: Caleb

*F*UU-UU-CC-KK!
I awoke with a start at 4:15 AM, springing from the bed and mentally cursing.

I hadn't swept the car for cameras, trackers, or listening devices. Usually when I left my car for any length of time while on a job, this was the first thing I did. Where the hell had I left my head?

Sweeping regularly was like dental flossing — good basic hygiene.

Not bothering with a coat, I grabbed my car key and the motel keycard, bounding down the stairs and out to the parking lot.

All was quiet, and the same number of cars that had been in the lot last night when we arrived were there now — fourteen. No one had moved. I always noticed these kinds of things.

But you didn't do a sweep, Cal.

I grabbed the bug detector from the trunk and slid behind the wheel, starting the car. Driving around a little, I set the detector on one of the two frequencies that detected a GPS tracker. I turned off the ignition, slowly scanning the whole car for a tracking device. Nothing. Adjusting the frequency, I repeated my sweep. Still nothing. That didn't mean there wasn't one. I found my jammer in the trunk and turned it on, setting it to charge.

Then I set the detector on its next-to-highest frequency and swept the inside of the car for a camera or listening device.

I found a pinhole cam the size of a screw head on the center console. And I detected an audio bug under the front passenger seat. My gut twisted as I detached both. So we'd been seen and heard for at least the time we'd been on the road last night. Possibly also on the way to Mom's.

Day one of my mission to protect Danya, and I'd already failed.

I racked my brains trying to remember when I'd last done a sweep. It must've been just before kidnapping the diva, seven days ago.

In the meantime, I'd had two sensitive conversations with Gideon in the car, and last night Danya had said, "I'll never tell anyone about Faye and Lucy." Just after we'd talked about my double identity.

Shit. If the spies had known where we were parked for the last two days, in front of the Germantown apartment, Faye and Lucy might not be safe either.

Never in my career had I made such a big mistake.

Either spending time with Mom and Faye or giving in to my overwhelming attraction to the diva had sapped my attention. I needed to get my head in the game.

Possible candidates for putting the camera, audio bug, and likely tracker in the car included Arnold Black and his associates, the Breadcrumb Client, and whoever had demolished Danya's apartment and quit her job for her—assuming those last two were the same people.

And the spy knew where we were now.

I wouldn't be able to use the jammer for long on the road before patrol officers would be all over me like a bad rash. I needed to drop whoever was following me and get somewhere where I could do another sweep for the tracker.

First to wake Danya and get us on the road again. We could fill the tank and put another hundred miles between us and the Pennsylvania border before stopping for something to eat.

As I took the stairs two at a time, I thought how any number of messages could've been written in that note to Walter. If the person who'd trashed Danya's apartment knew of the kidnapping and linked it up with me, then at this moment Walter might be hiding how much he knew about me. But what was the intruder's ultimate goal?

Entering the dark room, I padded over to where Danya's chest gently heaved and her soft breaths fanned the air.

Her warm, buttery body baking in the bed made me want to devour every inch of her. I spooned her, cupping her breasts and planing my hand along her belly to her heat.

"Mmmrrph," she hummed deeply, rocking her backside into my erection.

"Diva, we need to go."

My brain said, *Plenty of time for this later.* But my cock came back with, *Stay, asshole.*

She was more irresistible than a fresh-baked cinnamon roll. A starving man would need less willpower to turn down that temptation than it took to restrain myself now.

"Caleb. You feel so good." Her slurred voice dripped with sultry desire, and her endless curves drove me wild.

Fuck, this woman could be my undoing.

As she ground her hips into my thickness, my cock said, *Screw it.* It really meant *screw her.*

In seconds flat I'd wrenched our underwear down our legs, whipping her t-shirt off so I had full access to her tits. Fuck whoever was tracking us. The diva needed to be fucked now. *They* could go screw themselves.

I plunged into her depths from the back, groaning as I touched bottom. I groped every sinuous contour of her, biting her shoulder and latching onto one nipple with my mouth while twisting the other between my fingers. There was too much to attack and eat all at once, and the sensory overload made my head whirl. The compact globes of her ass, her perfect tits, her slender waist. Not to mention the hungry pussy that clamped around my cock as I speared it over and over. By now my mouth, nose, and lips knew that pussy as well as my dick did. Tight, silky, and hot, it was also sweet, tender, and spicy.

As our bodies jackknifed in sync, I felt her inner walls closing in on me.

I sank my teeth in her neck, using pain to prevent her from coming.

She cried out before I laved the bite with my tongue and blew on it. Pulling out, I let loose a guttural growl. "You may come, Diva."

I slammed into her, and her animal scream rent the air. Pleasure billowed out from our explosive joining like a mushroom cloud. She squeezed me in a death grip as I drove in and out, releasing plumes of jism in her channel. She flooded me, and I flooded her, our come mingling in one inbound tide. I groaned and shuddered, thoroughly spent.

Not for the first time with Danya, I thought I'd pass out.

But something was different this time. She felt more immediate and raw. Like I'd peeled off a few barriers and gone in naked.

I stiffened.

Fuck. I'd gone bareback.

Yes, she was on birth control. But there was still that six-percent chance of her eventually getting pregnant if I didn't use protection too.

But damn, it felt good to be inside her without a latex wall between us.

Sadly there was no time to enjoy it now. I pulled out, slapping her bottom. "Get up, Diva. We need to leave."

She must've heard the peremptory note in my voice. Rolling out of bed, she loped to the bathroom, returning a minute later to drag on her jeans.

Like a kid who'd scored treats at Halloween, she threw all the room's travel-size freebies into a plastic bag, an avid gleam lighting her eyes. Smiling, I pressed my hand into her lower back, leading her down past the front office, where I dropped our keycards.

A few miles down the road, we stopped to fill up on gas. Danya dumped Twizzlers, Snickers bars, peanut butter-filled cheddar crackers, soda water, and blue corn chips on the checkout counter.

"In return for my cooperation," she declared.

"I'll add it to your father's tab," I retorted, swiping my card. "Is this part of traveling simply?"

"It's part of traveling on the lam."

I scooped up the bag, pushing open the door. "Then only one of us will be eating this crap." Tossing the bag in the back seat, I arched an eyebrow, spearing her with a chastening look.

When I'd started the car, she grumbled, "Don't tell me, you're one of the anti-snack police."

"No junk food till the afternoon. It's five-thirty in the morning." Entering the service road, I checked the mirrors and blind spots for vehicles that might be following us.

"Did you have a strict upbringing?"

"My foster father was very strict."

"In what ways?"

I pulled onto the highway, switching off the jammer. "I followed a tight schedule, had to keep my room immaculate, did chores, had to do well at school . . . wasn't allowed any junk food."

I'd loved the discipline and routine of living with Clark. His years in the marines had shaped the way he'd raised me and his two daughters. His regimented lifestyle was everything I needed and craved after the upheavals of my own family life had driven me to steal, vandalize, get into fights, and skip school. And Clark had treated me like the son he'd never had, passing down everything he'd learned in the military and in his long career as both engineer and building inspector.

"Why were you placed in foster care?"

"I was a pissed-off juvenile delinquent." I switched to the fast lane. "After my third time getting caught, the probation department placed me with Clark." I smiled. "He would've whooped me if I'd tried to get up to trouble on his watch."

"You must've missed Lucy and Faye."

I shook my head. "At first I thought Mom didn't fight to keep me, and I was furious at her. That lasted a couple of years. Then I assumed she and Faye wouldn't want to see me because I was just a derelict who made them ashamed. I was determined to prove them wrong. So I worked my butt off at school and at whatever Clark was willing to teach me."

"So you didn't see your mom or sister at all?"

"Not till I was eighteen. Five years after I'd left."

After the gaping hole Dad had left in our lives, having Clark as a father figure meant the world. Looking back, I realized Mom had been in such bad shape psychologically that she'd probably suspected she couldn't raise one kid, let alone two. She'd suffered depression and alcoholism but hadn't wanted to raise an alarm, knowing Faye would be taken from her too. Even as she'd clung to Faye, she'd believed I was in the best place. And I found out later that she'd talked to Clark every now and then to make sure I was doing well.

I gradually realized, too late, that by making all those assumptions about Mom and Faye and not communicating with them over those five years, I'd done a lot of damage. I'd let Mom develop early-onset dementia, and let Faye suffer enough neglect to remain emotionally arrested at age 10.

The first of a few failures that showed I wasn't cut out for personal relationships, since I wasn't good at communicating outside my professional life.

"Where are we going?" Danya asked, pulling me back to the present.

I was relieved she hadn't probed further, as I would've had to shut her down. "I'm staying on Seventy-Six till we reach Youngstown. Then I'll take the turnpike west."

She tuned in to the classical music station, settling back in her seat. "When Mom and I took our cross-country road trips, she always loved listening to Beethoven. She brought CDs of his symphonies, piano concertos, string quartets, violin and cello sonatas, and piano trios. Maybe we'll get lucky, and they'll play some Beethoven."

A few minutes later, she crowed, "The Eroica symphony!" She turned up the radio.

I had no idea what she was talking about, but classical music in the morning suited me just fine.

At our first toll, just across the Ohio state border, I noticed a black Nissan Sentra and a blue Hyundai Elantra two cars behind us in line. They'd also been behind us on the service road heading from the gas station to the highway. The Nissan had one person in it, while the Hyundai had two.

Time to ditch both.

Weaving behind a few trucks and cars, I got off at the next exit, making a right at the first red light.

"Are we being followed?" The diva sat up, looking alert. "Mom and I got off here once."

My eyes darted to the rearview, where I saw the Nissan and Hyundai tailing us, one in front of the other. I hooked a sharp right, zipped down a narrow road, and turned left onto a boulevard. Flicking on the jammer again, I looked around for a few more shortcuts.

"If you make a left up here, there's a huge wildlife park about a mile down the road where you can lose them." Danya pointed.

It was worth a shot. "Hold onto your seat."

The boulevard had four lanes, and the light was just about to turn green. There was no left-turn arrow. In the split second after the light had changed, I gunned the engine, cutting off two lanes of oncoming traffic and putting them between us and our followers. Horns blared, but we made it through.

"There are a few entrances to this park," she recalled. "If you take the last and circle around to the exit, a little farther down, you can drive the wrong way, clockwise, around part of the lake. Then you can make a U-ey and ditch them in case they've followed you in."

I flicked up a brow, swinging my gaze to her. "You sound like you've done this before."

"Just the route. Not in this style." She twisted to look behind us.

For the moment, only a white Toyota Highlander and a green Subaru Outback followed us.

I entered the park, following the diva's suggestion by going the wrong way down the one-way road that led around a lake. A few cars swerved to avoid us, laying on their horns, but I ignored them, continuing clockwise. A few miles in, I stopped, blocked two oncoming cars, and did a quick U-turn.

When I exited the park, there was no sign of the Nissan or the Hyundai.

Turning right, I sped up down the winding road. "Any malls around here?"

"Yeah, as a matter of fact. Mom and I stopped at one off the main route. I think I can remember how to get us there." She trapped her lower lip in her teeth.

"Good. We're ditching this car."

Her eyebrows hit her hairline. "How?"

"Follow my directions."

The diva led us to a mall that was fifteen minutes away. I kept the jammer on while we found a parking spot on a suburban street near the mall's lot. While we waited for 10 AM, when shops would open, we consolidated everything in the car into two bags. Two hours into our wait, both our stomachs rumbled at once. Danya's crackers, chips, and soda water started to sound like a good idea.

"Hand me that bag of snacks." I tipped my head towards her plastic bag.

"Told you so," she chirped, grinning. "You never know when *junk food* will come in handy."

I laughed. "You called it this time."

At 9.50, I dropped her, holding our bags, near one of the exits to the mall parking lot.

"I'll be back in five."

Scoping the lot, I saw a silver Audi SUV pulling into a parking space, driven by a young woman who was blaring pop music.

Perfect.

I left the beamer in a nearby spot, sauntered over to the woman, who'd just climbed out of her car, and held my pistol to her lower back, clapping a hand over her mouth. "Give me the key."

She sucked in a sharp breath, dropping the key on the ground.

"Facedown, flat on the ground. Keep quiet, or I'll shoot."

Trembling from head to toe, she dropped to the asphalt in the empty parking space next to her car.

Popping open the car door, I started the engine, rolling down the window.

"Count slowly to sixty, and you can get up. Move or make a sound before then, and you're dead. Understand?"

She nodded, squeezing her eyes shut.

I tossed her purse—minus the cell phone—out the window, backing out and making my way towards the exit where

I'd left Danya. She stood in the exact same spot with our bags, a furrow creasing her forehead.

I leaned over the console. "Your new ride, Diva."

Her eyes rolled in their sockets as she took in the Audi.

Opening the door, she slung our bags in the back seat and climbed in. No sooner had she slammed the door than I took off, racing to beat the light at the major intersection ahead.

I handed her the woman's phone. "Throw this out."

She flung it out the window. "Is the owner okay?"

"She's fine."

Tugging the Audi's GPS tracker free, I tossed the device out my window.

"Won't the cops be on the lookout for you?"

"Stolen cars are their lowest priority. If they happen to know about us and they see us, they might try to pull us over. But if we run, the last thing they want is to get into a high-speed car chase. It's not worth the risk."

She pointed towards a road sign. "I think your best bet is to go back south and head through Akron, taking Two-Twenty-Four west to Indiana. That way, if anyone's on the lookout, they won't find you on the turnpike."

I signaled a lane change. "You really know these roads."

She flushed. "I kind of obsess over US roads."

The diva was getting more intriguing by the minute.

Chapter Twenty-One: Danya

Shit. We were in a spanking-new German car, and Caleb had picked it up the way most people picked out a frozen dinner at the grocery store.

"Just out of curiosity, is there anything you can't do?" I slid him a sidelong glance.

His eyes glittered. "Plenty. I just steer clear of it."

He merged onto the highway, speeding up to 70 to match the other cars.

"Like what?"

"Cook a lamb dinner. Write a two-page essay on someone's life in under an hour. Navigate the back roads of Ohio like the back of my hand." He shot me a devilish grin that melted my insides.

Pleasure simmered in the depths of my belly, and I felt as if I'd scored a bullseye on a target in archery. "Today you didn't exactly steer clear of navigating Ohio's back roads."

"No, but luckily I had you."

I gazed at a billboard advertising the Mid-Ohio Sports Car Course, showing a yellow racecar. "Do you think they'll still follow us?"

His jaw muscles jumped. "I plan to do a test once we get to Indiana."

We managed to make it through the rest of Ohio without getting pulled over.

Some three hours later we passed a sign that said, *More to discover in Indiana.*

He put on his turn signal at a light in Decatur. "Let's go

discover more of Indiana."

It was 2 in the afternoon as we parked in front of a grill off the main street.

"You hungry?" He pulled our jackets from the back seat, handing me mine.

"Starving."

Rounding the car, he opened my door, palming the base of my spine to lead me into the grill.

As we entered the cave-like interior, all eyes lasered in on us. At a glance I would've guessed about two dozen men took their suspicious measure of us, though a few women lurked in the background. Burly, bearded, and checker-shirted, the men nursed beers, baby back ribs, and whiskeys. After a few beats of silence that reminded me of old-west saloons in cowboy movies, they resumed their gruff conversations, though the air still crackled with tension.

Never in a million years would I have dared to come here without Caleb.

Eighties standards poured from the speakers, Paula Abdul's *Straight Up* currently ending and fading into Madonna's *Like A Virgin.*

"What can I get you folks?" the sandy-mustached guy behind the bar asked.

Caleb glanced up at the blackboard menu behind the barman. "Two of your barbecue lunch specials. With a root beer and—" he looked at me—"what would you like to drink?"

"Root beer sounds great."

The barman nodded, tapping our order into his tablet.

I lowered my voice. "There were two cars following us earlier. Is it normal for someone to send two cars? Are you considered that dangerous?"

Caleb's eyes flicked to the side in a way I'd noticed before that suggested he wasn't telling me the whole truth. "One of them may have been my client's hired men."

"And the other?"

He nodded at the barman, who set our root beers before us. "Might've been your stepbrother."

I sprayed my drink through my nose, coughing. *"Luis? How?"*

Caleb handed me a napkin. "He showed up at the farmhouse yesterday looking for you. There's an outside chance he followed Jeremy and Marisa and did some investigative work that led to our location at the Greensburg motel last night."

Luis had managed to find me! And he'd come close to catching up with us. My heart soared. Then it hit me how Caleb had destroyed my chance at freedom.

I parked my knuckles on my hips, raising my voice. "Luis found the farmhouse? Why didn't you tell me he might be following us?"

"Lower your voice, Diva, or we'll leave." Caleb's warning tone acted like a bucket of ice-cold water on my nerves.

"Why didn't you say anything?" I hissed.

"Because this is a kidnapping, not a family reunion." He drained half his root beer in one pull. "You'll have plenty of time to catch up with Luis once I return you. You wouldn't be safe with him. He doesn't understand the danger."

Suddenly his sharing all this with me now felt insulting.

"You used me to get what you wanted," I seethed. "Now that we're not being tracked, you'll go back to treating me as if I don't matter."

Hooking his shoe under the rung of my barstool, he dragged it towards him while cupping the backs of my knees and pulling me to the edge of my seat. His large thighs sandwiched my legs. "I didn't have to tell you now."

"Then why did you?"

His gaze plunged into the depths of mine. "Maybe today's experiences on the road made it feel like we're in this together.

Maybe I wanted to treat you as an equal."

Much as I wanted to believe his words, they seemed too good to be true. And their timing was too convenient for him. "*I* think you're telling me this now to test me. To gauge my reaction—see whether I'd try to escape if Luis did catch up with us."

"Would you?"

I knew it. "Maybe."

He stood, leaning forward and speaking in my ear. "Then I was right not to tell you till now."

His breath traveled straight to my core, waking my sensitive bits and setting them tingling.

He swaggered off, I assumed to use the restroom. As usual, when he left, he sucked all the air from the room, including the oxygen in my lungs.

I sipped my root beer, wondering how I should feel right now. Pissed? Suspicious? Pleased that he'd even had the idea to say those words just now, whether or not they were true?

It occurred to me to ask the barman if I could use his phone. I could call Luis now, telling him where we were.

Looking up to flag him down, I found a flannel-shirted arm attached to a warm body propping itself on the bar counter in front of me. My eyes followed the arm to its owner, a man of medium build with a reddish-brown beard, cornflower-blue eyes, and a crooked nose.

"I'm Dave. What's your name, darlin'?"

"Danya."

"Danya, I couldn't help hear you and your guy having a disagreement. Now, I don't like to butt in, but a pretty lady like yourself should be with someone who treats her right."

I opened my mouth to say that he'd misunderstood, when another man wearing a John Deere cap and ripped jeans edged in next to Dave. "Haven't I seen you in a magazine? Aren't you famous?"

"N-no," I stammered, looking away.

That was all I needed now, to be recognized, and for people to make a fuss over me. The only reason I'd told Dave my name was because I'd been certain that this small city was a world away from the glitz and glamor of the magazines. Now I wished I'd gone with the name Caleb had assigned me at his mom's place, Diva.

Dave's gaze never wavered from me as he spoke to his friend. "I was telling her she needs to ditch the guy giving her grief. Danya, if you need help dumping him, we'll be happy to assist." His hand rested on my thigh.

His friend snapped his fingers. "I know! I saw you in *People* last week. My baby sis leaves a copy around whenever she stops by. You're that girl whose daddy's a megamillionaire. What's-his-name, who had the terminal in Philly's airport named after him a few months ago."

The double onslaught of Dave and his friend jacked up my heart rate, and my thoughts sprinted to come up with an escape.

As I tried to remove Dave's hand from my thigh, he grabbed my wrist, pulling me off the barstool. "Let me buy you a drink, Danya. Paul and I'll make sure that other guy leaves you alone."

I tugged to free my hand, but he held my wrist tightly. "No, thank you. I don't need — "

"Danya . . . Danya Penwarren!" Paul broke in, his eyes widening. "My sister's obsessed with you. You're even more gorgeous in person!" He fingered a tuft of my hair, as if I were a museum piece. "Them pics don't do you justice."

Part of me believed these men had a right to touch me because I was public property, as Dad's daughter. That part wanted to keep things civil and polite, so I wouldn't ruin anyone's idea of him or me. But another part of me wondered what it would be like to be confident and self-assertive enough to holler and knee Dave in the groin.

Paul wrapped an arm around my waist, propelling me forward at the same time that Dave took hold of my other wrist, pulling in the same direction.

Suddenly, as if an alien force had seized him, Dave's body jerked and flew up against the wall opposite the bar. A second later, Paul went sailing in the same direction, landing on top of his friend. They slumped in a heap, groaning and rolling their heads from side to side.

Caleb's monumental presence filled the space around us like a destroyer. The electricity surging from him could've powered a factory, and the veins on his muscles bulged with challenge. Standing a few feet away in calm command, he warped the atmosphere.

The whole grill had gone quiet, and everyone held their breath.

Paul unfolded himself and pushed to his feet, lunging at Caleb. At the same time Dave rose and tried to grab hold of Caleb's knees. But Dave only managed to grip one knee, while Caleb shouldered Paul away and sprawled his own legs back, landing his pelvis on Dave's head. Paul's fist pummeled Caleb's ribs, but he seemed to be made of obsidian, he was so oblivious to the attack. He pushed Dave to the floor, putting him in a headlock and kneeing his back. When Dave lay motionless, Caleb sprang up and landed such a hard punch to the side of Paul's jaw that Paul crumpled to the floor like a marionette.

Unwinded, Caleb used the toe of his shoe to rotate Dave from his belly to his back. "Who hired you?"

Dave spluttered and coughed up blood. "N-no one. We were j-just having f-fun."

The barman had come over to stand on the other side of the men. "Paul and Dave are regulars here. But they overstepped today."

Caleb laid his foot on Dave's neck. "You got lucky this time. Next time I'll rip your balls off and shove them down your throat. We clear?"

Dave did the best version of a nod he could manage, under the circumstances.

Caleb turned to Paul. "Got it?"

Paul held up his hands as if in surrender. "Yeah."

The barman pointed to the door to the grill. "Out!" he barked to Dave and Paul.

Bruised and scratched, they peeled themselves off the floor and shuffled out without a backward glance.

Caleb turned to me. "You okay?"

"Yeah," I breathed. "Are you?"

He smoothed his shirt. "I could do with some barbecue."

I blinked as he pulled out my barstool for me. He was completely unfazed, after laying two strong men out cold. I felt half sorry for anyone who tried to steal me away on his watch.

The barman returned to his post, sliding our plates across the counter. "Can I get you more root beers? On the house."

"Sure." Caleb slit his cornbread, slathering butter on it. "Eat, Diva. We have a lot of driving ahead."

As I ate my mac and cheese, I couldn't stop thinking about Caleb's fearsome power and control. Nothing he did was too much—it was always just right. And so smooth, even when he was being brutal. The Werewolf's essence lived on, and it awed me more than ever.

"Tell me exactly what happened." Caleb pried a rib off his rack.

I related everything that had transpired while he'd gone to the restroom.

He twisted his lips. "They don't fit the profile of hired men, and they don't look the part. That's why I let them go."

We wolfed down everything on our plates.

"Will you teach me some self-defense moves?" I asked as

201

we crumpled our napkins.

His warm smile dazzled me. "With pleasure."

After paying, we left and found a park a few blocks away. There I showed Caleb what Paul and Dave had done earlier. He taught me that relaxation and surprise were key elements in self-defense. Letting the two men think I wasn't going to defend myself while relaxing into Dave's grip, I could've twisted my wrists into his thumbs, freed my hands, and grabbed his neck, kneeing him in the chest. Caleb showed me a few variations—one in which Paul was directly behind me and I needed to get him off me. Head-butting his face, I could hook my foot around his ankle, knocking him off balance and forcing him to loosen his grip on me. Then I could poke him in the eye, grab his crotch, or hit him in the nose.

Caleb demonstrated a few simple techniques for dealing with attackers, using the heel of my palm, my knee, the side of my foot, and my thumbs. He showed me the most vulnerable points on the body and the moves most likely to disarm an assailant.

We practiced for over an hour. By the end, I felt empowered and flush with endorphins. I also trusted Caleb in a new way. Not only was he trying to keep me safe, but he was ensuring that I could keep me safe. That felt like an even greater gift, because it gave me a boost in self-confidence.

"Can we do this again?" I asked as we walked back to the car.

"Why not?"

"For the rest of our time on the road, people will know me as Diva. No more pushing my luck getting recognized."

When we'd slipped inside the car, I twisted towards him. "Apart from Paul and Dave, how's your test in Indiana going?"

His eyes flicked to the rearview. "So far, so good."

"Where are we headed?"

He offered a lopsided smile. "I was hoping you'd have some ideas."

I licked my lips, remembering the routes Mom and I had taken on our eight trips through this part of the country. "What's our end goal?"

"To keep you safe till the end of my contract."

I swallowed. "But what if they grab me after you've turned me back over to . . . Dad?"

He shook his head. "I haven't figured that part out yet."

My stomach relaxed a little. He cared enough to be concerned about what happened after.

He started the engine. "If we can at least find out who ransacked your apartment and stole your identity, I'll be a little more ready to hand you back over."

So it wasn't a given that he'd even release me on the deadline three weeks from now. My chest expanded like a helium balloon. Why was I so euphoric to think I'd be in his thrall beyond the original date? It must be because I felt safe with him.

And you like submitting to him, Danya, a little voice piped up. Maybe that too.

"We could probably make it to Peoria, Illinois in five hours," I proposed. "Just stay on Twenty-Four."

He chuckled, pulling out. "You're better than Waze."

I found a classical satellite station again, taking it as a good omen that they were playing Beethoven. According to the screen, it was one of his piano trios.

"If the motel we stay at has a heated pool, can we swim later?"

"Sure."

"And maybe pick up a pizza?"

He sped up as we reached the open road. "Fine."

"And watch old TV shows and horror flicks?"

The rakish curve of his lips as he looked over melted my

panties. "Is this part of your ritual?"

"Mom's and my ritual." I gazed out at a lush forested area to our left and the glimpses of a large body of water through the trees. "I think that's the Wabash River over there."

"Important?"

"To Indiana's history, yes. It was the way early settlers got across the state. It's in the state song."

"If this is the kind of thing you learned traveling with your mom, your trips were very different from the ones I took with Clark." He rested his arm on the window edge.

This was one more reason I loved traveling. It encouraged people to open up. "Where did you go with him?"

His jaw flexed. "To the ten most violent cities in the US. As of the statistics thirteen years ago."

My mouth fell open. "But why?"

"It was the main reason Clark joined the marines. He saw that violence makes humans tick. If we want to know how the world works, we follow the violence. That's what he always said."

"Do you believe that?"

"It may not be the whole picture, but there's a lot of truth to it."

This was truly disturbing. "Is that why he encouraged you to become a fixer?"

His head whipped over. "How did you know that?"

"Jeremy told me." I hoped I wouldn't get Jeremy in trouble.

"Oh." His features and posture relaxed. "Yeah. Clark claimed my job wouldn't involve much violence—ironically enough. He said the calmest spot is the eye of the storm. I'm the before and after guy. Not usually the during guy."

My brow scrunched. "So you're saying he believes violence drives human affairs, and he wanted to shield you from it, so he pointed you in the direction of being a *fixer*?" It seemed paradoxical. Why not have his foster son become a botanist or some other peaceful profession?

"He also wanted to make sure I thumbed my nose at the law."

My puzzlement from that afternoon spent talking to Jeremy returned. "Why?"

"He said laws and lawmakers are by nature corrupt."

I twisted to face him. "What's the alternative?"

"Honor among thieves."

"Well what about those of us who aren't thieves?"

"You need to ally yourself with a thief." His eyes had a wolfish glint.

I blew out an exasperated breath. "Okay, sure, I'm traveling with you across America after you stole me, a car, and my sanity. But that doesn't mean I condone what we're doing in principle."

His lips twitched. "That's another thing Clark said. Principle is the cheerleader to action. Whoever dominates the field has the greatest cheers."

I groaned. "That in itself is a principle, isn't it?"

He smirked at me. "You need to start somewhere."

Chapter Twenty-Two: Caleb

I watched the diva strip out of her traveling clothes. Like me, she had two outfits for this trip — the clothes we'd brought to see Mom. In her case, a pair of white jeans and a figure-hugging long-sleeved black shirt, plus a powder-blue knit dress that also loved her curves.

When she'd gotten down to her red lace bra and matching panties, I said, "Stop."

She tossed her hair back, squaring her shoulders. Her nipples were tight nuggets crying to be plucked. Her intelligent eyes were bright sapphires darkening with lust. Her luminous hair maddened me with its coppery thickness. I was going to plunder her all night long.

I stalked over to her. "Turn around."

She obeyed.

"Walk slowly over to the window."

She did.

I padded to the floor-to-ceiling windows that faced out over the pool. My hands caressed her contours, dragging her panties halfway down her hips. "You see those people enjoying the pool? We're going to give them a show."

A full-body shudder greeted my words. "Some of them are teens."

My teeth sank into the meat of her shoulder. She tasted better than a ripe peach. "It's good education. Family-friendly, because it makes families."

She giggled, but stopped when my fingers skated over her folds, collecting her juices.

"Ohhh . . . "

I divested her of her bra and panties, plastering her against the glass and bending her arms the way she'd held them the night I'd abducted her, like a saguaro cactus. I breathed fire in her ear. "Let's give them something to record in their travel journal."

"Just promise you'll pull us away if you see anyone hold their phone up." Her voice was hazy with lust.

Using her nectar to wet my thumb and forefinger, I spread her buttocks and swirled my thumb around her puckered hole. She groaned as I inserted my finger an inch into her rosebud. A tight ring of muscles clamped around me.

"Breathe deeply and relax," I instructed.

As she breathed out, I screwed my finger in deeper.

"Ahhh!" She arched her back, giving me more access to her luscious, round ass.

I licked my way from her divide up her crevice to her crack, before biting a butt cheek and blowing on it. Naturally I couldn't let the other cheek go unattended. As an agonized cry tore at her throat, I pinched the second bite instead of blowing on it. I knew by now the diva liked a little pain.

I shoved my pants and boxer briefs down, my cock raging against my abdomen. This time I knew I was going in bare, but I didn't give a fuck. I wanted to revel in that sensation and confirm that it was as incredible as I remembered.

Slicking my finger over her hot center, I sank it all the way into her tight hole before she could reject it. I pumped it in and out, then withdrew, focusing on dicking her front entrance.

My strokes started out slow as I enjoyed the texture of her inner walls. But gradually her fluttering contractions blew my self-control to smithereens. Speeding up my thrusts, I drilled my finger in her rosette and held it there.

"Please, Caleb, I need to—"

I pulled out, waiting a few heartbeats.

"You may, Diva."

Slamming in, I felt her close around my cock, setting me spinning in a vortex of hot, destructive pleasure. I flattened her against the glass, picturing the way her nipples looked pressed into the window in full view of spectators below. The way her O-shaped mouth gave away her satisfaction. The way her dripping pussy leaked lust down her legs.

Yes, I did that to her, I felt like crowing. *And only I can do that to her.*

A searing bolt of possessiveness ripped through me. *Only I ever* will *do that to her.*

Whoa, where had that come from?

Pulling out, I laid a lingering kiss on her shoulder. "Let's go swimming."

We swam in our underwear, since that was all we had. The water felt like a bathtub that had been left to cool for a while. By the time we slipped into the pool, everyone else had gone inside. Maybe because of the show we'd given them earlier.

As I watched Danya do the breaststroke smoothly through the water, I recalled my strangely possessive thought before pulling out of her upstairs.

Territoriality was alien to me. I never claimed a woman.

Nor was this the time to start. For one thing, the diva was only in my care another three weeks. For another, every pore of her body screamed how much she wanted love. And in her world, communication and trust bound people together, not violence and fear. She believed empathy was a stronger driving force than greed. Even when her father provided a stark counterexample. Look at her willingness to care for Mom and her readiness to bond with Faye, in the midst of her own kidnapping. Her charity that allowed kids to travel and learn languages. Yes, I'd Googled it. Her insistence on trusting me even when I did my best to instill fear in her.

The diva was dangerous because she almost made me believe she was right. And she almost made me *want* to believe she was right. Right that I was missing out by not investing emotionally in a woman. Right that it was worth at least trying to communicate with people rather than pushing them away. Right that fear, violence, and greed were effective but not meaningful in the grand scheme of things.

Danya's soft, low voice broke into my thoughts.

"Splashing contest?" She climbed out of the deep end.

"How do you measure the winner?"

"By how far the droplets spread on the deck."

Palming the pool's edge, I surged out of the water. "Won't I win because I'm heavier?"

She shook her head, her eyes twinkling. "It takes talent to splash well." She stood back, folding her arms. "You first."

I backed up a few steps, lunging forward and leaping in the air. I landed on the water in a walking position with my arms spread wide.

When I emerged and climbed out, Danya was inspecting the spray. "Not bad."

I laughed, pushing hair out of my face. "You sound like you think you can do better."

"Maybe." She danced thirty feet away, turning and crouching into a sprint-ready pose. "And . . . go!"

She streaked towards the pool, sailing through the air and cannonballing into the middle of the water. Water spilled everywhere, and waves churned in the pool. I had to hand it to her. She knew how to make a splash.

Swimming to the edge, she stepped out.

Examining the damage, she pointed. "Look. This water wasn't here before."

As I tickled her ribcage from behind, she jumped, giggling and defending against me. "I think you win the splashing contest."

I picked her up, vaulting us in the air together. The last sounds before we sank in the water were her happy screams.

The Wi-Fi at the motel was crappy, but an hour before check-out I decided to attempt a video call with Gideon.

Since the diva and I had fucked like rabbits all night, neither of us had gotten much sleep, apart from the last four hours. I'd had my share of women in nice hotel rooms, but last night had opened my eyes to the unsung pleasures of a shitty motel, cheap pizza, and reruns of *MASH*.

Though admittedly Danya had everything to do with making it so enjoyable. She was like a kid going to the fair for the first time, finding delight in the simplest things. The complimentary bath salts provided by the motel had her dancing around the room naked. That had ended in me pinning her to the floor and plowing into her with her ankles on my shoulders. The jacuzzi setting on the bathtub had made her squeal and call me in to join her. Which had led to her sucking me off in the tub. She'd been so excited to find a Scrabble game in the cupboard, that I'd made an exception to my no-boardgame rule and played a game with her. When she'd won, I'd spread her legs wide and eaten her out. Slowly and torturously.

Now I left her seated at the balcony table, filling sheets of a pad with her writing. She was wearing her blue dress today, which left me permanently at half-mast.

Adjusting my pants, I set up my laptop on the desk and called Gideon.

For a while we shot the shit about Ginnie. Gideon had finally asked her out a year ago, and they'd been seeing each other since. Now he was nervous because she'd asked him to come to Maine for a weekend to meet her parents. Before, when he'd begged off meeting them, it had led to fights. I assured him he was prime son-in-law material and had nothing to worry about.

Gideon screwed up his face in doubt. "A rogue white hat with a bounty on his head the size of Kuwait's national debt?"

"Now you're just bragging."

"Well, it begs the question—what do I tell them I do?"

"What does Ginnie think you do?"

His dirty grin killed my semi for good. "I make sure she's not thinking about what I do for a living when I'm with her."

"How about IT consulting?" I suggested. "My mom and sister think I'm an operations management consultant. Which keeps them from asking questions, since no one knows what the fuck that is."

"True." Gideon balanced his stress ball on the tip of his nose. "No one knows what the fuck any consultant does. Not even them."

"Speaking of operations, let's return to Operation Screw Walter. What've you found over the last week?"

"Oh, man." Gideon sat up in his chair. "The guy's a full-on sleazoid. Besides what I already told you, I've got"—he consulted a piece of paper as if he had a list—"financial fraud, blackmail, tax evasion, theft of intellectual property, and plenty of cover-ups. He has a few people helping him, but he keeps his inner circle tight."

Salivating, I leaned back in my chair, resting an ankle on one knee. "Keep digging till our month's up. Any new proprietary ideas of GenRev that we could sell to their main rival?"

An avid glint kindled his eyes. "Yeah. I found a nonsteroidal treatment for eczema that looks to be a surefire cash cow. GenRev hasn't released it yet."

I whistled long and low. "That'd make billions. A lot of people suffer from that condition."

"*But.*" Gideon raised a palm. "Before you go selling it to SciPulse, you should know another development I discovered just yesterday."

"Okay." I scraped a hand over the stubble on my neck. I needed a shave.

"I found two emails exchanged by members of the GenRev board." He pulled something up on one of his laptops. "The first reads, *He's keeping it under wraps, but I heard he's trying to locate whoever kidnapped his daughter. He's distraught. She's apparently been gone for a week now, and she means the world to him. In his time of loss I think we should vote for the takeover. It would give him one bright spot in the darkness he's going through.* The reply to that reads, *I had no idea about the kidnapping. If you're voting for the takeover, I will too. Though I've expressed many doubts in the past as to the advisability of acquiring this company, I agree with your position now. I can't imagine what Walter must be suffering, wondering where his daughter is and whether she's okay. This will give him some much-needed comfort in his time of grief. I'll tell Frank about this too, so he can reconsider his vote.*"

I shook my head in grudging admiration. Walter was definitely followed by a lucky star. Even when his daughter was kidnapped, he was coming out on top. Over the last week I'd gathered that he was gunning for the board to vote for the takeover, but he'd worried that a leak about the kidnapping and the virus could ruin his chances. Now it looked as if everything was going his way after all.

But the show was far from over. By the time I was finished with him, he'd be begging for mercy.

I thought fast. "If GenRev is just going to take over SciPulse, we need to find another company to sell this idea to. Find a struggling startup biotech, sell the idea and its development processes to them for a price they can afford, and take whatever you earn from the sale."

Gideon was doing this job for me for free, so I was glad to find one way to reward him for his generosity. Though I also planned on giving him part of what I made from the kidnapping.

Gideon pumped a fist. "It's good to be da king." Gideon loved Mel Brooks's *History of the World – Part One.*

"Yeah, in our world, the hacker is definitely king." I tossed a licorice mint in my mouth. "The sooner you can put that sale through, the better. I want to take the wind out of Walter's sails."

He saluted me. "Consider it done."

We signed off, and I went to shave.

The diva and I seemed to have lost our followers—for now. For the rest of the morning I kept on the lookout for vehicles tailing us but spotted nothing. Danya directed us across the Mississippi to Mt. Pleasant, Iowa, where we stopped to eat. On the way, she counted the number of Beethoven pieces they played on the classical station, kept up a running commentary on the landscape and billboards, and speculated on the lives of the people in the towns we passed. Her memory for history and geography was impressive.

As we slid into a booth to have a late breakfast at a truck stop diner, I asked, "Did you learn all this from talking to people, or from reading?"

She smiled up at our waitress, who placed menus in front of us. "Both. But talking to a person makes me want to read up more on a place. Which makes me want to ask more questions of real people. So it's an endless cycle."

After Tammy, our waitress, had taken our order, the diva asked her if she'd recommend any shops around here for casual clothes, sunglasses, or bathing suits. Tammy seemed only too happy to take a break from placing orders and chat about shopping. By the time she'd sashayed off, we had the names of several places in town.

I leaned my forearms on the table. "Too bad you won't have a chance to follow up on any of her recommendations."

She looked at me sideways, as if trying to decipher whether

I was joking. "Don't we?"

Deciding to tease her, I kept a straight face. "Just what do you think this is? A shopping spree?"

Her eyes sparkled, and I could see she was going to try to convince me. "But we do need a few things. Sunglasses to remain incognito, swimming stuff for the pools, another change of clothes — or two." She leaned in. "And I need a few more panties if I'm going to keep spotting the two I have."

Cupping her chin, I had the overwhelming urge to crush her lips with mine. But still I kept my poker face. "And here I thought you were a cheap date."

She threw back her head and let loose a musical laugh that hardened my dick. "I'd say, at twenty million, I'm anything but cheap."

I cracked a smile. "Oh, you'll cost your father plenty. But I plan to come out of this a rich man."

Her expression turned innocent. "What *is* the going rate for kidnapping?"

I smirked. "Enough to bump me to the next tax bracket and allow me to hire the kind of accountant who'll keep me paying taxes at my current rate."

Danya's lips twitched. "Then you can afford a few necessary purchases in Mt. Pleasant, Iowa this afternoon."

I released her chin as Tammy returned with our breakfast.

When she'd left, the diva arched an eyebrow. "You can always write them off as business expenses." Her impish smile made me want to tackle her to the floor. "Or maybe you'll even be able to afford an accountant who comes up with a legitimate front for kidnapping."

I speared a sausage with my fork. "Consider yourself lucky, Diva. You have another nine hours before I torture you with my tongue. This time, I won't go easy on you."

"Is that a promise?"

I laid down my fork. Eight days into this kidnapping, and

I'd created a vixen. "Nothing's guaranteed. I may decide to hogtie you and have you suck my cock till I come, then tie you in a prone spread eagle and take you up the ass." I sipped my coffee, enjoying the way her eyes rounded. "So no, your pleasure is not a given."

She squirmed in her seat, sipping from the ice water Tammy had brought. "Can we skip driving today and get a room here in town?"

I smiled. "Patience, Danya. There'll be plenty of time for you to please me."

And a dozen other ways how.

After lunch, we headed to the first of the shops Tammy had recommended.

An hour and a half and three hundred and fifty dollars later, we returned to the Audi loaded with shopping bags. The diva had charmed everyone in the shops with her openness and curiosity. And we'd both found enough wardrobe that we wouldn't have to do laundry so frequently.

"If you want to go the route Mom and I often took, we could head north near Omaha and get to Sioux Falls, South Dakota in a little over six hours. It's incredibly beautiful. Going west from here, Highway Ninety is a lot prettier than Eighty."

I laughed. "Your enthusiasm is infectious."

A few hours later, as we skirted Omaha, the sky smeared with crimson, gold, and purple made a pretty spectacular effect.

As we drove north towards Sioux City, she studied me till I looked over. "I still wonder what you do for fun. When you're not fixing things."

"Work out, watch soccer and basketball, hang out with my friend, read." *Fuck.* "What about you?"

"Go out with people from work, read, run along the river,

explore the city. On weekends I have the charity." She gazed towards the horizon ahead. "But there's always something missing."

"Travel and writing?"

"Those too." She glanced back at me. "You don't ever feel like you're missing anything?"

Revenge. Which I'm about to get. "I'm trying to persuade Mom and Faye to come live with me."

Brightening, she nodded. "Yeah. That sort of thing. A gathering together of loved ones to make a family. Have you noticed how every story that's not a tragedy is basically about that? Drawing people into a community? I saw you had *Tortilla Flat* on your shelf. Those guys in the flophouse had a close, loving group. Or the tight-knit Paris-based artists in Hemingway's *A Moveable Feast*. Kerouac's *On the Road*. They all aim for the characters to live together, united by common goals. Like they have all they need in their own little world once they have each other."

I rested my hand low on the steering wheel. "I'm pretty sure that's just a fantasy. Not reality. People read those stories to escape."

"You don't think it's something to aspire to?"

"Harmony? Friendship?" I shrugged. "Sure. Ideally no one would ever die alone. They'd live with their friends in a retirement community and have grandkids who'd visit regularly. But life gets in the way."

"What if a person has a lot of love to give but never finds someone to give it to?" Her melancholy tone made me look over to find her expression just as sad.

I cocked an eyebrow. "I'm pretty sure there are plenty of people out there ready to receive any love being given out."

"Not just *people*, a special someone."

I shook my head. "You're asking for too much. Give love where you can and find meaning in the giving."

"But everyone else is pairing up. And they look so happy."

"They're actually lonely. They just feel pressured to follow the pack."

"And you?"

"I'm a lone wolf."

CHAPTER TWENTY-THREE: DANYA

Over the next few days, Caleb and I drove eight to ten hours a day, stopping for a late breakfast about two hours into our drive and eating a late dinner at a roadside restaurant or getting a pizza en route to our motel. In the afternoons, we found an area at a rest stop or park where he could show me some self-defense techniques. In the evenings, we talked, swam, played cards, and watched TV In the mornings, I wrote about our trip while Caleb worked on his laptop and made calls. Since I had no way to take photos, I tried to paint pictures with words.

Since last Thursday Caleb hadn't called Dad. The policy of calling him daily seemed to be part of the old *rules of this kidnapping,* as Caleb had called them after talking with his client. His new policy of *taking matters into his own hands* seemed to mean deciding when *he* next wanted to call Dad.

Sunday, Caleb and I made it as far as Billings, Montana. The stunning Black Hills gave way to the snow-covered cliffs of Billings and the Yellowstone River. The air was so pure and clean you could taste it like mountain spring water. A family of deer crossed in front of us as we headed to our motel. Caleb's reflexes were as good as a fighter pilot's as he laid on the brakes and swerved to avoid hitting them.

Monday, we drove only eight hours, since continuing past Twin Falls, Idaho would take us into the desert. And we stopped for an hour beside the black-watered Gallatin River. I told Caleb how in the hot summers this river felt like heaven when Mom and I took a dip in its frigid shallows. The towns along our route were saturated with history — human and natural. Livingston, Bozeman, West Yellowstone.

On Tuesday, we crossed the Nevada desert through Reno, climbing the steep ascent to the town of Truckee in the midst of towering pines, firs, and sequoias. When I closed my eyes, all I saw was the V of the disappearing lines of trees ahead on the road. Before coming into Nevada City, California, we stopped at a roadside restaurant about five miles out of town. It had the best chili con carne I'd ever eaten. Caleb drank one of the local IPAs, and I had a glass of a heavy red wine that bore the label of the Nevada City Winery.

That evening, at the inn, when we came in from our swim, Caleb read something on his phone before strolling over to his laptop and setting it up. I changed into my night tee and brushed my teeth, taking a seat at the table and writing in my travel journal — which was really just whatever pieces of paper I could rip from the notepads of the places we stayed at. I kept them together with a thick rubber band.

A devious smile curved Caleb's lips as he looked at his laptop. "Come here."

I couldn't believe he was inviting me to see his computer. He hadn't allowed me to see anything but the TV for the last eleven days. Laying my mini-pad on the table, I hustled over, standing before him in case he didn't want me to see the screen.

He patted his lap, and I sat down on his thigh. "Read."

He was in the business section of *The Philadelphia Inquirer*, reading an article titled *GenRev CEO Cries Foul Play As Biotech Startup Announces New Skin Treatment*. I read through the article, which quoted Dad furiously lashing out against Emergos, a new biotech company that, he claimed, had stolen one of GenRev's ideas for treating dermatitis. He vowed to rake the company over the coals. The article's writer interviewed Emergos's CEO, who claimed they had stolen nothing, and that they worked hard to create cutting-edge innovations to improve the health of the general public. He said he had all the evidence to prove that the idea had been developed and tested in the usual ways. My overall impression, after finishing the article, was that Dad was unfairly bullying a smaller company. And since in the past GenRev had been accused of monopolistic tactics, I suspected a judge or jury would favor the underdog in this case.

Caleb was pulsating with energy. "Give him a taste of his own medicine."

I twisted to meet his penetrating eyes. "What do you mean?"

"Your father's company—his whole career—is built on theft, lies, and coercion." He placed his laptop on the table, surging from the chair and seating me in it. Holding the armrests, he leaned over me. "Are you prepared to hear why I hate him?"

"Yes." And I meant it. Now more than ever I trusted Caleb to tell me the truth about Dad.

His eyes skipped between mine. "I think you are." He stood, shoving a hand through his hair and staring at the painting on the wall behind me. "Our fathers went to school together. When I was three, my dad, Nathaniel, invented a VR innovation for spine surgery. He thought Walter would help him develop and market it. Instead, your father stole the idea before my dad could patent it. Walter made a mint off of it, using it to found his company. Dad took him to court, and for seven long years he fought him. But he didn't have the means or the evidence to prove it was his idea. Our family grew much poorer, while your father grew rich."

My stomach clenched as waves of nausea lapped at my gut. This sounded plausible. After all, Dad had a head for finance—not for biotech. That he'd stepped on the shoulders of others to become the Titan he was didn't surprise me. What shocked me was his utter lack of conscience. I couldn't begin to imagine the emotional toll a seven-year-long lawsuit must've taken on Caleb's family.

Caleb popped a licorice mint in his mouth, stuffing his hands in his pockets as he paced. "Walter got my father blacklisted, forcing him to work for GenRev if he wanted to do anything in biotech. There, your father spied on mine and kept him under his thumb, paying him far below his qualifications. My mom also went to work for GenRev, in the design department. Two years into working there, Walter's hired hacker stole what my dad was working on—on his own time, on his own devices. It was an augmented reality treatment for Alzheimer's patients. Once again, your father beat mine to the punch, producing fabricated evidence that showed that the idea had been developed for GenRev. When Nathaniel challenged Walter, Walter fired him."

My eyes bugged out, and I gripped the armrests till my knuckles went white. "That's awful!"

In private, Dad had often spoken of the importance of *arming yourself with hackers in today's world.* Until now, I hadn't considered how this might play out in his own company.

Suddenly I had a flashback to the worst time Mom and Dad had fought, when I was maybe 6. Dad kept saying that anything people who worked for him did or thought was his. Mom's features had screwed up as if she was going to cry, she'd stalked out, and she'd stopped talking to Dad for a few days.

My mind returned to the present. To have stolen Nathaniel's idea once was unforgivable. To do so twice made Dad a beast. But to fire the man he'd had blacklisted made him an irredeemable monster.

Caleb's lips set in a grim line. "That's not all." He stopped pacing, glowering at the dark TV screen. "Now my mom was the only one supporting our family. Walter took advantage of his power and her vulnerability. He pressured her into sex. Three times." His jaw tensed, and his eyes narrowed to slits. "She was so afraid of losing her job that she gave in. But she wasn't protected, because my dad had long before decided he didn't want to have any more kids and had undergone a vasectomy."

The floor rose up and tilted like we were on a storm-tossed ship. Was this possible? Could my father have been such a brute? I'd thought he'd loved Mom, but I remembered how hurt I'd been when he'd remarried six months after she'd died. Had he cheated on her with Eve—and with Lucy? Right now anything seemed possible. My world was thrown upside down.

Icy tentacles wound around my chest and squeezed it. From Caleb's expression, I suspected Dad hadn't tried to set things right after his crime.

I braced myself for worse.

Caleb's fists clenched at his sides. "When she got pregnant, she knew it must be Walter's. She hid it for as long as she could. But when she started showing, Walter laid her off."

My jaw hit the floor, and I covered my mouth with my hand. If what Caleb said was true, then all signs pointed to my dad impregnating his mother. I could hardly believe Dad would be such an unfeeling cad as to then lay her off. But if he'd been able to do the other things Caleb was telling me, then he'd be capable of this too. After all, ever since Mom's death I'd wondered how well I really understood my father. That his ruthlessness could extend from his professional to his personal life now seemed frighteningly probable.

And Caleb's raw emotions told me that no way was he trying to manipulate me as a kidnapper might. He was exposing more of himself than he'd ever done before. He was trusting me with his truth—which increasingly looked like *the* truth.

My eyes stung, and tears threatened.

Caleb shut his eyes tight, as if to block out the painful images. "When Dad saw that Mom was pregnant again, he freaked out. His anger at Walter for doing this to Mom, the idea of raising a third kid, the stress of making ends meet when he and Mom were both laid off, and his depression over losing his creations to Walter drove him to hang himself." He swallowed. "I found him in the bathroom."

I couldn't breathe. I sprang from the chair, throwing my arms around Caleb's chest. The tears coursing down my cheeks flooded his shirt.

Caleb's voice cracked as he spoke. "My brother Luke was born a few months later. Stillborn. The doctors said it was from all the stress."

His chest heaved, and I didn't dare look up for fear of seeing the pain in his eyes. I squeezed him as tightly as I could, trying to close every millimeter of space separating us. For the first time in my life I wanted to absorb the pain of another human being. For him and his family to have endured such unspeakable suffering — one horrible tragedy after another in such a short time — and all at the hands of my father. It made me want to crawl through a crack in the ground and never emerge. Mortification at Dad's heartless, underhanded ways consumed me.

"I'm so sorry."

Caleb's body stiffened. "Don't pity me."

"I don't," I husked. "I'm ashamed and sad. About everything my father did and caused."

Relaxing a little, he wrapped his arms around me, resting his chin on the crown of my head. We stood like that for a while, his heartbeats thudding at my temple till I thought they were my own.

His voice was hollow and distant. "Every October second, on Luke's birthday, Mom, Faye, and I go visit his grave. It's next to Dad's. We fill them both in on everything that's happened since we last saw them."

His words tore my heart in two. A father and son stolen too soon from this life, leaving a family broken with all the reverberations of their grief. All the might-have-beens that never would be. A sob wracked me, and I buried my face in his warm chest.

No wonder Caleb had lashed out as a teen and welcomed Clark as a father figure. No wonder he hated my father so much. Right now *I* hated him. That he'd done those things to Nathaniel, Lucy, and their family without a backward glance or a word of regret made him unrecognizable to me.

Caleb took a step back, holding my arms at the elbows. Streaks of saffron jetted from his pupils. "I'll make sure he pays."

A full-body shudder seized me. Knowing Caleb, I knew he'd go big in his revenge. "How?"

He gave a slight shake of the head, his knuckles tracing my jawline. "That's as far as I can trust you, Diva."

I wiped tears from my lips. "I want to confront him on a video call. Tell him I know what he did and make him apologize to you."

His voice was surprisingly gentle. "Then you'll blow my cover. Right now he doesn't know who kidnapped you, doesn't know my old identity, and doesn't know my new one. Once he figures it all out, I won't be able to keep you safe."

"I don't want to blow your cover." *For your sake.* I looked down. I could never be the reason Caleb went to prison. I knew that now.

He tilted my face up. "I don't want an apology. I want to get even."

The next morning, Caleb and I had a full breakfast at a café at the top of one of the main streets in town. He'd just gone to use the restroom when a young woman with long black ringlets and a man with a nose ring approached with cameras and began to take my picture. I immediately regretted not wearing my sunglasses. I held up my hands to shield my face, but like most aggressive paparazzi, they continued to snap photos while asking me a slew of questions. "Why are you in Nevada City, Danya?" "Who's the lucky man?" "Is he your bodyguard?" "Does your father know where you are?" "Will you be attending Marcus James's party?" "Why won't you endorse Highet Crystals?" They wouldn't stop.

Too bad you can't use self-defense moves on paparazzi.

I stood and said, "Wait another minute and my bodyguard will be out. And he'll pound you both to a pulp."

That did the trick. They scuttled away like cockroaches, disappearing out the door.

Only when they'd vanished did it occur to me they'd gotten exactly what they wanted out of the encounter. They hadn't *wanted* to meet Caleb. They'd been afraid of him. That explained their careful timing that had them emerging only when he'd gone to the restroom.

A few minutes later, Caleb reappeared.

Still standing, he tensed. "What's wrong?"

My face must've been an open book to him. "Just some paparazzi who took my photo while you were gone."

In a flash he was out the door, scanning the street, up and down. He returned a moment later wearing his avenging-angel look. "No one with cameras out there now. Let's get on the road."

I was disappointed, because Mom and I had always stayed in Nevada City for a few days, it was such a special town. Tourists came for its old-west vibe, Victorian architecture, and gold-mining history, while regular vacationers came for its art, music, and theater. And every local I'd ever met there, native or nonnative, had fascinating stories to tell. I'd looked forward to showing Caleb the National Hotel, the pottery and photography shops, the antique stores, and the old Down-ieville Highway, a scenic five-mile walk just outside of town.

"Can I just show you the beautiful old Methodist church at the top of the street?"

He gripped the back of my neck, leading me out the door. "Two words—sex traffickers."

Jesus, he was brutal.

I shivered, leaning into him. "Okay."

After packing everything up, we headed out to the car.

Caleb muttered *fuck* under his breath.

"What's wrong?" Then I saw what he was talking about.

The rear tires were both flat as a pancake.

He crouched, examining the left tire closely and running his thumbs along the edge. "It hasn't been slashed." Rising, he rounded the car and looked at the other tire. "Neither has this one. Someone let the air out of the valves."

For some reason I thought of the two photographers. "Should we ask the front desk woman if she saw anyone?"

Our car was the only one in the parking lot.

"I'll stay here while you ask her." He pulled out his phone, tapping and swiping.

The ash blonde with the fashionable green-rimmed glasses smiled as I came in. "Hi, we've got a couple of flat tires. We were wondering if you saw anyone in the lot over the last hour and a half or so?"

She frowned. "Sorry to hear that. No. Just the mailman. But I had to step out for the last half-hour to check on a few rooms."

"Thank you."

I returned outside to find Caleb pocketing his phone. "What's the word?"

"She didn't see anyone. But she wasn't here over the last half-hour."

He shouldered one of the bags, gripping the other. "A

Greyhound bus comes through a gas station at the other side of town. It'll arrive in a little over an hour, bound for Colfax, where we can catch an Amtrak train. Our Uber should be here in a few minutes."

I was moved that Caleb was so determined to keep me safe that he'd resorted to three new modes of transportation to lose our followers. The fact that these modes were all a little awkward and difficult made his gesture more meaningful than the Audi carjacking. I could see his fixer's brain at work demolishing the hurdles in our path.

In the Uber, he kept looking back. Seeing that Caleb was preoccupied, our driver engaged me in friendly conversation about spring break crowds. On reaching the gas station, we found a bench to park our bags while waiting for the bus. I put my sunglasses on — maybe akin to closing the stable door after the horse had gotten out, but I figured I might as well.

"No carjacking this time?" I smiled up at him.

"This'll throw them off our scent." His eyes skittered around watching everything and everyone around us. "They obviously knew to look for the Audi. Maybe because they knew the location of the beamer once I'd taken the jammer out of it and connected it up with a stolen car report for that mall at that time."

"How did they know we're in Nevada City? The paps can't have published those pictures so quickly. And if the paps *are* the people following us, why would they alert us to their presence here by taking my photo?"

His intense gaze snagged mine. "Who knows that you often traveled this way when you were young?"

My thoughts raced. "A lot of people, actually. I used to write about this trip in high school and college. Not that I'd have expected anyone to remember. Besides my teachers and a few students, I guess Dad, Eve, Luis . . . oh, and Gladys and Innes at work, because I told them all about Nevada City and the breathtaking approach to it through Tahoe National Forest."

"A few new ground rules." He cupped the back of my neck. "One, we're not separating for a minute. Even when one of us uses the restroom. Two, we're not following any routes you've taken before. And three, at our next destination we're staying put for a few days and lying low. No point in running and giving them a better chance to follow us."

"Danya." A familiar tenor voice sounded from behind Caleb.

The next few seconds happened so fast, I barely registered them. Caleb whirled around, pulling his gun and pressing it into Luis's waist under my stepbrother's coat. "What do you want?"

My heart stopped, and I lost my speech. Luis had dark shadows under his brown eyes and furrows in his broad brow.

His eyes bulged as he stuttered, "I—I want to—to make sure Danya is okay."

Caleb's gravelly voice resonated with calm assurance as he spoke in Luis's ear. "Let's try this again. Who are you?"

"Caleb—it's Luis," I managed. I'd never seen someone pull a gun on someone else. The experience was doubly terrifying because it was Luis. "You can put down the gun."

"How did you know where she was?" Caleb nosed the gun into Luis's side, his body remaining as alert as if an open-jawed crocodile threatened me.

"I followed you in Ohio but lost you off the highway. Walter said Danya was in danger of being nabbed by sex traffickers." His throat processed a thick swallow. "I figured if you had any say in where to go, you'd head to Nevada City."

"Why are you *here*, at this gas station?" Caleb prodded.

"I just got into town and decided to fill up."

"Yours is the black Nissan Sentra?"

"Yeah."

"Hand me the key and your phone. Try anything, and you're dead."

Shaking, I found my voice. "Caleb, please, put down the gun."

"Now," Caleb snapped.

Luis fished in his pocket, passing Caleb the car key and his phone.

"Danya, get our bags and put them in the car. Then climb in." He handed me the key without removing his eyes from Luis.

I froze, not knowing what to do. I didn't want to endanger Luis or Caleb further by dragging my feet. But I couldn't leave things like this for my stepbrother.

"Caleb, he's only —"

"That was an order." His tone left no doubt that he would be obeyed.

Turning to pick up the bags, I heard Caleb demand of Luis, "Who were the people in the Hyundai behind you?"

"I didn't know there were people behind me," Luis stammered.

"Either you're lying or you're clueless. Either way, she's not safe with you."

"And she is with you?" Luis pushed back.

"As safe as she can be, under the circumstances."

I couldn't hear any more of their conversation as I stepped into the car, closing the door. I watched as Caleb maneuvered Luis so he faced the outside wall of the gas mart. Caleb slowly stepped back towards the car, covering Luis the whole way with his gun discreetly tucked inside his jacket. He rounded the hood, sliding behind the wheel and starting the engine. In five seconds he'd sped out of the gas station, and a minute later he'd entered the freeway heading south.

"No Greyhound for us just yet." Caleb pulled out his tin of

licorice mints, tossing one in his mouth. "Though I already miss the Audi's steering."

Wracked with guilt, I remained silent. What was going to happen to Luis? I'd been supremely disloyal to abandon my stepbrother when he'd only been trying to help me. Would he be more worried than ever now, or would he give up his mission and return to Philly? This was *not* how I'd imagined our reunion.

"He has his wallet. He can rent a car." Caleb broke into my thoughts as if he'd heard every word.

"You abused his love for me. He can't turn me in for stealing his car. And if he tries to report you, he'll leave me exposed to the traffickers."

A cocky smirk slid up his lips. "It was a neat solution, if I do say so."

I thought back to the tense moments at the gas station. "You don't really suspect him, do you?"

"We can't afford to rule out any possibilities—including him. His showing up where he did is pretty suspicious, for one. For another, he showed up just after those photographers snapped your photo and our tires were deflated."

"*I* think he's just the canary in the mineshaft for our real followers."

When we reached Rocklin, Caleb pulled over for gas and did a sweep of the car for trackers and other spying devices. He found a tracker embedded in the rear bumper.

"Your canary died." Caleb tossed the tracker in the back of a pickup truck as it left the station going in the opposite direction. "Now to outrun them if they tail us."

I steeled myself for another chase.

CHAPTER TWENTY-FOUR: CALEB

A round 1 o'clock, passing Roseville, I caught sight of the blue Hyundai three cars back from us in the far left lane. Adrenaline surged through me. Time to have some fun. Shifting one over, I changed lanes again, sped up a little, and passed an eighteen-wheeler, sliding in front to use it for cover. A minute later I spotted my next cover, a long tour bus in the next lane over to the right. Speeding up, I darted just ahead of it. After that, I found another tractor-trailer in the lane to the right, tucking us between its cab and a Jeep. Weaving and ducking among larger vehicles in this way, I covertly eased towards the next off ramp. Exiting, I immediately crossed under the freeway.

Danya volunteered, "There's a major road a few turns from here that takes you all the way south across the American River to Highway Fifty. Mom and I took it when we went swimming in Lake Folsom one summer."

Looking in the rearview, I saw the Hyundai scooting closer. *Damn*, these fuckers stuck to our scent like horseflies. Pulling my phone from my pocket, I unlocked it with my fingerprint and tossed it to Danya. "Locate where we are, because we're about to get lost."

I hooked the first right and then two lefts, entering a labyrinth of streets winding through a suburban development complex. Some of the streets looped around, some forked into smaller roads, and others led back out to through streets. I didn't care which way I went, so long as I lost the bastards on our tail.

"Take a left here, and then your first right," Danya directed.

She navigated us through the warren of back streets on the other side of the avenue that separated one development from the next. I kept watching and waiting for my chance to lose these jackasses. After a sharp turn, I spotted a truck hitched to a large boat blocking the bottom of a driveway. Pulling into the neighboring driveway, I turned and drove along the sidewalk, parking alongside the boat hitch so it hid us.

The Hyundai missed us and flew by, taking the only way they could take, which was to bear right along the road. No sooner had they passed out of sight than I pulled out into the street, did a U-ey, and drove back the way we'd come.

"To avoid running into them, take your first left, then an immediate right," Danya advised, consulting my phone.

I followed her instructions. As she directed me to Highway 50, I kept checking behind us. No one. We seemed to have shaken them.

At the stoplight directing cars to 50 East or 50 West, Danya chimed, "Instead of going through Sacramento, we could go east, climbing up into the Sierras."

"Did you and your mom ever go this way?" I slipped a mint in my mouth.

"No. We always took Eighty to the San Francisco Bay Area or Five to Los Angeles."

I met her eye. "Then we'll go east."

After we'd merged onto the highway, Danya told me, "I've got enough material from our trip so far to write five or six blog posts. And I know what the overall theme would be, as well as the topics of the posts. I thought maybe I could call my fellow traveler *the Werewolf,* to mask your identity. If I wait to publish it till after we're clear of the traffickers, do I have your permission?"

I rolled my tense neck. "As long as you don't give away

anything about me, my profession, or your kidnapping." I was shocked to find that I trusted her enough to know that she wouldn't intentionally compromise me.

Her eyes glittered, and a radiant smile spread across her face. "I'm really excited. I don't know whether it was being jolted out of normal life when we were at the farmhouse, or just retracing this trip I used to do with Mom, but I've got a hunger I've not had in a long time. I'm finally ready to just say *to hell with it* and write already. I have no idea what I'll do for money while I try to get the blog off the ground, but I'll manage somehow."

Remembering her usual barriers, I had to play devil's advocate. "What's to stop your perfectionism from rearing its ugly head?"

"I don't know. But I keep considering the alternative to publishing, which is never to be read. And that's far worse than being less than perfect."

"What if people criticize the hell out of you, and you make no money?"

She sobered. "Then I guess, at least I'll be able to say I tried."

She'd obviously been thinking about this a lot during our travels.

"What made you less cautious?" Signaling, I switched to the fast lane.

"You, actually."

I shot her a glance to see if she was joking, but her expression was dead serious.

Her face had pinkened. "Every time something happens that forces us to act, you're ready. Like last Thursday when we had to leave Philly, you had us heading out in fifteen minutes. Or when you discovered we were being tracked, you stole that car. And today, you were prepared for us to take the bus to drop our followers. Then you improvised and took my stepbrother's car. And now we just lost our tail for the third time."

I adjusted the radio dial to a country station. "What does any of that have to do with writing?"

She propped her elbow on the armrest. "As a fixer, you can't afford to hesitate much. Pretty soon you have to just act. I figure, what if I see travel writing in the same way? We have only a finite amount of time to do stuff in life. I might as well make my mistakes along with everyone else. At least I'll go down doing what I love."

Pride swelled in my chest at the thought that she'd been inspired by the way I handled my job. It hadn't occurred to me that as a fixer I could be a positive role model.

"Clark always said doing what you love keeps you eternally young."

Examining me from the side, she nodded. "I guess the opposite could be true too — if you're forced to do what you dislike, you age faster." She looked away, and then turned back. "Do you love fixing?"

Did I? I thought about the hundreds of different situations I'd negotiated a solution for over the years, and the many varied people I'd dealt with. I took pride and pleasure in both. I considered the freedom of not having a boss or a set schedule. The way it was easy to falsify my tax statements. The satisfaction of learning new things under pressure. Then I recalled the stress of last-minute unforeseen events and the annoyance of dealing with the dregs of humanity. The occasional anxiety over getting caught and the worry that I might not score a job in time to make a property tax payment. All in all, I decided the advantages of the job outweighed its disadvantages.

"I guess so. I can't imagine doing anything else."

Her lips quirked. "From where I sit, you're very good at it."

I offered a wry smile. "Hold your praise till we've gotten

rid of the traffickers."

She chewed her lower lip. "By the same token, I probably shouldn't assume I'll follow through with my new writing resolution till I actually publish the blog. A lot of things seem possible when you're traveling that don't come to pass when you return to everyday reality." She fiddled with my phone. "How far south are we going? I can program it in."

"Whatever's eight hours away."

"All right, we can get into Barstow at nine-forty-six. Not counting stops."

For the rest of the afternoon we climbed and climbed as the road grew twistier and more densely forested. At one point, the diva pointed to our left and said Lake Tahoe lay down below us. Even I had to admit the views took your breath away. To the right, we had peak after stunning snow-covered peak of the Sierra Nevada mountains. To the left, a vast arid basin stretched across the border into Nevada. We stopped at a scenic viewpoint where the plaque claimed we were at 8,143 feet elevation. Danya said that meant we'd climbed 8,000 feet since leaving Roseville four hours ago. While the air was thin, it was cleaner than any I'd ever breathed.

We stopped in Mammoth Lakes to fuel the tank and our stomachs. For some reason driving at high altitudes made me ravenous. I wolfed down two sandwiches and half a bag of chips, while Danya polished off the rest of the chips and a sandwich of her own. From there we descended steeply, keeping Inyo National Forest to our right and—according to Danya—the mountains surrounding Death Valley to our left. She pointed to the highest peak in the contiguous US, Mount Whitney, and then gestured in the opposite direction to indicate the lowest point in the US. A difference of nearly 15,000 feet in the space of fifty miles.

"If you didn't come this way with your mom, why do you know so much?" I cast a glance at her profile, defined by her round cheekbones and the subtle rise midway down the ridge of her nose. Perfection.

A smile pulled at the corner of her mouth. "I was just curious about the geography and natural history of California."

We reached Barstow late enough to find most eating places closing. But an all-night Mexican restaurant on old Route 66 fed us enchiladas and tacos with Mexican sodas.

After stacking our empty baskets, we lingered in our booth looking out at a horizon studded with dark mountains. Danya was using my phone to do more research on Barstow.

"Apparently those are the Bullion Mountains, and they extend only fifty miles to the southeast, north of Joshua Tree."

I stretched my arms. "Are we in Death Valley?"

"The Mojave Desert."

"I bet this place will be fuck-hot in a couple of months."

She nodded. "You'd win that. The temp now is forty-three. But apparently there are highs of one hundred and twenty in the summer."

"Have you ever traveled somewhere you'd actually consider moving for good?"

Her lips slid to the side. "That's a tough question. There've been a slew of places I've flirted with staying long-term. But the more I travel, the more I realize what makes Philly so special as a home base. Not to sound too Wizard-of-Ozzy, but a trip, however wonderful, always reminds me why I love home."

I smiled. "Now you sound more like a homebody than a travel writer."

"That said, if I had a family to travel with, I'd be carrying my home with me like a snail. That'd be the best of both worlds."

This jibed with how I'd come to know Danya over the last two weeks. While she obviously loved traveling, she was looking for love with just as steady a determination.

I slipped out of the booth, holding my palm out for my phone. "All right, let's go find our temporary home in Barstow."

No swimming that night—we were too wiped—but I trained the diva's ass a little more to accept my dick. Spreading two fingers wide past her snug hole to her rectum, I simulated the experience of taking my cock.

After we'd come like goats rutting in the fall—another nature channel image—she lay with her head resting on my chest and her back in the crook of my arm.

"I'd think those people would be sick of trying to catch me," she murmured, tracing her fingers over my abs. "Isn't all this time on the road just so much sunk money for them? Why don't they get on with finding some other victim?"

"There's more to this, I can smell it. Something beyond just the money." I strummed one of her peaked nipples, my girth swelling for round two. "And they may feel that having come this far, they've invested too much not to reap their reward. It's the same mentality—part hope, part desperation—that keeps casinos raking in the bucks. In poker we call it playing on tilt."

She looked up at me through her curly lashes. "How long will we stay here?"

"A few days at least." I straddled her, pinning her wrists above her head and tweaking her unstrummed nipple. "Long enough for me to leave you unable to walk."

Smiling, she arched her hips into my length. "That won't take long."

Danya

Caleb and I kept an extremely low profile in Barstow.

Wearing shades everywhere—necessary anyways because of the desert sun—we found one diner where we always ate breakfast, and we alternated between a grill and a Mexican place for dinner.

On Thursday, we did a load at a laundromat and visited a museum devoted to the history of Route 66 and the Mojave desert communities. Caleb showed me more self-defense moves in a park, and we spent an hour at a museum that displayed the history of railroading in the Southwest. Then we drove through Calico, a silver rush ghost town to the east of Barstow.

Friday was overcast—perfect weather for visiting the nearby Rainbow Basin, which I'd found on Trip Advisor using Caleb's phone. We drove a long, mostly-empty dirt road through the most bizarre multi-colored rock formations I'd ever seen. Green, tan, ruby, sable, and heather hues marked the sediments of rock that rolled, puckered, and poked out into the sky. Since we often pulled over and walked to the edge of the jutting cliffs to survey the basin more fully, our visit took four hours.

A geologist I was not. No matter how many times I read through a sentence about how the rocks came to be the way they were, my brain fuzzed over. After staring dazedly at the fourth placard, I decided to leave the basin a beautiful mystery.

"It's like watching geology in action," Caleb commented as we gazed at a huge layer of green rock tilting upwards like the prow of a ship.

I looked up at him. "Do you understand it?"

He spun us so we faced each other, pulling me to him by my hips. "It's the kind of information that's probably best shown in a video. Reading the blurbs, it's hard to picture the processes."

This moment with him, standing in the midst of awe-inspiring natural grandeur, made me long to capture it.

"Can we take just one selfie here?"

He chuffed a laugh. "For what purpose, Diva?"

"So I can remember sharing this experience with you. I promise I'll never publish it."

He thumbed my lips, his darkened eyes hinting at a hunger to kiss me. "How about I take your picture in front of that monster. I'll send it to you when everything's over."

When everything's over. I tried to ignore the hollow ache those words awakened in my chest.

"Kiss me," I said boldly.

He never had, though his eyes lingered on my lips often enough, as though he wanted to. A kiss would burn this moment in my memory even better than a picture. For six years I'd dreamed of him pressing his lips to mine.

His hand slid down to my throat. "A demand, Diva?"

"A request," I squeaked as his fingers squeezed my airways.

He gazed at my lips a long moment as if memorizing them. It was like that breathless moment in a raffle before the winning number is called out. *Please kiss me. Please close the space between us so I can taste your lips at last.*

His eyes shifting to mine, he released my throat, stepping back.

"Maybe when I say goodbye to you."

When I say goodbye. Four of the bitterest, saddest words I'd ever heard. *When* was so definite, *goodbye* so final.

Catching my breath, I looked away across the rainbow-colored ramparts. I was a fool to hope for anything more, I knew I was. Yet I couldn't stop myself from wanting more. Caleb was his own man, answering to no one, and until now I hadn't realized that was what I'd been looking for. He was courageous, smart, strong, and generous. And the fierce way he protected me showed that he was also compassionate. I'd allowed myself to imagine that such care might mean he cared *for* me. But he was just fulfilling the terms of his contract.

"Turn around and slant your arm upwards at the angle of the rock," he directed, holding up his phone.

I did so, unable to muster a smile.

"Flash one of your radiant smiles, Diva."

I pasted a smile on my face, and he took some pictures.

Me standing all alone in front of that rock seemed like both a symbol and a foreshadowing.

On Saturday morning after breakfast, Caleb and I hung out at the motel pool. No one else was using it, so we were able to play beach ball volleyball, shark and minnow—which Caleb won every time—and Marco Polo. On a chaise longue I read a historical romance novel I found in the motel lobby, while Caleb called Lucy and Faye.

When we came inside, those bright lights danced in front of my eyes—the ones you get on entering a dark room after being out in the sun for a while.

Caleb asked if I wanted to join him in the shower, but I said I was going to lie down and close my eyes for a few minutes.

He laid his phone, still open to the keypad, on the bedside table.

After he'd started the shower, my heart began to race. I'd never before been left alone with his phone open. I was quite certain he hadn't done it intentionally. I could check email—maybe respond to any pressing messages without giving anything away. And I could write to Luis, reassuring him that I was okay and he shouldn't worry.

I seized the phone, opening up a browser and typing in my email service. My hands were trembling as I filled in my username and password. I had only ten minutes or so before Caleb came out.

An email Dad had sent yesterday evening was the most recent, so I opened that. He wrote, *Danya, I know there's very little chance you'll read this for a while. But I hope you're okay, wherever you are. I haven't heard from you in over a week. I found this picture of you and your mom from when you were in London. You look very happy.*

My chest squeezed as I remembered Mom's and my time in London, just before we headed to the Continent and, eventually, Bulgaria. I opened the picture, my eyes pricking with tears. It was the photo I loved most, of the two of us on Tower Bridge. Gazing at it, I thought of how her spirit was everywhere I traveled. Her sense of adventure, curiosity, and willingness to engage with people inspired me every minute of every trip.

I closed the picture, tapping *compose* and filling in Luis's address. I typed a quick message. *I hope you got back to Philly okay. I'm sorry about what happened. I can't write much now, but I'm fine. Please don't worry. Te amo muchísimo.*

After pressing *send*, I scrolled through the rest of the unread messages, looking for anything urgent.

Suddenly I realized the shower wasn't going anymore. I hastily closed out the email service, reaching to put the phone back on the bedside table.

I inhaled sharply, dropping the phone to the floor.

Caleb stood in the bathroom doorway. A lethal fire flickered in his eyes, and his jaw muscles rippled with tension. His forearms radiated destructive power. Normally, when he wore a towel around his waist, I ogled his shoulders, pecs, and abs. Now, his whole body terrified me with its readiness to pounce.

"I—I was j-just . . ." I broke off, unable to continue.

"Stand." His sinister tone made my flesh prickle.

I stumbled off the bed, worrying my t-shirt in my hand. God, what was he going to do?

Prowling towards me, he stopped a foot away. "Arms at

your sides."

I obeyed.

Fixing me with a searing gaze, he took hold of the neck of my shirt and with one ferocious yank ripped it down the center. Gasping, I crossed my arms over my bare belly.

"Arms straight out behind you."

As I held them back, he whipped my shirt off. Then he tore my shorts down the middle so they slipped down and puddled at my feet.

"Please, not—"

No sooner had I gotten the words out than he ripped my nice black lace panties twice, so they too pooled at my feet.

"Please, Caleb—"

His lips twisted in a snarl as he tore my bra and wrenched it off me. My favorite underwear, gone. But I had bigger things to worry about now. Like what he was going to do next.

"Face down on the bed," he growled.

"I can explain—"

"*Now.*"

I scurried to lie on my belly.

I heard the zip of a bag and the swish of something being removed from it. Holding my wrists behind me, he manacled them with a rope so they were a few inches apart. Then he tied my ankles in the same way.

"Arch your back."

I did so.

Looping a rope between the wrist and ankle ropes, he hogtied me. My chest and shins were lifted off the bed in a contortionist's pose I never would've been able to hold without the ropes. Trussed up and unable to move, I was thoroughly abased.

He ran a finger along my slit, collecting my juices. Realizing how wet I was only made me leak more.

He fisted my hair, steering my body so I faced him as he stood beside the bed. Gripping the nape of my neck, he pulled me to the very edge of the bed. As I looked up at him, the smoldering coals in his eyes glowed with rage and lust. He had a double right—to punish and enjoy. My pussy flooded with need, and I knew I was in for it.

"Let down my towel."

There was only one way to obey him. That was to use my teeth. As I closed them on his towel and pulled, I could only imagine what I looked like. Like a roast pig with an apple in its mouth. The image set my clit drumming and my skin buzzing with heat. I looked ridiculous, but it was punishment, and it was for his pleasure.

I watched in slow motion as the towel whished down Caleb's legs, revealing his fully-erect cock bobbing against his abdomen. He was glorious to behold and delicious to breathe in.

With his index finger he swiped a drip of drool that had escaped my mouth. Mixing the drip with the pre-cum pearling his tip, he primed his thickness with his fist.

He held my chin. "Why are you being punished?"

I managed a swallow. "For using your phone while you weren't there."

He poised his purple head at my mouth like a mic. "And?"

White-hot want blazed through my core. "For emailing Luis."

His relentless gaze speared me. "Open wide."

Relaxing my jaw as I'd grown used to doing with him, I opened my mouth as wide as I could. I was completely in his power.

"Are you ready to please me?"

My body rocked as I nodded, and the pulse in my sex grew more insistent.

Twisting my hair about his hand and holding my head in

place, he fisted his shaft, feeding it into my mouth till he hit the back of my throat. My eyes welled with tears as I gagged. His lips twisted in a satanic smirk. He eased out and thrust in again to touch bottom. By focusing on the sweet rose scent of his soap, his clean masculine aromas, and his earthy taste, I soon forgot to gag. He drove into me, surfaced, and drove in again, sparing me no millimeter of his endless ridge. I sucked as he withdrew and lavished him with my tongue as he lanced me. Either I was hard-wired to crave giving him the best climax he'd ever had or his authority demanded it. Maybe both. But my humiliating position, the way he was using me and taking his fill of me, and the increasingly merciless slams of his cock down my throat drove me wild with arousal. My pussy clenched on air, contracting in spasms of desperate longing. Groans of frustration escaped me, and Caleb pulled out.

Much as giving him pleasure turned me on, this time was torture. I was sure my pussy lips were glossy with arousal, and my sex buzzed with hunger. Hunger that wouldn't be satisfied, if I knew my punisher.

His grip tightened so hard on my hair that sharp pains spiked from my scalp. His eyes were darkly blazing infernos. "Swallow every last drop."

He impaled my mouth, stroking it with irregular, unfocused thrusts as he spurted all over my tongue.

Knowing this was all the pleasure I'd get, I relished his tangy taste, gulping his come till no more was left. Seed spilled over my lips and down my chin, dribbling onto the bed.

He released my hair, stepping back to observe me. "Now I doubt you'll turn down a shower." A devil's smile touched his lips as he cupped my chin. "But I don't think I'll untie you for a while yet."

Chapter Twenty-Five: Caleb

Leaving Danya hogtied, I stepped out onto the balcony to make a few calls. When I came back in, she'd rolled to her side and edged higher so her head rested on a pillow.

Setting a chair by the bed, I took a seat facing her. "What else did you do besides email your stepbrother?"

I brought up her email, remembering her username and password from last week.

"I just read a message from Dad and looked for any pressing messages." She sounded exhausted.

"No other replies? No calls?"

"No."

Pulling up the call log, I saw she was telling the truth. I checked her outbox, reading through the message she'd sent to Luis.

"You've forfeited my trust, Diva. You've lost all rights to touch this phone, even in my presence."

"But it was only—"

"We don't know who to trust at this point. Even Luis is under suspicion. Do you understand?"

"Yes," she said in a small voice.

I turned her so she lay on her belly. As I unfastened the ropes, she shook out her arms and legs.

"Can I take a shower?"

"You may."

The diva knew that once I'd punished her, all was forgiven. But I wouldn't forget. Nor, hopefully, would she.

Over a dinner of fish and chips for Danya, and a burger and salad for me at our now-regular grill a few blocks away, Danya looked thoughtful. She was wearing a grey-and-brown plaid jumpsuit with flared legs that I wanted to rip off of her as I'd done to her underwear earlier.

Leaning her forearms on the table, she stirred her Coke with a straw. "Why won't you kiss me?"

Something told me she'd been turning over that problem since Rainbow Basin yesterday.

I put down my burger. "Kissing leads to emotions, which leads to attachment, which leads to trouble. As I've told you, I don't do strings-attached."

"Was that something you discovered yourself, or a rule you were told by someone else?"

I thought back to my year-long relationship with Gillian when I was 21. I wouldn't have continued seeing her after the third date if it hadn't been for the kiss we'd virtually been forced into having while we waited for the rain to let up in that narrow covered doorway. Apparently kissing under close cover in the rain was every chick's dream. After that, everything had been expected to lead with a kiss and end with a kiss, with plenty of kisses in between. In this way, one expectation had led to another, until I was in over my head.

Our relationship had been a train wreck in the making. I'd intended for us to break up when I told her not to wait for me while I went on a six-month assignment to Seattle. She'd apparently thought she was supposed to wait. Then she heard through others that I was seeing other women casually while I was away. When I got back, she was waiting in my apartment. She'd even gotten close to Earl, my traitorous doorman, who'd let her in. She hurled a porcelain vase, a glass plate, and a crystal decanter at me together with a storm of curses. Pounding me with her fists, she told me of all the men she'd passed up for dates, how many tears she'd cried for me, and how her heart would never mend. One black eye and six self-administered stitches later, I watched as she blew out the door.

But that hadn't been the end of it, because of course, strings had been attached. From the get-go she'd gotten close to Faye and Mom, and she seemed to be everywhere all the time. She knew my regular haunts, all the people I was close to — including Gideon and Clark — and all my habits. About the only thing she had no part of was my job. For a full year, I'd had to time everything so I'd miss her, substituting new places for my favorites.

A year later, she'd finally met someone and stopped stalking me.

Ever since Gillian, kisses meant pain, heartache, and breakups. They spelled the demise of freedom.

My thoughts returned to Danya and the present. "Something I discovered myself."

"From one experience?"

"Yeah."

"That's all one experience is, Caleb. *One experience.*"

I shook my head, taking a pull on my beer. "It's enough."

"Were you in love?"

I nodded.

I hadn't even tried to keep Gillian when I'd gone to Seattle, because I'd known we weren't compatible, even though I loved her. She did things too slowly for my tastes, so I was always getting impatient with her. She spent half an hour choosing a space in a parking lot, because she had so many conditions for feeling comfortable leaving her car. And she let people walk all over her — notably her boss and coworkers. I couldn't get her to be more assertive. If I'd been honest with myself at the time, I would've recognized that I'd seized the chance to break up with her when I'd left for Washington.

As the years had gone by, though, I'd suspected I had

failed to communicate enough with Gillian about the fact that I wanted to break up and why I'd wanted us to split.

Danya moistened her lips with her tongue, making my eyes stray to her mouth. "Maybe we could do an experiment and find out if kissing always leads to trouble."

I smiled. "That's like testing a nuclear bomb to see if it detonates."

She stood, rounding the table.

"What are you doing?"

She blushed scarlet. "Scoot back so I can sit in your lap."

"If this is part of your test, it's been aborted."

She dipped her head, looking at me through her lashes. "You won't regret it."

"Oh, I think I will." I tipped my head towards her chair. "Back to your seat, Diva. You're up to no good."

An adorable pout poofed out her lower lip, which I wanted to bite till it bled. "And you're cruel."

"To keep you in check."

She stopped and turned before taking her seat, puckering her lips tantalizingly. "You're going to kiss me soon, and you'll wonder why you didn't do it before."

The diva was showing more confidence by the day, and it was dangerous, because I liked this side of her. A lot.

"You said Clark loves puns." She held up the cocktail menu that stood in a plastic holder in the center of the table. "Would he like this one — *Jalapeño Face Margarita?*"

I laughed. "Yeah. What others are on the list?"

"How about *Orange You Glad*? Or *Whiskey Business. Bourbon Legends*. Oh! I like this one — *The Phantom of the Vodka.*"

"Any rum ones?"

"Egh. They're not very funny. *Good Things Rum to Those Who Wait. Girls Just Want to Have Rum.*' We can do better than that."

We sat in silence for a while, thinking. The diva rolled the end of a strand of hair between her fingers, which I found at once endearing and sexy.

"I know!" she said at the same time I said, "How about—"

I chuckled. "You first."

"*Time Flies When You're Having Rum.*"

"Nice. I was thinking *You Won't Rum-ember a Thing.*"

She laughed. "That's a good one. We should suggest these to the bar staff."

It being Saturday night in one of the most popular grills in Barstow, there was a five-piece band playing popular songs from the last sixty years. The dance floor had already filled up with patrons.

"Oh! I love this song," Danya said as the band started up *Stereo Hearts.* "Let's dance."

We'd be surrounded by people, so dancing seemed safe enough. I rose, leading her into the crowd with my hand on the small of her back.

As I watched the diva move and sing along to the music, a collage of carefree moments like this replayed in my brain. Danya crowing with triumph after leaning out of the pool and just barely tapping the beach ball back across our invisible volleyball net. Danya laughing at her mistakes in poker when I first taught her how to play. Danya shouting into the bathroom that she'd hidden the last piece of pizza—then her fizzy laughter when I'd later found it stuffed in a pile of dirty laundry.

Now, dancing with her, I realized this wasn't just a job anymore. It was a chance to spend time with the diva, to find out what made her tick. Not only did I rarely take vacations, but I clearly separated work and play. For once, work corresponded with fun and vacation, and I got to do it all with her. Teach her self-defense moves at rest stops, talk while we drove, play cards in motel rooms, do touristy stuff around Barstow, play pool games, work and write side by side on balconies. I enjoyed everything more than I would've imagined.

I remembered a comedian I loved, Chris Rock, saying that a relationship boils down to eating together and fucking. Till now I'd believed that, and it had been one more reason I'd never felt I was missing out. But the stuff I now recalled from my time with Danya wasn't so much the eating or the sex, though both were memorable. It was the experiences we shared on the road.

Danya knew how to turn stressful times into good times. Her smile and laughter were infectious. She was a good listener with an open mind and heart. She loved people, hungered to learn new things, and had a resilient, adaptable spirit. Her memory for places and history astonished me. And I admired the way she was turning a career setback into a new professional chapter, using her kidnapping to launch her blog.

And she appreciated my knowledge and skills. At last I understood Clark's drive to share his military and engineering knowhow with others. It was gratifying when the diva eagerly absorbed my stories and peppered me with questions. She trusted me to keep her safe, even when she could've doubted my motives. And she ate up all I taught her about self-defense, poker, and tying knots.

Now, as Danya and I danced to Cream's *Take It Back*, I spun her, and we rocked and swayed. I wanted to do the equivalent of Danya's writing in her travel journal—bottle up this moment and keep its memory for a time when fun was the furthest thing from my mind. I'd recall the sheen of her rust-colored hair, the sparkle of her eyes, and the fluid movements of her body in this jumpsuit. And yes, her sweet, rosy lips that tempted me, laughing when I twirled her, smiling when we pulled close, and parting in expectation when our faces drew inches apart.

We danced to song after song, the diva never tiring, as light on her feet after twenty songs as she was during the first.

During a slow dance I came closer to kissing her than I had to kissing any woman in eight years. All kinds of rationalizations for breaking my rule crowded my brain—it was impossible for us to have a relationship anyway, so there was no danger that a kiss would lead to one. I was immune to falling in love with Danya, so I didn't have to worry that a kiss would put me in over my head emotionally. In the years since Gillian, I had overblown the seriousness of kissing, and my memory was faulty.

If anyone's lips were made for kissing, the diva's were.

Just as I was about to cave and say *fuck it*, the song ended. And that was the last song the band played.

As the house music came on, I brushed my lips against her ear instead. "Shall we go?"

She forked her fingers through my hair. "Okay."

The gesture was so simple, yet so intimate. It reminded me of the feel of her fingers in my beard that night at the farmhouse. It recalled the many times she'd threaded her fingers through my hair after sex. It said, *You belong to me, and I belong to you.*

I should've found that idea frightening, but I liked it. A lot.

On Sunday, Danya and I walked through downtown Barstow, looking at murals that portrayed local history from the Stone Age to the present.

When we'd seen the last, Danya turned to me. "Which was your favorite?"

"I like the Mojave Runners." These were messengers of the Mojave tribe who sometimes ran a hundred miles a day to carry information to distant villages.

"I love the one done by local schools in one day, of parts of the Old Spanish Trail." The trail was an old pack mule route that went through Barstow from 1829 to 1848. "I know!" Danya hopped in front of me. "Let's buy each other a gift to remember Barstow and this trip by."

I smiled. "You want me to buy myself a gift with my own money?"

She held up a finger. "*I'll* be choosing yours. And after we get back to Philly, I'll send the money to whatever address you're okay with me using."

Of course I didn't give a damn about the money. Her idea, like so many of hers on this trip, was fresh and fun. "All right. How does this work?"

"Give me sixty dollars, and make a limit of sixty for your gift to me. When we're in a shop and we spot something for the other person, don't call attention to it. But at some point at each shop, we'll separate for a few minutes, in case we've found a gift. We'll come back together five minutes later. Tonight over dinner, we'll share our gifts."

"Fine. But as soon as we've found our gifts, we're not separating anymore. Try to find yours as soon as you can." Pulling out my wallet, I handed her three twenties. "Remember, safety above fun."

She stuck out her lower lip in another of her provocative pouts.

Our first stop was one of those old general stores with *mercantile* in its name. I imagined in the Old West this was the equivalent of a one-stop shop. It had everything from brooms and welcome signs to candles and flags. We walked around slowly, finding the kitschy, eclectic, useless, and mildly-practical all jumbled together in colorful piles.

After a while, we separated, agreeing to meet at the door in five minutes.

Since I didn't see anything that said *Diva*, I used those minutes to browse and marvel at all the junk people bought. Personally, I was a minimalist.

When we met up at the door, neither of us had purchased anything. On to the next place. I had to admit, I was enjoying this game.

A few doors down, we found a combined gift shop and art gallery. Right away we decided to split up, since Danya said she had a feeling she knew what she wanted to get me already, and I'd spotted something for her too.

In the jewelry section, a bright blue gemstone drew my eye. The gem's write-up said it was tourmaline, which local Native Americans prized for use in ornaments. It matched the diva's eyes, and the blurb said it signified the search for love. With the help of the shopkeeper, I found a chain to hang it on and bought both. Never mind that the necklace was way over our agreed-upon price point. I was glad to have discovered a gift that suited Danya so well.

I hung out by the door, waiting for her.

Danya emerged beaming from ear to ear with a large paper bag that was closed at the top with a sticker. "Found yours."

Since we'd both bought our gifts, we spent the rest of the afternoon browsing through the other shops in the area, commenting on art, cooking supplies, clothing, touristy knick-knacks, and antiques.

After a swim at the motel, we dressed and went for an early dinner at our Mexican place.

The diva was wearing her other major wardrobe purchase from when we'd shopped in Mount Pleasant—a skin-tight long-sleeved red mini-dress that reached to a few inches above her knees and showcased her shapely thighs and calves. The color highlighted her flaming hair. It made me ramrod stiff just wrapping my arm around her waist as we walked to the restaurant. I realized, as male and female passersby ogled her, that this might've been the wrong outfit for keeping a low profile. But I was hella proud of her.

We sat beside each other in a booth. Danya had ordered the

tamales, and I'd gotten my usual Mongo Burrito.

She leaned into me as I put my arm around her. "Since we're exchanging gifts, can we get margaritas?"

"Sure."

There was something festive about the evening. When the drinks arrived, we held up our glasses.

Danya toasted, "To surviving."

I laughed. "To surviving."

Clinking glasses, we took sips. Then Danya placed her large bag in front of me. I set my smaller one on the table before her.

"You go first," she invited.

Smiling, I opened my bag and reached in. Soft wool met my fingers. I pulled out an off-white sweater with a zip down the middle and intricate black embroidery on the zip, collar, pockets, and ends of the sleeves.

"It's handmade and hand-embroidered in Mexican wool," she said. "The lady at the shop said a local Mexican artist made it. It's burly, like you, with a little roughness, and a little softness."

"Softness?" My eyebrows lifted.

She laughed. "Well, you *do* have a soft side. It just takes some digging to find."

I squeezed her thigh. "I like it, Diva." I unzipped it and put it on.

Her breath caught. "You look . . . *very* sexy."

I nodded at her small bag. "Now you."

Opening her bag, she gasped. "Oh my God." She pulled out the necklace, holding the gem up to the light. "It's beautiful. What is it?"

I explained the significance of tourmaline.

"Searching for love," she repeated. "It's stunning. Would you put it on me?"

I unclasped it, fastening it around her neck. The chain was

just long enough for the pendant to fall above the neckline of her dress. She looked gorgeous. Granted, she looked gorgeous naked too. "It brings out your eyes."

She flung her arms around me. "I'll only take it off when I swim and sleep."

"I'll wear this instead of my jacket from now on." The sweater was breathable and comfortable and had plenty of pocket space.

As she pulled away, once more I was sorely tempted to kiss her.

But I held back. Just barely.

Since we'd just about exhausted the tourist attractions in Barstow, on Monday we decided to check out of the motel and drive Route 66, or 40, as it was now called, to Albuquerque. It was almost a ten-hour drive, but it was a good day to travel, since it was raining.

I had a few calls to make, so I had Danya pack all our things. Stepping out on the balcony, I first called Gideon to talk about developments on Operation Screw Walter. Then I called a potential client in Chicago who had a job for me in Philly. Finally, I contacted a past client who'd been calling about problems related to a previous job.

When I came back into the bedroom, I found Danya hastily putting one of my burner phones into an outside pocket of one of our bags. It was an old flip phone, the kind I only used for simple calls without video.

My jaw set. "Did you just make a call?"

"No. I was just . . . packing it."

"Give it here." I couldn't believe we were having this conversation again. I thought the diva had learned her lesson by now.

She handed it over. It had died, whether from a long call she'd made, or from previously. I'd been out on the balcony for about an hour, so either was possible.

"Look at me."

She met my eye, swallowing.

"Tell me you didn't make a call."

"I didn't make a call." Her voice was even. Too even? I'd be analyzing her tone for the whole drive to New Mexico.

I stared into her eyes for a full half-minute. She blinked a few times but didn't waver in her gaze.

The problem with this phone wasn't just that it died easily, but that it didn't always keep a log of recent calls. I'd had problems with that in the past when I'd wanted to call clients back.

For now, I decided to believe her. "All right." My eyes swept the room. "You got everything?"

She nodded.

"Let's go."

Chapter Twenty-Six: Danya

We had one last breakfast at our Barstow diner, in which I convinced Caleb to take a picture of *our* booth, the one we'd eaten in since last Thursday morning. I realized then how much I'd miss Barstow.

It was there I'd discovered I was falling in love.

On the one hand, I felt utterly foolish. How many other women had fallen in love with Caleb, when they didn't stand a chance? On the other hand, little glimmers of hope made me think I *did* stand a chance. The smoldering way he'd looked at me Saturday night when we danced. The amazing gift he'd given me. The way he was completely in tune with my body and mind—not just during sex, but when we were together, in public or in private.

Caleb remained cool for most of the drive to Albuquerque. Every time he looked over at me, he seemed to be dissecting my expression to see if I'd told the truth back in Barstow. I didn't know what to say to reassure him.

I was tempted, but I resisted the urge?

I wouldn't violate your trust again, after the punishment you gave me?

I know you're looking out for our best interests, so I defer to your will?

None of these seemed convincing enough. So I kept silent. Or rather, I babbled on about places I loved to go in New York City, hoping we'd find common ground there, since he'd mentioned having gone to the Big Apple a lot.

In the midst of a particularly awkward silence, I said,

"When have I ever lied to you?"

The effect of my words was like magic. His features relaxed, his shoulders lowered, and even his grip on the steering wheel loosened.

"To my knowledge, never."

I let out a breath I hadn't known I'd been holding. "I don't intend to start now."

He nodded, looking over at me with eyes full of calm green flecked with brown. "All right."

In the end, it seemed past deeds were the most effective form of persuasion.

We picked up pizza at a late-night place in Albuquerque, heading to a motel near the highway.

It might've been my imagination, but sex felt different that night.

Caleb kissed his way up my inner thighs, across the line of my pelvis, under the arc of my breasts, along my collarbone, and up my neck. His lovemaking — for that's what it felt like — was languid, sensual, and worshipful. His tongue swirled my nipples before he blew on them, only leaving them to lap at the hollow of my neck. He rolled his tongue down my belly to my navel. From there, he licked the line of my slit from crack to clit. After that, I lost track of what was happening down below, because I was gripping the sheets and trying not to moan too loudly. I knew he was using his fingers, tongue, and lips, but what he was doing became irrelevant once I began to uncoil like a tightly wound spring.

He paused in his ministrations. "Don't come yet."

I breathed deeply, trying to relax and pretend someone had just knocked at the door so as to jar myself out of the zone.

Looking down at Caleb, I wondered what it would be like to call him mine. To see him regularly and know that I was the only woman he wanted. To give him what he needed.

As he met my eyes, the knowing glint in his suggested he'd

read my mind.

After a long moment he continued to suck, pump his fingers, and swipe his tongue over my bundle of nerves. I lolled my head back, giving in to the ecstasy of the sensations.

I could feel my belly quivering and my pussy contracting.

He paused. "Now."

As he attacked my hot center, I exploded, rising off the bed like the girl in *The Exorcist*, with just as much demon in me. I no longer cared who heard me as I roared. The intensity of the pleasure was like no other climax I'd had. He continued to lap at me and plunge his fingers in as I spilled and spilled.

But coming down from my high, I was ready for his dick and for a second charged detonation.

He stroked me slowly, holding my gaze with almost unbearable intensity. I wanted to be eaten alive by him at the same time that I wanted to devour his lips. Power, passion, and fierceness melded in his features and movements, so that I existed only for him and that was more than enough.

"I see you, Diva," he murmured, "and you're breathtaking."

My eyes drooped closed as the rumbles of an orgasm gathered within.

He began to speed up, his cock swelling and biting me more sharply.

"Oh—*oh!*"

As he pulled out, my pussy fluttered in expectation.

"Come, Diva."

He stabbed me, and my orgasm sparked, ignited, and rocketed forth. My mouth opened on a scream as he drove into me, freezing on a downstroke, his neck muscles tensing. Then he thrust more heedlessly, packing it in so I could milk his every last drop. In that moment, gazing into his dark, savage eyes, I knew he possessed me completely.

I was in trouble.

But instead of running away, I ran straight into its jaws.

The rain continued as a drizzle on Tuesday. Caleb and I lay in bed till 10, wandering over to a café across the street for breakfast.

Apart from a few bakery items, the café only served one breakfast—Navajo frybread topped with venison, beans, cheese, lettuce, and salsa. Caleb ordered two of these and two coffees.

The frybread was delicious—fresh, poofy, and satisfying—and the taco mixture tasted incredible. We sat at a small, rickety wood table in a corner, among a dozen patrons who looked like regulars.

"After Albuquerque we should just continue on the old Route Sixty-Six to Tulsa," I suggested. "Then drive from Tulsa to Indianapolis on another day. And Indianapolis to Philly on the last day."

Caleb's brow had creased, and he scrubbed his beard. "I'm still working out what I'll do if we don't yet know who broke into your apartment and called in to quit work for you. Or if we don't know by then that the traffickers have been deterred."

I was flattered that he was confiding in me as he figured this out. "Maybe as we get closer to April second someone will show their hand."

He nodded. "That's what I'm hoping."

For the rest of the afternoon, we lounged around in our room. I read and wrote, and Caleb worked on his laptop and made phone calls out on the balcony. When the rain let up, around 5, it looked as if we could swim in the pool.

Caleb's phone buzzed, and he held up a finger as he slid open the balcony door to go take the call. Meanwhile, I changed out of my clothes into my bikini, pulling shorts and a t-shirt on over it and sliding into my flip-flops. It was about

60 degrees, so my clothes served merely for getting to the pool decently. I planned to spend the entire time in the warm water.

Caleb

Gideon's voice was deeper than usual, which meant he had serious news to share. "Cal, Walter knows we've hacked into his company's system. He had whoever detected us leave a message. It goes, *I know who you are, Caleb Scott. I know you're seeking revenge on behalf of your family for what you think I did to them. I know of Faye and Lucy, and I know where they live.*"

Fuck. I gripped the balcony railing so hard it looked like someone had flayed my fists to expose the knuckles.

My revenge blown to smithereens before I'd really gotten started. My sister and mom in danger. The fixer-kidnapper exposed. Walter triumphing yet again.

Thoughts zinged in my head on the possible ways he could know. He couldn't have found out through a hacker on his end. They wouldn't have been able to identify who'd broken into their system. I'd left no other trace for a PI to unearth. Walter on his own never would've come to this conclusion. He'd always been clueless about the horrors he'd caused my family. And even if he had recognized them, he never would've worked out that Caleb Scott was Callum Furness. Nor would he have connected me up to the hacking.

"There's only one way he could know all this now."

"Danya?" Gideon sounded hesitant, as if he was afraid of offending me. By now he'd figured out that I liked her.

The thought tasted bitter on my tongue. *Liked her.* I needed to expunge that feeling fast. She'd betrayed me to her father, ruining my chances at revenge and endangering Mom and Faye. After I'd done my damnedest to keep her safe. After I'd trusted her and taken her into my confidence. A weight dropped to the bottom of my stomach, squeezing my lungs in the process. She was Daddy's girl after all. Not mine. How could I have believed for a second that a few weeks with me would make a dent in her loyalty to Walter?

"Yeah," I rasped. "She used one of my burners to call him yesterday. She said she didn't. Clearly that was a lie."

"Why would she tell him? I thought she liked you."

"I did too." I felt as if I'd swallowed cyanide. "She must've been biding her time."

Gideon whistled long and low. "I'm sorry, man. That sucks. We can still proceed as planned until we know what he intends."

"His message suggests he plans to keep me from using the evidence by holding his access to Faye and Mom over me."

"Yeah. It does," Gideon agreed. "Well, I doubt he plans to actually go through with anything, because this message would point directly to him if he did. So it's likely a scare tactic."

"I need to think about what to do. I've got to get out of here."

"Go have a beer somewhere. Sharpen your brain."

"I will. Thanks for calling."

I ended the call, pocketing my phone. Now to deal with Danya.

Sliding the door open, I found her lying on her belly on the bed, writing on one of her small pads.

She looked up, her brows bunching. "Everything okay?"

My face must've given me away. "You told Walter everything."

Gaping, she sat up, her eyebrows soaring. "What? I haven't spoken to him."

I shook my head, scraping a hand through my hair as I slumped in a chair. "No use in lying this time, Danya. You've been found out."

"No!" She scrambled off the bed, approaching me with clasped hands. "I'm not lying. I would never lie to you, Caleb."

"What I want to know is why? I thought we were a team." I looked at her warily. *I also thought I was a good judge of character.*

"Tell me why you think I'm lying." Her voice was surprisingly calm.

She must've prepared for this exchange.

A bitter laugh rustled across my lips. "Why should I confide in you again? You've shown how trustworthy you are. How honest, caring, and grateful."

She was probably counting on reporting all this back to Walter when she next got the chance.

"Caleb, please. Listen to me. I never spoke to my father." Panic tinged her voice.

I pushed to my feet wearily. "I'm leaving for a few hours. I need to get some air. Alone."

Her eyes bulged, and she palmed my shirt. "Please don't leave me alone."

I brushed past her. "Isn't this what you wanted when you revealed all my secrets to your father?"

I strode to the door, pausing for a moment to look at the sweater she'd given me, before scooping up my jacket.

Danya

I was too stunned for tears. As the door closed, I blinked at the back of it for a good minute, staring at the *Rules In Case Of A Fire* printed on a laminated paper sticking to it. My legs were frozen to the floor, but my arms were numb, the numbness crawling up to my neck and face. I'd seen Caleb blazing with fury, cold with contempt, shaken with grief, and cool with doubt, but never, till now, had I seen him dry with bitterness. This side of him frightened me, because it suggested he'd given up on me. This time I'd lost his trust for good. The mere idea of my doing something to forfeit his belief in me made my stomach churn.

I didn't know how Caleb had planned to make Dad pay, nor did I need to know. But never in a million years would I have given Caleb away to anyone, let alone Dad. Caleb was in too precarious a position as a fixer and kidnapper. His mom and sister could only remain safe if he kept his two identities separate. And even if I shied away from *hearing* his revenge plans, I still would never deliberately cause them to blow up in smoke. Payback meant too much to Caleb for me to interfere with it.

I had to make Caleb realize this. When he got back, I needed to explain how much his trust and goodwill meant to me. How grateful I was for his protection.

This was the first time in two weeks that he'd left me alone, and it felt unnatural and out of joint. I was his captive, and he'd left without securing me or even locking me in. He'd completely abandoned me. If this was what it would feel like in ten days' time when he released me, then I was in for a lot of suffering.

The room without Caleb in it felt claustrophobic. I couldn't breathe or think straight. Maybe if I went down to the pool, I could stare into the water and make sense of things. Taking a towel and my book, I made my way downstairs and out through the gate to the swimming area. It was completely empty—not surprising, since the rain had only let up a little while ago and it was getting on towards dinnertime.

Though the air was chilly, I stood gazing at the gentle ripples on the surface of the water as the breeze blew across it. Trust was such a fragile thing, so hard to build and so easy to break. Right now, somewhere in the city, Caleb was doubting me and everything I'd told him. Would I be able to convince him I hadn't betrayed him and never would?

Suddenly a gloved hand clapped over my mouth, and something sharp pricked my neck. Blackness rose up and swallowed me.

Caleb

One beer had turned into three, which had turned into several glasses of whiskey. Though I didn't often drink more than one beer, I was no lightweight. But maybe it'd been too long since breakfast, or my gut had twisted a few too many times in the last couple of hours. The whiskey bit my blood like a thousand mosquitoes attacking me at once. Good thing I'd walked to this bar from the motel. I could stumble back after having a few more.

So far a white-bearded man in cowboy boots, three young women, and a motorcycle dude had tried to strike up a conversation with me. After my brief, gruff replies to their questions, they'd eventually gotten the message and shoved off. I needed to think, and I couldn't think with people talking at me.

The blonde barwoman knew better than to talk. She kept me steadily in drink, nodding when she met my eye as I finished off a glass, chatting only with the other customers. She seemed to silently empathize with what I was going through.

Depression was at the top of the heap of emotions. I'd never been depressed in my life. Angry, yes. Hurt, definitely. But having my chances at revenge pulled out from under me like a rug threw me off balance. Anxiety was next in the heap of feelings. This included worry about Mom and Faye, uncertainty about what to do next—something I'd never experienced — and dread for the fallout. Then came anger and resentment at Danya and her father. They both seemed to be laughing at me, crowing that her kidnapping had foiled my plans for vengeance.

Gideon had pointed out that if Walter had been going to hurt Faye or Mom, he wouldn't have blatantly announced his ability to do so. He must be using his knowledge as security against my leaking the evidence of his crimes. I decided to worry about all that when the time came. For now, it sounded as if my mom and sister were okay. I'd called them as soon as I'd left the motel.

I needed to focus on what I *could* do. I could return Danya intact to Walter on the 2nd, collect my pay, and let the two of them worry about break-ins and traffickers. I'd been trying to do too much. That must be why I was suddenly failing right and left. I had to finish this job and move on. Maybe, if I waited, another chance to get revenge on Walter would arise.

I stood, swaying a little. Checking my phone, I saw it was a little after 9.

I slapped a hundred on the bar, asking the barwoman, "Know of a place to eat around here?"

She leaned over the bar. "Across the street. Hank's Texas Barbecue. Get the slow-smoked pork ribs."

"Thanks."

Weaving across the street, I entered the crowded joint, snagging one of the servers and putting in one order of the ribs and one of the pulled pork, with sides of coleslaw, baked beans, and potato salad. I carried all this back to the motel, climbing to the second floor and keying the card in the lock to our room. The lights were off, and all was quiet.

I flicked them on, expecting to find Danya sleeping in the bed. I could immediately tell she wasn't in the room or the bathroom. Her distinct presence was gone. Crossing to the balcony door, I slid it open and leaned out over the railing to see the pool. I couldn't get a full view of it, so I left the room, taking the stairs two at a time, and stalking back through the gate to the poolside.

Though no one was here, a towel I recognized as the one Danya had folded next to her when she'd been lying on the bed earlier suggested she'd been here. I picked it up, catching her scent on it. I looked around, spotting the book she'd been reading on the chaise longue.

Where could she be? I raced back upstairs, confirming that all her things were still in the room. Wherever she'd gone, she hadn't taken anything with her.

There was one more place to check.

I returned downstairs, marching to the front office, which was at the far end of the parking lot.

The same mousy-brown-haired woman stood behind the desk as had checked us in last night.

"Excuse me, I'm missing the woman I came with. Long red hair, five foot seven. She disappeared over the last few hours. Maybe from the poolside. Did you see anyone come or go back there?" I took out a licorice mint and popped it in my mouth.

The woman's eyes bugged out. "Noo. I haven't seen anyone. Jerry was here till about seven. I could call him."

"While you're doing that, can you show me the camera footage starting at around five-fifteen?"

"For the pool?"

"Yeah."

She selected the time on one of the screens and pushed play. Then she called her coworker. I listened to their conversation while I watched the screen.

"Yeah, I think so. But there's a man here says he's missing the woman he came with. Wondered if you saw anyone go back to the pool between, say, five-fifteen and when you left."

She listened, humming. "Oh, I see. Okay. I'll tell him."

When she'd rung off, I said, "What's the story?"

"The repairman for the broken ice machine arrived around five-fifteen, and Jerry had to go help him with that. Took about half an hour. He might've missed something during that window of time."

I held up my hand as somebody came on the screen. Danya entered the pool area, shutting the gate behind her. She laid her things on the chaise longue, and then stood, fully clothed, staring at the pool from the deep end for a few minutes. I watched as two stocky men in ski masks opened the gate without her noticing. They crept up behind her, and one of them covered her mouth with his hand while the other injected her neck with a drug. She crumpled into the first man's arms, and they dragged her out. All within the space of a minute.

Fury coursed through my veins, spiking my heart rate. "Where's your camera for the parking lot?"

The woman flushed. "'Fraid it's on the fritz. Been meaning to fix it for a while now."

FUCK.

Chapter Twenty-Seven: Danya

As I came to, my head felt like a few sandbags had slammed into it. I was woozy, cold, and stiff in every joint. I lay on a dingy carpet in a dark room. The only light came in from the streetlights streaming through two large windows. Ropes bound my ankles and wrists, and I had a cloth gag in my mouth. Now I remembered the hand over my mouth and the needle in my neck. A tremor of fear shot through me.

No time for fear. I have to think.

I sat up, scanning my surroundings. It looked like a motel room with an unused bed and no bags, jackets, or other signs of occupancy. I murmured behind my gag to see if anyone was in here.

No sound.

All kinds of thoughts blazed through my head. I'd been left here and forgotten, to starve and rot in a dingy motel room. Or, worse, this was just a holding spot till I could be taken to where I'd be sexually abused. The thought that once they'd used me this way they'd never let me go made queasiness well up in my gut.

I had to get free while I could.

With great trouble I pushed to my feet, my eyes skittering around the room. If I could find something sharp to rub my wrist ropes against, I might be able to sever them.

I hopped over to the heating-and-air conditioning unit in front of the window. The sharp corner at its base was a possibility. Gazing out the window, I saw I must be about three

269

floors up.

I dropped to my knees, getting to work sawing at the rope using the corner of the vent.

No. This was too soft a corner. I needed something sharper. Desperation made my brain lightning-fast as I scanned the room again.

I rose and lurched over to a sharp-edged fake-wood bedside table that looked fixed to the floor. I was elated to discover that this made a slight dent in my ties.

After moving my wrist ropes back and forth over the table's corner for about ten minutes, I had a kink in my neck and back. I straightened, taking a breather. Then I stood to the other side, bending over in the other direction. Ten minutes later, I looked at the rope. I estimated I'd cut about a thirtieth of its diameter.

At first this slow progress made me despair. Then I realized that one thirtieth was still *one* thirtieth. It was better than nothing. Rather than think about how much time it'd take me to cut through the whole thing, I focused on how lucky I was to have a sharp edge at my disposal, a little time on my own, and no physical pain to fight. So far, they hadn't harmed me, apart from drugging me.

Rolling my shoulders and neck, I set to work again.

While grinding down the rope, I wondered why I'd been left alone. How many people were behind this? What did they plan next for me?

I wasn't sure how much time had passed when I heard voices coming down the hall towards the room. I quickly hopped back to where I'd first woken up, sinking to the floor into a sitting position. I held my wrists against my raised knees to hide the work I'd done.

After a click, the door opened and two men piled into the room, switching on the light. Both muscular, they were only a few inches taller than me, one with dirty blond hair and a mustache, and the other with a red crew cut and freckles.

The blond's eyes landed on me. "Awake, huh?" Crossing the room, he flopped into an armchair by the window, turning on pop music on his phone. "What a day." I'd heard his deep voice somewhere before.

The redhead set a paper bag on the desk, pulling out a six-pack of beer. *Shoot.* They planned to stay awhile.

"Wanna Bud? We've got an hour." The redhead's voice came from the nose. That was when I realized I'd heard both of them on the recording of the two men talking in the bar.

The blond held out his hands, catching the redhead's toss of a beer. He opened the bottle on the edge of the desk, glugging a good amount in one pull. "What's the score?"

"He's meeting us at eleven at a place called The Bitter End." The redhead shot me a look. "He'll check the pictures, and we can turn her over to him tomorrow morning at eight at the same location."

"We should take a few now she's awake and sitting up. In case he makes a stink about not seeing her eyes or something." The blond tipped back his bottle, finishing it. "Throw me another."

The redhead lobbed him another beer. Then he turned and pulled his phone out, holding it up and snapping pictures of me from various angles. "That oughta do it."

"Lemme see."

"Why?"

The blond leered at me. "She's hot."

"She's right there. You can look your fill. Just don't touch."

"The guys who'll touch her are no better than me," the blond argued.

A violent shiver wracked my body. It was all I could do to hold my wrists and legs in position.

"Then pay your way, and you can have a piece." The redhead took a swig of beer. "Your money's as good as theirs."

The blond groaned. "Roddy's charging a hundred grand a pop. Who's got that kind of money?"

The redhead shrugged. "Plenty. Just not us."

Throwing me a lewd look, the blond licked his lips. "We have a whole night before we turn her over. I'm not jerking off."

"Yeah. You are. Cuz business doesn't open till she gets back to Philly."

"No one'll be any the wiser. She's already tied up and gagged. I'll use lube."

The redhead shook his head. "Save it, Ivan. We can hit the strip club tomorrow after we've finished this job."

Please, Ivan. Listen to your friend.

Ivan strode over and crouched down in front of me, brushing hair off my forehead. My pulse shot through the roof as he trailed his fingers along my cheek to my ear. "She's hot as Hades." He grabbed a breast and squeezed it. "I could fuck these titties and come all over her face."

I shivered violently.

His friend shuffled over and smacked his forehead.

"Ow! What the fuck did you do that for?"

"You're a dumbass, that's why. What did I say about not touching her?"

"She likes it, see? Her pupils are dilated."

The redhead scoffed. "From fear, you moron."

Ivan straightened, turning up the music on his phone. "Fine, asshole. We need to get more beers when we go out."

Only once they'd moved away did I let out a breath I hadn't realized I'd been holding.

As they talked and drank, my trembling slowly subsided. At least this time it didn't look as if Ivan was going to rape me.

I swallowed, trying not to think what would happen if I didn't escape. I couldn't think that way.

They stayed for another half-hour, as I guessed, then left the lights on when they went out.

No sooner had the door closed than I stood, shimmying my hips to shake out the cramps. My heart ramped up as I jumped my way over to the bedside table to resume my work on the rope. Now it was pretty clear what they planned to do with me.

But if I could get this rope free, I might be able to escape while they slept.

Caleb

I stomped across the room for the fiftieth time. Nothing to go on. No license plate, no names, no address. No time for guilt or regret over leaving her alone.

The only thing left to do was to call Arnold Black.

I hadn't spoken to him since the Thursday we'd started out on this trip, almost two weeks ago. He'd called a few times at first but had stopped after a while when I didn't call back.

The phone rang a few times before he picked up. "Scott?"

"Do your hired goons have Danya?"

"You don't have her?" His tone conveyed that he was in the dark. But he could be a good actor.

"She was taken about seven hours ago."

"Where are you?"

"Never mind. Do. They. Have her?"

"First of all, I'm offended that you still think I'd have anything to do with trafficking," he huffed. "Second, you haven't contacted me in twelve days. Now you say you've *lost* her?"

I exploded a breath of frustration. "Can you help me or not?"

"Fine. I'll look into this. I have a few contacts who might know something. In the meantime, don't do anything stupid."

"Whoever's responsible for taking her will be feeling pretty stupid soon." I hung up.

Heading back to the balcony, I kicked a bag of barbecue aside. My appetite was long gone, and I was completely sober.

What was the best course of action? To check out and head back to Philly? To wait for her here?

I plonked myself into a chair, propping my head in my hands and leaning my elbows on my knees. I wasn't going to get any sleep tonight anyways. I might as well start out for Philly and drive all night, stopping when I got too tired to be safe.

How the hell had they found us here? We'd ditched them in that Roseville development complex.

Plenty of hours behind the wheel to consider this. It was time to go.

Danya

Ivan and the redhead returned when the clock on the bedside table read 12.29 AM I'd sawed off another chunk of my wrist rope, but when I heard their footsteps, I scurried back to lie down on the floor in my place. Turning on my side and facing the wall, I closed my eyes, pretending to be asleep.

The redhead announced, "Ivan, you're sleeping on the floor in front of the door. I'll take the bed."

"Nuh-uh. If I don't get the bed, you don't either. You can take the chair."

"What kind of sense does that make? How 'bout this? We'll set up the cot so it blocks the door, and you can sleep on that."

"I'll wake you up at four, and we'll switch places," Ivan bargained.

The redhead's nasal laugh ricocheted against the walls.

"Fine. If you're able to get up at four, we'll switch."

I was relieved they didn't bother to check on me. I heard the creak of a cot being opened and Ivan's complaints about how hard it was. Soon they turned off the lights, and not long after, Ivan's bass snore rumbled from the door.

Rolling over, I pushed quietly to my feet. I wished Ivan had been the one sleeping in the bed, since he'd be less likely to hear me chafing away at the bedside table corner. The redhead seemed much the sharper of the two and was probably a light sleeper.

I watched the clock turn to 1 before I shuffled across the carpet towards the table and resumed my work on the rope. I had to saw more gently, because if I went too quickly, I'd likely wake up the redhead.

My heart jumped into my throat when he turned over in his sleep, facing me and stirring. *Please, don't wake up!*

Now that he faced me, my heart rate skyrocketed. Only desperation gave me the courage to continue. That and Ivan's snores, which covered the scratching of the rope against the wood.

Channeling the patience of a mouse, I worked for several hours, stopping every so often to gauge how much of the rope I had left and to stretch out the kinks in my shoulders and back.

At 4:30, only a few rope strands remained.

That was when I heard Ivan stir as if he was going to get up.

Shit!

I dropped down to the floor, rolling over and over till I reached the wall where I'd been lying last night.

Ivan flicked on the light. "Wakey, wakey, Mick. Time to take the cot."

Please don't come check on me! I held my wrists as close together as possible, though the way the rope was abraded, one more minute of sawing would undo it.

I heard them shuffling to switch places. One of them stopped to look down at me on the way. *Don't notice anything!*

Someone—I suspected it must be Ivan—stroked my hair. It took all my concentration not to spasm at his touch.

"At least *she's* getting a sound sleep," Ivan grumbled.

"Back to sleep, Ivan. *No touching.*"

"Fine, jerkface."

After what seemed like forever, they got settled and turned off the light. I waited till their breaths were steady before I hobbled on my knees over to the table.

I had the rope off after a few rubbings.

I'd worry about the gag later.

Now to figure out the complicated knot around my ankles.

Caleb had shown me five or six standard military knots. This one seemed to be a variation on one. I began to undo it, praying I could get free before one of them woke again.

It took me a good half-hour, but at last I'd untied my ankles.

Since there was no question of leaving through the door, I crept to the window, looking out. We were high up, but there was a trellis of sorts at the second-story level and, beneath it, some thick shrubbery. If I could just get down to the trellis, I could say a prayer and jump.

I laid out the rope that had fastened my ankles. It was about six feet long. Using it judiciously, I could just reach.

That was when I got a brainwave. Opening one of the windows and pushing up the outer screen as quietly as possible, I let down the rope, holding one end at the sill. Then I closed the window, clamping the rope firmly in place. I removed my flip-flops, which would only hinder me at this point. I opened the adjacent window, again quietly, shoved up the screen, and grabbed hold of the rope. Then I swung out, holding on for dear life. I hadn't shimmied down a rope since eighth-grade gym class. Luckily I had some upper-body strength from swimming two or three times a week at home. I slid down, aiming my feet for a slightly wider beam in the center of the trellis.

If I missed, I'd go flying to the concrete in front of the motel. My clammy hands started to lose their grip on the rope. I couldn't think about alternatives to making it. I had to land safely.

Taking a few deep breaths, I let go of the rope, landing with one foot on the center beam and the other on a parallel beam. I reached out for the building to steady myself. I was shaking all over, and my heart was sprinting in my chest.

I'd made it!

Take a few more breaths, Danya, before you go leaping again.

I rested like that for a few minutes. Then I balanced myself along the cross slats of the trellis to its very edge, touching the building for support when I needed it.

Oh God, it was such a high fall. The bushes were about three feet tall, and I estimated I had about nine feet to accelerate before hitting them. And they were full of spiky twigs.

I thought of Caleb and pretended he was going to catch me in his arms when I fell.

He'd want me to try. He'd say this was better than getting taken by traffickers.

There was no turning back now.

I jumped.

Caleb

I was somewhere in the Texas Panhandle when it occurred to me that if by some chance Danya broke free of her captors, she'd try to find me again. I was still her best bet for keeping safe at this point. *Fine job you've done of it too, Cal.*

Yeah, I'd been furious at her. Yeah, I'd wanted to punish her by leaving her alone. And yeah, I'd needed to get away from her. But now I was prepared to make a deal with the devil if it'd bring her back to me. My revenge meant nothing compared to sparing her from the horrors of sex trafficking.

"I don't care if I have to do time for this kidnapping, just so long as I find her," I bargained with whatever force out there might be watching over a rogue fixer.

Driving east into the dawn, I realized I no longer suspected Danya of betraying me. Her honest, kind, loyal nature had made far greater an impression on me than the few times she'd sneaked a communication. There had to be another explanation for what had happened to make Walter leave that message for Gideon.

I pulled over to relieve myself by the side of the road, marveling at the humongous sky arching above me and the billions of stars winking from it. Where did they get stars like this? If I ever grew lonely, I could just think of the Texas sky, peopled with intelligent lights watching from their set posts at set times during the night.

I remembered visiting nearby Lubbock, Texas with Clark when I was 17 — one of the violent cities he'd wanted me to experience. We hadn't seen anything remotely resembling violence for our whole three-day visit. In fact, a young man had stopped me and handed me a fifty-dollar bill that had fallen from my wallet when I'd bought a taco from a food truck. And an older lady had invited us to a card party at a neighbor's house, flirting with Clark and telling him he had the prettiest brown eyes she'd ever seen.

Now, climbing back into the car, I decided I'd go only as far as Tulsa, in case Danya was looking for me.

After all, that was the last route she'd planned out for us.

Danya

I landed, stifling a cry as sharp twigs dug into my skin. Thousands of pinpricks of pain lanced my bare arms, legs, and face. But the good news was, testing my limbs, I didn't think I'd broken or sprained anything.

My heart pounded as I realized someone might've heard me thump into the hedge.

I had to keep moving.

Tumbling from the bush, I ran as fast as I could on bare feet. I saw a road up ahead and rejoiced. *Slap, slap slap!* My feet hit the cold asphalt as I sprinted to the roadside. It was only when I'd started gasping for breath that I remembered I had a gag in my mouth.

Maybe some good Samaritan would remove it and save me the trouble of trying to undo the knot.

Reaching the road, I kept running a ways. I didn't care if it was in the wrong direction. I just wanted to get as far from that motel as possible. Still panting, I stopped at last, opting to use my thumb.

Several large trucks thundered by, obviously on a schedule that prevented taking in hitchhikers. I began to shake violently from my congealing sweat and the wind on the highway.

But after about twenty vehicles had passed, a dark-green pickup truck pulled over.

The driver, a round-faced man with a friendly smile and a warm voice, leaned over, opening the window. "Where you headed?" I pointed to my gag, mumbling, and he nodded. "Hop in, and I'll take it off."

I was a little nervous, as I'd never hitchhiked before. I'd only seen it done in movies. But it seemed to fit traveling on the cheap. Not to mention, I was desperate.

"Mmm. This is a stubborn knot. Gimme a sec." I heard a

rustling and a click, and the gag dropped into my lap. He'd cut it!

"Thank you!" I breathed.

"You okay?"

"Now I am."

"Whoever tied that wasn't taking any chances. So where to?"

"Albuquerque. The Motel Six on Route Sixty-Six."

He laughed. "Triple sixes. Should I be afraid?"

"I think tonight the devil was after *me*."

Pulling out, he glanced over a few times. "You're pretty banged up. Don't suppose you wanna talk about it?"

I gazed out the window at the increasingly dense settlements as we approached the city. "I escaped a kidnapping. They planned to hand me over to someone who'd sell me for sex."

A breath hissed through his teeth. "You want me to take you to the police? Hospital?"

"No, no." I needed to find Caleb. "I'll be fine."

His eyes skittered over me again. "Will you be safe where you're going?"

"I don't know. I'm not sure the man I was with will still be at the motel."

"My name's DeShawn, by the way."

I smiled at him. "Danya."

"Danya, where were you two set to travel?"

"To Philly."

"How 'bout, if you don't find him at the motel, I'll drop you a little farther east. I'm going to Amarillo."

DeShawn was so kind, I wanted to fling my arms around him. "Thank you. That would be amazing."

That was when I realized I'd been dripping blood all over his seat. "I'm sorry, but I'll have to clean this for you when we get to the motel."

Chuckling, he waved a hand dismissively. "Don't worry about it. That's what Lysol's for." His brow furrowed. "You look cold. Reach behind your seat and you'll find a jacket."

I pulled out a leather jacket. "I'll get it bloody."

"Keep it. It's a size too small for me, and it never fit. My brother-in-law gave it to me two Christmases ago."

When we reached the motel, DeShawn parked in the lot and waited while I padded to the front office. My heart battered my ribcage, trying to get out. Was Caleb still here?

The same brown-haired woman was at the desk who'd been there last night.

"Excuse me, is Caleb Scott still checked in? I was with him earlier."

Her face expanded like an inflating rubber ball. "Oh my God, you're the lady who disappeared yesterday."

"Yes. Is he here?"

Her gaze danced over my gashes. "No. He checked out a little after midnight."

Shit. "He didn't mention where he was going?"

She shook her head.

Of course he hadn't. This was Caleb, not Mister Rogers.

I closed my eyes tiredly. "Thanks."

Had he wanted to leave me here? Or was he trying to get back to Philly to prevent the worst from happening to me?

I trudged back to DeShawn and opened the passenger door to his truck. "He's gone."

"Did y'all have a route you were following?"

Butterflies sprang up in my chest as I remembered our talk at the café yesterday. Maybe Caleb had recalled it too. At least it was a lead. "Yes! We were going to do Route Sixty-Six as far as Tulsa."

He nodded. "I'll get you to Amarillo. I'm sure you'll find a way to get to Tulsa from there."

I tamped down my anxiety about not finding Caleb once I

got to Tulsa, assuming he had indeed gone there. I'd worry about that when the time came.

I sighed, nestling back into the seat. "Thanks again. This is wonderful of you."

"At your feet there's a bag of energy bars, case you're hungry."

I was more tired than anything. "Can I take a few for the road?"

He flashed a half-grin. "Take some bottles of water too. I work for an energy supplement company, and I can't get rid of the stuff fast enough."

Too wired to sleep, I also wanted to keep DeShawn proper company, since he'd been kind enough to pick me up.

For the next four and a half hours he and I talked about a huge range of subjects. He was really interested in my charity, and from there we got to discussing problems with public education. After that, it came out that his niece was going to cooking school. And so we whiled away the trip to Amarillo, from pre-dawn darkness till 11, when he parked alongside the highway and gave me a plastic bag full of nutrition bars, water bottles, and alcohol wipes for my wounds.

He patted my shoulder. "Get to Philly safely. And good luck finding your man."

"Thank you."

As he rolled off, I said a silent prayer of thanks to the traveling god who'd looked after me so far. Hermes? Mercury? I was sure every culture had a god of travel.

It was too risky a business for travelers not to need someone's protection.

CHAPTER TWENTY-EIGHT: CALEB

I decided to stop at the first motel I saw on the old Route 66 in Tulsa. It was dilapidated as shit, but I wasn't taking any chances at reuniting with Danya. I'd stay here for a day and see if by some miracle she blew in.

After making a flurry of phone calls to people I knew who might have a lead on the traffickers, I came up with nothing helpful.

Unpacking, I inhaled the aromas of her clothes like an addict snorting lines. Her bras and panties, her powder-blue dress, her plaid jumper. That sweet marjoram scent made her even more present than the pictures on my phone, the sweater she'd given me, or the pieces of paper bound with a rubber band that made up her travel journal. She was everywhere. Even in the trashy romance novel she'd snagged from two motels ago. I'd listened to the classical stations all the way from Albuquerque to Tulsa, in hopes that they'd play some Beethoven.

As I lay down on the bed, closing my eyes, I wondered where the diva was now. For the twentieth time, I made my own twisted kind of prayer, offering up something in exchange for her safe return to me.

When I awoke, it was 4:30 PM, and I'd slept three hours. Springing out of bed, I had an idea. It was crazy, but it just might work.

I hoped I wasn't too late.

Danya

Tenzin had a red beat-up Toyota Corolla with a stick shift. He wasn't very talkative, but that suited me, since it'd now been more than 33 hours since I'd slept. I suspected anything that came out of my mouth would be gobbledygook. I'd hitched rides with four people today, joining up with Tenzin outside Oklahoma City. As we approached Tulsa, I crossed all eight fingers in my lap.

We'd just passed a sign for Arnold's Old Fashioned Hamburgers when I saw a motel to our right with a huge white cloth sign that read *Diva* in red letters.

Joy sprang up in my chest. "Stop the car!" I cried.

Tenzin jammed on the brakes. "What's wrong?"

So far he'd proven very calm, but this time I could see I'd riled him a little.

"The man I'm looking for is in the motel back there."

Watching for a break in the traffic, he did a U-turn, driving back. He pulled into the lot. "I'll wait here."

"Thank you."

I jogged into the front office, where a portly man was reading a newspaper. "Hi, how are you?"

"Fine, thanks."

"I'm Diva."

He put down his newspaper, a smile stretching from ear to ear. "You are? It's great to meet you, Diva. You've got someone waiting for you."

"Is it Caleb Scott?"

He checked his logbook. "Sure is. You wanna surprise him?"

I beamed. "Yes. Let me just say goodbye to my ride."

I ran back out and thanked Tenzin for all his help, telling him I'd found the man I was looking for.

"Good."

"Get to Springfield safely," I said. "See you on the road."

Nodding, he put the car in gear and pulled out. I raced back to the office with newfound energy. "Can we go knock on his door?"

The portly man was already pulling keys from his pocket to lock up the front office. "Right this way."

Caleb

From the second-floor balcony I gazed out over a pool filled with people. Danya would wait till all the kids had pissed in it before using it, as long as it meant she had the pool to herself. I smiled, thinking of her auburn waves plastered to her shoulders when she emerged from the water like a mermaid.

A knock sounded at the door. I padded to the keyhole, looking through. Bryan, the guy from the front desk, stood there, looking down at his shoes.

I opened the door.

"Hi, Caleb?" he greeted in his soft voice. "I have a delivery for you."

In a rundown motel outside Tulsa?

I cocked my head, getting ready to pull my gun. "I didn't order anything."

Suddenly, from out of nowhere, the diva leapt into my arms.

"I hope I'm the *Diva* you were looking for," she said into my hair.

Instant relief and joy flooded me. I clung to her as a ship-wrecked survivor clings to wreckage. "The very one."

Looking pleased, Bryan coughed. "Well, I'll leave you folks to it."

"Thanks, Bryan." I let the door fall shut, still holding the diva with her legs wrapped around my waist.

"You're a hard man to find." She pulled back, her eyes scrolling over my features as if she were memorizing them.

"You're an easy woman to catch."

Before I knew it, I was pressing my lips to hers, drinking in their salty, savory taste. Plump, ripe, and firm, they were like cherries in June. My tongue opened them at the seam, delving in to taste more of her. Her tongue responded to mine as if we were dancing. I led, and she followed, and it was smooth and easy to enjoy her. But I wanted more.

Turning us, I walked us over to the bed, tipping her back without breaking our kiss.

A moan rose from her throat as I explored her mouth more fully, rolling my tongue with hers, batting her tip to tip, and teasing her by drawing her out, pulling away, and devouring her in one voracious swipe. I coated her lips with my tongue before diving back in to consume her again. She was hot and full of passion, and I wondered why in hell I hadn't done this before.

When I pulled away, we were both breathless. I dropped more kisses up the ridge of her nose and across her brows, down her cheeks and along her neck.

I tasted caked blood, sweat, and her unique aromas of marjoram and sun-baked rock.

I stood, taking her in. Barefoot, haggard, dirty, and scratched almost beyond recognition, she looked like an earthquake survivor.

She'd never been so beautiful.

"I never spoke to my father." She gazed up at me gravely. "I would never betray you."

Her beauty intensified by the minute. Even if I hadn't come to the same conclusion on my own over the last twenty-four hours, I'd believe her now.

All evidence to the contrary be damned.

I kissed her lips. "I believe you."

"I'm grateful for your protection."

I drank from her lips again. "I know."

"And I feel safer with you than anyone else."

This time my lips crashed into hers, and I pillaged her mouth. I could see getting addicted to this. I began to pull her clothes off—her jacket, shirt, bikini top, shorts, and bikini bottoms. It was all I could do not to ravish her. "Let's get you cleaned up."

She yawned. "Then let's sleep and never wake up."

"When you do wake up, you're not safe from me."

After our shower, but before we took a nap, we went outside and removed the *Diva* sign.

No use in tempting fate.

As we lay in bed later that night after a nap, the diva told me the whole story of her abduction and escape. A batty music teacher named Matilda with a carload of junk had given her a ride from Amarillo to Shamrock. From there to Oklahoma City, she'd ridden with a florist named Athena who was so tall she'd had to cut a hole in the ceiling of her Mazda to drive comfortably.

"Why didn't she just buy a Jeep?" I asked.

"She was very superstitious. She'd inherited the Mazda from her late husband and believed that as soon as she traded it in, bad things would start to happen to her." She rubbed her thumb along my beard, sending tinglings of heat to my groin. "I also had a few near misses. Men who invited me to hop in but who my gut told me weren't safe. One guy looked strung out on something." She twisted to look at me. "Tell me about your call with your friend."

She meant the call with Gideon that had sent me into a tailspin and ultimately separated us.

"First I have to explain how I've been seeking revenge on your father." I told her how Gideon—I didn't name him—had been hacking into the records of Walter's company and finding evidence of his various crimes. I explained how I'd orchestrated the sale of GenRev's skin treatment to the biotech startup. Then I quoted the message Walter had embedded in one of the hacked files for Gideon to find and relay back to me.

She propped her head on her hand. "You realize what it means that I didn't tell my father anything, right?"

"What?"

"It means he still doesn't know who my kidnapper is. That message was just a separate occurrence that had nothing to do with the kidnapping."

I cupped a breast, squeezing it. "That's true." I was grateful at least one cover wasn't blown.

She nuzzled my neck. "I can't believe he would mention knowing where Faye and your mom live. I feel as if I don't know my father at all. As if all these years he's been hiding behind a façade of decency while acting like a rat."

After that night in Nevada City when she'd been so compassionate about my family's sufferings at the hands of her father, I should've known she wouldn't reveal my identity or my family to Walter. Her actions so far had all pointed towards trustworthiness, honesty, and loyalty.

"While driving here, I decided I'm going to dig up different damning evidence against your father. I'll talk to people directly." Never mind that I wasn't very good at that sort of thing.

She twined a leg around mine. "And if you can get Faye and Lucy to move in with you, that'll take care of the other problem."

Her optimism infected me, inspiring me with more hope.

Grabbing her hips, I pulled her on top of me, poising her at my tip and lancing her with my dick. She laughed as I controlled her from the bottom.

Until she couldn't laugh anymore.

The next morning we were both famished, as neither of us had eaten a solid meal for two days. I drove us into town, where we found an all-day breakfast café overlooking the river. Over biscuits, roasted potatoes, gravy, sausages, and poached eggs, we decided to spend a few days in Tulsa. On Sunday, we could move on to Indianapolis and stay there till next Thursday, when we'd drive to Philly. Gideon had offered to put us up on Thursday and Friday night. By Saturday morning, April 2nd, when the handover was scheduled to take place, I hoped to have enough leads to return Danya in good conscience.

Gideon and I had been to hell and back together, like Aeneas and Achates, a story Dad was fond of telling from Virgil. There was no way Gideon could ever be the leak to Walter. I'd gotten him out of several jams when he was first starting out as a hacker, and he'd returned the favor several times over the twelve years we'd known each other. Besides always having my back, Gideon had zero motives for getting me in trouble. I provided a lot of business for him. His secrets were mine, and vice versa.

I still hadn't heard from Arnold Black, which either meant he was still working on finding out about the traffickers, or he was letting them follow us in hopes of nabbing Danya again. There was no reason to think if they'd tracked us in Albuquerque they wouldn't be able to track us here in Tulsa.

We spent the rest of the day at the Tulsa zoo, where I never took my hand off the diva. I told myself I was just protecting her, but possessive pride played a part too. In her lilac skirt and white blouse that flared at the hips she looked classically feminine. When I took her picture in front of the grizzly bears, the photo was more for me than her. We watched rhinos, penguins, leopards, giraffes, iguanas, and parrots bathe, feed, and exercise. But I knew I'd remember best watching her appreciate the animals.

After the zoo, to celebrate our reunion, I surprised her by taking her to a nice Creole restaurant. I knew she liked simple stuff, but for once I wanted to spoil her.

For starters, we ordered fried alligator, crawfish remoulade, and a cup of gumbo, and for entrées, we ordered shrimp étouffée and jambalaya.

"This place *knows* their New Orleans cuisine!" Danya exclaimed after swallowing a spoonful of gumbo.

"You've been to New Orleans?" I crunched a piece of fried alligator.

"Once, when I was eight, with Mom." She sipped her Sazerac, which our waitress had recommended as the original New Orleans cocktail.

I'd stuck to beer, since I was driving. "Clark took me there when I was seventeen, as part of his violent cities tour."

"What were your impressions?"

I shook my head. "That city is way too vibrant to reduce to crime statistics. The history, the people, the music, the food . . . "

"That's what I remember too." Sighing, the diva laid a hand on her belly. "Its cuisine is my new favorite."

When we left the restaurant, I scanned our surroundings for hints of anyone following us. My shoulders relaxed, as no one and nothing stood out. Danya looped an arm in mine. Walking south along a greenway, we traversed the city, skirting a massive riverfront park that seemed to be the equivalent of Tulsa's Central Park.

"Can we come back tomorrow when it's open?" she asked as we stood in front of a sign listing the opening hours for the Gathering Place.

I gathered her in my arms, guiding her face to mine. "If you like." I brushed my lips to hers, catching whiffs of the anise in her cocktail and smiling. My old favorite flavor lacing the diva's tongue, my new favorite. Unable to rein in my hunger anymore, I caught her bottom lip in my teeth and bit down.

She moaned, braiding her fingers through my hair. "I thought you didn't kiss."

"Every rule has its exceptions." Sucking her tongue, I began to fuck her mouth with my tongue. Tenderness flew out the window, and insatiability took its place. I couldn't get enough of her smell and taste, her diva-ness.

When our lips separated, she looked drunk. Her eyes were glazed-over, her lips swollen, and her cheeks flushed. "What makes me an exception?"

I brushed her hair behind her ear. "I don't know."

Despite my unsatisfying answer, a quiet smile unfolded across her lips.

Danya

On Friday, Caleb and I visited the Philbrook Museum of Art and the Gathering Place. Caleb's tastes in art aligned with his literary tastes—he enjoyed American artists of the nineteenth and twentieth centuries. After the museum, before driving to the Gathering Place, we stopped at an outdoor market, buying salads and sandwiches.

While picnicking on a lawn beside a pond, we saw people rowing boats on the water.

"Let's rent one!" I proposed.

Stuffing our plastic containers into a paper bag, he crooked a wry smile. "What do you think this is, *The Notebook*?"

Rising on my knees, I scooted towards him on the grass, cupping his face with my hands. "How do you know that film, Caleb Scott?"

A blush crept into his cheeks. "Faye. It's one of her

favorites."

"Hmm. Seems suspicious you should recall it now."

Grabbing my wrists, he pinned them behind my back, taking me in a searing kiss. He kissed as if years of pent-up kisses were being unleashed. Before I knew it, I was on my back, and he hovered over me, caging me in with his arms.

I loved him. Yes, I did. Foolish me, but it was the truth, and I couldn't deny it. Driven, badass, forceful Caleb. Going above and beyond the call of duty to protect me. Giving everything he had at every minute to get us safely back to Philly. Solving the problems we faced like simple math equations. Making love to me as if my body were his instrument. A lone wolf whose wolfish kisses made me swoon.

"I just saved us a rowboat ride by cutting to the chase." He caught my top lip in his teeth and pulled.

"You're not very romantic, are you?"

"Romance, for me, is eating you out till you scream."

"I don't think sex counts as romance." I rose up to meet his tongue with mine, but he pulled back.

"Why not? You're giving to the other person. Your thoughts are full of them. You're deferring your own gratification for their pleasure. What could be more romantic?"

My heart sank. "You have a lot of experience with that sort of romance?"

His eyes were almost completely forest-green edged with brown. "Only one girlfriend in my past."

"But other women?"

He smiled. "Of course, Diva. But none were romantic attachments."

"And I am?" I held my breath.

His eyes skipped between mine before dipping to my lips. "You're as close as I've come in eight years."

Woww! I did an inner fist pump. I wouldn't say anything more, not wanting to ruin this moment. But later I'd dissect everything about his expression and tone as he'd said those words.

He painted my lips with his tongue, inserting it so our tongues coiled and meshed.

I was in heaven.

But for how long?

We spent Saturday at a museum devoted to art of the American West and Native American artifacts and artwork. Its gardens were full of intriguing statues and trails running alongside a turtle pond.

After a Mexican dinner, we went to an outdoor country music concert in a park. Caleb bought us beers, and we sat on his sweater and the jacket I'd acquired from DeShawn. Since every love lyric made me think of Caleb and there were a lot of these, it was all I could do not to stare at him the whole evening. Eventually, as it got cooler, I slipped his jacket on, inhaling its musky, Caleb-y aromas.

When the band took a break, three young women in Daisy Dukes and crop tops strutted over to us, laughing amongst themselves.

One tossed her long brown waves, batting her eyelashes at Caleb. "You look like you could use another drink. I'm Sam."

Her friend, a blonde, thrust a Solo cup out to Caleb. "I'm Megan. Here's the beer that cost eight dollars."

Their third friend, an athletic black-haired woman with a pixie cut, nudged Megan in the shoulder so the beer spilled. "It's the ale. The local one."

Megan rolled her eyes. "There're like four of them, Erica."

Erica knotted her arms over her chest. "Four local beers? Or four beers on offer here?"

Caleb spared Megan having to work out an answer to that question. "Thanks, but I'll get my own."

"No, here!" As Megan bent over to place it on the lawn next

to Caleb, her large breasts spilled out of her knotted top. "I tried it. It's not too bitter."

Sam struck the classic pin-up pose, jutting out a hip, gathering her hair high with her arms bent behind her head, and puckering her lips as she thrust out her chest. "We're going on to a club after this, if you wanna join us."

Erica nudged her chin in my direction. "You can even bring Ginger. If you want."

If you must was what she meant to say.

I couldn't believe the nerve of these women. Acting as if I weren't even here as they tried to pick up Caleb in the most blatant ways I'd ever seen.

He coiled an arm around me, pulling me close and kissing my temple. I could feel the lust oozing from the three women as they watched his movements. "Thanks for the offer, but I have all I need right here."

Angling my face to his, he kissed me passionately, as if we were in our own little world. A direct line of warmth and wetness sluiced through me to the fire beating at my core.

When our lips parted, I was surprised to see that the three women were still standing there with slack mouths and rounded eyes.

Erica seemed the first to realize their campaign was over with. She straightened. "Well, enjoy the rest of the concert. Come on, Meg, Sam."

When they'd trooped off, Caleb raised the beer in the Solo cup to his nose, sniffing.

That was when I realized—he suspected they'd drugged his drink.

"Do you smell anything?"

"No. But that doesn't mean it's not spiked." He poured it out on the lawn.

A white lab trotted over and started lapping it up.

"Hey! Apple! Get back here. Now," a man's voice called

from a picnicking group near us.

Apple raised his head and loped back to his master.

"I didn't know dogs drank beer," I puzzled.

"Some. There's a guy I know in South Philly whose dog gets drunk on beer at the bar every Saturday night. They put out a dish specially for him."

"Do you think those women were hired by the men who took me?" I sat back on my heels.

"Maybe. A twenty each would do the job for women like that."

I shivered. "Then, once you were out cold, they'd try again?"

"No doubt."

"Why not just take Sam, Megan, and Erica?"

His gaze delved to the depths of mine. "That's what I'm trying to figure out."

CHAPTER TWENTY-NINE: CALEB

The nine-and-a-half-hour drive on Sunday to Indianapolis was interesting only as far as St. Louis. The next three and a half hours were monotonous and flat, full of farm fields and none of the fascinating hills and trees I'd grown used to while traveling in the West. But to save time I'd opted to take 70 instead of a less direct route that might've been more scenic.

Yet Danya made the day fun with The Radio Game, as she called it. She rolled two dice we'd found at one of the motels. Depending on the number, she'd surf among twelve radio stations with different kinds of music. The first person to name the tune being played on that station got a point. If neither of us knew it, we moved on. I had oldies, classic country, and country locked down. She cornered classic hits, easy listening, and the college station, which was playing jazz and folk that afternoon. The other six stations she'd selected were hit or miss for both of us — top 40, adult contemporary, contemporary Christian, classical, Latin, and gospel. By the time we stopped for gas near Terre Haute, I'd won by four points.

"You learn so much about places from their radio stations," she observed.

"Like what?" I offered her a licorice mint across the console, and she took one.

"Their values, the stories they tell about themselves, their lifestyle. I'd guess, from listening to these stations, that the area we've passed through is more rural than urban. Not just from the kinds of music, but their presentation."

"Wouldn't you learn even more by listening to talk radio?"

She tilted her head. "I don't think so. A song is worth a thousand words. And it represents thousands of listeners."

We found a motel on the eastern outskirts of Indy, so we'd have less driving on Thursday. After eating burritos we'd gotten to go from a Mexican restaurant near the highway, we swam in the pool. Standing to one side, I watched her do the crawl up and down for a while. Then she swam over and hooked herself around me like a koala.

Her scratches from Albuquerque were healing, but there was still a large one along her jaw that served to remind me how I'd failed her, though it heightened her beauty. I ran my thumb along it now.

"Are you sick of motels and pools?" She nuzzled her nose to mine.

My dick swelled in my swim shorts. "That's like asking an Old-West cowboy if he's sick of pork and beans. It's what we have to work with."

Her laugh sent another kick of heat to my groin. "We've both got cowboys on the brain from the museum yesterday." Then she grew serious. "I had an idea. What if we called Dad tomorrow, and I spoke to him. I'd ask him whether the police found out anything about who broke into my apartment."

I cupped her chin. "Only if you stick to scripted questions. Don't veer off from what you show me beforehand."

Her luminous eyes looked into mine unwaveringly. "I won't. I'll write them out when we get inside."

I moved her hips from side to side over my rigid length. "No, you'll write them out after I fuck you."

Putting the call through to Walter, I turned the phone to face the diva, who sat in an armchair in our room.

"Danya! You're not tied up or gagged. Where are you?" Walter opened.

"I'm with my kidnapper. He's allowed me to call you so I

could ask you a few questions."

"It sounds as if you're on good terms with him now."

Danya stuck to the script. "He let me do this in the interests of delivering me safely back to you. If the people who broke into my apartment are coming after me, then there's no guarantee that I won't just be taken again."

Walter chuffed a dry laugh. "He's a very considerate kidnapper, I must say. What's his name, Dani?"

Danya ignored his question. "Do the police have any leads on who broke in?"

"They've caught the perpetrator." There was a rustle as he looked through some papers. "Name of Heinz. Bill Heinz."

Danya moistened her lips. "Please tell me everything they found out."

"The man was arrested for identity theft in the past, so he was in their system," Walter relayed. "Heinz stole your identity by hacking into one of your credit cards. Apparently he was even able to hack your phone when you used an unsecured Wi-Fi network. He took samples of your voice and quit your job for you."

"Why would he do that?" Danya's jaw had dropped.

"To scare you. He had planned to blackmail you by stealing your identity. Then apparently he found out you were my daughter and he decided to kidnap you. He broke into your apartment hoping to take you. When he found it empty, he ransacked it to scare you and me. He looked for more information to hold over you—your driver's license, your credit cards, your bank statement, and so forth. Then he left a note to scare us both further."

"What did the note say?" Danya queried.

"It was addressed to me and said he'd be back. He'd decided to negotiate with me for much more money than he could've gotten from you."

"How did they catch him?"

"He was filmed on the apartment cameras coming and going in broad daylight." Walter cleared his throat. "Now, Dani, tell me who your kidnapper is. You could save me fifteen million."

"That's all I wanted to ask you, Dad. I'll say goodbye now." I ended the call.

Danya was shaking her head. "He really only sees the money in all this. The losses that he and his company could suffer."

"It looks as if the vote of the board will go his way on Friday and he'll get to take over SciPulse."

The diva stood, coming over and wrapping her arms around me. "You'll find a way to make him regret what he did."

I avoided thinking of my own losses in the revenge department, instead focusing on the good that had come out of that call. "At least we know who broke into your apartment. Now we have to make sure the traffickers aren't after you anymore."

"If you return me late because of this, will you still get paid?"

"Oh, I'll get paid."

The diva and I spent the next few days doing touristy things in Indianapolis—a museum devoted to American Indian art, a museum of Western art, a couple of monuments, and a state park where we hiked all afternoon on Wednesday. I took more pictures of her, way more than I should've. But as the possible return date approached, I realized this would be all I had of the diva come Saturday.

On Wednesday evening, as Danya and I were getting dressed to go to dinner, Black called.

Stepping out onto the balcony, I slid the door shut. "What's the deal?"

I was prepared to hear his words from two angles—one that treated him as guilty, and the other that allowed for him to be telling the truth.

"Someone hacked into my secure line and overheard you and me talking a few times. He offered the information on the kidnapping to a guy named Roddy Stensen, who works with Vic Amargulo. The two deal in flesh. They figured they'd get in on the action. I found this out through a man I know who knows them, Abe Weiser. I can put you in touch with him so you can confirm what I'm telling you."

"Do they know you found them?" I leaned back against the railing.

"Yeah. I talked to Roddy yesterday and told him I had enough evidence to close down his entire operation. I said we knew his men took Danya, warning him we'd take action if he didn't release her. He said she'd already escaped near Albuquerque. Did you find her?"

"Yeah."

"Good. I told him to call off his hired men immediately, who apparently were in Tulsa. He promised he would."

"Give me Roddy's number."

"Abe's won't be enough?"

"I want it from the horse's mouth."

"All right." He paused. "Here you go." He texted me the number. "I'll see you on Saturday at noon at the fountain?"

"If everything checks out with Stensen."

Soon after that, we rang off.

Danya

Caleb came in from the balcony looking thoughtful.

"Everything good?" I stood in front of him with the necklace he'd given me, so he could fasten it around my neck.

He moved my hair to one shoulder, clasping the chain at my nape. "It would seem the men hired by the traffickers have been called off our tail."

"Oh?"

He told me the gist of the conversations he'd had with his client and the man named Roddy whom Mick and Ivan had mentioned in the bar.

"This means I'll be returning you to Walter on Saturday morning at ten."

I should've been relieved. But now that my return was imminent, I felt only dismay and sadness. It was like being told schools had opened again after a snow day.

Caleb and I were heading back to Philly at last, after three weeks on the road.

That same dull ache throbbed in the pit of my stomach that had appeared before whenever I'd contemplated Caleb leaving me.

Logically I knew this wasn't a tenable long-term lifestyle, staying on the road with him. But many times on our trip I'd pictured us driving around for another six months or so while I built my blog and wrote up our experiences.

"Oh. That's great," I croaked.

As he stood behind me, his hands roved the curves of my red mini-dress, rounding my breasts, waist, and hips. "I plan to make the most of our last three nights together."

His fingers traced light circles over my crotch before he cupped it.

As if summoned by him, my pussy gushed, and I ground my rear into his bulge. "Please."

He threw me face down on the bed, hiking my dress up to my waist and wrenching my panties down my legs. I heard the click of his belt and the swish of his pants and boxer briefs.

Pulling me so I hinged at the hips over the bed's edge, he bent over and growled in my ear, "On our last night I'm going to light this ass up."

I tried not to hear the first part of his declaration. I wanted him forever to be commanding me, controlling me, possessing me. He was the Werewolf, he was my kidnapper, and he was Caleb. I would always belong to him.

In one thrust he stabbed my sheath, and already my pleasure welled like a geyser from deep within me. Several strokes later, I felt it surfacing.

All his intoxicating aromas surrounded me — wine-soaked wood, anise, and his musky sweat. His heat was like the corona of the sun.

He held my hips steady, easing out. "Come."

Slamming in, he activated the surge of rapture waiting to burst forth. His groans filling the air drew out my bliss, and our hips continued to rock as a unit till our release had subsided.

He withdrew, pulling me to a standing position and swatting me on one ass cheek. "Don't wear panties to the restaurant."

Caleb seemed unfazed by the fact that we were parting in two and a half days. In fact, he acted pretty upbeat. I'd spent the meal swirling my soup around with my spoon, while he'd wolfed down his burger and fries. After I'd been silent for a while, he'd asked our waitress to tune the TV to soccer and had watched the women's match for the rest of dinner. When he'd gotten up to use the restroom, he'd been whistling.

He'd turned back and said, "No need to come with me this time, Diva."

He must be delighted that this long, hard job was nearly over. He was about to become rich — and deservedly so, after everything he'd been through on my behalf. He was about to have his much-prized independence back again, his routine, and his family.

And I was happy for him.

But the cold fist of dread squeezed my chest as I thought of what lay ahead for me.

Caleb

We arrived at Gideon's at 8:30 on Thursday. He pulled Danya into a bear hug and kissed her cheek as if they'd known each other since childhood. Typical Gideon. He was very responsive to human touch.

I saw he'd closed the door to his office and likely put the rest of his computers in there too, since his living room was usually cluttered with electronics. As far as Danya knew, Gideon was just a friend of twelve years. Not a much-sought-after, much-hunted hacker.

"Danya, do you drink white wine?" he asked.

"I do."

"Lemme get you guys some drinks. Come on into the kitchen."

Gideon's kitchen, like the rest of his place, was riddled with a chaotic assemblage of things that should've been elsewhere — or in a garbage heap. A folded-up camping chair stood next to a telescope where people usually kept their brooms, beside the refrigerator. A dusty, empty aquarium, a globe of the world, and a backgammon set crowded the counter where cooking prep normally took place. An old-style rolodex filled with contacts, a red boule ball, and a motherboard filled a plate on the small center island where most people had a dish of fruit.

Gideon handed me a beer and Danya a glass of wine, and we all took seats on the barstools at his island.

"Where the hell do you cook?" I gulped my beer, glad not to be driving anymore.

He hitched a shoulder. "I cook once in a blue moon. The Chinese restaurant down the block keeps me alive most days." He turned to Danya. "I heard you're a travel writer."

A shy smile illuminated her face. "Yeah. I'm hoping to get a blog underway."

"Nice. You using WordPress, Blogger, or something else?"

"WordPress."

He nodded. "Good choice. It's got a ton of free plug-ins."

"You're an IT consultant?"

He coughed. "Yeah, that's right."

"Well, maybe I can hire you if I need help with the site?"

Gideon whipped out a card from his shirt pocket, handing it to Danya. "It doesn't say what I do, but it has all my contact info."

Examining it, the diva smiled. "Thanks."

I scrolled through my phone, looking for the Middle Eastern restaurant near here. "I'll order us some food."

Half an hour later, our takeout bags arrived, and I set them on the island.

Gideon and Danya helped serve everything onto plates.

"Did you meet Ginnie's parents?" I dipped a falafel in white sauce.

"Yeah. They're cool." Gideon swallowed some grilled fish. "Their house is right on a lake, so we did some boating and fishing."

"I'd never have guessed Ginnie came from such a remote area." I thought of how outgoing and at home in the city she was.

"Me neither. She must've been escaping her origins when she fled to Philly."

"Where is she from?" Danya sipped her wine.

"Rangeley, in western Maine."

"Oh, my stepmom's first-cousin-once-removed lives up

there, near the Quebec border. In the proverbial cabin in the woods." Danya cut up a piece of lamb, turning to me. "I told you about him. The serious man who lost his mother to Alzheimer's. Eve says he uses a generator, septic tank, and rain catcher. He basically lives off the grid."

"Can you imagine what that'd be like?" Gideon stabbed a piece of chicken, holding it up. "Raising your own goats, chickens, and vegetables? Only making a pit stop into town for the occasional bag of sugar or flour? Cooking everything on the woodstove that heats your house?"

She smiled. "Yeah, apparently he was escaping in the other direction. From the urban rat race of Philly to the peaceful rural existence of Maine."

Gideon gulped his beer. "You guys have been away from the rat race for a while. Tell me some stories from the road."

Danya smiled. "We played *lots* of pool games."

I tipped back my beer. "And watched a few horror movies."

"We hiked for a day near Indianapolis."

"We did a shit-ton of touristy things."

"And shopping," she added. "And eating local stuff."

The diva told him about the three women who'd tried to pick me up and drug me in Tulsa. I told about the paparazzi and the tire sabotage in Nevada City, followed by the car chase in Roseville. Then she related her escape from the traffickers in Albuquerque.

Gideon's jaw slackened. "*Damn*. You've been through some serious shit. Are you putting all this in your blog?"

Danya shook her head. "I'm just describing the parts that have nothing to do with kidnapping or trafficking. And I'll wait awhile to publish even those."

"You must be looking forward to getting back to your life again." Gideon split a look between Danya and me.

The diva's brow creased. "I'll be glad to see my stepbrother and stepmom again." She looked across at me. "Maybe not so much my father."

I smiled at her. "No more pork and beans."

A wistful smile curved her lips. "No more pork and beans."

Was I looking forward to getting back to my life? I dipped pita bread in baba ghanouj. I'd resume my exercise routine. I'd see Mom and Faye. I had some interesting jobs lined up in upcoming weeks. And it'd be nice to sleep in my own bed again. So yeah, it should be good to return to normal.

"You guys are gonna stay in touch, right?" Gideon double-dipped a radish in hummus.

I shook my head. "First rule of being a fixer—never bring a job home with you. Second rule—never bring home to the job."

Gideon waved a dismissive hand. "Egh. Rules like that are meant to be broken. You have a friend—me. You've got a family—Clark, Lucy, and Faye. You've managed with us till now. You may have met Danya under unusual circumstances, but why can't you continue seeing her?"

As the diva's eyes ping-ponged between me and Gideon, hope leapt in them.

She *wanted* to continue seeing me. It was written all over her face.

Too bad I had to put the kibosh on that. The last thing I wanted was a reprise of Gillian. Or to have one more woman to worry about when it came to enemies like Walter. Or to have the diva constantly reminding me—in her trusting outlook, forgiving spirit, and gentle presence—that my violent, lawless job was more parasitic than symbiotic to much of society.

No, I had only let myself kiss Danya for the rest of the trip after reuniting with her in Tulsa because I'd known I had a finite amount of time left with her. I'd known the kissing couldn't lead to anything serious. She was part of a job, and when that job ended, so did our time together.

"She has her life, I have mine, and never the twain shall meet." I finished my beer. "This was a job, not a dating show. We found a way to get along out of necessity. Now that it's over, we'll say our goodbyes like honorably discharged soldiers who've fought together but fully intend to leave their connection behind them."

It was brutal, but it had to be said. I couldn't leave Danya hoping and longing for things that would never be. Maybe just now I'd falsified the last month by making it sound as if the diva and I didn't get along, but after all, kidnapping and vacation modes were one thing, and real life something completely different.

She looked as if I'd socked her in the solar plexus. Paling, she swallowed a few times before reaching for her wine and downing the rest of it in one gulp.

Gideon poured her some more before heading to the fridge and taking out more beers. "You know what your problem is, man?"

I accepted another bottle of beer from him. "No, but I have a feeling you're about to tell me."

"You're too goddamn practical." He held up his bottle, poising its mouth at his lips. "The whole time I've known you you've never really let loose and had fun. I mean, sure, on Saturday nights at Finney's. But that's just Saturday nights with me and my weirdo friends. The closest thing I've seen to you letting your hair down was this trip. You guys were playing pool games, watching movies, hiking, visiting tourist attractions, eating local food, shopping."

Taking a swig of beer, he set it down and snagged a shish kebab, brandishing it. "It took me the longest time to get up the courage to ask Ginnie out. But when I did, I wondered why in hell I hadn't done it sooner. We laugh and have fun, we fight, and we drag each other to the films we like and the other person hates. Then we fuck and do it all over again." He grinned. "So all I'm saying is, you gotta recognize a good relationship before it passes you by. It's never perfect, but then, nothing is."

I sat back in my stool. "You just contradicted yourself. You started out by saying a relationship is about being impractical. And you ended up saying you have to be practical about relationships."

Danya shook her head. "I think Gideon meant that a light heart and a willingness to have fun are the basis for a good relationship."

He pointed his fork at her. "Bingo. So you gotta ask yourself, Cal, do you have a place in your life for having fun on the regular? For laughing sometimes, instead of always fixing other people's problems? For being romantic instead of laser-focused on goals?"

Anger flared in my chest. I snorted, standing to take my plate to the sink. "Spoken like someone who doesn't know what my profession requires. *On the regular*? There's nothing regular about my times or jobs. *Laughing*? I laugh plenty when I want to, often while *fixing other people's problems*. And no, I don't see myself losing my laser focus on goals anytime soon. In my career, that'd be suicide. Save your speech for a nine-to-five accountant whose highest ambition is to have a white-picket fence, a wife, and three kids."

Dumping my plate in the sink, I took my beer to the living room and flopped onto the couch, very much done with the conversation. I switched the TV on to a Costa Rica—US soccer match.

Inside, I fumed, thinking of Gideon's critique. That I didn't know how to have fun or laugh. That I had tunnel vision. That I wasn't romantic. Okay, maybe I'd cop to the last. At least, going by the conventional views of romance. But that was the problem with relationships. Those who were in them tried to conform to social dictates. Valentine's Day dinners, anniversary jewelry, three-hundred-guest weddings. On and on till you croaked. And in between, there was no time to live the way you wanted to live.

Danya and Gideon remained in the kitchen talking for a while.

Finally, I rose, stretching. "Diva. Time for bed."

Breaking off what she was saying, she turned. "Gideon and I are in the middle of something."

I arched an eyebrow. "You want to test me?"

She hesitated, her eyes sliding to the side. Then she climbed down from her stool, taking her plate to the sink. "Can we continue this tomorrow, Gideon?"

He shrugged. "No problem. If you guys need anything, let me know."

Danya looked nervous as she joined me to find our bedroom.

As well she should be.

CHAPTER THIRTY: DANYA

He pushed the door closed, flicking on a lamp. The gleam in his tiger eyes and his kingly stance made me wonder why I'd ever dared to question him.

"Face me."

I turned, struggling to meet his glinting eyes.

"Who's in charge, Diva?"

"You," I croaked.

"Did you think that had changed because we'd returned to Philly?"

"No."

He rolled up his sleeves, exposing his forearms. "What was rule number one?"

"As long as I'm in your care, I obey you without question."

"And if you don't?"

I swallowed. "I should expect punishment."

As he took a step towards me, his muscles bunching beneath his clothes reminded me of the leopard we'd seen in the Tulsa zoo, crouching to leap for the bone hanging in the tree.

"Stand facing the bed."

Padding to the bed, I stood waiting. My heart palpitated, and warmth spread up my thighs. What was in store for me this time?

Yet I welcomed anything he gave me. For these were our last days together. Who knew if I'd ever see him again?

I heard a rustle as he handled one of our bags, and his steps as he approached from behind. Unbuttoning my skirt, he unzipped it and slid it down my legs. Then he peeled my panties off. The drag of his palms over my naked hips made my channel slick.

Sitting on the bed, he laid me facedown over one knee so my torso rested on the mattress and my hips hinged between his legs.

He kneaded my buttocks, slapping them lightly and rubbing them. Then his palm came crashing down on one cheek, making me jump and cry. Warmth bloomed around the place of impact, spreading through my center and seeping up my spine.

He cracked his hand against the same cheek once, twice, three times, before soothing the sting with the heel of his palm. With hardly a rest, his hand slammed down on my other buttock, lighting me on fire with a barrage of slaps. When my legs jerked up to escape the onslaught, he penned me in with his outside thigh, holding down my back.

After a while, I not only grew used to the pain, but longed for more.

Of course, that was when he stopped.

I badly needed release from the throbbing in my sex.

He gathered my copious leakage on his fingers, screwing them into my tight hole. Then he laid me on the bed in the child's pose, my ass in the air. His belt clinked, his zipper rolled down, and his clothes rustled. The pop of a cap sounded, and his fingers worked cold lube into my rear passage.

Oh boy. Here we go. I was nervous. He had a large dick, and that hole was very small.

"Breathe in and out, Diva."

I did so. On my exhale, he eased his tip through my hole.

"Breathe again."

As I breathed deeply, he worked his shaft into me, inch by inch, till I felt so filled I thought I'd burst.

Groaning, I relaxed into the invasive sensation. He rose up

and sank into me again, filling and emptying me. Now that I knew it was possible to hold him, I wanted more. Pushing back into him as he packed me, I relished the sparks flying from every nerve he touched along the way.

"That's right, Diva. Give me every inch of your tight ass." He manhandled my hips so I was nothing but a vessel to receive his cock at the rate he chose to give it.

Strange stirrings I'd never felt before were at work inside me. Pleasurable, not painful.

"Oh, *ohh!*"

He sped up his thrusts, acclimating me fully to his girth.

Then he pulled out, holding his tip at my entrance and plunging to the bottom. With a scream I came unraveled like a ball of twine, spooling outwards and spinning, spinning till nothing remained of my core. It was torturous, unholy bliss, coating every cell in my body with awareness. Growling long and low in satisfaction, he slowed his prods, sinking his weight over me and plastering us both to the mattress.

His body draped over mine felt so right, I wished we could stay like this all night.

His lips moved against my scalp. "For coming without permission, you have another punishment due soon."

Soon. Not tomorrow, our last day together, but soon.

A slip of the tongue, or a promise?

Friday went by all too fast. Gideon, Caleb, and I walked around Gideon's neighborhood, getting pizza at an old Italian place and eating it in a nearby park. The day was breezy, sunny, and warm, with daffodils fluttering on the fringes of the park and ducks mating beneath the willows by the pond. Spring was in full bloom, and it should have made me happy. But sadness festered inside me the more I counted down the hours I had with Caleb.

Most of his harsh words at dinner last night hadn't

surprised me, so much as reinforced how I'd suspected he felt. But hearing him say we'd found a way to get along out of necessity had jarred me, because it didn't ring true. At least not from where I stood. But my perception was one-sided. *I* felt so strongly about *him* that no doubt I saw what I wanted to see.

On the way back from our long walk, we picked up takeaway from a Filipino restaurant, setting everything out on the coffee table in the living room. Gideon put on a playlist of eclectic songs from Harry Nilsson to Bad Azz Yella Boy.

After my second beer, I was feeling a little tipsy. Gideon passed me another open bottle, and I raised it. "To the weirdest last night of a kidnapping ever."

"I don't know." Gideon tilted his head. "The end of the Patty Hearst kidnapping was pretty bizarro."

"True," I agreed. "At least I won't end up in prison."

At 11:30, Caleb opened his phone to make sure Dad had wired the money to the account set up by Caleb's client.

At midnight, Caleb nodded. "He sent it."

As he gazed at me, I couldn't tell whether triumph or fondness sparked his eyes.

The last hurdle to going home had been removed. I tried to swallow the tightness in my throat, but it stubbornly stayed put.

"Should I send the things Jeremy and Marisa packed at the farmhouse to your apartment or to Walter's?" he asked.

It made sense to stay at Dad's mansion for a while. At least as long as Luis was in town and until the broken locks on my apartment door had been replaced.

"I guess to my father's."

Caleb and I spent most of the night making love, only drifting off around 5. He spooned me as we slept, neither of us moving till his phone woke us. I tried to commit to memory the masculine scent of him surrounding me, his solidity and warmth. The way his large hands molded to my breasts, ass, and hips, making me feel his. The scratch of his beard against my cheek.

After saying goodbye to Gideon, we drove to Center City. Caleb parked, holstered his gun, and popped open his door. He rounded the car, opening my door for me. He backed me up against the car, bracketing me with his hands. "I promised you a goodbye kiss."

The tears that had been stinging my eyes as we drove now spilled down my cheeks. "Why does it have to be goodbye?"

He thumbed away a tear. "You know why."

"But we're good together."

"I'm not the man for you, Diva."

"Let me decide that."

His eyes darkened. "Is that a demand?"

Hope fluttered in my chest. "Yes."

His lips crushed mine with bruising force, his tongue punishing me for my boldness. He assaulted my mouth, flicking my tongue, trapping it, and pulling it between his lips. It was the most brutal kiss imaginable, and I ate up every bit of it. It was so like Caleb, so unlike my fantasies of the Werewolf, that it marked the present as nothing else could. A present where I was not who I'd been a month ago.

My knees weakened, and I melted into his body.

He bit down on my lip, drawing blood, so I tasted my own metallic tang.

Disjoining us, he took a step back and pulled something from his pocket.

My wallet!

"I took this the night I took you. When you receive your box of belongings, you'll find you're richer than that night."

I refused to be distracted by money or even his conquering kiss. "But about what I said —"

"Time to go meet your father, Diva." He gripped my nape, steering me towards Washington Square.

My last time to be shepherded by him. I dashed a few more tears from my cheeks.

At the northwest corner of the park, Caleb said, "Walk slowly down the path to the fountain. I'll be covering you the whole way from behind the trees. After your father has picked you up, I'll watch to make sure nothing happens till you're in his car."

I nodded. "Thank you."

"The pleasure was all mine."

The salacious notes in his tone made my skin tingle.

I love you. "Goodbye."

"Goodbye, Diva."

I started the lonely walk towards the center of the park, grateful for the crowds to help hide me. It being Saturday, the park was bustling with people. Young kids on scooters, elderly couples, groups of teens, moms pushing strollers, and joggers.

Nearing the fountain, I spotted Dad in a navy wool Tom Ford suit, facing the other direction. He kept fit, looking ten years younger than his 55.

"Dad!" I called out.

He swiveled, his raised eyebrows the only sign he'd seen me. "Danya."

I approached with my arms spread wide to hug him. But his frigid stance made me drop them again.

"No need to make a show of it, Dani. The kidnappers said no photographers."

This was supremely embarrassing. Caleb was watching Dad snub his daughter after she'd been kidnapped for a month.

Why did he even bother to pay the fifteen million?

Glancing at his watch, he nodded towards the northeast

entrance. "My driver's waiting this way."

Struck dumb, I hastened to keep up with his long strides. Finally, as we exited the park, I found my voice. "How are you, Dad?"

"We'll discuss that in the car." He waited for his driver to open the door to the Range Rover for him.

Was he angry at me?

I cast one last glance around, looking for Caleb. Of course he was invisible. But I felt his fearsome presence keenly. Rounding the back of the car, I climbed in on the other side.

Dad's driver, René, pulled out into traffic.

Dad closed the barrier between René and us.

"Did you enjoy your very expensive vacation?" Dad opened.

My jaw dropped. "What?"

Dad slapped a manila folder on the seat between us. "A few pictures from your trip."

As my stomach plummeted, I tremblingly took up the folder, opening it to find pictures of me and Caleb. Photos of us at the tollbooth in Ohio, taken from just behind the car. Pictures of us sitting at the café in Nevada City, taken by the paparazzi. Pictures of me alone that they took up close when Caleb had gone to the restroom. A photo of me and Caleb standing close together at the gas station in Rocklin. Pictures of Gideon, Caleb, and me in Gideon's neighborhood yesterday.

My ears burned, while my fingers went numb. "Why do you have these?"

"Time to lay my cards down, Dani. I want you to marry Drake Arthur, give up your apartment, give up working, and give me grandkids." He said it as coolly as if he were asking me to hand him an umbrella.

The sinking feeling in my gut worsened. "But I don't want to do any of that."

His malicious smile made me momentarily forget he was my father. "That's too bad, Dani. Because you're going to. Otherwise, the man you seem so fond of will be spending his life in prison. And you'll get several years for conspiring in your own kidnapping."

"Conspiring — *what?*"

He smoothed out his trousers, folding his hands in his lap. "This kidnapping has been a long time in the making. Caleb's so-called *client* and I hatched the idea in January, just before your birthday. He and I have known each other a long time, and he knew I wanted grandkids. He joked that I should go about it the old-fashioned way, selecting a suitor for you and marrying you off. As you know, Drake Arthur has always been my pick — rich, successful, full of sound business sense, and a family man. A fine son-in-law. I approached him, proposing the match. He said, if you were willing, he'd be glad to. But all the times I tried to get you to go on dates with him, you refused. So I came back to Caleb's client and proposed that we hire Caleb to kidnap you. Apparently he's quite the lady killer, despite his rough profession. It was a safe bet that you'd fall for him and become a willing participant in your own kidnapping."

He paused, rubbing a finger over his jaw. "To allow enough time for this to happen, and to gather sufficient evidence against you, I set the time frame as thirty days. I timed it so the board vote would happen just before you were returned to me. And I knew the board would sympathize with me as a bereft father. Just as I'd hoped, we took over SciPulse yesterday." He smirked. "My plan was to set up the kidnapping and then nearly sabotage it at every turn. I started by having my hacker make a deepfake of your voice and call in to quit your job the day after you left."

"That was *you?*" I could barely contain my rage.

"Once you were kidnapped, it was very easy. I also hired

someone to ransack your apartment and leave a generic blackmail note addressed to me. Like your supposed call into work, this added to the evidence that you conspired to have yourself kidnapped. Since nothing was taken from your apartment and the note was a cliché, a DA would likely find the circumstances highly suspicious."

My chin wobbled. "How could you?"

"Then I sent Luis after you, having my two hired men, Mick and Ivan, tail him. The way you let Caleb steal that car from Luis in Nevada City was pretty damning, Danya." He tsked. "Stockholm Syndrome at its worst."

"Mick and Ivan were *your* hired men?" I felt as if I were slowly suffocating.

"Oh, yes, the trafficking." A villainous glimmer lit Dad's eyes. "That scare was to send you two on the road and keep you there. Until finally you called that day without a gag or ropes on. I recorded that call, of course. Excellent evidence to suggest you were on your kidnapper's side. You kept on refusing to name him, and he'd authorized you to do all the talking. Highly irregular, under the circumstances. Anyway, when you asked about the supposed break-in at your apartment, I fed you both a pack of lies about police reports and identity thefts and a made-up man named Bill Heinz." He chuckled.

I struggled to keep calm enough to think. "How did you think we'd find out about the break-in?"

"I knew Caleb was monitoring my communications. He'd get wind of the police call."

I seethed. "And the call with Caleb's client?"

"Also full of made-up stories about traffickers named Roddy and Vic." He rasped a dry laugh. "Of course Mick and Ivan made that recording in which they were supposedly overheard in the bar."

Suddenly light dawned. "That attachment! Of Mom and

me in London."

He nodded with a smile. "Full of malware that tracked Caleb's phone to Albuquerque—and, in fact, all the way to Philly. I banked on the fact that eventually he'd let you check your email."

Chills shot down my back. "But why did you have Mick and Ivan drug and kidnap me?"

"Ah, that. I was furious at Caleb for selling GenRev's skin treatment to Emergos. And angry at you by association, for falling for someone like him. I decided to punish you both. I also wanted to humble you. You both seemed to be getting smug and over-confident."

Trembling with fury, I barely managed, "What if I hadn't gotten free?"

He tossed his head. "Then I would've had Mick and Ivan bring you back early. And I wouldn't have had to pay Caleb."

"But you *will* pay him." I was still reeling from the idea that *Dad* was the real client in this kidnapping—not whoever Caleb thought hired him.

Dad scoffed. "In an hour, Caleb's supposed client will deal with that problem. I refuse to give him the three million promised. He wasn't polite to me, he didn't call me every day, he touched you right out of the gate, and he lied in every single call." He chuckled. "Granted, I set him up to fail on all counts. I knew he'd fall for you."

Rage on Caleb's behalf seized me. "Be prepared to pay the full amount or suffer Caleb's wrath."

Dad looked amused at my outburst. "You seem to forget I know where his mother and sister live."

I had forgotten. "How did you find out his identity?" I quavered.

Dad's lips curled in a sneer. "That was easy. I had a camera, audio bug, and tracker put in his car when you were first kidnapped. He didn't detect them till a week into your abduction. I heard Caleb and his friend talking about hacking into my company's systems and about Lucy and Faye. It didn't take long to figure out that it was the same Lucy Furness I knocked up seventeen years ago, whose daughter Faye was ten at the time. And it didn't take an Einstein to realize Caleb and his friend were plotting to bring me down with the evidence they found through their hacking. Caleb's idea of revenge, I suppose."

I knotted my arms across my chest. "You need to apologize to every member of that family. In person, with humble sincerity."

His lips set in a grim line. "Dani, if you think you can make demands of me, you're wide of the mark. You're in a tight spot. And your man is in an even tighter one. Prison is a cold, lonely place, with few amenities. This afternoon we'll head to City Hall to get your marriage license. Drake is meeting us there."

"You would never turn me in." *Though he would turn in Caleb.*

"Try me, Dani." Dad's glacial tone froze my bones.

I shivered. "We can find evidence that you were behind the kidnapping."

A grin slashed his face. "There you're also wrong. I've left absolutely no trace. And you don't have a phone, so you can't record any of what I'm telling you." He leaned back in his seat, crossing his legs. "You looked very smitten with Caleb. Unfortunately you two won't see each other in prison. You'd do better to cut your losses and follow my instructions to the letter."

I lashed out. "How can you be so hateful? So vicious? To orchestrate this whole thing, just to — what, get me to marry a rich guy and have babies?"

He held up a finger. "And to have you under my thumb. You've been getting too independent over the last six years. It was time to rein you in. Drake will toe the line, and now, so will you."

"But to hire all these people and go to all this ridiculous trouble of chasing us across the country for weeks!"

He chuckled. "It was just Mick and Ivan, and they come cheap. Oh, and the man I had Caleb call to confirm the truth of his client's story." He sobered. "True, I did lose Luis's work in Singapore, since he was hell-bent on rescuing you. But that couldn't be helped."

I gnashed my teeth. "You're inhuman, you know that?"

It was as if Dad had stripped himself bare for me to see him at last as he was.

He straightened his collar. "If you mean I'm not hampered by the usual liabilities — emotions and human attachments — I'll take that as a compliment. It takes ruthlessness to be as successful as I am."

I tried a different tack, adopting a softer tone. "Please, Dad. I'll come back and live at the mansion, I'll work from home as a travel blogger, and I'll . . . date. If you promise not to turn Caleb in."

He tutted. "Dani, the first rule of negotiation is to come from a strong position. Unfortunately, by that rule, neither you nor Caleb is in a position to negotiate."

I turned towards the window. Dad had thought this through from every angle. He was determined to win, on his terms. I couldn't let Caleb go to prison. Whatever it took, I needed to save him. I could always divorce Drake.

"So, Dani. What's it to be?" To me, now, Dad's voice resembled a serpent's. "And in case you're planning to divorce Drake, you have to remain married to him for seven years and try for children for me to withhold my evidence. Just remember, there's no statute of limitations on federal kidnapping."

I ground my molars. "I need you to put everything in writing."

He smiled. "Ah, there's a glimmer of my own daughter. Now you're learning how to negotiate."

How ironic that all these years I'd been so determined to gain Dad's approval and love. And now that he'd given his approval, I wanted to throw it right back at him.

Chapter Thirty-One: Caleb

A t noon at the fountain in the center of Washington Square, I strolled, watching parkgoers and waiting for Arnold Black. I had a premonition that things weren't going to go smoothly. But since I'd never yet failed to get my full pay from a client, I wasn't too worried.

He showed five minutes after the hour, nodding towards an empty bench, where we both headed, sitting down two feet apart. He was a bald man of medium stature with droopy jowls and a hook nose.

"So, Scott, the handoff went well?" he breezed.

"Yeah."

He nodded. "So I heard, from Walter."

I whipped my head around. Keeping an impassive expression, he gazed out at the pigeons collecting around the fountain.

"Walter is your client, Scott."

My brain whirled like a spinning top. *Walter.* For something that made no sense, it made too much sense. All my critical information from day one had come from either Walter or Arnold Black. The break-in — filtered through Walter's phone. The traffickers — overheard by Walter's men. The solution to the traffickers — presented by Black. The solution to the break-in — relayed to us by Walter.

They'd been playing me.

I disguised my irritation that I hadn't seen through them before this. "What's his motive?"

"I can't tell you."

"Can't or won't?"

"Won't."

I took a deep breath, focusing on why we were here now. "You have the money?"

He took out a suspiciously small case, setting it between us. "Half a million."

I clenched my teeth. "Where's the other two point five?"

"The price of the kidnapping was reduced as soon as your double identity came out. Once Walter discovered Lucy and Faye and where they live, he figured you wouldn't press the issue."

"He figured wrong," I gritted. "He's already using that threat to keep me from publishing evidence against him."

Black shrugged. "Apparently he felt the threat was strong enough it could do double duty."

I snorted. "It doesn't cover you. Or him. I know where both of you live, and you both have wives."

He paled. "We could broadcast your real identity every-where."

"And I can make sure no one in Philly trusts you." I rose. "You'll want to rethink your position, Black. Otherwise, there's no place you can call safe now."

Walking back towards my car, I already had a few ideas for how to get that money and teach Black not to screw with me. But they'd take some working out.

I stopped suddenly. Walter had arranged for Danya to be kidnapped. I'd had no time to think about that part when I'd been sitting next to Black. Now it began to register. Why the fuck had he done it? Was Danya safe with him? How would I know, since I'd severed all communication with her?

Thoughts of Danya—dreams of her—haunted me for the rest of the day and all through the night. My practical side told me not to worry. The job was over and I'd completed my part of it. But the side that had been awakened by being with her for a month—Gideon would probably call it my impractical, fun, romantic side—said I should follow up and make sure she was okay.

I was thinking of her while pounding weights at the gym the next morning when a call from an unknown number came through on my burner. Dropping the barbell I'd pressed overhead, I toweled off my sweaty hands before swiping up.

"Scott." I still breathed heavily.

The Breadcrumb Client's familiar voice sounded over the line. "This is Mr. J. Am I catching you at a bad time?"

"No. It's fine. What can I do for you?"

"You remember I was keen to see you enact revenge on Walter Penwarren. It was my understanding that you planned to find evidence of everything I revealed to you and publish it."

I worked my jaw back and forth. "That may be harder than I originally thought."

Walter had found out who I was, who my mother and sister were, and where they lived. And he'd found out I'd hacked into his company. He was using his knowledge to keep me from publishing the evidence.

"I see." He paused a moment. "Well, if you can swing it in the next thirteen days, I'll give you a million."

"Why thirteen days?"

"It's the timeline that works best for the person I'm acting on behalf of."

"And if it takes me longer?"

"Then the million is off the table."

I knew he wouldn't give it, but I still had to ask. "Can I have your contact information?"

"Sorry. I'm very private. I'll speak with you again on the fifteenth."

He hung up.

One million for a two-week job. Not bad.
But how in hell was I going to complete it?

Danya

Eve's shiny black bob darted among fellow shoppers as she
pulled dozens of dresses from racks. Dad had told us to "go
buy wedding clothes," giving us a black AmEx card, René,
and the Range Rover. I'd begged Luis to come too, but he had
emails to write, since it was now early Monday in Singapore.

"Come on, Dani, we'll start with these." Eve's arms were
laden with dresses in different shades of white for the ceremony and reception, evening gowns for the rehearsal dinner,
and cocktail dresses for other wedding-related events Dad
had listed as obligatory.

Dad had started cracking the whip and telling me how
high to jump as soon as we'd arrived at the Marriage License
Center yesterday. I could see what life would be like for the
next seven years—of indentured servitude, I thought wryly.
He'd corrected my posture, instructed me on topics of conversation to introduce with Drake Arthur, and rattled off the
schedule of events for the next two weeks leading up to the
wedding.

Drake had arrived dressed in a perfectly tailored dark-grey
suit, his charcoal-black wavy hair slicked back and a modest
smile on his face. I felt bad for him. He had no idea how evil
Dad was. Or if he did, he was even less equipped to deal with
his evil than I was. I could see Dad had partly picked Drake
because he loved family so much. He was always talking
about his immediate and extended relatives.

I was relieved Dad didn't force us to marry three days after
getting our license, for he could've. But he was old-fashioned
enough that he wanted to go through a few of the proper

rituals leading up to the marriage.

Now, as I tried on dresses with Eve, I dreamed of wearing them for Caleb. I tried to think from his point of view and guess which ones he'd like best. Knowing he liked my ass and breasts, I figured anything that highlighted those would appeal to him.

"Ohh, that one's lovely." Eve circled me as I stood in an ivory silk dress that clung to my curves and had a draped bust. It reminded me of styles worn in 1920s silent films.

"I like it." I hoped she'd okay it, as my feet were already getting sore from standing for so many hours.

"Very classically feminine." She linked her arm in mine. "You look gorgeous, Dani. Let's get it."

Looking in the mirror at us, I appreciated the contrasts. Eve had an olive complexion, a pert nose, and bright brown eyes.

"Tell me why you're marrying Drake." She met my eye in the mirror.

"Dad's holding something over my kidnapper," I replied.

"You're in love with him." She stated it as a fact.

I nodded.

"I knew it was some form of blackmail. Otherwise why Drake, out of the blue and in just two weeks' time?" She drew my hair behind my head, swirling it into a loose, low bun. "This is a nice look with this dress." She let it fall, wrapping an arm around me. "Tell me about him."

My heart revved. "He's got a very dangerous job. He's ruggedly handsome. He solves people's problems and makes them go away. And he's got an incredibly strong will." I could've gone on for a while, but I didn't want to abuse Eve's patience.

"Solves people's problems, eh?" Eve looked thoughtful. "What kinds of problems?"

"Practical problems of all kinds." That fizzy feeling that skated around my chest when I thought of Caleb returned.

"You mean a fixer?"

Seeing I might've given away too much, I backtracked. "Something like that."

"Why don't you call him and have *him* deal with Walter's blackmail?"

"He doesn't want to hear from me again." I sat down on the cushioned ottoman beside the dressing room. He'd made his wishes very clear over the last few days, and I couldn't go against them without risking his anger. Though I was pretty sure this kind of situation was exactly what Caleb excelled at.

"Treat it as a job. His pay will be my *non*-wedding gift." She winked. "Seeing as how he'll get you out of the wedding."

"How much would you offer for that sort of job?" I wondered aloud.

"See if twenty grand does the trick." She held up a sheeny purple-blue-green Cinderella-style ball gown. "In the meantime, let's keep spending your father's money. God knows what it'll go towards otherwise."

"What about your and Dad's fifteenth anniversary? Shouldn't we be planning something for that?"

She frowned. "No, no. I have a special surprise for him. We'll keep it simple."

As I tried on more dresses, I mulled over what she'd suggested. I decided I'd call Gideon once we got home and see if I could get a number for Caleb from him.

After all, this *was* an official job.

"Hello?"

"Gideon? This is Danya."

"Oh, hey, Danya. How you doing?"

"Good. Do you have a moment?"

"Sure."

"I've got a job for Caleb. Only I don't know how to reach him."

"Ah. I can tell him you're trying to reach him, if you give me a number."

I guessed Gideon was only protecting Caleb by not giving out his number. Since Eve and I had just bought me a new phone yesterday, I gave Gideon my number. "Tell him he can call or text anytime."

Something in my chest was doing grand jetés like Anna Pavlova straight from my lungs across to my heart. He was going to call or text me!

"How's the blog going so far?" Gideon asked.

"It's on temporary hold for two weeks. Hopefully no longer than that."

Hopefully Caleb would foil Dad's plans to marry me off and to keep me from working.

When we'd rung off, I curled my legs under me on the chair in my old bedroom. I was just getting ready to have a good think-about-Caleb session when Dad texted to summon me to his study so we could hammer out the terms of our contract. Given the mansion was as big as a small city, it'd take a good ten minutes to reach his study from my bedroom.

On my way there, I stopped in the library to recall the evening of the Werewolf. So many times I'd re-enacted him pushing me against the bookcase and questioning me. But now I refrained. It seemed like a childish fantasy, compared to the realities I'd experienced over the last month.

On Tuesday a box arrived containing all my belongings that Caleb had packed when he'd kidnapped me, including the composition book I'd written in for that first week. And nestled in the midst of all my things were two stacks of hundred dollar bills. A total of twenty thousand dollars.

A hastily-scrawled note read, *Your reward — for being taken and for keeping my secret when we first met.* C Underneath another pile of clothes I found five photo prints of me in different places — Rainbow Basin, the Tulsa zoo, our hike near Indianapolis. I fingered my necklace, kissing the pendant. Caleb was so near with this note, these pictures he'd taken, and this gemstone. Even the money was a bridge linking me to him. Holding two crisp stacks of ten thousand dollars each, I felt close to his shady underworld.

I decided to spend the rest of the afternoon typing up some of my notes from the trip.

Before dinner, Luis and I headed out on a walk around the estate. A dense forest in back of the house stretched for two miles in one direction and one in the other, its packed gravel paths winding amidst the tall pines. This was our first chance to talk alone since I'd gotten back.

"How did you get home?" I asked.

"I flew out of Sacramento." He twisted towards me. "That guy. Man, he has good trigger reflexes. No pun intended."

I shuddered. "I'm just glad his reflexes were good enough *not* to pull the trigger."

"I realized he was only protecting you when he fired off questions after you'd climbed in the car — had I let the air out of your car tires? Had I sent paparazzi to snap your picture? And so on. He's thorough. By the way, the answer was no to all those questions."

I squeezed his arm. "Of course I know you'd never do any of that. Did you ever suspect that *Dad* was behind the kidnapping?"

"Honestly? It seemed a little weird that he was sending me off in search of you instead of having the FBI handle it. I know he's looking out for the company and all, but that's taking fear of publicity too far." Luis helped me over a fallen log in our path. "I quit."

I gawked. "Because of what Dad did?"

He nodded. "On Sunday, after you told me and Mom. I don't want to have anything to do with him professionally. I know he's family, so it's hard to avoid him at gatherings. But anyone who'd have his own daughter kidnapped is not right up here." He tapped his temple. "Or here." He placed a hand over his heart. "That's why I haven't been eating dinner with you guys."

"I think what's even stranger is the reason he did it. To marry me off and keep me under his thumb."

Luis shook his head. "He's always been super paranoid. This is probably just another way of asserting control. *Oye*, Dani, if you need any help getting out of this marriage, *estoy aquí para ti.*"

I turned, embracing him. "*Gracias*, Luis. I'm working on it. I'm just so grateful to have you."

"That's what *hermanos* are for."

By Wednesday, I'd begun to grow antsy. Would Caleb never call? I carried my phone with me to the bathroom, kept it beside my pillow, and held it in my lap at meals, checking religiously to see if I'd missed any calls or texts. Nothing.

For most of the day I worked to finish typing up the notes from my travel journal. Luis and I took another walk before dinner, talking about his upcoming trip to Singapore to pack his things and what he'd do next in biotech. He had an interview with Emergos tomorrow.

That evening was the first of several cocktail parties scheduled as lead-ups to the wedding. Dad announced my engagement to Drake to a hundred *intimate* friends. They were really mostly coworkers at GenRev, so that for him the whole thing was about flaunting my new fiancé to the company and the press. Of course he'd called in paparazzi. Dad ordered me to mingle with various important people and never leave Drake's side.

By the time we got back, at midnight, I was exhausted. And still no word from Caleb.

On Thursday, I thought of calling Gideon again. But I didn't want to treat him as a message relay service. Still, it'd been five days, and no communication. I knew Caleb must be very busy, but the idea of marrying Drake next Saturday filled me with increasing dread.

In all my waking moments when Dad hadn't claimed my time I'd been racking my brains for ways I could get out of this trap. If I went to the police, I'd be endangering Caleb. If I tried to warn Drake about my father and it got back to Dad, I'd be violating the contract. No matter which way I turned, I hit a wall. I had to come up with some workaround.

During my talks with Drake, he'd confessed that he'd agreed to this marriage for the prestige and money, above all, but also because apparently he'd had a crush on me for years. At least he was honest.

Tonight we had a charity event in the city. I had no doubt Dad would carefully stage our appearances and direct me in everything, as he'd done last night.

If this was life for the next seven years, prison might be better.

CHAPTER THIRTY-TWO: CALEB

Money — king of everything. Power — money's throne. Violence — money's oxygen supply.

Parking my new beamer in the driveway after a six-and-a-half-hour drive from the North Shore of Massachusetts, I checked my account again. I was three point five million richer than this time last week.

Smiling, I climbed out and stretched my limbs. It had taken five days and a trip up to Black's neck of the woods, but I'd taught him a lesson and scored half a million extra as a reward for my pains.

Lurking on shore, I'd bribed the staff of his mansion as they'd come to town for supplies. I'd ridden a boat with one of them to Black's island, staying out of sight while conducting my operation. Then I'd had him and his wife slowly poisoned over the course of a few days. Not enough for them to go to the hospital, but enough to make them violently ill. Like a moderate case of salmonella.

When Black was finally starting to feel better, he'd woken to find me sitting by his bed enjoying a glass of his most expensive Scotch and one of his Cubans, while holding a wedding picture of him and his wife. She was sleeping in a separate room while they were both sick.

"Nice picture," I commented.

He startled, groaning. "Get off my island."

I clicked my tongue. "Not very welcoming words, Black."

"How did you get in here?"

I placed the whisky on his bedside table, leaning back in my chair so he could see my packed holster. "Your staff were very accommodating. With a little persuasion."

"What do you want?"

I blew smoke out of my nose. "My due. Plus half a million for my troubles."

He looked like crap after suffering a high fever, vomiting, and chills for four days. His voice was as weak as a ninety-year-old pneumonia victim. "Fine. You'll never disturb me again?"

"Once I've got my money, I'll never see you again."

Black had the money wired to my account, and I paid one of his staff to motor me back to shore.

Isolated islands had their advantages, but a quick getaway wasn't one of them.

Now, entering my house and tossing my bag on the rug, I noticed a call from Gideon last Sunday evening. Cell phone reception on the North Shore had been spotty, even on Black's island. Apparently I'd missed a lot of calls.

I called Gideon.

"Hey, Cal. What's up?"

"Just got back from a trip to Massachusetts."

"Oh, to pay a visit to Black? Did you get your money?"

"I did."

He chuckled. "It's always the rich dudes who try to pull that kind of crap. Anyway, listen, Danya was trying to reach you."

I paused with my hand on the doorknob to my bedroom. "Oh, yeah?" Why the fuck did I have a fluttering in my chest? Was I about to have a heart attack? I placed a hand on my sternum.

"Yeah, apparently she's got a job for you."

My eyebrows jumped. *Really.* "What's her number?"

"I'll text it to you now. Just so you know, she doesn't sound so good."

Apprehension tied a knot in my stomach. "What do you mean?"

"She mentioned maybe not being able to do her blog after all, and she seemed depressed."

Fuck. This had *Walter* written all over it.

"I'll call her."

After showering and dressing, I went down to the kitchen, where Marisa had made me a roast beef sandwich.

I called Danya. After a few rings, it went over to voicemail. Her voice message stirred still-glowing embers deep in my core.

When it beeped, I said, "Danya, I'm just returning your call."

An hour later, as I stood out on the deck enjoying the view of Jeremy's garden, she called back.

"Hey."

She sounded as if she was speaking in an echo chamber. "Hi, Caleb. Thanks for calling back. How are you?"

"Okay. Where are you?"

"I'm at a party. I had to sneak to the restroom to call you. Sorry I missed you earlier."

I'd been prepared to worry about her well-being. But it seemed she was doing just fine, attending parties and calling me back when she could spare a minute. I adopted a cool tone. "What can I do for you?"

"I have a job for you. Can we meet at a café in the city tomorrow morning?"

"What kind of job?"

"Blackmail."

I gripped the deck railing. "Who's blackmailing you?"

"My father."

Fucking Walter. He was next on my hit list. If he was

blackmailing the diva, it was time to make mincemeat of his hide. "Where do you want to meet?"

"Konditori Coffee. At nine?"

"I'll be there."

The diva wore a white dress that made her look like a fresh-blooming flower. It had been only six days since I'd seen her, but she was more beautiful than ever. This despite the black rings under her eyes and the furrow between her brows. She seemed a little thinner and paler too.

She blushed as I kissed her cheek. "Thank you for coming."

"You look gorgeous."

Her gaze caressed my features. "You look ready to slay."

Smiling, I guided her to the counter. "What would you like?"

After getting us drinks and pastries, I led us to a table, pulling out a chair for her. When we'd settled in, she slid some cash across the table.

"What's this?"

She smiled. "The money for my gift to you in Barstow."

I chuckled. "I'd forgotten."

She fingered my necklace. "I hadn't."

I'd worn the diva's sweater the whole time I was in Massachusetts. I leaned in. "Tell me what's going on."

She took a deep breath. "When I got into Dad's car last Saturday, he told me he'd orchestrated the kidnapping."

I nodded. "I know."

Her hand shook as she brought her cup of coffee to her lips. "He did it so he could frame me."

My heart took a nosedive to my belly. "*What?*"

"He's got a ton of evidence showing that I conspired in my own kidnapping. He's holding it over me so he can make me marry Drake Arthur." She swallowed. "And it could put you behind bars."

"Never mind about me. How is he threatening you?"

"He forced me to get a marriage license with Drake. I have to stay married to him for seven years before Dad will withdraw his evidence. And I have to try to have children." I'd never heard her sound so stressed. "The whole week has been nothing but wedding preparations and parties. We have one every night this weekend. And I have to check with Dad every time I leave the house. Right now he thinks I came into town to meet a former coworker for coffee."

Tension shot like a high-voltage current from my arms to my neck. I narrowed my eyes. "It's time to rain on Walter's parade."

"What can we do?"

I decided to take the diva fully into my confidence. "I have a client who wants Walter's neck on a platter for reasons of his own. He's offering a million if I can publish evidence of Walter's early white-collar crimes by Friday April fifteenth. Now your father's committed kidnapping, I plan to take him down on both counts, so he'll spend the rest of his life in prison."

"How can you catch him for the kidnapping? He's covered all his tracks." She gnawed on a fingernail.

"There's no such thing as covering all tracks. There must be some kind of evidence. I just need to find it." Finishing my coffee, I turned in my seat, drumming my fingers on the table.

She folded her arms on the table. "How do you usually go about it?"

"Follow the money. Who was paid and how."

She frowned. "Tell me about your other client."

"It's that mystery client I mentioned when we were driving. He knows about my identity from following my family's history over the years." I crossed my legs. "If I could find out who he was, I'd be able to name him to other potential sources, get more evidence to expose Walter."

"What do you have to go on?"

I chuffed a laugh. "Not much. I have no idea where he lives. He disappeared seventeen years ago. Used to work at GenRev in the finance department. I thought his name was Ian MacLamare . . . "

Danya's eyes rounded, and she gasped. "Did you say Ian MacLamare?

"Yeah."

"That's Eve's first cousin once removed. The one I told you was so serious and lives off the grid in northern Maine. I've met him! At his mother's funeral."

I sat up straighter. "Do you know where he lives?"

"Eve will know."

I looked at my watch. "Can you call her now? The sooner we get things rolling, the better."

She pulled out her phone.

Danya

Eve answered after the first ring. "Dani?"

"Eve, hi. I'm sitting with the man I told you about."

"Mr. Hot Fixer?"

"Yeah. He has a mystery client he thinks is Ian MacLamare."

Her voice lowered. "Really? Tell me more about this mystery client."

"He says he disappeared around two thousand and five, so all . . . um, Mr. Hot Fixer has to go on is that he worked in the finance department at GenRev. Apparently this client somehow knows all about the fixer and his family."

Eve cleared her throat. "And why does the fixer want to get in touch with Ian?"

"If he could get in touch with him, the fixer might be able

to save me from marrying Drake."

"How so?"

"Apparently Dad committed a lot of crimes, especially early in his career when starting the company. The mystery client wants the fixer to get Dad charged with these crimes by Friday April fifteenth. That's the day before my wedding."

"This fixer wouldn't be named Caleb Scott?"

Though shocked, I just barely managed to avoid giving him away. "What makes you say that?"

"I'm his mystery client."

My face muscles pulled back, and I goggled at Caleb, who was listening intently. "Um . . . maybe I'd better put him on the phone."

Caleb

Danya passed me her phone. "You'd better speak to her."

"Hello?"

"Caleb Scott?"

"Who's speaking?"

"Eve Penwarren. Ian MacLamare's first cousin once removed."

"How do you know my name?" I knew the diva never would've told her.

"I've hired you for five jobs over the years. Now six, if you count what Ian spoke with you about on Sunday."

The Breadcrumb Client! At fucking last. "*You're* my mystery client?"

"I am."

"Why are you only now revealing yourself?"

"Because I have a feeling you're not going to be able to bring my husband down without my help."

I folded an arm across my chest. "You mean, you can help

me find evidence of his white-collar crimes?"

"Those and evidence of this kidnapping."

My heart sped up. "I'm listening."

"Can you and Danya meet me in Rittenhouse Square at eleven?"

"We'll be there." I hung up, pushing to my feet. "Let's go."

She stood. "Where are we going?"

"To earn your ticket to freedom."

Spotting her stepmom, Danya called out to her. After she'd introduced us, the three of us walked around a circle of trees and found a bench next to a statue of a lion with its paw on a snake.

Leaning forward and propping my elbows on my knees, I told Eve, "We're limited in what we can do. Walter threatened that if I use the hacked evidence against him, he'll do something to my sister or mother."

Eve's eyes had a steely glitter. "What if you went about exposing him the old-fashioned way?"

"What's that?"

She turned to Danya. "You write an investigative piece about his crimes. After following the leads we can find."

Danya's eyes widened. "Me? I haven't done journalism since junior year."

Everything suddenly clicked into place. Of course this was the way to go. I twisted to face the diva. "In his threat, Walter never said anything about not writing an article —" I snapped my fingers — "an exposé."

She swallowed. "But don't we only have a week?"

Eve nodded. "You can do it, Dani. Ian and I together have a dozen sources you can contact. And they'll name other people."

My thoughts swirled. "Gideon can give you plenty of clues to follow up on from what he's found over the last month."

Danya's chest heaved. "An article. In a week."

"It's your ticket to freedom," I urged.

"It's *your* ticket," she insisted.

"If that gets you writing, then fine," I allowed. I turned back to Eve. "You mentioned you had evidence of this kidnapping."

Eve smiled. "If you can get him charged with those crimes by next Friday, not only will I give you that million I promised, but I'll give you evidence you can use to put him behind bars for life."

"How about you give me the evidence now, so I can start working towards that while Danya's writing the article?" I prodded.

She mused for a moment. "Why not? I think I can trust you two to complete this by the time I divorce Walter on the fifteenth."

Danya tilted her head, her brow crinkling. "Divorce him? I thought you were so happy."

Eve smiled grimly. "Divorce papers will be my fifteenth anniversary gift to him."

"How long have you been planning to divorce him?"

"For six years. That's why I started hiring Caleb for jobs five years ago. I wanted him to expose the fact that Walter stole intellectual property from employees and committed other fraud that significantly boosted his assets by the time we married. He didn't list any of this in our prenup, of course. On the basis of this fraud, I can have the prenup declared null and void by a judge and walk away with tens of millions of dollars more than I otherwise would." She looked at me. "But in case you think I'm just a money-grubbing ex, I'm giving it all to my Alzheimer's charity. This will be poetic justice, since I first started having doubts about Walter when I was working for the charity and discovered his company was gouging Alzheimer's patients for GenRev's medical treatments. I confronted Walter about this, but he refused to reduce costs. He laughed and said if GenRev had a monopoly on these products, it behooved them to make the most of it. He boasted he'd gotten the idea *for free from one of his employees.* I saw what a louse I'd married. But I also began to be curious about this idea he'd stolen." She gazed ahead at an elderly woman pushing a man in a wheelchair. "When I looked into it, I heard rumors that during my time at the company, Walter had stolen an innovation from an employee, Nathaniel Furness. I did some more delving and found out it was likely he'd committed a similar theft years earlier, and that Furness's invention had started the company. I remembered a Lucy Furness working in the design department while I was at GenRev. After talking to Ian and a few other employees and former employees of GenRev, I pieced together everything I told Caleb over the years. The more I dredged up on my husband, the more I loathed him. I used Ian to hire Caleb because Ian had a few jobs he needed a fixer for, Ian had it in for Walter for reasons of his own, and I wanted to remain incognito till everything was in place to divorce Walter."

I was satisfied to finally have the Breadcrumb Client's story. It was as if a critical piece of the jigsaw puzzle had slotted into place. "If Danya can put together the whole story in the next week and sell it to a news source, what evidence can you give me now to follow up on—about Walter's kidnapping?"

Eve held my gaze. "I have access to an account of Walter's that shows unusual activity over the last five weeks. Large payments to various accounts just before and after Danya's kidnapping. I can provide you with the account numbers."

The men Walter had hired. Mick, Ivan, *Roddy.* Maybe even my good old pal Black.

Sniffing the sweet smell of triumph, I smiled. "That oughta do it." I turned to the diva. "If you use evidence from Gideon that would've been accessible to various employees of the company, we can start with those sources."

A keen hunger shone in her eyes. "I'll start right now, while I'm in the city. I can probably talk to a few of the sources before the day has ended. Maybe get contact info for others I can call over the weekend."

Eve added, "I'll call Ian, and together we'll draw up another list of sources you can contact."

I pulled out my phone to call Gideon. "The key to this enterprise is not letting Walter know what we're up to."

Eve turned to Danya. "I'll try to distract him this whole week to take some of the heat off you so you can work. It'll be tricky, since he wants us to plan the wedding."

Danya rubbed her eye. "I don't need much sleep. I can write at night and do my research during the day. If you can convince him to confine the wedding-related events to the evenings, I should have enough time."

Pride swelled in my chest at the thought that Danya could take down her father with her pen, saving both our skins in the process. "Let's get cracking."

CHAPTER THIRTY-THREE: DANYA

Keiko, my roommate in college, once said that in order to get me to write something you had to light a fire under my butt. Not only did I need a deadline, but I needed the stakes to be high for me to write a paper.

Talk about a deadline and high stakes.

Time was of the essence, and Caleb's and my freedom was on the line.

I didn't actually begin outlining the article until Monday. Too many demands crowded the weekend, starting directly after I'd said goodbye to Eve and Caleb. As Dad's daughter, I was able to get into GenRev without a problem. I told security at the entrance that I wanted to surprise Dad by writing a history of the company to give him for his fifteenth wedding anniversary. In order to do my research, I claimed, I'd need to come and go freely for a few days. They bought my story, hook, line, and sinker.

Gideon had provided me with the names of two dozen people he felt sure knew something about the various pieces of evidence he'd unearthed on Dad's crimes. I devised several tricks for getting these employees to talk. First, I assured them that Dad would applaud this project, even though it was a surprise. I said I'd title the article something like *The Challenges of Remaining a Biotech Giant In Today's Ever-Changing World*. The article would present some of the shadier practices big biotech firms used to stay ahead in a competitive market—but, I claimed, it would still cast GenRev in a sympathetic light. And none of this was a lie, since it was Dad I was after. I promised the employees they'd be cited as anonymous sources without any added descriptors about the departments they worked in or other identifiers. Then I encouraged them to speak as freely as they wished, since the audience for the journal I was writing the article for was relatively small — academics in the biotech sector. I steered well clear of questioning any employees who, according to Gideon, were known to be directly involved in these crimes.

To cover myself, I contacted an academic journal to see if they'd be interested in my story. They invited me to send it when I'd finished. Not that I planned to do so — I was aiming for *The New York Times* — but just in case one of the employees I interviewed followed up on my claims and checked me out. Regarding *The New York Times*, I knew that an editor might consider I had a conflict of interest, as Dad's daughter. But I hoped that if my article was incendiary enough, it might squeak through.

By the time I left GenRev's building at 6 on Friday, I'd spoken with sixteen of the people Gideon had mentioned, and I'd gotten names and contact info for another four dozen. I would call them over the weekend, hopefully getting another list of names to contact from these. While I'd gathered a massive amount of information, I knew the lion's share of the work remained ahead — sifting through their responses for usable evidence, organizing it, and framing it in a persuasive way.

That night Dad invited all the extended family and friends of Drake and me to the mansion for cocktails and dinner.

No sooner had the party ended at midnight than I began typing up notes on the interviews I'd conducted that day.

After four hours of sleep, I walked with Luis to a nearby café in Elkins Park, where we worked all day. Since he still hadn't heard from Emergos after his interview on Thursday, he put in more applications at other biotech firms. Meanwhile, I called another eighteen potential sources and typed up more results from my interviews.

That evening Dad had me and Drake attending another charity gala. At one point, when photographers swarmed the two of us, Dad said, "Drake, Dani, let them get a picture of you kissing." Flames filled my cheeks, and anger shot to my toes. Mercifully, Drake didn't drag out the moment. He gave me a quick peck on the lips — the sort of kiss European friends give one another. When we next had a moment without Dad or the photogs breathing down our necks, I said, "Thanks for that." He replied, "No problem. We'll have plenty of time to get to know each other after the wedding."

No offense to him, but I hoped not.

Luckily, the event only lasted till 11. Afterwards, as soon as I'd changed into my sweats and t-shirt, I got to work entering more notes into my laptop. I fell asleep at my desk at 5, waking at 8 and closing the laptop to sleep another hour in my bed.

All day Sunday, working alongside Luis in the café and calling more GenRev employees, past and present, I drank cup after cup of coffee to stay awake. But still I yawned and periodically found it hard to focus. At least that night Dad had nothing scheduled for me. In the interest of regaining my sharpness, I went to bed at 9.

Drifting off, for the first time in days I allowed my thoughts to wander to Caleb. Seeing him Friday had been like slaking my thirst at a well after traveling in the desert. I'd missed his capable approach to tackling problems, the way he made me feel secure and safe, his commanding presence, and don't-fuck-with-me aura.

When would I next see him? Could this plan to bring down my father open a door to something more between us?

Caleb

With Gideon's help, I traced the names of the account holders who had received large payments from Walter before and after the kidnapping. The names Bob McCann, aka. *Mick,* and Ivan Ferlov stirred memories from early in my career. Since I'd recognized their voices in Walter's recording, I had no doubt I'd dealt with them before. *Roddy* turned out to be Ray Hough, someone I'd never met, to my knowledge. The fourth payee was Arnold Black.

I spent Tuesday and Wednesday hunting down the three new men and bribing them to tell on one another, assuring them I was only bringing down Walter. Fully wired, I had Mick give me information about Roddy, Ivan fill me in on Mick, and Roddy spill about Ivan. All of their stories clearly pointed back to Walter. Directly after Danya had filed a report of her kidnapping, I would send these recordings, together with the evidence of the money transfers, to the police.

Since Danya was working nonstop every day this week to get the article in, she planned to put off filing the report until Saturday.

I felt secure that once Walter was forced to deal with the furor over his white-collar crimes, he'd call off the wedding. The police would come knocking on Walter's door, causing him to do one of two things — break his contract with Danya and reveal the evidence against the two of us, or try to keep to the contract in hopes that he could then clear himself of all charges and still force Danya to marry Drake.

If he did the first, Danya would claim that she had escaped the kidnapper Walter had hired and run off with me until it was safe to return. If Walter withheld the evidence and claimed he was innocent of the kidnapping, his chances of getting off were slim to none. Danya's exposé would publicize his criminal character. She would testify that Walter had coerced her into marrying. And the evidence I'd sent the police would finish the job of sinking Walter thoroughly.

Sitting in my kitchen on Wednesday afternoon, I called the diva to see how the article was coming along. She was apparently working at a café near Walter's mansion, where she'd been conducting interviews, doing research, and writing since the weekend.

"I've got more than enough evidence of seven separate crimes, and plenty of instances of each," she told me. "And I've started writing up the long version of the article. Tomorrow I'll spend the day cutting it down to a newsworthy size. But I'll send the *Times* editor both versions, so she feels more confident publishing the reduced one."

"Once your article comes out, you're not safe at your father's." I wouldn't trust Walter as far as I could throw him. There was no telling what he'd do once he discovered Danya had exposed him. "And you're not safe at your own apartment, since he may come after you there."

"Oh. I hadn't thought of that. The thing is, in order to fulfill the terms of my contract, I have to attend Drake's and my rehearsal dinner on Friday evening. It's at the mansion." She was silent for a moment. "I could ask the editor to release the article at a set time."

"Tell her you want it published at eleven-thirty. I'll pick you up at eleven and bring you back to my house." That same fluttery feeling arose in my chest as I thought of having her safely under my watch again. "Be at the front door of the mansion then."

"All right. I'll bow out of the party at ten-fifty-five."

Danya

I was too wired to sleep much on Wednesday and Thursday nights. Too keyed up to think about how I'd be seeing Caleb again tomorrow night. Too pressed for time to revel in the fact that I'd be *staying with him at his house!*

I used every waking minute, apart from dinner, which Dad required me to attend, to write. At last, at 3 on Friday, I took a deep breath and clicked *send* on the two documents I'd prepared for the *Times* editor I'd communicated with on Tuesday. In my message to her, I requested that she not publish the article until 11:30 tonight.

Twenty minutes later, she replied. "Hi, Danya, Thank you for this article — the long and the short version — both of which I will carefully review. If I have questions, I'll call you. As for publication time, I'll do my best."

I sagged in my chair, suddenly overcome with exhaustion, but equally elated. I'd done it! I'd written a piece of investigative journalism in a week on a subject I'd known very little about before starting. Imagine what I could do in a travel blog, writing what I loved and knew about, with more time.

I leaned my head against the wall by my table. I planned to remain at the café for another few hours in case the editor called, then dress for the rehearsal dinner, and pack for Caleb's.

I was talking to Drake, his mother, and Luis about Lyme disease, which one of Drake's cousins suffered from, when a wave of gasps and mutterings rippled through the guests. The three of us turned to find practically everyone at the party gawking at me. Instinctively I looked down to see if anything was amiss with my dress or shoes. I patted my mouth in case a stray piece of smoked salmon was stuck to the corner.

I realized that half the guests were looking between me and their phones. The rest were shaking their heads and sucking in their breaths. *Oh no.* Had the editor published the article already? I checked my watch. It was only 10.35!

Like Moses parting the Red Sea, Dad cut the crowd in half

as he stalked towards me, his face and lips ashen and his eyes colder than the Siberian tundra.

Watching him approach was like watching an angry hornet fly at you in slow motion. I waited for the pain of the sting.

"Never in my life," he ground out, "have I been so ashamed of you. Disgracing me, the family, and the company with this—this pack of lies!" He held up his phone, a vicious snarl curling his lip. "This is what comes of giving you too much freedom. Of letting you go to college and hold a job. Of not vetting the company you keep." His eyes narrowed to slits. "You're going to issue a statement retracting everything you wrote. And you'll do it now."

I gathered strength from Luis's supportive presence beside me. "I meant everything I wrote in that article, and every word was true. I won't retract it."

He took a step closer, sneering. "If this is about you trying to prove you are a writer, you'll never make the cut, Danya. This?" He waved his phone. "This is the press snatching at anything they can get from Walter Penwarren's daughter. Presses will print any drivel by a celebrity. And that's all you are, thanks to me."

"No." My chin wobbled, and my lips trembled. "I used to believe that. But that article—" I nodded my head towards his phone—"is well researched, well documented, and well written. You did steal people's ideas. You did gouge consumers in dire need of your products and innovations. You did give kickbacks. You lied to shareholders and the IRS. You blackmailed and coerced people, and you covered everything up. And now you'll pay the price."

"You forget who your father is," he grated. "A few of my lawyers will have *The Times* quaking in its boots. Your article will dissolve into thin air over the next few days, the cry of a spoiled brat who knows nothing of the world and never will."

I thought of how in a few days he would likely be arrested

for my kidnapping. "If that's how you feel about me, then you won't mind if I leave. I don't have to stay where I'm not wanted."

Never in a million years would I have believed I could speak to Dad this way. But some dam had burst inside me, letting the pressures of years come crashing down. My sense of never being good enough, my desperation to please, my image of my father as untouchable. I saw him as he would be in a few weeks' time, greying in a prison cell, his heart a dust heap drier than the Mojave desert Caleb and I had driven through. I remembered the evils he'd done to the Furnesses. The way he'd made me feel guilty for Mom's death. The damning stories of him that dozens of employees had told me over the last week.

The kidnapping.

Shaking my gaze from his, I turned and shouldered my way through the guests, fleeing towards my bedroom. It took me awhile to reach it from the ballroom, but when I did, I didn't bother to change out of my dress or shoes. Grabbing my packed bag, I legged it towards the front entrance. I was a few minutes early for Caleb to pick me up, but I could wait out on the veranda.

"Just where do you think you're going?" Dad caught up with me as I emerged onto the front porch, his long strides matching my hasty steps.

Shit. I hadn't wanted to make a scene. I'd wanted to escape undetected.

"Where I'll be safe and cared for." I avoided looking at him, staring out into the night.

"That's here. You're staying put." His tone was a death knell.

Not so long ago, his tone would've cowed me.

I shook my head. "If I never see you again, it'll be too soon."

"You think that because you've published an article exposing me you can escape our contract?" His metallic laugh jarred my spine. "You're marrying Drake tomorrow, Danya."

"You've got bigger things to worry about now." *The FBI coming after you. Me turning you in to the police. Your wife divorcing you.*

"You're definitely not going to *him*."

That was when I saw Caleb putting his car in gear at the base of the steps.

My heart soared. "Yes. I am."

"That's what you think," Dad countered.

I began to step forward, when I heard the cock of a gun. At my temple.

Freezing, I slowly registered that my father held a gun to my head.

Caleb

Since the gates were open, I drove straight up to the door, parking in the midst of a few cars that were preparing to leave. Stepping out, I rounded the trunk. Then I stopped dead.

My heart stopped.

Thirty feet away Walter was pointing a pistol at Danya's head.

My own pistol was in my holster.

"Walter, put it away," I urged. "She's your daughter."

"That's right, and you're not taking her." His gaze never veered from Danya. "It's your influence that's ruined her. Before you took her, she was tractable, willing, eager to please."

"Put the gun down, Walter," I said again in as soothing a tone as I could manage.

"Not till you've driven away."

At that moment Danya surprised both of us. Using a self-defense move I'd taught her, she jabbed Walter in the gut with her elbow, forcing his right arm away from her head. That action gave me the second I needed to whip out my gun and fire it into Walter's right shoulder. His pistol fell before he tumbled backwards onto the terrace. Bounding over, I leapt up the stairs, grabbed his gun, and pulled Danya to me.

I had hesitated momentarily before pulling the trigger, thinking I'd aim for his head. It would've been a simple, satisfying solution to my revenge. The culmination of five years of plotting his suffering. But killing him would've meant hurting the diva. However much she thought she hated him, seeing him die a violent death would've forever scarred her. And scarred her opinion of me.

I chose her over revenge.

"You okay?"

She was trembling like a leaf in my arms. "Yes."

"That was brave."

Burying her face in my chest, she shivered in response. I removed my sweater from Barstow and put it around her shoulders.

I wanted to carry her to the car and drive off. But this wasn't a job I'd planned out in advance. I'd stumbled into this situation, and now I had to resolve it the conventional way.

I pulled out my phone, calling 911 to relay our circumstances. Having heard the gunshot, guests rushed out onto the terrace, fussing over Walter. Twenty minutes later, sirens blew through the gates as medics and a patrol car arrived together. Fully conscious, Walter rattled on about this being his property and his daughter. About Danya being *under contract*. Finally they closed the doors on his babbling, whisking him off to the hospital.

The police questioned us for another half-hour before letting us go.

When we'd settled into the car, I turned to Danya. "Do you want to go see your father?"

She looked down at her hands in her lap. "Honestly? No. I don't feel anything for him right now." As she glanced up at me, I saw how tired her eyes were. "I'd rather go to sleep."

I was relieved. "Then that's what we'll do."

The diva fell asleep halfway to my house. After pulling into the driveway, I watched her softly breathe for a few minutes, amazed at her courage and quick thinking earlier. A UFC fighter couldn't have made a better move. Not wanting to wake her, I slipped out of the car, carrying her through the front door and upstairs to my room.

I undressed her, pulling a t-shirt over her head and tucking her in.

I kissed her forehead. "You're mine once again, Diva."

All mine.

The thrill I felt should've alarmed me, but it only made me feel more alive.

CHAPTER THIRTY-FOUR: CALEB

The scents of marjoram and granite baking in the afternoon sun awoke me. My arms encircled the diva, and my nose breathed in her hair.

She stirred, nestling into me. "Mmm. Caleb."

I kissed my way along her jawline. "Morning, Diva."

Groping every voluptuous curve of her, I made sure to taste her arousal on my fingers before taking her slowly from behind. I wanted to savor the moment, relishing her purrs and puffs of breath as I stroked her. To bask in the silkiness of her warm skin. The fiery heat of her pussy. To inhale her sweet, earthy aromas. Having her again was like coming home. She made me never want to leave again.

No longer able to rein myself in, I thrust in faster until I felt her walls tightening around me.

"*Please* . . ." she begged.

I drilled my tongue in her ear. "Come, Diva."

Wildfires rolled up my spine as my balls lifted and tensed. We exploded together, my climax barreling through me like a cannonball, ripping through everything in its path. Our hips continued to rock till we'd ridden out our highs.

I couldn't remember ever having such an intense release. I suspected it was because I knew the diva so well and took such pleasure in every sensitive part of her.

Over breakfast, Danya showed me the texts her father had sent over the last twelve hours. Even though he was still recovering in the hospital, he insisted she marry Drake this afternoon according to their agreement. "If you don't," he wrote, "I'll turn over all the evidence to the police. You and Caleb will go to prison."

"He's getting sloppy in his pain-killer-induced haze," I remarked. "This text alone is proof that he's coercing you."

She sat up straight. "I'd better go file that report of the kidnapping."

I drove her to the station, where she made a full report of the last six weeks, including the trafficking rumor that sent her running with me, her father's framing her for the kidnapping, and his forcing her to marry Drake. Detective Lee, who took Danya's case, asked her to describe her kidnapper. She said he was wearing a ski mask the whole time she was with him. She only knew he was of medium height, with a brassy voice. She claimed she'd escaped him a week after he'd abducted her, and she'd hitchhiked with me. She gave her driver's name as Caleb Scott, saying I worked as an independent strategist and had a job that had taken me out West for a few weeks. She'd been so afraid of the traffickers, she'd hung out with me until it was time to return to her father. She told Lee she didn't trust her father to keep her safe from them.

As soon as she'd concluded her report, I sent Lee an anonymous email of all the evidence I'd gathered over the past week.

When we left the station and climbed into the car, Danya called her stepmom, putting her on speaker.

"Congratulations, Dani!" Eve gushed. "Your article has been *the talk* of every social media site and several major news shows. On the basis of your carefully-documented report, the FBI showed up here an hour ago looking for your father. I served him his divorce papers before dinner last night, warning him he was facing a legal battle over his fraudulent prenup."

Meeting my eyes with hope gleaming in hers, Danya crossed her fingers. "What's happening with the wedding?"

"I managed to call it off. Contacting everyone took every minute from this morning till now, but I got everyone." She exploded a breath. "Thanks to the evidence you dug up, Dani, I'll have enough to walk away from this divorce with another thirty million at least. All of it going to Friends of Alzheimer's Research."

I cut in. "The million you wired me last night for meeting the deadline will go to Danya, Eve." She'd certainly earned it by the sweat of her brow. And what a talented brow it was.

Beaming, Danya blinked, as if processing that she was a million richer. Then she sobered. "Dad still seems to think the wedding is on. His last text, an hour ago, read, *Even if it's just you, Drake, and the pastor, be there.*"

The manipulative paranoiac was still trying to control Danya from his sickbed.

"The ceremony is scheduled for five this afternoon," Eve pointed out. "The DA has already charged Walter with assault for last night. If the FBI doesn't catch up with him for his white-collar crimes before the ceremony begins, it sounds as if the police will arrest him for the kidnapping. One way or another, your father will be out of commission by the time you're supposed to walk down the aisle."

The diva's shoulders relaxed at the same time I felt all tension leave my neck.

"Stay with Caleb, though, because knowing your father as I do, if he can commission something nasty beyond the grave, he'll do it." Eve's bitter tone was grim.

Danya's eyes questioned mine, and I nodded.

"I will," she promised.

After they'd said their goodbyes, Danya hung up, her brow wrinkling. "What if the police put Dad's and my stories together and come up with you as the kidnapper?"

"It's his word against yours." I started the engine, pulling out onto the road. "They can't prosecute me if you keep claiming the man in the photos is your driver and lover."

Her head snapped around. "Are you my lover?"

"That depends, Diva." I checked the mirrors, deciding to drive us to a park where we could walk to the Schuylkill River. "Are you prepared to follow my rules?"

In my side vision, I caught a slow grin spreading over her face. "If they're the same rules from the farmhouse, then yes."

I made a right onto the winding road edged with thick trees that led to the park. The diva seemed made for me. Pleasure or pain, she ate up whatever I dished up for her. I slid my gaze to hers. "You're my willing captive?"

She gave a decisive nod. "Yes."

Maybe it was time to make an exception to my rule against girlfriends and do as Gideon had suggested—just take the plunge. I could still see the diva being clingy and the two of us having our share of miscommunication. I could see myself worrying about her whenever I had an enemy. But I realized I had to accept all that as part of the deal of attaching myself to her—to anyone.

What I couldn't see was letting another man move in and snap her up. Because she was a prize catch. I'd known that since some motel between Iowa and Nevada. She was adventurous, spirited, warm-hearted, and passionate. Not to mention Fuck-Hot, with capitals.

And what she'd done over the last few weeks—escaped who we thought were traffickers, exposed her father to the world as a criminal, and fought against him at gunpoint—showed she had courage, spine, and resilience.

If the diva required a boyfriend, then I'd have to step up to the plate. Because I sure as hell wasn't going to let any other asshole try for the position.

The only thing that still bothered me was the possibility that she thought my job was wrong—that she would want me to quit.

That I couldn't do.

The news blew up our phones as we stood among the flocks of grazing geese in Flat Rock Park, looking out over the river. Walter was apparently under federal investigation for forty-two crimes, including the kidnapping of his own daughter.

The diva wrapped an arm around me, leaning into me. "You must be glad that your revenge is finally coming to pass."

I pulled her closer. "It's coming about in stranger ways than I ever could've predicted."

It didn't matter, so long as Walter would be suffering long and hard. Which he already was.

She gazed out at the water, where a lone rower was sculling with broad strokes. "This feels like the end of an era. Dad has been ousted from his own company. Eve is divorcing him. Luis has quit. Everything's breaking up."

I thought of how the Breadcrumb Client had said my revenge would be like an explosion that would reverberate across many lives.

I spun the diva so we faced each other. "Do you regret being kidnapped?"

Her lake-blue eyes seemed bottomless. "Not anymore. I can't imagine not knowing what it feels like to have an article published in national news or to stand up to Dad. Not knowing what Dad is really like, under his polite veneer. Not knowing who you really are, beyond the Werewolf."

Maybe that was what made the diva most courageous — that she wasn't afraid to look the truth in the face.

Having decided to make her my girlfriend, I'd committed to kissing her. Now seemed as good a time as any to resume what I'd started in Tulsa.

Gripping her nape and pulling her face to mine, I caught her up in a ravenous kiss, storming her mouth with my tongue. When I surfaced for air, I growled, "I meant it last night, Diva. You're *mine*."

Her eyes shone like the Texas stars. "Then you're mine too."

My knuckle skimmed her jaw. "Is that a demand?"

"Yes."

I grabbed her chin. "I'll allow this one exception to my second rule. Though I'm sorely tempted to punish you."

Her eyes flared. "Please."

I swooped on her lips again, coating them with my tongue and diving through to reach hers.

I crushed her body to mine, needing to feel every inch of her against me that I could.

I was either the luckiest fucker alive or totally fucked.

Danya

My weekend stay with Caleb turned into a two month-long stay. That was how long it took for a jury to find Dad guilty of orchestrating my kidnapping, coercing me into marriage, and assaulting me. On June 16th he was sentenced to life imprisonment.

By then, GenRev's board had voted to make Luis their new CEO. Accepting the position, he announced his aim to improve the company's policies and conduct and redress the crimes that had been uncovered.

Drake had been frequently photographed with an actor who'd won a TONY award and seemed to be moving on easily from our whirlwind engagement.

In the meantime, Caleb and I worked, played, slept, and ate together like a regular couple. We went to movies, ate out occasionally, ran around Ardmore, visited the gym, and met up with Gideon, his girlfriend, and his friends at a bar in

Passyunk Square.

Being under Caleb's rule was very different from being under my father's. For one thing, I *wanted* to follow Caleb's commands. Usually. Well, often. For another, he had long ago earned my respect. Since the night of the Werewolf. And for another, when I did rebel against his orders, I accepted my punishment as my due. Doing otherwise earned me his wrath, which I avoided at all costs.

Most of all, I loved him.

And he, in turn, respected me. Fair, honest, and loyal, he exercised his iron will on me in a way that showed intense focus and care.

June 16th was double cause for celebration, as it was Caleb's birthday. Gideon and Ginnie were meeting Caleb and me at a seafood restaurant on Walnut Street by the river. Since Caleb had only one errand to run in the city and I had several, I drove the beamer in, dropping him in Center City and continuing to my apartment to pick up a few things, including mail. From there I drove to a pharmacy for some necessities, and then to a bookstore, where I purchased five books I'd chosen for Caleb's birthday gift.

Parallel parking in a tight spot had never been my forte. Doing so on a downhill was a complete nightmare. I faced both challenges on the steep downward slope of Walnut Street near the restaurant. I accidentally tapped the rear bumper of the shiny red Porsche convertible in front of me. Either my stomach rose up into my throat or my throat dropped to my belly when I realized the owner was in the car.

Oh, shit!

I chewed on my pinky nail, afraid to get out of the car.

The Porsche's driver's door opened and slammed shut behind possibly the most livid man I'd ever seen. His eyes glowed like furnaces, he breathed fire through his nose, and he cracked his knuckles as he approached. I put him in his

mid-thirties. Sporting the tattoo of a king of diamonds playing card on his shoulder, he wore a tight white t-shirt that
hugged his gym-built torso.

Swallowing, I crept out of the beamer, nudging the door
closed. I guessed it was time to own up to my mistake and
exchange insurance information.

"Sorry, I—" I began.

He launched towards me, pointing at his car.

"You bitch!" he snarled. "Do you fucking know what this
car is? It's a nineteen-eighty-four Porsche 911 Carrera. Cost
me eighty grand just last week. They only made a thousand
of the red ones. Now look what you've done." He gestured
toward the bumper. "You don't use a bumper to figure out
how close you are to the next car. Go back to fucking driving
school if you don't know how to park! Women drivers don't
belong on the road." He stepped into my personal space, jab-
bing a finger at me. "You're gonna pay. Big time. Gimme your
name and number. And insurance." He slapped a hand on the
top of the beamer. "How'd you like it if I did your car that
way, huh? Fucking bitch."

He kept on shouting insults and accusations, till my head
pounded with blood and my palms grew clammy. And he
was so close, I had no room to open the door to get the papers
from the glove compartment.

A large hand landed on the man's tattoo, causing him to
jump.

"You'll want to watch your car." Caleb's voice vibrated
with barely suppressed rage, and the arteries in his neck
bulged.

My foe's Porsche was rolling down the hill straight towards the intersection at the bottom.

"FUUCCKK!" He tore at his hair, sprinting after his car.

We watched in slow motion as the car crashed into the back
of a dump truck parked at the base of the hill. My antagonist

shouted at the top of his lungs, throwing his fists in the air and hurling a stream of curses at us.

Satisfaction brewed in my belly, bubbling forth as a relieved giggle.

Caleb nodded at the beamer. "Climb in, and I'll re-park."

After I piled in, he backed up along the one-way street, turning onto Front Street at the top of the hill and parking in a garage a block down.

I turned to him. "Did you release his handbrake and pop his car in gear?"

Caleb

Shit. The diva knew me too well.

I'd been trying to show her I kept my fixer mode separate from everyday life. Now she must think I couldn't rein it in. That this was my default mode, and I was only playing at being a normal person the rest of the time.

A deep-seated instinct to protect and avenge her had kicked in when I'd seen that asshole hollering at her. It seemed I couldn't turn that reflex off, ever.

If I kept on reverting to that second nature, she'd want to change it, to make me more socially acceptable.

Yeah, I'd sent his car careening down the hill. And I'd do it again.

I reached for the flowers I'd brought her, hoping these would soften my image. Maybe make me look sweet. "Here. These are for you."

Her gaze jumped between me and the flowers. Then, pushing the bouquet aside, she crushed her lips to mine, wrapping her arms around my neck. I met her tongue, greedily plundering her mouth.

She pulled away, her gaze snaring mine. "I love you,

Caleb."

I thumbed her lip. "Because I brought you flowers?"

She shook her head. "Because of who you are. Flowers aren't who you are. Teaching jerks a lesson is who you are. Taking no bullshit is who you are. Protecting me is who you are. And I love that about you. I always will."

She didn't mind what I'd done. She liked it. Something emerged from its chrysalis in my chest, unfolding its wings. "It doesn't bother you that I'm a fixer?"

"I'm proud of it. At least the way you practice the profession."

She didn't know the worst of it. But I wasn't about to tell her that now. She'd find out eventually, if she stayed with me.

Could the diva be that unicorn among women who accepted me as I was, without any changes?

Her love was an unexpected gift, a surprise outcome of all the crimes committed and brought to light in the last two and a half months. And I soaked it up like a freshly watered plant.

Danya

Now that Dad was locked up, I returned to my apartment. I wanted to give Caleb some space, figuring he hadn't signed up to have me move in with him two months ago. The last thing I wanted was to frighten him off by being clingy and needy. Moving back to my place for a while would demonstrate that I could be independent and allow him his freedom.

When he asked why I was going, I told him I had a lot of people to interview for my next few blog posts, which were about summer staycations in Philly. I said it'd be easier to use my apartment as a base of operations while I conducted my research and wrote up the entries.

My heart was hollow as a drum as I packed my bag to leave

him. However good this separation might be for him or us, it felt all kinds of wrong to go.

He looked thoughtful as he kissed me goodbye at my apartment door. "Text whenever you go out, telling me where you are."

"Okay."

"Call whenever you get home."

"All right."

"Double bolt this door when you're home."

"I will."

When he'd gone, the hollowness worsened, so I busied myself working on my blog. Using my notes from our trip west, I'd published my first posts three weeks ago, finding instant success. It seemed a good number of those who'd liked the *Times* article were following the blog, which I called *The Traveling Diva*. Within a few days I reached a hundred thousand followers, and the numbers had steadily grown since. My notoriety no doubt had a lot to do with my popularity. But now that I knew I also had talent, I didn't worry as much about distinguishing between my famous name and my professional accomplishments, which seemed a futile exercise anyway.

I decided to throw myself into work, easing the dull ache in my chest with writing and research.

I texted Caleb as I stepped out of the apartment. *Headed to my usual café to meet my former coworker, Innes. Talk to you when I get home.*

While walking towards Konditori, I recalled the day Caleb and I had met there to discuss the job I had for him. Even though it was only nine weeks ago, it seemed like an eternity. Over the last two weeks, I'd slowly gotten used to living apart from Caleb. But it hadn't become any easier. I missed him while interviewing people about their summer plans in

Philly, wondering if Caleb knew about the places mentioned or if he'd enjoy the events. I missed him while swimming or running by the river, thinking of our motel swims and our runs in his Ardmore neighborhood. I missed him while writing on my laptop, remembering our work sessions together on the trip and more recently at his house. I missed him when going to bed, waking at night, and getting up in the morning.

Maybe seeing Innes would distract me for a couple of hours at least.

I spotted him reading at a table outside on the terrace by the café's large window.

I sneaked up on him, standing above him a moment before he looked up.

"Danya!" He stood, throwing his arms around me and kissing my cheek.

"Innes. It's wonderful to see you again."

"You look amazing. Blogging agrees with you."

I laughed. "Thanks. You look as if you've gotten a lot of sun."

He chuckled. "Yeah. I'm covering Guatemala and Belize for our next Latin American edition, and I just got back from there."

"Wow! I want to hear all about it."

"Let's get something to drink first." He wrapped an arm around me, leading me towards the counter.

Talking to Innes was easy and fun. We both traveled for similar reasons—to learn about the world, meet people, and come back with a fresh perspective on home. And we could discuss writing strategies for hours. He had some ideas for my blog's design, and I suggested a few additional ways he could improve on the previous edition's coverage of Belize.

At some point the conversation drifted to my kidnapping. I told him the version I'd told the police, calling Caleb *my traveling companion.*

Innes whistled low. "Man, Danya, you've been through a lot. Is your traveling companion the Werewolf you refer to in your blog?"

"Yeah." Warmth swirled in my chest as I thought of him.

"You wrote that the nickname comes from the werewolf costume he kept in the back of his car."

"And from the way his bearded face looked in the moonlight when we drove at night," I added.

Innes shook his head. "I don't know. I'm not sure I would've gotten back inside a car with a guy who carried around a werewolf costume." He winked. "Or is that what a man has to do these days to turn a woman's head?"

I laughed. "If he has good lungs for howling, he should absolutely try it."

He leaned in, a flirtatious grin hovering over his lips. "If you give me a second chance at that date we had planned, I may give it a whirl."

"Oh, actually I'm—"

I was going to say *seeing someone.* But a deep gravelly voice behind me finished my sentence for me.

"Taken."

I spun in my seat to find Caleb standing over me, a dangerous glint flashing in his eyes as he glowered at Innes. Though my heart took wing at his presence, a trace of nervousness pinched at my belly. Was Caleb the jealous sort? I had a feeling I was about to find out.

"Stand, Diva."

Without hesitating I pushed to my feet, joy leaping in my chest at being commanded by him again.

Kicking the chair aside, Caleb slammed me against the café window, grabbing my throat and mauling me with a rough desperado's kiss. I felt his teeth on my tongue, his tongue on my lips, and his lips everywhere, catching, capturing, and claiming me.

"Come home," he rumbled into my mouth. "Now."

Breathless and flushed, I husked, "I need to gather my things at my apartment."

He scooped me up in his arms, knocking the last breath from my lungs. "We'll stop there on the way."

As Caleb carried me off, I twisted to meet Innes's eye. "Sorry, Innes."

His brows had hit his hairline, and his eyes had rounded. "That's fine, Danya. We'll talk soon."

In a few strides Caleb deposited me in the beamer, and a moment later he slid behind the wheel, starting the engine.

"What was that about?" I ventured as he pulled into traffic.

His eyes flicked to me before returning to the road. "You're mine, Diva. Understand? No more living separately. No more sleeping apart. No more laughing with men who want to fuck you." His jaw pulsed. "You captured me. Now you won't get rid of me."

I held my breath, afraid to hope. "What do you mean?"

We were waiting at a stoplight.

"You want me to say it?" He held the steering wheel in a death grip, looking out the window.

"Yes," I croaked.

The light changed, and he crossed the intersection, pulling over and parking at the edge of the square where I lived.

He switched off the ignition, turning towards me, his tone fierce. "I love you, Diva. You're like the song of the birds in the morning. I can't begin my day without you. I need to see you when I come home from a job. I need you across from me at every meal and beside me in my free hours. Your smile lights up my world, and your laughter fills my dreams. I love you, and I'm keeping you captive for always."

His words were the caressing ripple of a fountain, filling my heart with happiness.

"Always?"

He fisted my hair, pulling my face to his and tilting it so our lips brushed. "Till the end of our journey together."

Caleb: One year later

When Gideon and I got off the phone, I parked my elbows on my desk, burying my head in my hands. This would be my most dangerous assignment yet. But I had to do it. Gideon had helped me too much over the years for me not to return the favor now. And anyway, I owed him as a good friend.

"What's wrong, Caleb?" The diva's soft voice floated from the door. Padding over, she placed a mug of tea beside me, wrapping an arm around my shoulder.

I sat up, swiveling my chair and pulling her down into my lap. "It's Gideon. He's in trouble."

She nestled into my chest. "What kind of trouble?"

I'd never failed to confide in the diva when she asked outright about any of my jobs.

"A group supporting the oppressive regime in Muldavia has discovered Gideon's identity as the Weissritter. They've threatened to out him unless he rigs the upcoming Muldavian elections so their party remains in power, winning by a landslide. Otherwise the opposition will win hands down and replace the regime with a tolerant, humanitarian leader." I scrubbed a hand over my beard. "If Gideon says no, he'll go to prison for life. If he says yes, he'll cost hundreds of thousands of people their lives, liberty, and happiness."

She sucked in her breath. "We have to expose this group."

I had come to the same conclusion. I also planned on taking out every last one of the bastards threatening Gideon. There was just one problem with her phrasing.

"*We*, diva? I'm going to Muldavia alone."

A crease appeared between her brows. "No, Caleb. We've

never once traveled alone since we met."

It was true that I had always timed my jobs so I could remain with Danya when she took work trips. She'd always accompanied me on my away jobs too. And we'd married and honeymooned in the Scottish Highlands three months ago.

"This is different. It's too dangerous. Besides, Faye and Mom need you to help them settle in and get used to life here."

My mom and sister had moved in three weeks ago—a major triumph for me. In the end, Danya had persuaded Mom, and Mom's insistence had worn down Faye's longstanding resistance to the idea. Having convinced Faye to join the local softball league, Danya was helping Mom put in applications to a few biotech companies. Marisa, Jeremy, and Danya were doing everything they could to make the two feel at home.

The diva covered my hand with hers over my jaw. "Where you travel, I travel. Remember what we vowed?"

"Not when my target may get wind of your existence and harm you or hold you hostage." I shook my head, capturing her hand and spinning her so her back was to my chest. "This time you stay home."

"But I could help," she persisted. "I could write another exposé."

"Write the story after the fact, once I've brought down the group."

There was no way I was taking Danya with me and risking her life.

She squirmed to climb off my lap, but I held her tightly in my arm, cupping her throat.

"When I came to live with you, I told you I accepted your job and lifestyle as a fixer. And when I married you, I said I loved your rough, underhanded ways of solving problems," she asserted. "And you said you didn't want to change me either, that you loved my spirit and strength. Now I'm fighting to come with you. I promise to do whatever you say to keep us safe. I'll abide by your rules. I'll keep quiet while observing everything and wait to publish our findings until you give me the go-ahead."

"It's not that I don't trust you to obey me, Diva. But this would involve leaving you alone for long periods of time." *I'd be worried about you the whole time.*

"I can help you, Caleb. While you're gone, I can take care of necessary tasks you don't have time for. Take photos, if it's safe. Talk to people casually to gather information." A swallow traveled down her throat beneath my hand. "Write up what you find."

"Already Gideon's and my lives will be on the line. I can't risk endangering yours too." I released her, and she slid off my legs, turning to face me. "End of discussion."

"Please, Caleb—"

I pinned her with a look that silenced her.

Mom appeared at the door. "Dinner's ready!"

All through dinner the diva was quiet. By now I knew better than to think that meant she'd given up. I could practically see the wheels spinning in her head as she thought of things to say to make me change my mind.

Later, as we undressed for bed, she said, "I'll go on my own if you don't let me come with you. I'll go undercover. I researched Muldavia after dinner, and I can't in good conscience stand by and do nothing to prevent this political party from prevailing. Gideon is my friend too, and I owe him a lot."

"I said end of discussion." I placed my watch on the dresser. I would let her air her grievances for about another minute before I shoved her against the wall, wrapping her thighs around my waist. After rebelling, she really needed the flogger, but I was too impatient tonight.

"I *could* go alone, but it would be such a waste, when we

could pool our resources and knowledge. Like a team." She tossed her slacks on the chair.

"You have ten seconds to finish stripping, and I'm taking you right here."

"I researched getting a visa for Muldavia, and I applied for one."

"Fine. But you're still not going."

"You can't stop me." She folded her arms across her bare tits.

I pushed her against the door, hooking her legs around me. "I have all kinds of ways to make it impossible for you to leave the country. Try me."

She gasped as I impaled her in one thrust. "If you're going to play dirty, then I will too."

"Play dirty, Diva." I pulled out and slammed in, feeling her smooth, tight walls around me. This was home.

"If you leave me here alone on this trip," she whispered brokenly, "I'll leave you to stay with Eve and Luis when you get back."

Pure fury drove me to finish, stabbing her with a frenzy I hadn't felt since Walter had held a gun to her head. She screamed as I brought her to climax without giving her permission. I wanted to have an excuse to compound her punishment later.

Plastering her against the door, I breathed into her mouth, "Remember, Diva, you're my captive. I won't let you move back with Eve and Luis."

"Then *keep* me captive," she begged. "Take me with you. I'll obey your every command."

Still embedded in her, I fisted her hair and pinned her hand above her head. "If I lose you, I have nothing."

"You won't lose me."

My beautiful diva with the flaming hair and indigo eyes. "I need to get you pregnant so you can't travel anymore."

Her eyes widened. "I thought you didn't want children."

"Plans change. With you I intend to make several babies."

A lopsided smile tilted her lips. "In the meantime, can I come with you?"

It was irresponsible, impractical, and mad, but faced with her determination I gave in. "Don't make me regret it."

Combing her fingers through my beard, she smothered my cheeks, lips, and neck with kisses. "I won't! I promise, I won't."

My dick surged up for round two, and I carried her to the bed, lowering her without disconnecting us. "You, on the other hand, will regret it. Your clit and pussy are mine to control. And you have three punishments due now."

She arched her back and ground into me as I teased her divide with my tip. "Do your worst."

"Oh, Diva," I chided, "you should know by now. This is far from my worst."

And I proceeded to remind her just how bad it could be.

The End

ABOUT THE AUTHOR

A former academic, I love everything to do with language and literature—teaching, learning, writing, and reading. My favorite novels are historical and contemporary romances with alpha heroes. I've self-published *Rivals In Restraint, He's Digital, I'm Analog, The Scornful Heart*, and *The Vulnerable Heart*, all contemporary romances. All the novels I write feature music, travel, and food in abundance. I prize strong heroines who love and trust themselves—or who learn to in the course of the story. I live in Berkeley, California with my dachshund-Chihuahua, Pooh-bah. When I'm not writing or teaching, I like to cycle in the nearby hills and play piano.

www.ingramcontent.com/pod-product-compliance
Lightning Source LLC
Chambersburg PA
CBHW060153260626
47160CB00001B/243